Kidnapped by a Rogue

MARGARET MALLORY

ALL RIGHTS RESERVED

BOOKS BY MARGARET MALLORY

THE DOUGLAS LEGACY
CAPTURED BY A LAIRD
CLAIMED BY A HIGHLANDER
KIDNAPPED BY A ROGUE

THE RETURN OF THE HIGHLANDERS
THE GUARDIAN
THE SINNER
THE WARRIOR
THE CHIEFTAIN

THE GIFT: A Highland Novella

ALL THE KING'S MEN
KNIGHT OF DESIRE
KNIGHT OF PLEASURE
KNIGHT OF PASSION

PROLOGUE

Drumlanrig Castle
The Lowlands of Scotland
1522

Margaret's husband, the 7th Baron of Drumlanrig, stormed into the bedchamber, banging the door against the wall, even before the maid had time to change the bloody sheets.

"You failed again, you useless woman!" He leaned over the bed and shouted in her face, "Have you and your family not made me suffer enough already?"

Margaret curled into a ball and covered her ears. Another miscarriage. Another lost babe. Her heart could not bear it.

"For God's sake, stop your damned weeping," he said. "I'm speaking to you."

Could he not show her some mercy for once and leave her alone?

"Nay, you're worse than useless!" William continued his ranting as he paced back and forth beside the bed. "You're a rope around my neck tying me to your traitorous family."

"Please, laird, your lady wife must rest," the elderly maid spoke up. "She's lost too much blood this time."

The poor woman's attempt to intervene earned her a shove from William that landed her on the floor. Margaret tried to get up to

1

help her, but she was too weak to rise from the bed. Frightening the elderly servant appeared to calm William for the moment, and he sauntered over to the side table to pour himself a whisky.

"I was the envy of every man in Scotland when we wed. A rare beauty, they called you," William said, raising his cup to her in mock tribute. "But what good is a beautiful wife if she's a cold fish in bed and too weak to bear an heir?"

Margaret made no effort to placate and soothe him as she usually did. She was too lost in grief to care what William said.

"Of course, it wasn't your looks that made ye such a dazzling marriage prize," he said. "'Twas that your brother was Archibald Douglas, Earl of Angus, the sly devil who wheedled his way into our widowed queen's bed and persuaded the lovesick cow to wed him."

Why was William droning on about this now? Did he feel no sorrow for the child they'd lost?

"Your brother outmaneuvered all the other powerful magnates by becoming the stepfather of the infant heir to the Scottish throne." William held his clenched fist inches from her face. "He had it in his grasp to rule Scotland."

His sour breath in her face made her uneasy stomach turn. When she tried to roll away, William pinned her arms.

"Not one of the men who envied me would have ye now." William's voice was low and dangerous. "You're nothing now that the men of your family have been charged with treason and fled to France."

"William, please…" She suspected she was still bleeding, judging by the growing dampness beneath her, and she just wanted him to leave.

"In truth," he said, nodding to himself, "'tis a blessing ye lost the child."

A fresh flood of tears streaked down the sides of her face. *A blessing?* How could he say that? For the sake of a peaceful home, she had made excuses for his behavior and forgiven him time and again, but this was too much.

"Since there will be no child, I'm free to be rid of ye," he said. "Even if it costs me a damned fortune in bribes, I'll obtain an annulment from Rome."

A cold sweat broke out on her brow, and she felt so light-headed she could barely follow what he was saying.

"I'll not risk losing my lands and title for a barren woman and her treasonous brothers." He grasped her shoulders and shook her. "Do ye hear me? I want you out!"

She fell back on the bed when he released her. Her head swam, and her fingers had gone numb.

"Get her out of here," he told the maid as he headed for the door.

At last, he was leaving.

"Of course, laird," the maid said. "I'll prepare another chamber for her right away."

"Nay, I want that woman gone from the castle," William shouted. "Gone! Tonight!"

"But Lady Margaret ought not be moved," the maid said.

"I'll not allow her to endanger me another day," he said. "Nay, not another hour."

"But laird," the maid said in a hushed voice, "I fear she may not survive a journey."

"That would save me a good deal of trouble and expense," he said before slamming the door behind him.

A short time later, Margaret had the odd sensation of looking down at herself from a great distance. There she was, Lady Margaret Douglas, sister-in-law to the queen, leaving Drumlanrig Castle in the midst of a howling storm in the back of an open horse cart that smelled of hay. Her sole guard was Old Thomas, the stable master.

Her mind drifted back to the day she arrived at the castle as a young bride, full of hope and dreams and accompanied by two dozen warriors and several carts that carried her trunks.

How far she and her mighty family had fallen. Not that it mattered.

She slept in fits and starts, waking when the cart hit a bump that jostled her head against the bare boards of the cart. The wind

3

and rain slashed at her face, but the cold seemed to come from deep inside her.

Margaret had no notion how much time passed, whether it was days or hours, when she awoke to find Old Thomas peering down at her with a worried expression on his wrinkled face.

"Ye must hold on, lass," he said. "Blackadder Castle isn't much farther. You'll see Lady Alison soon."

Alison. Margaret smiled at the thought of her sister, but she could not muster the strength to speak.

"Your sister will nurse ye back to health," he said as he tucked the rough, wet blanket around her. "You'll be safe at Black-adder Castle under her husband's protection."

Safe from what? The worst had already happened. She had lost another babe.

The next time she awoke, it was to the painful tingling of warmth creeping into her hands and feet.

"Blankets! And more peat on the brazier, now! God have mercy, she's so cold."

She heard her sister Alison giving instructions and people scurrying about the room.

"Her gown is bloody," Alison said. "Why did ye travel with her in this condition?"

The voices faded, and Margaret's mind drifted again until her sister squeezed her hand.

"May William burn in everlasting hell," Alison said. "I wish I could send him there myself."

When Margaret felt Alison's tears falling on her hand, she forced her eyes open.

"She's awake, praise God!" Alison cried out.

"I lost the babe," she told her sister, her voice coming out in a whispered croak. "I wanted it so much."

All she had ever wanted were the ordinary things most women had. A home, a husband, children. Children most of all.

"I'm so sorry, sweetling," Alison said.

"I'm glad I made it here to you," Margaret said. "I didn't want to die alone."

"You're *not* going to die," Alison said. "Ye must fight, Margaret."

It would be a relief to let go and join her lost babes.

"I know what it is like to despair, to feel so beaten down ye lose hope." Alison brushed Margaret's hair back from her forehead as their mother used to do. "One day, everything will be better. I promise."

How could it? She would never have the life she wanted. And she was so very tired...

"Don't let that whining, selfish, cowardly, poor excuse for a man take you from us," Alison pleaded. "You mustn't let him defeat you."

Margaret forced her eyes open again. It pained her to see her dear sister so distressed. She wished she could comfort her.

"Now that you're free of him, you've everything to live for," Alison said with tears streaming down her face. "Do ye hear me, Margaret? You're free of him!"

Freedom seemed a poor substitute for her lost dreams.

But it was all she had.

CHAPTER 1

Girnigoe Castle, Caithness
The Scottish Highlands
November 1524

The Orkney men sailed right into Sinclair Bay, the brazen bastards, and tossed Finn over the side of the ship within sight of the Sinclair clan stronghold, Girnigoe Castle. Finn broke to the surface gasping and struggled to stand in the heavy surf.

Laughing, the men on the boat tossed the bag containing the head of the Sinclair chieftain into the sea after him. As Finn lunged for it, a wave crashed over his head and slammed him against the rocks on his wounded leg. Still, he managed to catch the bag before it hit the water.

"A' phlàigh oirbh!" *A plague on you!* Finn shouted and raised his fist at the Orkney men as they sailed off.

He staggered onto the beach, then sat down to catch his breath and consider his future.

"What would you advise, uncle?" Finn said, turning to the bloodstained bag beside him, which contained the head of his great-uncle on his mother's side. "Will your son kill the messenger?"

The other warriors who sailed across the strait to retake Orkney were all dead, either slaughtered on land or drowned at sea. Finn had only been spared to deliver the chieftain's head to his family.

He looked up at the imposing Girnigoe Castle on the cliff above him and considered the wisdom of completing that task. His Sinclair relations were a suspicious and violent lot, even by Highland standards. And George Sinclair, the dead chieftain's son and heir, was the worst of them.

What the hell. Finn was desperate for a drink, so he picked up the bloody bag and started for the castle. As he climbed up the steep bluff from the beach, dragging his injured leg, he reflected on lost causes—the dead chieftain's and his own.

The Sinclair chiefs had been the Earls of Orkney until the king of Norway gave the Orkney Islands to Scotland in the marriage contract between his daughter and the Scottish king. As part of that royal exchange, the Sinclairs were forced to trade their rich lands on Orkney for Caithness, a region with vast expanses of infertile moors in the northeast corner of Scotland, a few miles by sea from their former home.

Though this occurred over fifty years ago, the Sinclairs had long memories, and the loss of Orkney still rankled. When the Sinclair chieftain decided to defy the Scottish king and fight to retake Orkney, his pride outweighed his common sense.

The same could be said of Finn.

He winced when a shot of pain ran up his leg like a hot blade, as if he needed a reminder of the consequences of his error in judgment. He had no obligation to fight for the Sinclair chieftain. Though Sinclair blood ran through his veins, it came from his mother's side.

Nay, he was lured to fight for his Sinclair kin by a foolish desire, a desire he did not even realize he harbored until his mother's uncle dangled it in front of him: lands of his own if they won the battle.

The guards at the outer gate were surly, as usual. The Sinclairs were wild and ruthless fighters, but sorely lacking in humor. Though Finn was a close kin of their chieftain, his father was a Gordon, which made Finn a Gordon and a member of an enemy clan. Marriages like his parents', which were intended to ease the tension between the two powerful clans, had only made things worse.

The guards sent word of his arrival ahead and let him pass through the gate into the west barbican. From there he crossed the first drawbridge, passed under the iron portcullis of the second gate, and crossed the courtyard with the guest hall and lodgings.

Finally, he reached the sliding drawbridge. They would take him over a moat to the main part of the castle, which was built atop a long, narrow outcropping of rock that extended into the sea. It contained the tower, additional lodgings, the chapel, bakehouse, and other essential buildings surrounded by a perimeter wall.

Finn paused to take in the sheer cliffs that fell to the sea beneath the wall. If the new Sinclair chieftain decided to make him a prisoner here at Girnigoe Castle, he'd have a hell of a time getting out.

By the time Finn was escorted into the great hall to give his accounting of the battle to the chieftain's family, he was unsteady on his feet from loss of blood. He was starving as well since his Orkney captors had not seen fit to feed him in the three days since the fighting. Though he was trailing blood, he did not expect the Sinclairs to ask him to sit, and they didn't.

The Viking blood was strong in these Sinclairs. George and his three sons were all well over six feet and looked like men who preferred to slice their meat with axes and eat it raw. Though George was nearing fifty, he was the most dangerous and least predictable of the family—except perhaps for his daughter.

Barbara, who was George's eldest at thirty-two, was considered a handsome woman. Like her brothers, she was tall and looked as if she could hold her own in a fight. When their eyes met, Finn had a vivid memory of ten-year-old Barbara watching him with those same cold gray eyes while she strangled his puppy. He had seen many men die in the years since. And yet the memory of that pup's death when he was a lad of five stuck with him like a burr.

The dead chieftain's wife, Mary, a petite, gray-haired woman, entered the hall then, and the weight of the bag suddenly felt heavier. She was both the reason he had climbed the hill to the castle to deliver the news instead of walking off and the reason he'd dreaded coming. Mary was a Sutherland, so Finn was somehow related to her as well, and he'd always been fond of her.

Finding her in this family was like finding a kitten in the midst of a wolf pack.

"Where is my husband and the others…" Mary's voice faded as her gaze took in the state Finn was in and then fixed on the bloody bag. Her low moan tore at his heart.

Though it was not his place, when no one else offered any comfort to the widow, Finn limped to her side and rested a hand on her shoulder.

"Thank you for bringing us something to bury," she said, looking up at him with watery eyes.

She was the only Sinclair to shed a tear. George had been waiting a good twenty years for his father to die and did not bother hiding his satisfaction. With a flick of his hand, he motioned for one of his men to take the bag away, then he nodded for Finn to speak.

Though Finn was itching to be done with this task and leave, he took his time telling the tale of the battle, as was expected. He spoke at length of the courage and fighting skills of the Sinclairs who had fallen, though in truth they had suffered a thoroughly humiliating defeat.

"The witch prophesied that whoever's blood was drawn first—Orkney or Sinclair—would lose the battle," George said when Finn finished. "Did my father fail to heed her warning?"

Finn had hoped they would not ask him about that.

"We came across a young lad herding sheep soon after we landed," he said. "Your father ordered him killed."

The murder of that innocent lad was the worst part of the whole damned ordeal. Finn knew then he'd made a grave mistake. If he'd had his own boat, he would have turned around right then.

"I'll have the witch put to death for her false prophecy," George said.

"Her prophecy was true," Finn said. "As it turned out, the lad belonged to one of the Sinclair families who still live on Orkney."

"How is it that you survived?" George asked, and slapped him on his shoulder, which George could damned well see had been badly cut in the battle.

Finn clenched his teeth to keep from wincing.

"Can't ye see the poor man is injured?" Mary chastised her son, then she turned her gaze to include her grandsons. "Unlike the rest of ye, Finlay sailed to Orkney to fight at your chieftain's side."

Finn felt a wee bit guilty that she credited him with loyalty to her husband when he'd only done it for the promise of lands.

9

"I'm chieftain now," George said, his eyes burning bright as he looked down at his mother. "You'll not speak that way to me again."

"Grandfather's attempt to take Orkney was a foolish quest that did nothing but waste the lives of Sinclair warriors and invite our enemies to attack us here at home in Caithness," Barbara said. "We remained here to protect what is ours."

"Come, Finlay," Mary said, and took his arm. "Let me tend to those wounds."

He gritted his teeth with the effort not to lean on the elderly woman and topple them both as she led him up the stairs to one of the bedchambers above. His leg and the cut across his shoulder hurt like bloody hell.

Mary sent for food and drink, which he wolfed down while she cleaned, sewed, and bandaged his wounds with an expertise born of practice. When she was done, she helped him into a clean shirt that belonged to one of her grandsons.

"Ye ought to stay in bed for a few days to let these wounds heal," Mary said.

Remaining with the Sinclairs seemed the worst of the bad choices before him.

"I'd like to," Finn lied, "but I ought to let my family know I'm alive before news of the battle reaches them."

Mary did not contradict him, though they both knew there would be no weeping from his family if Finn never returned.

"The Sinclairs will expect ye to stay at least another day to avoid crossing the Ord on a Monday," she said.

Sinclairs were even more superstitious than most Highlanders, and that was saying something. It was on a Monday that the Sinclairs had crossed the Ord of Caithness, the pass that marked the boundary between Caithness and Sutherland, on their way to fight the English in the Battle of Flodden. Because most of them died in that disastrous battle, no Sinclair had crossed the Ord on a Monday since.

"My luck could not get much worse than it already is, so I'll risk it," Finn said with a laugh.

"Ye misunderstand me." Mary's tone carried an urgency he had not picked up on before. "Though I wish ye could stay and let your wounds heal, ye must go tonight. 'Tis not safe for ye here."

He took her at her word. Still, he asked, "Why?"

"My son is a dangerous man, and ye know how he feels about ye," she said.

"What does George have against me?" he asked.

"I doubt even he knows, but there's no changing his mind."

Finn sensed she was not telling him all she knew, but George was an easy man to offend, so it could be anything. Most likely, George wanted some woman who had gone to bed with Finn instead.

"George would not harm ye while his father lived," Mary said. "But now that he's chieftain, he can do what he wants. No one will dare cross him."

"Except his mother," Finn said with a wink.

"I've given up on my son and his children, except for John," Mary said in a choked voice. "There's still hope for John."

There was once. The two other boys had held Finn down while Barbara murdered his pup. When John found them, he tried to stop Barbara, but he was too late.

"His father mistakes John's decency for weakness." Tears glistened in her eyes.

Finn nodded, though he feared that John had been trying to win his father's approval for so long that the good man he might have become was lost.

Despite Mary's dire warning that his life was in danger, Finn slept like the dead until she returned to wake him in the middle of the night.

The old woman led him down a back staircase and into a small chamber, where she opened a secret door disguised as a panel. It opened onto a dank tunnel.

"This comes out in a cave above the shore on the next inlet," she said. "My nephew is at Old Wick Castle now. He'll give ye a horse."

Her nephew, Sutherland of Duffus, had several castles. Luckily, Old Wick was just a couple of miles down the coast.

"Take care of yourself, Finlay," she said, rising on her toes to kiss his cheek. "Though ye may fool others, and even yourself, I know ye have a good heart and an honorable soul."

He had no notion why she thought that.

"You'll return to the Gordons?" she asked.

"Aye," he said, though he was not at all certain his father's clan would take him back. Even if they did, the Gordons would not trust him after he'd fought for an enemy clan.

Finn had no notion what they would require him to do to prove his loyalty, but it was bound to be painful.

Mary felt her age as she watched Finlay disappear into the darkness. She closed the secret door and rested her head against it, lost in her memories. Perhaps she should have told him what she knew. She was old and tired and may not have the chance again.

But what good could come of it?

Nay, 'twas best he never know.

CHAPTER 2

"Come, Lady Margaret," the farmer said when she handed him two pennies for the apples, "I've told ye time and again ye mustn't pay the first price I ask."

"Why should I bargain when ye always give me a fair price?" she asked with a smile.

"Because others will take advantage of your good nature." He thrust one of the pennies back into her hand and shook his head in exasperation.

They had this same exchange every week on market day. The man was widowed with five children to support, and yet he would not take an extra penny from her. As soon as the farmer turned to argue with his next customer, Margaret slipped a silver coin to his daughter, as she also did every week.

"Hello, Brian," she called out to a rail-thin lad of about twelve as she approached the last stall.

The boy's eyes lit up when he saw her—probably because no one else would buy the pathetic dolls his mother made from rags. Margaret bought one every market day, even though by now her nieces and every servant's child in Blackadder Castle had at least two.

"You're visiting Old Thomas?" Brian asked.

"Aye." She came to the village often to visit the former stable master of Drumlanrig Castle. "Is your mother unwell again?"

Brian nodded. His poor mother was married to a man who drank away what little they had, and she would never escape. Only rich and powerful men like Margaret's former husband could rid themselves of an unwanted spouse with the church's blessing.

"How is your precious sister today?" Margaret asked when she saw the little girl hiding behind him.

Ella was a shy child of three with large blue eyes and tangled fair hair. Margaret's heart melted when the girl peeked around her

13

brother and gave her a small smile. What she would not give to have a child like this. She pushed aside the old, familiar ache. There was no use in wishing for what she could never have.

What good is a woman who cannot give her husband heirs? You're useless! Worse than useless! Margaret pressed her fingertips to her temples. Would she never get William's voice out of her head?

"This one will make a lovely addition to my collection," Margaret said, picking up one of the rag dolls at random and handing Brian a coin.

Margaret started to leave, but then she paused, uncertain whether to make an offer that might embarrass the lad or seem like an empty promise.

"If there is ever anything I can do to help you," she said, "please ask me."

She continued through the tiny village until she reached the last whitewashed cottage.

"Thomas!" she called, and rapped on the door.

The old stable master's wrinkled face broke into a wide smile when he opened his door. "Lady Margaret, ye shouldn't trouble yourself coming to see an old man."

This old man had saved her life. After she'd been mistress of Drumlanrig Castle for seven years, Thomas was the only member of the household who volunteered to accompany her the night her husband threw her out.

"I enjoy visiting you," she said, "and it will be my last chance for weeks."

Thomas was leaving today to visit his niece and her family, and they chatted about the visit while she helped him pack.

"I'd best be off while I have plenty of daylight," Thomas said.

Margaret's stomach felt queasy as she helped him load his things into the same wagon that had carried her from Drumlanrig. She shivered as she remembered the rain that pelted her face, the cold that penetrated the wet blanket and seeped into her bones, and the despair that nearly destroyed her.

Thomas touched her shoulder. "Are ye all right, lass?"

"It's just that I'll miss you." She gave him a bright smile and kissed him farewell on his weathered cheek. "Have a safe journey."

She sat on the bench by Thomas's door to wait for Alison.

"I'm sorry I'm late and missed Thomas," Alison said when she arrived, breathless and smiling. "I had to change my gown after my younger two got sticky fingers all over it."

Her sister was a month from giving birth—again—and radiated good health.

"When you're with child, you're like a flower that's come into full bloom," Margaret said, then she took Alison's arm and led her to stand in front of the empty field next to Thomas's cottage. "I asked ye to meet me here because I want ye to see where my cottage will be built."

The thought of having a home of her own made Margaret's heart swell.

"I don't understand why ye want to live here in the village rather than in the castle with us," Alison said. "Won't ye be lonely?"

"The village is but a short walk from the castle." Margaret squeezed her sister's hand, willing her to understand. "We'll see each other almost every day."

It had taken her months to build up the courage to ask for this for herself. To persuade her sister's husband David, she had to agree to let him build a larger house than she needed and to accept a married couple of his choosing as live-in servants. She was unsure of the wife's skills, but the husband had the arms of a blacksmith and carried an axe in his belt.

Persuading her sister was a more delicate matter. She struggled to find a way to explain it without hurting her feelings.

"We love having ye live with us," Alison said. "Our home is yours."

"You've been nothing but kind to me," Margaret said. "I am so grateful."

But living in the midst of their happy, boisterous family was a constant reminder of the family Margaret could never have for herself. She needed something of her own, a place she could make into a home.

"Then why leave us?" Alison pressed.

"I don't want to become the old, unmarried aunt who lives in the top of the tower."

"Don't be ridiculous." Alison laughed. "You're bound to marry again. Besides being the sweetest and kindest Douglas sister, you're the most beautiful."

What good is beauty if a woman is a cold fish in bed? Margaret winced as she heard William's voice in her head again. What made it worse was knowing that the words were true. Unlike her sisters, she simply was not a passionate woman.

"I'm afraid there are not many men who want to wed a barren woman who has no property," Margaret said, "*and* whose brothers are banished traitors to the crown."

"Our brothers' status is a complication," Alison admitted, tapping her cheek in thought. "But when you're ready, you'll find a worthy man who's not afraid of the queen's wrath."

"My sisters have already wed the only men in Scotland who meet that description," Margaret said with a smile. "Besides, since I can't have children, why would I ever want another husband?"

"To warm your bed?" Alison asked with a gleam in her eye.

God save her from that. Margaret had always found her marital duties unpleasant at best, and usually far worse. All the hurt and humiliation she suffered when her husband threw her out and annulled their marriage was outweighed by the relief she felt from knowing she would never have to allow him to touch her again.

She squeezed her sister's hand as she remembered how, when she was close to death, Alison told her she was finally free of William.

She had come a long way since that terrible night. While she would always be grateful for the love and shelter Alison and her husband gave her in her time of need, Blackadder Castle was also a reminder of the state she had arrived in and the long months of recovery. She had regained her health, but the wounds to her heart—and her pride—still festered.

But she did have her freedom. And now, she would have a home of her own as well.

She did not mind that it would be a humble one, rather than the sort of grand castle she'd always lived in, and she had given up the dream of a kind and loyal husband a long time ago. But she had wanted children with every fiber of her being, and the loss of that hope left a hole in her heart that would never heal.

Still, she was determined to forge a life for herself. A quiet, peaceful life. Aye, it might be lonely at times, but she knew well that there were far worse things than being lonely.

Her thoughts were interrupted by the sight of a familiar figure galloping toward them through the village.

"You'd think her witch of a mother would have better control over her," Alison said with a sigh.

Lizzie, their sixteen-year-old cousin, pulled her horse up and slid off in one smooth motion. She was dressed in a lad's breeches and had her hair tucked into a cap.

"Don't tell me ye rode here alone again," Alison said, using her most severe mother's tone.

"All right, I won't tell ye I did," Lizzie said with a grin.

"'Tis not safe." Alison was not ready to let it go. "You're getting too old to pass for a lad."

"But I had to bring ye the news!" Lizzie said.

Icy fingers of premonition crawled up Margaret's spine.

"We Douglases are on the rise again!" Lizzie took Margaret's hands and danced her around in a circle. "Your brothers and my da have returned from exile!"

"What?" Alison asked, catching Lizzie's arm.

"They're here in Scotland," Lizzie said. "Archie has the backing of his brother-in-law, Henry VIII of England, and half the Scottish nobles. All the Douglas lands and titles have been returned to us."

"The queen agreed to take Archie back?" Margaret asked.

That was hard to believe. The woman had been so angry with Archie that it was rumored she had even asked her brother to seek a petition of divorce on her behalf.

17

"King Henry demanded she be a good wife and reconcile with Archie." Lizzie's eyes sparkled with amusement. "But when Archie approached Holyrood Palace, the queen had the cannon fired on him!"

Archie was always so sure of himself that Margaret could not help being amused, but her smile soon died on her lips, and she exchanged a worried look with Alison.

"I hope Archie has learned from the past," Alison said, "but I suspect he's as ambitious as ever."

Twice now, their brother, Archibald Douglas, had reached for the power of the crown, and twice he had lost and suffered a dramatic fall. The first time, he persuaded the newly widowed queen to wed him in secret without the permission of Parliament, which caused such a stir that the queen fled to England and the Douglas men holed up in their mighty fortress, Tantallon Castle, until the political winds changed again.

The second time, the conflict between the Douglases and their rival magnates descended into a bloody battle right in the streets of Edinburgh, which came to be known as the Battle of the Causeway. With the country on the brink of civil war, her brothers and uncle were charged with treason and fled the country to save their skins.

Margaret had bad memories of her own from that terrible day of bloodshed in Edinburgh.

"You'll have your revenge on Wretched William now," Lizzie said, using the nickname she had given Margaret's former husband. "Archie will have him boiled in oil for what he did to you."

"I don't want vengeance." That would give him too great a place in her thoughts, after she spent the last three years trying to forget. "All I ask is that I never have to see his face or hear his voice again."

"Ye needn't worry about that," Lizzie huffed. "Wretched William doesn't have the bollocks to show himself now that our family is on the rise again."

"One thing is certain," Alison said, turning to look at the empty field behind them, "ye won't be living in a cottage in the village."

Margaret felt the blood drain from her head.

"Now that the treason charges have been dropped," Alison continued, "the queen cannot accuse the rest of us of being complicit and threaten us with imprisonment."

The queen's fury with Archie extended to the entire Douglas family. Alison's husband, however, was such a powerful laird that they were safe from even the queen on his lands.

"You can live at Tantallon Castle," Alison said. "But I expect you'll spend a great deal of time at court again."

"I don't want any of that," Margaret said.

"I doubt ye can convince our brothers of that," Alison said. "Now that Archie is back, he'll not have his sister—particularly his only unwed sister—living in a cottage."

Margaret felt as if the ground was opening up beneath her. She wanted to argue that the men of her family had no right to tell her where and how to live. They had not cared what happened to her when they fled Scotland and left the rest of the family to face the consequences.

But Archibald Douglas, the 6th Earl of Angus, was not just her brother. He was the head of her family, the chief of the Douglases, and—most importantly of all—their young king's stepfather. Now that Archie had returned with the backing of Henry VIII and many of the Scottish nobles, he was again one of the most powerful men in Scotland.

"If ye don't wish to go, you can stay with us at the castle," Alison said, putting an arm around Margaret's shoulders. "Ye know my husband will not let Archie take you."

That would cause a dangerous conflict between her brother and brother-in-law, which would be a poor way to repay Alison and her husband for all they had done for her.

"I won't worry about it now," she said, to calm herself. "I expect Archie will be too busy to bother with me for some time."

19

"He's already sent men to fetch you," Lizzie said. "I rode hard to get here first to warn you, but they'll be here soon."

Margaret's hand went to her throat. "They're on their way?"

"Aye," Lizzie said. "They weren't far behind me."

Margaret pushed through the door of Thomas's cottage and sat down hard on one of the kitchen stools. Could she go back to the life she had before?

Did she have a choice?

She had grown up in one of Scotland's most powerful families, accustomed to a life of great castles, fine gowns and jewels, and frequent visits to court. Her family's fall—and everything she lost with it—had been hard, but she had gotten through it and survived.

She missed nothing of her former life. It had brought her too many sorrows.

The sound of pounding hooves of twenty horses arriving in the village filled the cottage, like an echo from her past, trampling on her hope of making a small, quiet life for herself.

Finn stood outside the door to the great hall of Huntly Castle, the seat of the mighty Gordon chieftain, the Earl of Huntly. A month ago, he'd been a member of the earl's guard, a respected position for a warrior of the clan. And he gave it up for naught.

Asking Huntly to take him back was a humiliation he'd rather not face sober. Though he'd been drinking steadily all day in diligent preparation, he took out the flask for one last pull.

Ach, this could not be that bad. Even if Huntly threw him in the dungeon for fighting for a rival clan, at least Finn didn't have to deliver a severed head this time.

Still, a man who underestimated the Gordons was a fool. The Sinclair clan would burn down a village over a small slight, but no one could match the Gordons for cunning self-interest. While the Sinclairs stood their ground and died with the king in the Battle of Flodden, the two Gordon earls—Huntly and Sutherland—foresaw the outcome, took flight, and saved themselves.

A serving woman he suspected he had slept with greeted him when he entered the hall.

"Thought you could use this, Finlay *Aluinn*," *Handsome Finlay,* she said, and handed him a large cup of whisky.

"*Ach*, lass, ye must have *the sight*," Finn said and gave her a wink.

"'Tis been dull as dirt without ye." She leaned close to speak in his ear. "I could meet ye in the stables tonight."

He gave her a noncommittal smile. He could be in the dungeon by nightfall. Besides that, he had no interest, which was a startling revelation as she was precisely his kind of woman: a buxom and willing lass with no expectations beyond a good roll in the hay.

The hall was even more crowded than usual and abuzz with conversation, which made him wonder what had happened. Perhaps Huntly had negotiated a betrothal for his granddaughter. Whatever it was, Finn hoped it was good news that would make the earl receptive to taking him back into his guard.

He groaned when he saw his mother stalking across the hall toward him with his father in her wake. Damn it, it was too late to escape. She'd seen him. People said his mother had been a great beauty, but her firm belief that she married beneath her had imprinted a permanent frown of resentment on her face.

"We didn't expect to find you here," his mother said, jutting her chin out. "Thought you'd be living on Orkney."

"Lovely to see you too, Mother," he said, then nodded to his father, who was probably too drunk to notice.

"What did ye do to make my uncle Sinclair decide not to give ye the lands he promised?" she asked.

"The Sinclairs lost the battle," Finn said.

"*Ach*, I told ye it would all be for naught," his mother said, shaking her head.

She appeared to have forgotten she'd encouraged him to go.

"I have bad news, I'm afraid. Your uncle was killed, along with most of the Sinclair warriors who sailed to Orkney." He told her about delivering the head as well, since she was bound to hear of it.

"Then my cousin George is chieftain now," she said, narrowing her eyes. "He'll make a strong chieftain."

Finn was not surprised she took the death of her kinsmen in stride. His mother was not a sentimental woman.

"How did you survive the battle when so many others were lost?" she asked in the same tone George Sinclair had put the question to him.

"Sorry to disappoint you, Mother," he said.

"Ye know that isn't what shhe meant." His father spoke in a slurred voice. "Ansswer your mother."

"They had to pick someone to deliver the head. Guess I was just lucky," Finn said with a shrug. The Orkney men said they chose him because of how bravely he fought, but his family would never believe that.

"So now you've come crawling back here to beg the Earl of Huntly to take ye back," his mother said. "*Ach*, why did I expect more of ye?"

Lord above, he needed a drink. Where did that lass with the whisky go? Finn looked over his shoulder, hoping to see her, and instead saw his brother Bearach and his wife Curstag were here as well—and fast approaching. Nay, not them too.

Clearly, God had decided not to wait until he was dead to punish him for his sins.

"Unlike you, Bearach is a credit to this family," his mother said when the couple joined them. "He was a hero in the fight against the Douglases at the Battle of the Causeway."

Finn just smiled, which he knew would irritate her, and kept silent. But when his gaze caught Bearach's, he could not avoid the bitter memory of finding his older brother cowering in a doorway during the battle.

Pull your sword and fight, damn it! Finn had shouted at him as half a dozen warriors came running toward them down the narrow street. While Finn fought them off, his brother took the opportunity to run.

The incident hung between them, poisoning the air like a fish gone bad. Bearach resented that he owed his life to Finn and hated him for witnessing his cowardice. Though Finn would never stoop to tell the tale, it would change nothing if he did. He had long ago given up trying to persuade his family that he was anything other than a wastrel.

"What will ye do now?" Bearach's wife, Curstag, asked.

Finn could no longer avoid looking at her. Curstag was a black-haired beauty, and despite his best efforts, he still remembered the feel of her voluptuous curves beneath his hands and the purr of her voice as she told him she loved him. He'd been sixteen and believed her.

She only asked the question to make him remember all of that, so he gave her a lazy smile to show her he had long since put that heartbreak behind him.

"I've come to speak with Huntly," he said. "But first I have a lady waiting for me, so I'd best be off."

"You're too late," his mother said before he had taken two steps.

He turned back to face her. "Too late for what?"

"To speak with Huntly," his mother said.

"He's left the castle?" *Damn it.* "Where's he gone?"

"To his grave," she said. "The Earl of Huntly is dead."

Finn could almost hear the faeries laughing in their faery hills at his bad luck. Hell, what could he do now? As a skilled warrior, he could always go to Ireland or France and fight for the highest bidder, but he'd hate to leave Scotland.

"Why don't ye come home to Garty?" his father asked. "Just until ye figure things out."

Jesu, he hoped he had not sunk that low. He would rather live by his sword in a strange land or spend the rest of his days in one of his relatives' dungeons than live at his parents' home.

"I appreciate the offer, Father," he said, "but—"

"For God's sake, Finlay is a grown man," his mother interrupted, planting a hand on her hip. "He neither needs nor deserves our charity."

At that moment, like an angel from heaven, Janet Kennedy, the former mistress of King James IV of Scotland, appeared at Finn's side to rescue him from his family. Janet was a woman not even Finn's mother would dare challenge.

"I have need of Finlay," was the only explanation she gave them before taking his arm and leading him away.

"God bless ye," Finn said as they crossed the hall.

"How did ye manage to know that woman for twenty-seven years and not murder her?" Janet asked.

"Drinking helps." He picked up a flagon of wine and two cups as they passed a table. "Where are ye taking me?"

"Upstairs," Janet said. "You and I need to have a talk."

"Only a talk?" Finn smiled and cocked an eyebrow. Though he was in no mood for flirtation after hearing the news of Huntly's death, Janet expected it as her due.

"Aye, just a talk," she said with a laugh.

Janet Kennedy was an extraordinary woman, still vivacious and beautiful at five and forty. In her youth, the strong-willed lass with flaming red hair had attracted powerful men, including the king. She was married three times, though the king had her first marriage annulled when he made her his mistress, and her third husband divorced her. Having outlived them all, she now reveled in her independence.

When Finn was twenty and full of himself, Janet had taken him to her bed and taught him lessons that every woman he bedded since should thank her for. Years had passed since their affair, but they remained good friends.

She led him up the enclosed circular stairs to a richly furnished bedchamber. As the mother of two royal bastards, she was an important guest and given one of the best chambers. She was also related to the Gordon chieftains, which probably made her and Finn third or fourth cousins, once or twice removed.

Janet took one of the chairs before the hearth, and Finn sprawled in the other and put his feet up.

"Damn Huntly for dying on me," he said. "*Ach*, he probably wouldn't have taken me back into his guard anyway."

When Janet refused the cup of wine he poured for her, he drank it himself.

"Becoming a drunkard like your father," she said, "will not solve your problem."

"It serves him well enough," he said, giving her a smile.

"Unlike your father, ye have no lands," she said. "Consequently, you must make yourself valuable to someone who can give them to you."

"I tried that and was nearly killed on Orkney for my efforts," he said, raising his cup to her. "I suppose I could offer my sword to Huntly's son. *Ach*, no, he's dead too. The next Earl of Huntly is the sniveling grandson, isn't he?"

An image of the fat-cheeked lad stuffing his face with sugared plums and shouting at the servants came into Finn's mind's eye.

"Sniveling Huntly is eleven years old and presently is in the queen's care, so he won't be adding you to his guard." Janet leaned forward to rest her hand on Finn's arm. "Besides, you can do better. You underestimate yourself and aim too low."

"I'm a second son of a second son, with no lands of my own," he said. "I have no prospects except to live by my sword."

"That's where you're wrong." Janet leaned back with a knowing smile. "A widow with a title and lands is easily within your reach."

"If this is what ye brought me up here to discuss," Finn said, "I'll need something stronger than wine."

"You're everything a land-rich, highborn widow could want in a husband." Janet ticked off the points with her fingers as she continued. "You're close blood relations with three earls, and you're a renowned warrior who could protect her lands."

"Janet, please," he groaned.

"Add to those qualities soulful blue eyes, a devilish smile, and a muscular physique, and I believe ye can do quite well for yourself." With a coy smile, she added, "Not as well as I did, of course. But you could gain what you want through a well-planned marriage."

"The only problem with your plan," Finn said, "is that I don't want a wife."

He especially did not want a wife of high status. His mother never let any of them forget she had married beneath her. His brother's wife was an ambitious schemer cut from the same cloth, except that she wrapped it in an appealing facade.

"Please tell me you're not still pining for that horrid Curstag," Janet said. "She was cruel to toy with ye, but it was inevitable she'd choose your brother. After all, he's your father's heir and you own nothing but your horse, your sword, and the clothes on your back."

"That was a long time ago." He'd been naïve to believe she would have him, despite his lack of prospects. He would never make that mistake again.

"Women must marry to acquire the home and position they expect in life," Janet said, "which is why we must find ye a widow who already has the wealth and lands ye both need."

"And have her lord it over me the rest of my life?" he said. "Nay, a night under the blankets and a few laughs is all I want from a lass."

"Not all women are like your mother and Curstag," Janet said. "Or me, for that matter."

"You're not like them," Finn objected.

"Oh, but I am," she said with a twinkle in her eyes. "I'm just far more charming and clever in how I go about getting what I want."

Finn laughed. One of the things he admired about Janet was that she was utterly honest, a decidedly rare quality in highborn women. She was, however, not easily deterred once she set her mind to something.

"Now to find the right woman of property..." Janet tapped her chin. "She shouldn't be too old, nor too young. And definitely not the small-minded sort who would complain about other women."

No matter what Janet believed about him, he'd feel bound by his vows. That was one more reason never to marry.

"I appreciate your concern for me, but marrying for land 'tis not worth the misery," he told her. "I'd rather the Orkney men had drowned me or hung my head off the mast of their boat or—"

"All right." Janet laughed and held up her hands. "Let me speak with my son. He may be able to suggest another way."

Her son was the Earl of Moray, a royal bastard of King James IV of Scotland. Moray was an exceedingly clever young man of twenty-four. Those who liked him called him politically astute; those who didn't called him conniving. Either way, Moray was a good man to have on your side. And a dangerous one to have against you.

Janet meant well, but her son was an important player at the highest level of royal politics. His interests were driven by forces far greater than Finn's fate, and Moray never gave a favor that did not advance his own interests.

Surely Finn had nothing to offer that Moray would want.

CHAPTER 3

"By the saints, I missed you," Margaret's brother George said as he lifted her off her feet and spun her around.

After he set her down, Archie gave her a stiff embrace. Her handsome brothers seemed unchanged, except that Archie's features had grown harder. Despite all the trouble her brothers had left in their wake when they fled the country, Margaret was overjoyed to see them.

"You're as gorgeous as ever." George grinned as he looked her up and down. "But, my God, what are ye wearing? Ye dress like a grandmother."

Margaret felt herself blush. George had always teased her about dressing as if she hoped to join a nunnery. When she was thirteen and painfully shy, her family had dressed her in exquisite gowns and paraded her in front of the king in hopes that she would catch his eye. Although the king failed to show an interest, she'd had so much unwanted attention that she preferred to dress to avoid it. Her husband had preferred that as well.

"I thought our escort was taking us to Tantallon Castle," Margaret said to change the subject. "I didn't expect to meet ye here in Edinburgh, especially at Holyrood Palace."

She had been looking forward to seeing her childhood home, and she had deeply unhappy memories of the last time she was in Edinburgh.

"We must be where the king is," Archie said, "and the king is here."

"How did ye manage to get past the queen's cannon fire?" Lizzie asked.

Archie's jaw tightened, and he shot a heated glare at Lizzie, which did not appear to bother her at all.

"The queen has withdrawn to Stirling, under pressure from the King's Council," Archie said. "The king is now free of his mother's overbearing and unfortunate influence."

That sounded like a significant victory for Archie over his estranged royal wife.

"I, for one, am glad the queen is not here," Lizzie said. "While ye were away, she called us all in for questioning and threatened us."

"We heard it was not pleasant for you," Archie said.

That was hardly an apology, but Archie had never been one to admit blame.

"Not pleasant?" Lizzie said. "Ye must have heard what Wretched William did to Margaret. I hope ye take a hot poker to his eyes and put his head on a pike."

"You're a bloodthirsty lass," George said with a laugh.

"And Sy—"

"Enough, Lizzie," Margaret said, and discreetly stepped on Lizzie's foot to stop her from telling them what her sister Sybil had done to escape the queen's wrath. For the time being, it was best her brothers not know where Sybil was.

"Do ye think exile was *pleasant* for us?" Archie snapped. "We had to live on the charity of the French court and then on my brother-in-law's."

"France wasn't all bad," George said, tilting his head. "Ahh, those French women…"

She and George had always been the peacemakers of the family, though their methods were different. While she soothed tempers and accommodated others' demands, George employed his sharp wit and easy charm—and got what he wanted.

"There's no profit in dwelling on the past," Archie said, brushing his hands against each other. "The Douglases will soon have everything we had before and more."

"I still don't understand how ye came to be residing here at Holyrood Palace with the king," Margaret said.

"The King's Council has recognized that, at thirteen, our king is too young to rule without the protection and guidance of more mature men," George explained. "They've decided that custody of the king's person shall be rotated every three months among the most important noblemen of Scotland."

This complex arrangement was obviously designed to prevent another fight like the Battle of the Causeway among the Scottish magnates for control of the young king. Still, Margaret could not help but feel sorry for the lad, separated from his mother and shifted from one set of guardians to another every three months.

"Archie has the king for the first three months," George said, and exchanged a look with Archie that she could not read.

"I want to see my father," Lizzie said. "Where is he?"

"He's keeping watch on the king," Archie said.

Keeping watch. That was an odd turn of phrase. It almost sounded as if the king was their prisoner.

"He's giving the king lessons in sword fighting in the courtyard," George told Lizzie. "The king is so impressed with your father's skill that he's given him the nickname of Greysteel."

After Lizzie left to join their uncle, Archie narrowed his eyes at Margaret and said, "I suppose she'll require new gowns for court."

"That fool William was so jealous he made her dress to hide her beauty." George grinned and flung his arms out. "I say, let our princess shine, as she always should have."

"New gowns are not necessary," she said. "I won't be staying long."

"You will," Archie said. "I require your presence here."

Margaret's stomach lurched at the thought of staying here at court and getting caught in her brothers' political machinations. "Why do ye want me here?"

"As the queen has refused to play her part as my wife," Archie said between thinned lips, "I need a woman to serve as my hostess."

"Wouldn't you prefer Lady Jane?" she asked, referring to his mistress. At least, Jane was his mistress before he was banished, and they had a daughter together.

"Having Jane play that role at the royal palace would be inappropriate," George said. "More importantly, it would upset the king, and we must all do our best to make him happy."

"But Alison will have her baby soon," Margaret said, managing to keep the edge of desperation from her voice. "She needs my help."

"Alison breeds like a rabbit and has a castle full of servants if she needs help," Archie said. "I need you here. The Douglases need you."

Margaret felt their expectations closing around her like a trap, making it hard to breathe.

"And while you're here, we can find you a new husband," George added.

"I don't want a husband." Never, never would she let them marry her off again.

"Nothing need be decided now," George said, putting an arm around her shoulders. "We're together again, and that is what's important. Please stay for a few weeks so we can spend time together."

That sounded so reasonable. How could she say nay? They would not let her refuse anyway.

"Of course I will," she said, because her mother had taught her that when you could not avoid an unpleasant task, you may as well be gracious about it.

"I knew ye would," George said. "Ye always do what's best for the family."

"Just for a few weeks," she said. "I won't stay longer than that."

Her brothers, however, were no longer listening.

###

Finn sat in a tavern a few miles from Huntly Castle with a lass on his lap, another beside him, and a drink in his hand. Not long ago, this would have been enough to make him happy, but he was just killing time, delaying the inevitable, as he had been for the last few weeks.

God's bones, he dreaded leaving Scotland, but what choice did he have? He was nearly out of money. After buying one last round of drinks, he had just enough left to pay for his passage across the sea.

"Which shall it be," Finn said, holding up a coin for everyone to see, "Ireland or France?"

Wagers were quickly placed. As he flipped the coin high into the air, shouts of "Ireland!" and "France!" filled the tavern. With all eyes on the spinning coin, no one else appeared to notice the two warriors who came through the door wearing their weapons and dead-serious expressions. They were the Earl of Moray's men, and their gazes were locked on Finn.

The shouting in the tavern turned into a roar of complaint when Finn let the coin bounce off the table and disappear into the filthy straw that covered the dirt floor.

A coin would not decide his fate, at least not today.

An hour later, Finn was ushered into the small room behind the hall that the former Earl of Huntly had used to conduct private business. He was surprised to find Moray here alone and sitting at Huntly's table with a stack of parchments before him.

The Earl of Huntly's death left a lad of eleven as the new earl and chieftain, which meant the Gordons, like Scotland itself, had no clear leader. Finn had wondered which of his Gordon uncles would fill the void, but he should have known it would be Moray instead. The Earl of Moray was a close Gordon ally and was the young earl's royal uncle. The boy's mother was another illegitimate offspring of King James IV.

"You smell like an alehouse," Moray said, in lieu of a greeting, and gestured for Finn to take the seat across the table from him.

"I suppose that comes from spending time in one." Finn slid into the chair and picked up an apple from a stunning silver bowl on the table, feigning indifference. It never paid to show you were desperate, especially to a man like Moray.

"Archibald Douglas returned to Scotland a few weeks ago, with the backing of Henry," Moray said.

"Henry who?" Finn asked.

"Ye know damned well who," Moray said. "His brother-in-law, King Henry VIII of England."

"What does Douglas's return matter to us?"

"My nephew was placed in royal guardianship when his father died," Moray said.

"Even though his grandfather was still alive then?" Finn asked.

"The queen followed my father's practice of making orphans who were heirs to important titles wards of the crown," Moray said. "That served to protect them and their lands during their minority."

Finn suspected that keeping the young heirs close during their formative years also served to ensure their future loyalty to the crown. James IV had been a wily ruler.

"Douglas was in exile at the time, so we agreed to it," Moray said. "Our understanding was that the boy would live in the queen's household, where he would be the king's close companion, as the two are near in age."

Unease prickled at the back of Finn's neck, though he could not guess where this was leading or what it had to do with him.

"But now Douglas is back and, as the queen's husband, he's claimed guardianship over my nephew." Moray fisted his hands on the table and leaned forward. "Young Huntly should be in *my* care, rather than in the hands of that grasping Douglas."

Grasping? That was the pot calling the kettle black.

"If Douglas would steal from a Tudor," Moray said, "he'd surely do it to his Gordon ward."

Finn remembered hearing that when the queen was forced to flee to England after their marriage, Douglas collected the rents from her estates for himself and lived on her money with his mistress in one of her castles. Folk said the queen was even more enraged over the rents than the mistress and that she'd hated her husband ever since.

"I have an unusual task I need done." Moray folded his hands and smiled as if he knew he had Finn over a barrel, which he did. "I believe you are uniquely suited to accomplish this task due to your particular talents and…attributes."

What in the hell did that mean?

"We need leverage," Moray said. "Something that will persuade Archibald Douglas to release young Huntly."

"What is it ye have in mind?" Finn asked.

"I want you to kidnap a Douglas."

"Kidnap a Douglas?" Finn repeated, not quite believing he had heard correctly.

"We need a hostage to trade for my nephew," Moray said.

By the saints, nothing could persuade him to do that.

"Why not just take young Huntly?" Finn asked.

"Because Huntly is always with the king," Moray said. "And the king is extremely well guarded, night and day. You'd never get close to him. It has to be a hostage."

"A lot can go wrong in taking a hostage." Finn leaned back in his chair and pretended not to sweat. "What happens if this hostage—an important noble who is close kin to the king's stepfather—puts up a fight and gets hurt?"

"I've given a good deal of thought to that problem," Moray said. "We can't risk spilling blood and starting a war with the Douglases. His brother George and uncle Greysteel are both skilled swordsmen and are usually in the company of a large force of Douglas warriors."

Finn relaxed, pleased that Moray had just talked himself out of the hostage plan.

"There is an uncle who is a bishop and another who's an abbot, but we don't want to take on the Douglases *and* the church." Moray paused and cleared his throat. "That leaves the Douglas women."

"Ye want me to kidnap *a lass*?" Finn sat up straight and raised his hands. "Nay. I can't do that."

"From what I hear, you have considerable charm with women," Moray said. "You ought to be able to seduce one of these Douglases and persuade her to run off with you."

"I never deceive women to bed them," Finn said, folding his arms.

Moray raised a skeptical eyebrow.

"I don't," Finn said. "And I won't."

"Well then," Moray said, "you'll simply have to capture her."

"I can't, not a lass," Finn said. "If I'm the one who takes her, I'll be responsible for whatever happens to her afterward."

"I assure you she'll be treated as an honored guest while she is here," Moray said, "and returned safe and sound to her family."

It was Finn's turn to raise a skeptical eyebrow.

"Mistreating the hostage would cause a blood feud with the Douglases, and that would not serve my purpose. All I want," Moray said, spreading his hands out, "is a simple exchange. A hostage for a hostage."

If Moray had claimed some high-minded reason for protecting the hostage, Finn would not have believed him, but his pragmatic explanation was persuasive. Still, Finn did not want any part of this scheme.

"There could be no better way for you to regain the trust— even the gratitude—of your clan than by being the man responsible for the return of their earl and chieftain," Moray said. "Young Huntly will be grateful as well. And remember, he's only eleven and likely to be your chieftain for the rest of your life."

This was *almost* enough to persuade Finn. But the notion of dragging a lass from her home didn't sit well with him, and the prospect of a long journey of rough travel with a spoiled Lowland noblewoman was worse.

"I understand you have an interest in acquiring lands." Moray steepled his hands and tapped the tips of his fingers against his chin. "If you succeed in this task, that could be arranged."

Ach, Moray knew exactly how to tempt Finn. Janet must have told him.

"The property I have in mind is not large, but sufficient to support you in comfort." Moray paused. "I'm afraid it's quite a distance from your family, up on the north coast of Sutherland."

If Finn could live anywhere he wished, it would be in Sutherland—and at a very great distance from his family. With property, he could sleep under his own roof, in his own bed, before his own hearth. He could be his own man.

"I'm giving you the chance to make amends with your Gordon clansmen and gain lands of your own," Moray said. "But if you would rather leave Scotland and fight for foreigners…"

Finn sighed inwardly. Moray was offering him everything he wanted. He demanded more assurances that the hostage would be well treated, but they both knew he would do it.

"Which Douglas lass do ye want me to take?" Finn asked, dread settling in his stomach like a lump of lead.

"Three of the sisters are married to powerful men. Not only are they well protected, but it would be foolhardy to bring their husbands into this dispute," Moray said. "That leaves Archibald's sister Margaret and his cousin Elizabeth."

"What do ye know of them?" Finn asked.

"Margaret was married for several years to a distant Douglas relative, William of Drumlanrig," Moray said. "But he had the marriage annulled some time ago."

Finn shuddered as he envisioned a sour middle-aged woman who would make the rough journey a misery for both of them.

"What of the other lass, the cousin?" he asked.

"From what I hear, Elizabeth—they call her Lizzie—should be fairly easy to take," Moray said. "She's loosely supervised, considering she's a sixteen-year-old virgin."

"I'm not kidnapping a sixteen-year-old virgin!" The thought gave him hives. Besides that, traveling alone with him would destroy the lass's reputation and hurt her chances of a good marriage.

"Then it's settled," Moray said, folding his hands with a small, satisfied smile. "You'll kidnap Lady Margaret."

CHAPTER 4

Margaret stared out the window at the gardens below, wishing she could leave Holyrood Palace and never return. Though she had only agreed to stay for a short visit, she'd been stuck here for weeks. She was sick to death of being paraded before men her brothers viewed as potential allies for them—and husbands for her. Lately, however, they had ceased pressing suitors on her, which gave her hope that they had finally accepted her refusal to wed again.

Her thoughts of escape were interrupted by Lizzie, who came storming into the bedchamber they shared in the palace and slammed the door behind her.

"If I have to spend another day with the king and that Gordon brat, I swear I'll punch one of them in the face," Lizzie said, and flung herself down on the window seat.

"Those two certainly can be a trial." Margaret sat beside her cousin and smoothed her hair back from her face. "Try to remember, 'tis not entirely their fault. Everyone caters to their whims because they're a king and an earl. At their age, 'tis bound to go to their heads."

Unfortunately, Archie did nothing to curb their behavior. If he would fill their time with worthwhile pursuits, the boys would not have so much leisure to spend on frivolous ones. The king's father would be so disappointed. James IV had been a well-educated man who spoke several languages and supported artists, musicians, and universities.

Lizzie's father did train them in sword fighting, which endeared him to the boys, but Margaret sensed that the men of her family were more concerned with keeping the king entertained than with training him to be king.

"Hopefully," Margaret said, "the king and Huntly's behavior will improve as they grow older."

"They're old enough now to know better." Lizzie folded her arms and pressed her lips together.

"What's wrong?" The anger in Lizzie's voice made Margaret suspect the boys had done something worse than usual. "Did something happen?"

"You're too nice to the king," Lizzie said, and fixed her gaze on the floor.

"Too nice?" Margaret felt sorry for the king, being separated from his mother and passed from guardian to guardian. Though he was difficult, she tried to be kind to him.

"Aye," Lizzie said. "Ye must stop it."

"Stop being nice?" Margaret asked with a laugh. "Why?"

"The king talks about you," Lizzie murmured.

"Talks about me?" she asked. "How?"

"He's always saying how beautiful ye are." Lizzie cast a furtive sideways glance at her. "He brags that he's going to take ye to his bed."

Good heavens, the king was not yet fourteen. Though this infatuation could not be serious, it was best to nip it in the bud. Time and distance would solve this problem.

"I must leave Edinburgh, at least until Archie passes the king onto his next set of guardians," Margaret said, getting to her feet. "I'll speak with my brothers at once."

She could barely contain her glee. The king had given her an excuse to escape court, one that her brothers would have to accept.

Once she was away, perhaps she could stay away.

Margaret found her brothers in the royal solar, which Archie had taken over for his own use.

"I've had a new gown made for you to wear tonight that will be stunning," George said. Then he winked and added, "Without my help, ye might be mistaken for a laundress."

"I'm afraid I've something more important than gowns to discuss with ye," she said.

Her brothers listened closely as she explained the problem and did not interrupt her with either expressions of disbelief or criticisms. This was going better than she had hoped.

"As I'm sure ye can see," she said, clasping her hands in front of her, "I must leave Holyrood at once."

"Ha! Our Margaret has the king wrapped around her little finger." A teasing smile tugged at George's lips as he held his finger up. "What did I tell you?"

If George anticipated this, why did he not forewarn her? Margaret stifled her annoyance and said in a pleasant tone, "I'll go pack my things now."

"This is no time to leave," Archie said.

"But I just told you the king wants to"—she felt herself blush—"take me to bed."

"Then give the king what he wants," Archie said.

Margaret was so shocked she could not find her voice to object.

"'Tis unfortunate the king takes after his mother in looks, but I bedded her," Archie said, making a face as if he had something bitter in his mouth. "We all must make sacrifices."

"You cannot be serious," Margaret said. "For heaven's sake, the king is half my age. He's still a child."

"He's old enough to want a woman," Archie said. "No matter how unappealing he is in appearance and disposition, he is the king and will have his choice of bedmates."

"What Archie is trying to say is that some lass is going to be his first mistress, and her family will benefit," George said. "Should it not be a Douglas?"

"You want to make me a...a...whore to that *boy*?" She should not have been so surprised.

"If you're unwilling to bed him, then just give him the hope that ye will," George said. "Keep him diverted so he doesn't choose a lass from one of our rival families, who would be only too happy to have a royal bastard."

Margaret's heart raced. She hated to argue, but this time she had to stand up to them.

"I can't do this," she said. "I won't."

"Ye don't have to do anything ye don't want to," George said in a soothing voice, and put his arm around her.

"You used to understand the importance of putting the family first and doing your duty," Archie huffed.

She looked up in time to catch the cautionary look George shot Archie.

"Do this for the family," Archie said, attempting a more conciliatory tone, "and I promise that after the king tires of you and moves on to someone else, I'll find you a good husband."

"By *good* husband," she said, struggling to keep her voice even, "ye mean a powerful man ye wish to make an ally?"

"Of course, he must be that as well, but we'll find a husband who will make ye happy," George said. "You deserve that after what happened with William."

"After what happened with William, I *never* want another husband." She'd told them that a hundred times in the last weeks, but they never seemed to hear her.

When George attempted to put his arm around her shoulders again, she stepped out of his reach. She usually avoided confrontation and swallowed her anger. But not today.

"William must have been a dreadful husband," George said, "even before he left ye."

"William did not leave me. He threw me out," she said. "And if ye knew he would be a terrible husband, why did ye marry me to him?"

"Marriages are like any alliance," Archie said. "Ye need not like your partner."

"I'll not marry again." She dug her fingernails into her palms with the effort to maintain her composure. "I will *not*."

"For God's sake, Margaret, control of the crown is at stake, and we need allies." Archie leaned over her as he spoke, in a way that reminded her far too much of her former husband. "I will choose a good man for you, and when I say so, you *will* marry him."

"We can discuss this another time," George said as he drew Archie away from her and refilled his cup. "Is everything ready for our special guests and the feast tonight?"

"King Henry's emissaries have already arrived," Archie said. "Margaret, make certain the food and music are the very best tonight, or they'll tell tales in London about the inferiority of our Scottish court."

Without waiting for her to respond, her brothers began discussing their strategy regarding the emissaries from Archie's brother-in-law, the English king. Margaret hid her shaking hands in the folds of her gown. She had not realized until this moment how determined Archie was to force her to marry again.

She never realized the toll her marriage had taken on her until long after William threw her out. During her marriage, she had focused on getting through each day as best she could. Soothing her husband's temper, coaxing him from foul moods, listening to his lying boasts, enduring his constant criticism and demands. Worst of all, suffering his invasion of her body, even when the midwife warned it was too soon after her last miscarriage.

She might not survive another marriage. She feared she would fade away altogether until there was nothing left of her at all.

But what could she do? She dug her nails into her palms and forced herself to keep an outwardly calm expression while she struggled to think of a plan.

Her dowry. If she was to have any control over her life, she needed her own resources. Her dowry included lands, jewels, and gold that would provide her the independence she needed to live her life as she saw fit.

Provoking Archie had been a mistake when she would need his help to force William to return her dowry. She chastised herself for her brief display of anger. That never served her well. She waited for a pause in their conversation to speak again.

"I'm sorry I reacted poorly to your suggestion that I marry again," she said, casting her gaze to the floor. "I know ye meant well."

"We are only trying to do what's best for all of us," George said.

Archie and George did what was best for Archie and George. Though they may persuade themselves that what was best for them was also best for her or the family, she knew better from bitter experience.

"Alison also urged me to consider remarrying." Alison was wrong, but at least her sister truly did have her best interests at heart and wished Margaret to find the kind of happiness she had. "Perhaps I will warm to the notion with time."

She would never agree to remarry, but her sister Sybil said the key to lying was to not make it too far-fetched—and Sybil knew about such things.

"You've always been a sweet-natured lass," George said, and put his arm around her shoulders again. "Any man would be lucky to have you."

By sweet-natured, he meant compliant, which was what men wanted. But she was not going along with her brothers' plans for her this time.

"There is something I would ask of you," she said.

"What is it?" Archie asked in a clipped tone, clearly impatient for her to leave.

"Insist that William return my dowry," she said. "He has no right to it."

"Have no worry about that," Archie said with a self-satisfied smile. "He's already returned every last penny."

"God bless you!" She was so relieved she would have thrown her arms around Archie, if Archie was the sort of brother one could embrace. This meant she could have her own home.

"We'll need the dowry for your next marriage," Archie said. "Until that's arranged, I will, of course, hold your property for you."

Margaret rarely lost control, but she had to struggle to overcome the urge to beat her fists against Archie's chest. He was making it plain she would never pry his hands off what should be her property until she agreed to marry when and whom he bade her. And once she did marry, control of her property would pass directly to her new husband.

She felt her life spinning out of her control again. Her brothers were so confident they could bend her to their will. She did not want to be the meek and submissive younger sister her brothers remembered, the one who married as she was told without complaint or question.

But how could she fight them when they held all the power?

"I must dress for the feast," she said, because she needed to get away from them before they saw how shaken she was.

She hurried toward the door, but Archie's voice stopped her when her hand was on the latch.

"I have important state business to conduct with our guests from England," he said. "I can't have my stepson interfering in matters he doesn't understand."

She waited with her back to him, knowing what he was about to say, and yet not quite believing he would have the gall.

"Remember, I'm relying on you to keep the king entertained tonight."

Finn emerged from the darkness of the tavern and fixed his gaze on the imposing gatehouse to Holyrood Palace at the base of the Canongate Road. The hour was early for drinking, even for him, but his guess that the tavern closest to the palace would be frequented by palace guards had proven correct.

A few whiskies after a long, tedious night of guard duty loosened the men's tongues, and Finn learned the palace would be full of guests for a great feast tonight. Once he was inside, Finn could easily blend into such a large gathering. Everyone would assume he was a low-ranking member of some other guest's party.

The challenge, however, was getting inside.

The palace was attached to the much older Holyrood Abbey, which was Finn's next destination. Moray had told him more about the abbey than he needed to know. Since its founding hundreds of years ago by King David, the abbey had had a strong relationship with the royalty of Scotland. The early Scottish kings stayed in the abbey's guest lodgings so frequently that eventually royal lodgings were built to accommodate them. More recently, James IV expanded those lodgings into a royal palace to welcome his bride, Margaret Tudor.

As Finn entered the abbey's church, his eyes were drawn upward to the graceful arches and intricate carvings. This was a very wealthy abbey, thanks to royal patronage and to the noblemen who joined their brotherhood, took vows of poverty, and gave their property to the abbey. And yet common people of the parish also worshipped in this church, which made it easy for Finn to enter without drawing notice.

Like all great churches, it was built on the lines of a cross. Finn passed through the long nave along the north aisle to the transept, where a screen separated the public from the monks during services. A young novice was sweeping the floor in front of the screen.

"I've a message to deliver to Brother Ansel," Finn told the novice. "His father is gravely ill."

"I'll give it to him." The young man held out his hand.

"I promised Ansel's mother I would put the message into his hands myself and wait for his reply," Finn said.

The novice withdrew into the dim interior on the other side of the screen. A short time later, a monk appeared. He had sharp, coal-black eyes that discerned at a glance Finn was not there to deliver a message from anyone's mother.

When he saw the seal on the parchment Finn slipped to him, the monk darted a glance over his shoulder. "Not here," he said, glaring at Finn.

Finn followed him out of the church through a low side door that led into the walled area that contained the abbey's extensive gardens. Once they were on the other side of the row of tall trees that separated the church from the gardens, the monk glanced around once more to be sure they were alone. Then he quickly broke the seal, read the message, and hid it inside his robes.

"Moray wants me to help you enter the palace in secret?" the monk hissed in a low voice.

"All ye need do is get me inside," Finn said. "I'll make my own way out."

"Moray asks too much!"

"'Tis his royal blood that makes him so bold," Finn said, shaking his head. "Truth be told, I'm not keen on the task he's given me either. But what else can we do?"

Finn sensed the monk's resistance weakening with the reminder of Moray's status, but the man needed one more push.

"Sooner or later, there's bound to be a cost to saying nay to the king's brother"—Finn paused and lifted an eyebrow—"or a reward for saying aye."

"If you're caught," the monk said, "I'll deny I had anything to do with it."

"Don't worry," Finn said. "I won't get caught."

###

Lizzie was waiting for her outside the solar, but Margaret did not pause to talk.

"I must warn ye—" Lizzie started to say.

"Not now," Margaret said, and hurried down the corridor to the hall. She was intent on reaching the privacy of their bedchamber before she lost her composure in the middle of the palace. "My brothers will do *nothing* to save me from the king's silly infatuation."

Thank heaven the king would move to his next guardian in a few days. She ought to be able to keep the boy at bay that long without offending him.

But how would she avoid another marriage? Archie had regained his power in the country—and over her. He was the head of her family, her chieftain, an earl, stepfather to the king. God help her!

When they reached the entrance to the hall, Lizzie pulled at her arm, but Margaret could not stop. She could barely keep herself from running through the courtiers milling about the hall to reach the stairs that led to the private chambers above.

"Listen to me," Lizzie said in an urgent whisper. "Ye need to know…"

Suddenly, the people between Margaret and the stairs shifted, and she saw a too-familiar profile she had hoped never to see again. It was William, the man who was her husband for seven interminable years, the unfeeling beast who threw her out in a storm in the dead of night while she was still bleeding from miscarrying his child.

Her feet forgot how to move. She was vaguely aware that Lizzie was speaking to her in a hushed voice, but she could not hear the words. The noise and the people in the hall faded and blurred as her vision narrowed so that she saw William as if through a tunnel.

God give me strength. I cannot do this.

She swallowed hard when she saw a very pregnant young woman attached to William's arm. His new wife could not be more than sixteen. The poor thing.

For a moment, she thought she would escape before he saw her. But he turned, and when their eyes locked, memories flooded through her like a raging river threatening to drown her. The countless nights she gritted her teeth while he pushed, prodded, and grunted over her. What he said to her the day she suffered the stillbirth while the Battle of the Causeway raged outside the shuttered window.

At least it was only a girl ye lost. Ye must give me a son. Do ye hear me, Margaret? I need a son!

William started walking toward her with a smug look on his face. Unlike her, he was prepared for this meeting. He had known she would be here.

"I have my dirk hidden under my skirts," Lizzie said under her breath. "Say the word, and I'll stick it in his belly."

"That won't be necessary." Margaret straightened to her full height, pasted a serene smile on her face, and walked right past William as if he was not worthy of her notice.

Margaret did not think they would ever reach their chamber. When they finally did, she began pacing the floor. She needed a plan. She could not stay here. But what could she do?

"We must tell your brothers," Lizzie said. "I can't wait to watch them kick Wretched William out on his arse."

"William is too cowardly to come without the assurance he would be welcomed." The truth was as clear to her as it was hurtful. "My brothers invited him here."

"They wouldn't!" Lizzie said.

"That is exactly what they did."

William would never have taken the risk unless the invitation had come directly from her brothers. Margaret tried to think the best of people, but there was no escaping the truth about Archie and George.

Her brothers valued the support of the Lord of Drumlanrig in their play for power more than they valued her. While they may be fond of her, she was an asset first and always, a pawn they could use and discard.

After all she had been through to further their ambitions, and the price she'd paid when those ambitions failed, they thought they owed her nothing.

They thought they owned her.

Hurt welled in her chest. She held her fist to her mouth as she fought back the bitter tears. Just like her husband, her brothers—the men who were supposed to love and protect her—did not deem her worthy of even the smallest sacrifice or consideration. She rarely got angry, but she felt it simmer and spark beneath the painful disappointment.

After this, she would be a fool to expect them to give up any advantage for the sake of her happiness. She could have no doubt now that her brothers would ignore her objections and do their best to force her to make a marriage alliance for them.

She could not let that happen.

"I'll tell my father," Lizzie said. "He'll make Archie do the right thing."

Greysteel was close to Archie and George and undoubtedly knew of this already, but Margaret did not have the heart to tell Lizzie that. Better to let her keep her faith in her father a little longer.

"'Tis too late," Margaret said, regaining control over her emotions. "Archie has already made his deal with William."

Lizzie kicked the side of the bed. "'Tis not fair!"

Margaret could not even recall when she had expected life to be fair.

A few hours later, Margaret looked at herself in the looking glass and tugged at the bodice of her gown while the maids did the finishing touches to her hair. The silvery blue silk gown George had the seamstresses make specially for the feast tonight was magnificent, if a bit daring.

"I've never seen anyone look more beautiful," one of the maids said.

"'Tis the gown, to be sure," Margaret said with a smile.

For once, she was glad to be dressed in a dazzling gown that showed her best features to advantage. She needed all the confidence she could garner tonight.

"Thank you for helping me dress," Margaret told the maids, and dismissed them.

She could not delay going down to the hall much longer. Lizzie had grown impatient and gone to wait for her downstairs some time ago. When she heard a knock on the door, she knew George had come to prod her.

"Aren't ye ready yet?" he said as he opened the door, then he came to an abrupt halt and gave her a broad grin. "I knew that gown would be perfect. You'll outshine every other lady at the feast."

Margaret was in no mood to be flattered by her brother.

"How could you invite William here?" she asked. "How could you forgive him after what he did to me?"

"He's necessary to our plans," George said in a quiet voice, and shifted his gaze to the side. "But we should have warned you."

"Aye, you should have," she said. "How am I supposed to face him in front of the entire court and all the guests at this feast?"

As soon as she entered the hall, the room would be abuzz with her humiliation.

"I'm sure you'll handle it with grace and calm," George said. "You always do."

With grace and calm? As she always did? Anger roiled under her skin. Her brothers were so certain that she would suffer this slap in the face, this last hurtful betrayal, quietly and without causing them the least inconvenience.

Tonight, she would teach them a lesson.

"Let's go, then," she said, and took George's arm.

When they reached the bottom of the stairs, Lizzie was waiting just inside the stairwell and watching the people in the hall.

"One of your ribbons has come loose," Margaret said as she reached for a bow in Lizzie's hair. "George, you go ahead. I need just a moment to fix this."

As soon as he left them, Margaret took both of Lizzie's hands in hers. She felt uneasy involving her younger cousin, but Lizzie was her only ally at the palace.

"I need your help," she whispered.

"Of course," Lizzie said. "I'll do anything."

"I'm afraid it might be a bit dangerous."

"Dangerous?" Lizzie's eyes lit up. "What is it ye plan to do?"

Finn returned to the abbey that evening at the appointed hour. Hidden by darkness, he followed the wall that encircled the grounds until he reached the back gate behind the abbey's kitchen gardens. He found a monk's habit hidden behind the bush next to the gate, tossed it over his clothes, and tied the rope belt. Holding his breath, he leaned his shoulder against the gate, then smiled as it creaked open. Until this moment, he had not been sure the monk's courage would hold and he'd leave the gate unlocked.

After pulling the hood low over his face, Finn quickly crossed the garden and entered the abbey church through the side door the monk had shown him earlier. Keeping to the shadows beyond the reach of the church's burning candles, he moved on silent feet along the wall until he reached the opposite side of the church and the decorative arched doorway that was the king's entrance from the palace.

He ducked through the arch and ran up the steps that the king would walk down to enter the church. The stairway was black save for a flickering candle at the top, where he found the monk waiting for him in front of a heavy oak door reinforced with iron.

"Thank you for your help," Finn said in a hushed voice as he pulled the habit off and gave it to the monk. Beneath it, he wore his best tunic and breeches. When the monk made no move to unlock the door, he said, "Ye do have a key to it?"

"Nay," the monk said. "The lock is on the palace side of the door, and it's only opened when the royals come into the church to pray."

Finn waited, hoping the monk did not bring him here for nothing.

"With the queen's hurried departure and custody of our young king changing hands, however, all is in confusion," the monk said. "No one seems to be responsible for locking the door."

"Then luck is on my side," Finn said.

"I doubt that verra much," the monk said before he snuffed out his candle and slipped away into the darkness.

CHAPTER 5

Finn walked down the long, dimly-lit corridor, pleased to find it empty, and followed the sounds of voices and music that should lead him to the great hall where the feast was being held. As he neared a corner, he suddenly found himself face to face with a pair of burly palace guards who came around it from the other direction.

"What business do ye have back here?" one of them demanded, moving his hand to the hilt of his sword. "Ye should be in the hall with the rest of the guests."

"A lady invited me to slip away to her bedchamber. If ye saw her," Finn said, spreading his arms out, "you'd know I couldn't say nay."

"I see no lady," the guard said.

"She returned to the hall before me." Finn lowered his voice. "She didn't wish her husband to see us return together,"

"Men who look like him have all the luck," the other guard said with a sour expression.

Finn tilted his head and grinned. "I won't be so lucky if her husband catches me."

"Ah, go on, ye bastard," the first guard said with a laugh, and waved him on his way.

Finn smiled to himself. The hard part was over. He was in.

His chances of carrying Lady Margaret Douglas out of the palace under the noses of the royal guards and half the Lowland nobility were slim to none. If the opportunity presented itself, he'd take it, but his goal tonight was simply to study his quarry so he would recognize her and know how best to approach her when she was outside the palace.

Surely the woman had to leave it sometime to visit a shop on King's Street or to ride in the wood next to Holyrood. If he was lucky enough to get a chance to speak with her tonight, he might even persuade her to meet him for that ride. She would not be the first woman to decide to meet him against her better judgment.

When he reached the great hall, it was crowded with nobles dressed like peacocks in colorful silks and velvets. They were all milling about, presumably waiting for the king to arrive and take his seat at the high table. Finn moved along the fringes of the crowd, picking up snatches of whispered conversations.

"I thought we were rid of the damned Douglases for good."

"The Douglases are like the weeds in the garden. They always come back."

"The queen is furious about losing control of the king."

"God help us, what kind of king will the lad make? He's thirteen, and they say he wept like a babe when he was separated from his mother."

"Perhaps he wept about being put under his stepfather's thumb. I'd weep too."

Heads turned toward the doorway nearest the high table, and a murmur traveled through the hall like a wind blowing through a field. The king must have arrived. While Finn was curious to see the lad, finding Lady Margaret in this crowd was a more pressing matter.

He caught the attention of a young serving woman as she passed by. When he took her arm and drew her aside, she blushed to her roots and batted her eyelashes rather furiously.

"Do ye know who Lady Margaret Douglas is?" he asked. "Is she here?"

"Lady Margaret?" The lass's face fell, and she nodded in the direction of the high table. "That's who they're all looking at."

When Finn turned and followed her gaze across the room, the woman's beauty struck him like a punch in the chest, knocking the air out of his lungs in a *whoosh*. She looked like a faery queen, slender and graceful in a gown that shimmered a silvery blue. Fair hair the color of moonbeams was piled on top of her head and fell in loose tendrils to frame an exquisite face.

A woman as beautiful as she was must be accustomed to all the attention, but he sensed she was uneasy with it. She glanced around the room with a distant expression. In contrast to her fair hair and skin, her eyes were a deep brown. When she looked his way, he thought her gaze caught on his for just a moment.

That moment made him think of the time a doe looked up and met his gaze through the leafy wood just as he pointed his arrow at her heart. He had lowered his bow and let the doe go. For some reason he could not fathom, this lass tugged at his heartstrings the same way. He had the urge to leave the palace and let her go too.

Finn had known his share of beautiful women. More than his share, truth be told. But this Douglas lass had an ethereal quality that was different from the others. Though she was tall, there was a gentleness, a fragility, about her that made her seem vulnerable—and made a man want to protect her.

Then Finn remembered that he was the man she needed protection from.

He shook his head to break the spell she cast over him. He knew what highborn women were like. *Ach*, no doubt she practiced that doe-eyed expression in her looking glass, knowing what it did to men, just as she calculated how low to make her bodice. The gown revealed enough of her breasts to make a man's mouth water while leaving enough a mystery to make him hope to be the one she allowed to uncover them.

Finn told himself that if he did not kidnap her, Moray would find someone else to do it. This was his chance to acquire lands of his own, and he did not expect to have another. If he failed to even attempt to do as he'd agreed, Moray would see that he suffered more than the loss of that opportunity.

Now that he'd cleared his head of foolishness, Finn took in the talk around him.

"Thought she'd be past her prime, but she's even more beautiful than before," a man behind him said. "Heavens, she must be seven and twenty now."

"Wonder who will be the lucky man she's married off to this time?" his companion said. "One thing is certain—he'll have more warriors to support her brother's ambitions than I have."

"Sad to think of such a fine lass in some old goat's bed," the other said. "But she's barren, so the husband will be someone who has heirs to spare."

"Aye. A man can always have beauty in a mistress," his companion said, "but for a wife, he needs a good breeder."

"Still, who wouldn't be tempted—"

"God's blood, this will be interesting," the other man interrupted. "That's Drumlanrig, her former husband."

The buzz of gossip spread through the hall like a swarm of bees. Lady Margaret must hear it, but her placid expression did not waver. Not a faery queen, then, but an ice maiden.

The more Finn examined her, though, the more he wondered if she was as unaffected as she pretended. Her ivory skin seemed a shade paler. In the end, it was the slight tremor of her fingers against the skirt of her gown that gave her away.

It took inner strength to face this crowd of nobles, who were all hoping for a dramatic scene, and show nothing of her true feelings. While Finn admired her for it, he also tucked away the knowledge that this lass was damned good at deception.

During the feast, Finn kept watch on the high table from his distant seat with the lowest-ranking guests. Music floated down from the gallery, and even at his lowly table, the wine was good. By the sixth or seventh course, he'd had more than enough to eat, but the food kept coming.

When the last course was finally removed, a tall, dark-haired man stood up from the high table. He looked to be in his mid-thirties, and he wore a trim, pointed beard, a bejeweled velvet tunic, and a stiff, self-important manner. This had to be Archibald Douglas, the 6th Earl of Angus, himself.

"The king calls for dancing," Douglas announced, and clapped his hands. Once the servants folded and moved the lower tables against the walls, he turned to the king and swept his arm out to the side. "Which lady will you honor as your partner, your grace?"

"Lady Margaret!" the king said, his voice cracking.

The lady took the awkward youth's arm with a smile, but the slight creases at the corner of her eyes looked strained. Unfortunately for the king, his choice of a partner who was half a head taller and as graceful as an angel only emphasized his clumsiness. It was painful to watch.

The moment the king released her at the end of the dance, Lady Margaret disappeared into the crowd. Finn was taller than most, and he soon caught sight of her standing against the wall and began to make his way toward her. He was just a few feet away when the room suddenly went quiet. He turned to see the king standing in the center of the hall with his arms raised.

"With the help of Lady Margaret, I've come up with a grand surprise for you, my honored guests, this evening." He paused a long moment for effect, then shouted, "Stand back! Make room for the lions!"

Lions? Finn had heard that the lad's father, James IV, kept lions at the palace and even had a house built for them in the gardens. Finn edged to the front of the crowd.

Several women shrieked, and everyone moved back as two lions were brought in on heavy chains with thick leather collars. Finn had never seen anything like them. Drawings did not come close to capturing the magnificence of the beasts. When the male roared, the rumble reverberated through the hall and in Finn's bones. Even a few men screamed.

What a marvelous beast!

Curious to see how the cool Lady Margaret reacted to the lions, he turned to look at her. She had moved from where she had been standing, but so had everyone else when the lions were brought in. Finn scanned the hall, trying to catch sight of her.

O shluagh, she was gone. How long had he been distracted by the damned lions?

He ducked out of the door that was closest to where he last saw her. Hoping to catch her before she returned to the hall, he half ran down the corridor, glancing into rooms as he passed them. Though he had not planned to take her hostage tonight, if he found her alone while everyone else was distracted by the lions, he just might be able to sneak her out through the abbey.

He slowed his pace to a walk as he passed a serving woman so as not to draw attention to himself. He did not want to be remembered.

###

Margaret found Lizzie donned in her breeches and cap and waiting, as planned, with her horse in a dark corner of the courtyard behind the stables.

"Ye told your father you're staying at your stepbrother's house tonight?" Margaret asked. Lizzie's stepbrother from her mother's first marriage was a successful Edinburgh merchant. "I don't want anyone to find out ye had a part in this."

"Don't worry, I've done this before," Lizzie said. "My stepbrother and father don't speak, so neither ever finds out."

Margaret mounted the horse behind Lizzie and averted her face as they approached the gate. Unfortunately, the guards were more astute than Lizzie's father.

"Lady Elizabeth, where do ye think you're going at this hour?"

"This poor servant's mother is near death and asked to see her," Lizzie told the guards. "'Tis on the way to my brother's house, so I'm taking her. We've no time to waste if she's to hold her dear mother's hand before she expires."

Lizzie could spin a tale like no one Margaret knew.

"With such an important feast tonight," the guard said, narrowing his eyes at Lizzie, "I would not expect a servant to be allowed to leave before the guests are abed, dying mother or no."

"Lady Margaret gave her permission," Lizzie said. "Ye know how soft-hearted she is."

"All right. But ye shouldn't be allowed to go out and about the way ye do," the guard grumbled as he waved them through the gate. Then he called after them, "You be careful and go straight to your brother's!"

"We'll be at Blackadder Castle in a couple of hours," Lizzie said as they started down the cobblestone street.

"'Tis not safe to ride there in the dark," Margaret said. "We'll need to find a tavern where we can take a room for the night."

"We'll be fine," Lizzie said. "My horse knows the road to Blackadder Castle, and he's faster than any bandit's horse."

"Lizzie, ye worry me," Margaret said, which made her cousin laugh.

"Alison and David will be furious when they hear that your brothers welcomed Wretched William back," Lizzie said. "David won't give ye up no matter what Archie threatens."

Relations between the two men were already tense. David was still angry with Archie for fleeing the country and leaving Alison vulnerable—even though it was David who had taken advantage of that and laid siege to her castle. When two powerful magnates with hundreds of warriors at their command have a dispute, it could too easily escalate to bloodshed.

What had she done? Acting rashly was unlike her, but she was so desperate to escape she had not thought through the repercussions. The last thing she wanted was to cause trouble between her brothers and David, especially with Alison so close to her time.

"Let's leave Alison and David out of this if we can," she told Lizzie. "Instead of the castle, we'll go to Thomas's cottage in the village."

Margaret knew she could not escape for long. How could she? Running off like this would buy her a few days' reprieve, at best. But perhaps her bold act of rebellion would persuade her brothers not to attempt to force her to wed again.

Finn could not find Lady Margaret, so he returned to the great hall, where she was bound to return eventually herself. He relieved a passing servant of a silver carafe and a cup. While he waited for his quarry to reappear, he may as well avail himself of some of the palace's fine wine.

"Where's Lady Margaret gone?" The king's thin, petulant voice a few feet away told Finn he was not alone in his vigil.

Out of the corner of his eye, he saw Archibald's subtle nod to a man who bore a strong resemblance to him. This second man put his arm around the king's shoulders and led him to a group of bonny, but very young lasses. While the man talked and the lasses giggled, the king's gaze continued to search the hall for Lady Margaret.

Finn had the nagging feeling he had missed something, some telling detail he had seen but ignored. When Lady Margaret failed to reappear after an hour, he drank down the rest of his wine and left. He paused on the palace steps and drew in a deep breath of the cool night air. That nagging thought was just out of his reach…

The image of the serving woman he passed in the corridor when he was searching for Lady Margaret came into his head. The woman carried a tray, wore a servant's gown and an old woman's kerchief, and walked with her head down. He was so intent on finding a lady in a sparkling gown and headdress that he barely saw her. And yet, somewhere in the back of his mind he had noticed something was not quite right about that serving woman.

It was the hands that clasped the tray. They were not the red and chafed hands of a servant, but the smooth, elegant hands of a noblewoman. He could kick himself for missing that clue. As he mulled over the memory, he was certain the graceful walk and slender shape beneath the drab servant's gown belonged to Lady Margaret Douglas.

Now, that was intriguing. He smiled at her inventiveness. His amusement faded as he recalled the king's petulant voice and her brother's irritated expression when she did not return to the hall. If Finn's suspicion was correct and her brother wanted her to initiate the young king into the pleasures of the bed chamber, it was no wonder she left the feast.

Perhaps she used her disguise to escape for a few hours solace in a lover's arms. Finn certainly was never one to judge a woman for seeking pleasure.

So why did the thought of Lady Margaret meeting a lover unsettle him?

A couple of hours later, Finn returned to the nearby tavern to see if he could learn something useful from the guards about her habits. He settled in, expecting he'd have to buy a few rounds before he could casually bring Lady Margaret into the conversation, and then buy a few more before he could get them to tell him when she usually left the palace to visit friends or shops in the city.

As soon as he sat down next to some guards, however, he heard them complaining that if Lady Margaret did not reappear by morning, Archibald Douglas would send them to Blackadder Castle with orders to find her and bring her back.

"I don't relish the notion of asking the Beast of Wedderburn to hand over his wife's sister," one of the guards said. "The last time a man crossed him, the Beast tied his severed head to the market cross by his hair."

"Let's look in the village near the castle first," one of the others suggested. "That's where we found her the last time, after we learned she visits the old man in the last cottage on the road."

"Aye, we'll go to the village first," another said, "and pray we find her there."

It must have been near midnight when they reached the cottage. While Lizzie tied her horse in the brush behind the cottage where it would not be seen, Margaret got a fire going in the hearth.

"You can have the bed," Lizzie said, stifling a yawn. "I'll sleep in the loft."

Margaret was too tired to argue and quickly stripped down to her chemise. When she pulled down the extra blanket Thomas kept on the shelf above his bed, a small leather pouch fell onto the mattress. She started to put it back on the shelf, but then stopped herself. It was an ordinary pouch, the kind used to carry coins or a talisman. She did not know why she felt compelled to open it.

She untied the leather lace and upended the bag into her palm. As shining bits of black stone poured out, memories filled her head from the night William tore her pendant from her neck and smashed the stone into these tiny pieces. Her mother had given her the stone, a black onyx, believing it held magic that would protect her and bring her good fortune.

It had done neither.

Two years later, she had left Drumlanrig with nothing but the night shift she wore, a rough blanket, and a handkerchief with these smashed bits of onyx clutched in her hand. She had told Thomas to throw them away. But dear Old Thomas had known better, that one day she would want them, and he kept them for her.

Rap.

Margaret tilted her head. Was that a knock at the door?

Who would visit Thomas at this hour? She wrapped the blanket around her shoulders and hurried to the door. But when she reached it, she hesitated. Could her brothers have already discovered she'd gone and sent men to fetch her?

Rap. Rap. Rap.

She leaned her ear against the door.

"Please, help me!" a frantic voice called from the other side. It sounded like the lad Brian from the village.

As soon as she opened the door, Brian rushed past her carrying his sister.

"Quick, shut the door before anyone sees us," he said.

"Mercy!" Margaret cried when he turned around and she saw smears of blood on his face and clothes. "What's happened to you?"

His eyes were wild, and little Ella had her face buried in his neck.

"I saw ye ride in," he said. "Ye said I could come to ye if I needed help."

CHAPTER 6

"You were right to come to me," Margaret told Brian. "Now tell me what's happened."

"Da killed her this time!" Tears streaked down his face. "He's killed my mum."

Margaret swallowed. She was afraid to go into the boy's cottage with his violent, drunk father there, but his mother might still be alive. "I'd best go see."

"Nay!" Brian said. "I don't know how soon he'll be back, and he mustn't find ye there."

"Your father's gone?" she asked. "Where?"

"To bury her," the lad choked out. "Said he knows a place where no one will ever find her body."

Good God. Margaret's hand went to her throat.

"Da said he'll tell everyone she left him, and if I say otherwise, he'll kill me too."

"I'll get my cloak and take you and Ella to the castle at once," Margaret said. "You'll be safe there."

"I'll not be safe so long as Da knows where I am," Brian said, shaking his head violently. "I'm going to go as far away as I can."

Margaret eased Brian onto a stool and tried to calm him. Ella still clung to him with her face pressed into his chest and her tiny fingers clenched on his bloody shirt.

"Come, Brian, ye can't manage on your own," she said. "How will ye live?"

"Ye know I'm a hard worker. I can find a place on a ship," he said. "I'll go to sea and never come back here."

Margaret could not blame him for wanting to escape to a different life.

"But I can't take care of Ella too." His eyes pleaded with her for understanding. "Will ye take her?"

61

"Take her?" she said.

"Please!" Brian said, fighting tears.

She was not sure what he meant. "As I said, I can take her to the castle, where my sister and the laird will—"

"Not the castle! People in the village work there," he said. "They know Ella, and Da will find out and get her back. Ye must hide her from him."

Margaret looked up to see Lizzie listening raptly from the doorway.

"With no proof of murder and the only witness gone," Lizzie said, "David will have no justification for keeping Ella from her father."

"David will do it if I ask him to," Margaret said.

"Da would find a way to steal her back, I know it," Brian said. "My mum always said how kind ye were. She'd want *you* to have Ella."

"Me? Have her?" Margaret was taken aback.

"I know you're fond of Ella, and you'd take good care of her," he said, his voice cracking. He rubbed his cheek against the top of his sister's head. "Please, can't ye be her mother now?"

Ella looked up at her then with wide blue eyes, and the air went out of Margaret's lungs in a rush. She would not allow the violent man who murdered this sweet child's mother to ever have her back. A fierce determination filled her to do whatever she must to protect her.

When Brian lifted his sister onto Margaret's lap and the exhausted child leaned heavily against her chest, Margaret's decision was made.

"Of course I'll take care of Ella," she said.

"I can't stay any longer," Brian said. "If Da catches me trying to leave, he'll beat me—or worse."

"I'll take care of you as well," Margaret said. "We should stay together."

"Ella and I have a better chance of escaping him apart," Brian said. "Da will travel the roads and search everywhere, asking after a boy and a wee girl."

Though Margaret tried to persuade him he would be safer with her, in the end, she could not make him stay. And the lad deserved a chance at a new life, far from the village where he would always be known as his father's son.

"I left our things outside," he said.

While he brought in a dirty cloth bag and a large rectangular basket from outside the door, Margaret and Lizzie gathered what few coins they'd brought with them.

"Hide these coins well," Margaret told him, then she gave him one of her pieces of black onyx. "This is for protection."

A tear slid down Brian's cheek as he pressed a soft kiss to his sister's cheek.

Margaret suspected he'd been shown little affection in his life. She put her arm about his bony shoulders and held him. For a moment, he leaned into her, then he stepped away and hoisted his bag over his shoulder.

"You're going to grow up to be a fine man," she told him. "When you're ready to find us, Ella and I will be waiting for you."

"Bwian! Bwian!" Ella cried out, her small arms reaching toward the door.

Margaret was grateful Ella had not understood her brother was leaving without her until after the door closed behind him. The parting was already so painful for him without hearing his sister's heart-wrenching cries.

"Hush, sweetling, hush," she cooed as she rubbed Ella's back and rocked her on her lap.

Margaret's heart wept for the little girl in her arms. How could she fill such a gaping hole in Ella's life? The poor child had lost both her mother and her brother tonight. Margaret squeezed her eyes shut and prayed Ella had not actually witnessed the bloody murder. Even if she had not, Ella most likely had seen violence in her home before this.

Ella's cries gradually subsided to soft hiccoughs, and eventually she fell into an exhausted sleep in Margaret's arms. Being careful not to wake her, Margaret laid her in her basket.

Her heart swelled as she watched Ella sleep curled up on her side in the basket, which was meant for a babe, not a child of three. Even sound asleep, she clung to her ragged blanket and a dirty doll her mother had made, all the poor thing had from the only home and family she knew.

"By the saints, what will ye do with her?" Lizzie asked, leaning over the basket.

"I'm going to keep her."

She touched Ella's soft cheek. Tears swam in her eyes. She was a *mother*. After years of longing, she had given up on her dream of having a child. Ella was the answer to her prayers.

"I'm your mother now," she whispered. "I'll take good care of you. Always."

Ella changed everything. This could no longer be a temporary escape from court. Margaret could not go back. Ever.

"I can't wait to see Archie and George's faces when they find out," Lizzie said with a grin. "Adopting the child of a penniless villager, and a murderer at that, will ruin their plans of making the kind of marriage alliance they hoped for."

"They must never find out. Never," she said, gripping Lizzie's arm. "They would take her away from me."

"What will ye do?" Lizzie asked.

"I don't know yet." Where could she go that her brothers would not find her? How would she care for the child once she got there? She rubbed her forehead, trying to think.

"Ye can't stay here in the village long without being found out," Lizzie said.

Brian's father would assume Brian took Ella with him when he disappeared, and the other villagers would assume their mother took both children with her. That bought Margaret a little time. Still, she could not keep Ella hidden in the cottage for long without being discovered by a villager, if her brothers' men did not find them first.

"I'll have to take Ella somewhere I'm not known," Margaret said, more to herself than to Lizzie.

"I know," Lizzie said. "Ye can go live in the Highlands with Sybil and her MacKenzie husband."

"If only I had a way to get there." MacKenzie lands were far away and difficult to reach. Her brothers could track her down anywhere in the Lowlands, but no one in the MacKenzie clan territory knew her except her sister. She could pretend to be someone else there.

"Ye could hire a man to take ye." Lizzie screwed up her face in thought. "He'd have to be someone who knows the Highlands well and who can wield a sword if you're attacked."

How would she ever find such a person—and quickly? Even if she did, the man would probably take her straight to Archie. Any fool would know he could gain more by revealing her plan to her powerful brother than by helping her escape.

Lizzie yawned and stretched her arms. They were both beyond tired.

"We can't do anything before morning, so let's sleep on it." Margaret brushed Lizzie's hair back from her face. "Thank you for helping me tonight. I don't know what I would have done without ye."

After Lizzie climbed the rope ladder up to the loft, Margaret set Ella's basket on the floor beside the narrow bed, then she paused to marvel again at the girl who was now her daughter. Though she had no right to this dear, sweet child, Ella needed a mother, and Margaret was determined to keep them together.

She had no idea how, and she did not have much time to figure it out.

In the morning, her brothers would discover she was not in the palace. How long would it be before they sent men to Blackadder Castle and the village to look for her?

God help me, what can I do?

She picked up the bag with her shattered onyx from the bed and dropped to her knees beside Ella's basket. Though she doubted the stone retained its magical qualities after it was shattered, if it ever had any, she was desperate. The jagged pieces poked into her palm as she squeezed the bag and prayed for a way to escape with Ella.

When no answer came, she rested her head on her folded arms on the bed.

Her mind was foggy with exhaustion when she felt a slight draft and turned to see the lamp on the table in the other room flicker. She meant to have that door fixed for Thomas because the latch sometimes stuck open. With a deep sigh, she got up to blow out the lamp and shut the door. When she stepped into the other room, she came to an abrupt halt, too stunned to move as her mind tried to make sense of what her eyes seemed to see.

A huge Highland warrior sat with his feet propped on the table, a long dirk across his lap, and a wicked smile on his face. Margaret blinked, expecting the inexplicable vision to disappear. But the vision—or rather, the man—remained.

He had coal-black hair that fell past impossibly broad shoulders, a square-jawed face with the shadow of a beard, and startlingly blue eyes that watched her closely. Despite his smile and relaxed posture, his long, muscular body exuded an animal power that reminded her of the king's lions. She knew instinctively that if she attempted to run, he would spring from his seat and pounce on her before she took one step.

She forced back the almost overwhelming urge to scream. That would wake Ella and Lizzie and alert the Highlander to their presence. She had to protect them, no matter what it cost her. Her heart beat so frantically that she felt lightheaded, but she was determined to keep her wits about her.

"This will be easier on both of us if ye cooperate." The Highlander spoke in a deep, soft voice, as if soothing a frightened animal, but everything about him pulsed *danger, danger, danger*.

"Cooperate?" she asked, her own voice coming out in a thin whisper. "What is it ye want?"

"You, lass," he said. "I've come for you."

CHAPTER 7

"I've come to kidnap ye," Finn said.

He let out his breath when the lass did not awaken half the village by screaming—at least, she had not yet. He'd gambled on her being a steady lass and not given to hysterics. After how coolly she reacted to seeing her former husband while half the Lowland nobles watched, he figured she either had ice in her veins or was extremely adept at pretending she did.

Of course, he could have avoided the risk by grabbing her from behind and muffling her screams with a hand over her mouth. But they had a long journey ahead and that certainly would start them off on the wrong foot.

The lass had been beautiful from a distance in her glittering gown, but this close—and, God help him, in just her shift—she stole his breath away. Hair the color of moonlight spilled in waves over her shoulders and breasts, which were firm and high.

Ach, what was wrong with him? He was frightening her enough without gawking at her breasts, fine as they were. With an effort, he dragged his gaze back to her face. He had the odd sensation of falling when he found himself staring into her deep brown eyes, but he shook it off.

"I give ye my word I won't harm ye," he said, and gestured to one of the stools at the small table. "Now can we talk this situation over quietly?"

She hesitated, but then she perched on the stool, all the while watching him warily with those large brown eyes.

"There's no cause to make this difficult," he said. "But one way or another, you're coming with me."

"Ye can't kidnap me," she said. "Do ye know who my brother is?"

"As it happens, that's the verra reason for kidnapping ye," he said. "You're a valuable lass."

"You're mistaken if ye believe my brother places a high value on me," she said. "He did not give a thought to what might happen to me when he fled to France."

Finn had seen how her brother used her as a lure for the king and other powerful men. Archibald Douglas would want his beautiful sister back.

"As soon as your brother does what we want," he said, "you'll be returned home, safe and sound."

"What if he doesn't do what ye want?"

"He will," Finn said. "Until he does, I give ye my pledge ye will not be harmed."

"I'm to take your word for that?" she asked.

"Aye." He gave her a smile that usually won over the lasses.

She arched one delicate eyebrow. Apparently, she was not fully persuaded.

"Look, lass, I don't want to do this either. As neither of us has a choice, let's be off," he said. "We've a long journey ahead of us."

The lass did not give away much, but Finn sensed a subtle change in her. Perhaps his admission that he was forced into this kidnapping had worked to ease her fears, as he had hoped.

"A long journey?" she asked in a soft voice that had the effect of fingertips brushing against his skin. "Where are ye taking me?"

She appeared to accept that she was going with him. This was going surprisingly well.

"I can't tell ye where just yet," he said.

"But it is *far*?" she asked.

"Aye." He found it odd that his answer did not appear to upset her. But then, she was a cool-headed lass who did not reveal much.

"Since you're a Highlander"—her gaze darted to his kilt, which had the dual effect of making her cheeks go pink and his cock spring to life—"ye must be taking me somewhere in the Highlands?"

"Aye." He saw no harm in telling her what she already knew. He unwound the rope he'd brought from around his waist. "I'm sure ye understand I must take the precaution of binding your hands."

"I'll make a bargain with ye, Highlander." She stood up and backed away from him with her hands raised. "If you'll agree not to bind me, I'll give ye my word that I'll go willingly."

"*Ach*, I cannot do that."

"Did ye not say this would be easier on both of us if I cooperated?" she asked, tilting her head in a verra fetching way. "On such a long journey, surely there will be many opportunities for me to attempt to escape or cry for help."

"That would indeed make the journey tedious," he said. "But I'm afraid you'll have to earn my trust."

"*Me*," she said, "earn *your* trust?"

"All right, I'll give ye one chance," he said, holding up his finger. "If ye try anything, I'll bind ye hand *and* foot. Now, we must leave."

"I can't go in my shift," she said, sounding more shocked at this than at being kidnapped.

When she looked down at the offending garment, his gaze followed hers and lingered. He could not see through the damned thing, and yet his throat went dry imagining her naked body beneath it.

"If ye care nothing for my discomfort," she said when he failed to respond, "anyone who sees me like this will know something is amiss, and you'll be caught for certain."

Traveling with this lass in a night shift would certainly draw unwanted attention. When she started for the other room, he suspected a trick and caught her arm.

"You may not come into the bedroom with me," she said in a quiet but firm voice.

Did she have a man in there, waiting for the opportunity to attack him? Finn drew his dirk. Holding her by the wrist, he eased the door open with his shoulder.

The room was tiny and sparsely furnished with a narrow bed built into the corner. After finding nothing under the bed but a large basket, he relaxed. The opening to the loft above was too small for a grown man to fit through. And if a man did manage to squeeze through there to hide instead of protecting his woman, he wasn't anyone to worry about. There was nowhere else to hide and no windows to offer Lady Margaret an escape.

"Whose cottage is this?" Finn asked.

"My friend's," she said. "He's away."

Finn was curious who this friend was to her and why she came here. Sometimes bored noblewomen found it exciting to bed men not of their class. Lady Margaret was sinking low indeed if she was carrying on an affair with a villager.

The room was so small that they were mere inches from each other and the narrow bed. He eyed the bed and imagined it would be a tight squeeze for two, but—

"I need privacy to dress," she said, interrupting his untoward thoughts.

She glanced meaningfully toward the door, and yet his feet failed to carry him out. He was still imagining her lifting her night shift to reveal slender calves and thighs that stretched to…

When his gaze reached her primly folded hands, he snapped his gaping mouth shut.

This time, she gave him a stern look and pointed toward the door.

"Ye don't need help with the hooks on your gown?" he asked. "I'm good at that."

"I've no doubt you are," she said, and it did not sound like a compliment. "But I can manage on my own."

Margaret's heart was pounding in her chest so hard that she thought the Highlander must hear it. She was terrified he would discover Ella and Lizzie. Praise God for Lizzie's quick thinking—she must have heard the voices and hidden Ella with her in the loft. Lizzie even had the wits to pull the rope ladder up behind her.

The Highlander grinned at her as he finally backed out the doorway. As soon as he closed the door, Lizzie's head popped through the opening overhead. When Margaret put her finger to her lips, Lizzie nodded, then dropped the rope ladder and scurried down with Ella in one arm.

Margaret took Ella, who was furiously sucking her thumb, into her arms and held her close. She glanced up just in time to see Lizzie start toward the door with a small dirk in her hand.

Good heavens, Lizzie meant to stab the Highlander. Margaret grabbed Lizzie's arm to stop her. Then she conveyed her plan to Lizzie with gestures, pointing to herself and Ella and then to the door.

You're going with him? Lizzie mouthed.

Margaret bit her lip. She wished she had more time to think it through! But she'd wanted to find a man to take her to the Highlands. Now one had found her—albeit a kidnapper—and she was going to use him to get away.

When she nodded that she was going, Lizzie's eyes lit up, as if Margaret was embarking on an exciting adventure rather than making a desperate escape that could end very badly indeed.

"He's a Highlander and verra handsome," Lizzie whispered, as if these were redeeming qualities that made this ridiculous plan worth the risk.

"When we travel through MacKenzie lands, I'll try to escape and find Sybil," Margaret said in Lizzie's ear. MacKenzie lands stretched from sea to sea across the Highlands, so they ought to pass through them.

She nearly jumped out of her skin when a deep male voice called through the door.

"Are ye having trouble with those hooks, lass?"

"Nay! I'm nearly ready." Margaret quickly donned the servant's gown and cloak she had borrowed—or rather, stolen, now that she could not return them. She felt bad about that, but it could not be helped.

"What if ye can't get away from him?" Lizzie asked in a low voice as she fastened the hooks at Margaret's back.

"Then I'll be a hostage." Highborn female hostages were usually treated well, even as guests.

Weren't they?

"If you're waiting for Archie to pay a ransom," Lizzie whispered, "ye could be gone a long time."

That was her best hope. The longer she was away, the better her chances of avoiding her brothers' schemes altogether. It may be wrong to wish they would be forced into exile again, but she did.

She retrieved the basket from where Lizzie had shoved it under the bed. Ella immediately climbed into it and curled up, still sucking her thumb, which gave Margaret a sick feeling that Ella was accustomed to hiding in the basket. The poor child!

"Shhh," she warned Ella, then kissed her forehead and gently pulled the blanket over her head.

She could not hide Ella from the Highlander for long. Her hope was to delay the discovery until they were too far away for him to want to turn back. Luckily, Ella was an unusually quiet child—Margaret could not let herself think about why that was now—and the night was dark. If she could just get Ella out of the cottage without the Highlander seeing her, her plan should work.

Margaret blinked back tears when she and Lizzie embraced to bid goodbye.

"I'll miss you. Tell Alison not to worry," she whispered in Lizzie's ear. "I'll send word when I can."

Lizzie held up her dirk, then dropped to her knees and strapped it to Margaret's thigh before she could object.

"What are ye up to in there?" the Highlander said through the door. "Fair warning, I'm coming in to fetch ye."

"Don't!" she called out.

Margaret's heart raced as Lizzie scrambled up the rope ladder and pulled it up behind her. As she picked up the basket, her gaze caught on the pouch with her shattered onyx lying on the bed. Without pausing to think why, she slipped it into the side of the basket.

Then Margaret opened the door to her kidnapper—and whatever fate would bring her.

CHAPTER 8

The Highlander, who was pacing the small room like a caged animal, came to an abrupt halt and swept his gaze over her, which did nothing to calm her nerves.

"Ye can't take that," he said, pointing at the basket. "We're on horseback."

Sudden panic made her limbs weak and her throat tight. She had to persuade him to let her bring the basket.

"Surely, ye cannot expect a lady to go on a long journey without a second gown, extra stockings, and"—Margaret turned to put her body between him and the basket while she fumbled for what else she could say was in it—"and…other things a woman needs."

He heaved a sigh and gave her a lopsided smile. "All right, princess."

With his easy smile and that twinkle in those deep blue eyes, fringed with impossibly long dark lashes, this Highlander was far too good looking to trust. Handsome men were the worst.

While she was shamelessly staring at him like a girl half her age, he took the basket from her before she realized it.

"By the saints, lass, what do ye have in here? Rocks?" he said, hefting the basket.

She barely managed to stifle a gasp as Ella began to wiggle beneath the blanket. Moving quickly, Margaret leaned over the table to blow the lamp out.

A steel grip clamped around her arm. "I hope ye weren't planning to slip out in the dark and escape."

"This is my friend's home," she said. "I don't wish to risk setting it afire by leaving a lamp burning."

"Just who is this *friend*?" he asked.

"He—" She stopped speaking because the Highlander was no longer listening for an answer. With her heart sinking, she followed his gaze to the wriggling blanket covering the basket.

"Sh-i-t-e," the Highlander said on a long exhale.

God grant him patience, did the lass have a dog in there? Ladies like her were fond of those wee snappy ones with sharp teeth. Finn whipped off the blanket before the damned thing could bite him.

A bairn with curly blonde hair, rosy cheeks, and enormous blue eyes stared up at him. He was so stunned that words failed him. Slowly, he dragged his gaze from the apparition to Lady Margaret.

"What in the hell is this?" he asked. "No one told me there would be a bairn. They said you were barren."

She winced slightly at the word *barren*, but he was too upset at the moment to apologize.

"Whose bairn is this?" he asked.

"Mine." Lady Margaret picked the child up and clutched her to her chest. "She's mine."

"I meant, what man does she belong to," he pressed her. "Who's the father? Is it your husband, Drumlanrig?"

"He's not my husband any longer," she said. "And Ella is not his."

Then the child was the result of an affair. An adulterous affair. This must be the true reason her husband discarded her.

"Who is the father, then?" he asked.

"She's mine alone," she said, and pressed her lips firmly together.

"*Ach*, ye haven't told him, have ye?" he said. "A man has a right to know."

"You're a kidnapper, and ye judge *me*?" she said.

"'Tis wrong to take a child from its father."

"Sometimes," she said, rubbing her cheek against the child's curly blonde head, "'tis the only right thing to do."

"*O shluagh*," he said, calling on the faeries for help as he ran his hands through his hair. "'Tis bad enough I have to take a highborn lady unaccustomed to rough travel. I cannot take a bairn as well."

"You'll not take me without her," she said, and the iron in her voice surprised him. "If ye try, I promise ye I'll fight every moment of every day to get back to her."

That would surely make for an unpleasant journey. And if Lady Margaret did manage to escape, she would be in danger until he found her again. *Damn it.*

"Besides," she said, "'tis to your advantage to bring her along."

"To my advantage?" He gave a dry laugh. "I cannot wait to hear this."

"The men my brother will send to search for me will not be looking for a woman with a child," she said.

"Why not?" he asked, though he suspected he already knew the answer.

"Archie doesn't know about her," she said. "No one does."

"How did ye manage to keep your daughter a secret from your family as well as the father?"

"Ella has been living with a woman here in the village," Margaret said. "Everyone believes she's her daughter."

"Well then, this problem is solved," he said, relief pouring through him. "Ye can leave the wee bairn with her."

"The woman died suddenly...of a fever," she said. "That's why I had to rush here in secret at night from Holyrood."

The faeries were surely laughing at him in their faery hills tonight. What in the hell was he going to do? He shuddered at the prospect of tearing the child from her mother's arms and carrying a screaming and wailing Lady Margaret off over his shoulder. And then the lass would give him no end of trouble with her attempts to escape.

He glanced down at the child. Though he knew next to nothing about bairns, even he could see this one was too young to be left on her own. He could leave her on the doorstep of one of the neighboring cottages, but he had no way of knowing if the family would take good care of the wee thing.

He was tempted to walk out the door and not look back, but there would be grave consequences if he did. Moray and the Gordons would lose the leverage they needed to force Archibald Douglas to release the young Gordon chieftain. And then, once the lad came of age and returned to rule his clan, he'd hold a grudge against Finn for the next fifty or sixty years. Finn would have to leave Scotland and never return.

"Shite!" What choice did he have? He spewed a long string of Gaelic curses interspersed with a few more *shites* until he noticed that Lady Margaret's eyes were wide with alarm and she was holding her hands over the bairn's ears.

He did not mean to frighten her—at least not more than he needed to.

"All right, ye can bring your daughter, but only"—he paused and pointed his finger at her—"if ye promise to give me no trouble."

Lady Margaret broke into a smile that made him feel as if he'd just walked into a valley filled with sunshine and birdsong. *Jesu*, the lass was dangerous.

Margaret peered into the darkness, afraid that someone would see them—or hear the Highlander muttering more colorful Gaelic curses. She could feel that Ella was frightened, but she neither cried nor whined as any other child of three would do. Instead, she merely sucked her thumb and held tightly to Margaret's hand.

"It will be all right, sweetling," she leaned down to whisper, and hoped she was right.

"Must we take this damned basket?" the Highlander asked again from the other side of the horse.

"Aye," she said. "Ella cannot sleep without it."

The Highlander had already tried to persuade her to leave it behind, but it would comfort Ella to sleep in it and the child had lost everything else, so Margaret held firm.

"All I wanted was to get this journey over with," he said under his breath as he tied the basket behind the saddle, "and now we'll be traveling at the pace of a peddler."

Margaret sucked in a startled breath when the Highlander suddenly appeared behind her. He stood so close that she felt the heat from his body. He lifted her and Ella onto the horse.

When he swung up behind her, she was suddenly surrounded by brawny male Highlander. A blade of grass could not have fit between them anywhere. The hard muscles of his thighs rubbed against hers, his breath ruffled a loose strand of her hair on the side of her face, and her backside was pressed against his...

She would just have to do her best to ignore him.

"One peep from you as we leave the village," he whispered in her ear, "and the bairn stays behind."

Margaret refrained from pointing out that she'd been quieter than he had. She'd learned long ago that men resented being told of errors in their thinking.

They rode into the black night and left the village behind. Despite the uncertainty and dangers that lay ahead, when she felt Ella's heartbeat beneath her palm, a wave of happiness spread through her. She and her daughter were making their escape.

CHAPTER 9

Margaret awoke from a deep sleep to find herself lying flat on her back with the Highlander leaning over her.

"Have a good sleep, *m' eudail?*" *my treasure*, he asked with a wicked grin.

She had no notion where she was or, more importantly, how she came to be in this position. The last thing she remembered was riding through the night. She blinked, struggling to clear her head, but it was hard to gather herself while staring up into those deep blue eyes.

"Please move so I can get up," she said, doing her best to pretend she did not feel the least bit awkward about finding herself practically lying under her kidnapper. "And I am not your treasure."

"Ye are a treasure to me—or ye will be once I deliver ye," he said with a wink, and offered his hand to help her sit up. "So ye speak the Gaelic? I suppose that means ye understood all my cursing as well."

"Quite well, as a matter of fact." After their former king learned Gaelic to win the hearts of the Highlanders, her family required her to learn it in the hope of winning his.

"That will make things easier for ye where we're going." With a smile in his voice, he added, "*M' eudail.*" *My treasure.*

"Where's Ella?" she blurted out, suddenly remembering she had a daughter. Her hand went to her chest. "God forgive me, I'm a terrible mother!"

"'Tis all right. The wee lass is right here." The Highlander put an arm around Margaret's shoulders and turned her to the side.

When she saw Ella a few feet away busily playing with a pile of sticks, Margaret was able to breathe again.

"She helped me gather moss for our fire, didn't ye, Ella?" he said. "Now she's sorting the sticks for me, big to small."

Ella looked up from her task and gave the Highlander a serious nod. Margaret was surprised he made such an effort to entertain Ella and succeeded so well.

"She's a fine helper, she is," he said.

Ella swelled with the compliment. This Highlander certainly knew how to win over her daughter. Though Margaret would not succumb to his charm herself, it warmed her heart to see Ella so content.

"Shall we make some porridge?" he asked Ella. "'Tis almost noon, but we slept so late we missed our breakfast."

We *slept?* She swallowed hard when she looked down and saw a long dent on the other half of the blanket. Good heavens, the Highlander had slept right beside her. And there were more nights ahead. She really had not thought this through when she decided to escape with him.

Before she could recover from that revelation, Ella started to run past her. She caught her for a moment and gave her a hug, a sweet reminder that Ella was worth the risks she was taking.

A short time later, the Highlander and Ella were side by side before the fire, in deep contemplation of the bubbling oats.

"Would ye say 'tis ready?" he asked.

Ella answered by holding out her bowl.

"Careful. 'Tis hot," he warned as he gave her a scoop, then he scooped up another bowlful for Margaret.

"Thank you." Margaret felt awkward having him wait on her. She was accustomed to being the one who took care of others, and she did not know any men, other than servants, who cooked.

When Ella got up to chase after a butterfly, Margaret decided to use the opportunity to learn more about this Highlander who, at least for a short while, held their fate in his hands. Men always enjoyed talking about themselves, so it should not be difficult.

"I don't know your name," she said, thinking his clan name would give her a clue as to who he was and where he was taking her.

"Finlay," he said. "Most people call me Finn."

So much for that. She would have to try another tack.

"Ye seem like a good man, Finn," she began, hoping flattery would help.

"Do I?" he asked with a gleam in his eye. "Women don't usually tell me how good I am until after we've been to bed."

She refrained from rolling her eyes. "What I mean is that ye don't seem the sort to kidnap women, and ye made it clear ye didn't want to. So why are you doing this?"

"'Tis a long tale, but it comes down to this," he said. "I agreed to kidnap ye in exchange for lands of my own."

She was surprised he did not gild his answer in a pretense of duty to his clan or some other high-minded justification. That saved her from having to gently probe until he revealed his true reason.

"So," he said, giving her a devilish grin that made her stomach do a strange flip, "don't go mistaking me for a good man."

At least he was honest about it, which was better than most men.

"Ye make a fine porridge," she said, as she scraped the last of it from her bowl. "You're a man of many talents."

He gave her that grin again and waggled his eyebrows.

"I know," she said before he could speak, "most women tell ye that *after* you've spent the night together."

She did not know what made her say that out loud. William never took teasing well, but the Highlander responded by throwing his head back and laughing.

"Well, lass," he said, "we did sleep together."

Her cheeks went hot. She thought again of that dent in the blanket beside her and wondered how many more nights they would share that blanket. What would she do if he tried to seduce her? While she was contemplating that prospect, he took her bowl from her.

"I can clean up," she said, and started to get up.

"Even after I kidnapped you and your daughter, ye cannot help being polite, can ye?" He gave her an amused smile. "Well, we kidnappers have our rules of courtesy as well, and I'll not put ye to work."

With quick efficiency, he washed their bowls in the stream and then returned to sit beside her.

"You're good with Ella," Margaret said as she watched the small girl try and miss catching the butterfly again. "Have ye children of your own?"

"*Ach*, no!" He gave a dry laugh. "At least I've succeeded in avoiding that."

"But ye must want children one day," she said.

"Nay."

She was taken aback by the certainty of his tone. The men she knew considered it their duty to sire heirs and took pride in the number of their offspring as a reflection of their manhood.

"Why not?" she asked, turning to look at him. The question seemed a bit rude, but she was curious.

"I might turn out to be a father like my own," he said. "I wouldn't do *that* to a child."

"What is your father like?" she asked.

"Drunk and miserable," he said with a laugh.

"Ye need not be like him."

"Alas, I fear I would, as a bairn comes with a mother," he said. "The bairn would bind me to her. As a wife, even." He actually shuddered.

"Would that be so terrible?" She couldn't help smiling.

"Aye, it would," he said. "A wife would be like an anchor around my neck."

Her smile died on her lips. His words were too near to what her husband said of her the night he threw her out. Before she could hide her reaction, the Highlander touched her arm. It was a light touch, and yet his hand left a heated imprint on her skin right through her sleeve.

She shifted her gaze away from him and called to Ella. "Don't go too far!"

"What have I done?" he asked.

"Other than kidnapping me and carrying me off in the middle of the night?"

Her attempt to divert him with a jest did not succeed, judging by the furrow between his dark brows. Another man would never have looked past her smile. She would have to be more careful with this Highlander.

She stood up and for the first time really took in her surroundings. In the distance, she could see the sea coast, which made no sense at all.

"Ye must have taken a wrong turn," she said. "We're not on the road north to Stirling."

"Nay, we're not," he said.

She recognized the coastline now, and they were not far from Tantallon, the Douglas stronghold. Had he lied to her from the start and intended all along to deliver her to Archie?

"But ye said ye were taking us to the Highlands," she said, keeping her voice light with an effort.

"We're sailing there," he said.

She was relieved he was not taking her to her brothers, but any hope she had of escaping her kidnapper and finding her sister Sybil when they crossed MacKenzie lands were dashed. If they traveled to the Highlands by boat, rather than through the interior, they could end up as far from her sister and MacKenzie lands as when they started.

"But…why go by sea?" she asked.

"'Tis faster to reach our destination by boat," he said.

She remembered now that in her last letter Sybil had written that her family planned to stay at Eilean Donan Castle in the west until after their new babe was born. The kidnapper was taking her up the east coast to the opposite side of the Highlands.

"The sooner we get there, the sooner I'll be done with this miserable task," the Highlander said, "and the sooner you'll be returned home."

But Margaret had no home with her brothers.

And she was never returning.

Finn could have sworn Lady Margaret was dismayed when he told her they were traveling by sea, though she hid it well. Perhaps she had hoped to escape if they traveled north through Edinburgh and Stirling. Or maybe she suffered from seasickness. God, he hoped not.

"Who's Brian?" he asked. "Is that Ella's father?"

"Brian is the son of the woman she lived with in the village," she said. "How do ye know his name?"

"She was crying for him when she woke up."

Lady Margaret looked so stricken that Finn had a bad moment, fearing the lass would start weeping on him.

"They were verra fond of each other," she said with only a slight quiver in her voice. "He's gone to sea."

Ella returned then, sat down, and clutched her empty bowl, which he'd left out for her. *Ach*, she was such a quiet, wee thing. From the way she dove into the first bowl as if the porridge was the best meal she'd had in a long while, he thought she might still be hungry.

"More?" he asked her.

Ella held her bowl out tentatively, as if she did not expect him to give her the second helping. It was not his business, but it seemed to him that Lady Margaret had made a verra poor choice in the woman she'd left Ella with in the village. Besides being thin and dressed in rags, the bairn was too quiet.

He was surprised he did not mind the wee bairn's company at all. In truth, she was a welcome distraction from Lady Margaret. The damned woman sparked his curiosity. He wondered if there was a hot, passionate woman beneath her calm exterior—and the devil in him was tempted to find out.

Sailing to the Highlands had another advantage—on an open ship, he'd never be alone with her.

"Time for us to find a boat sailing north," he said once Ella had finished. "The sailors will all be in the tavern next to the harbor."

He packed up their things and bridled the horse to lead it down. He was uneasy taking Margaret and Ella into a gathering place for rough, seafaring men who were mostly pirates, but, promise or no, he could not trust Margaret not to run off if he left them.

He glanced sideways at her as they started down the slope toward the harbor. Despite the servant's clothing, she would stick out in the tavern like a rose growing in the midst of a pigsty. Besides her pearly-white skin and slender hands that had never scrubbed a pot, she carried herself with a quiet dignity that set her apart.

Worst of all, the lass was too damned beautiful. If she had half the effect on other men as she did on him, there could be trouble.

"Some of these men are unsavory," Finn warned her. "You'll be safe in the tavern and on the boat so long as the men think you belong to me."

"*Belong* to you?" she asked, raising an eyebrow.

"I'll tell them you're my wife." He ignored Margaret's startled expression. "You'll fit in better as a Maggie, so that's what I'll call ye."

"All right," she said without any hesitation.

"And you, wee one," he said, picking up Ella, "will be our daughter."

"You'll be her father?" Margaret said. "Does this mean you're going to be drunk and miserable?"

He laughed and put his arm around her. Now that they were in sight of the boats and the tavern, he may as well play the part. But he had no business enjoying it.

He'd misjudged the lass when he saw her at Holyrood Palace and thought she was cold and humorless. Still, Lady Margaret did not seem the sort to engage in a brief and frivolous affair. He was beginning to think that was a shame.

A damned shame.

When they reached the tavern, Margaret took Ella from Finn and ducked under the low threshold behind him. Inside it was dark and noisy and had a foul stench that made her gag.

"Stay close to me," Finn ordered and clamped a hand on her elbow. "I'll make this as quick as I can."

Margaret thought he was warning her not to attempt to escape—until her eyes adjusted to the gloom. Men at court made her uncomfortable with their suggestive remarks and attempts to lure her into dark corners, but these men with their hard expressions and scarred faces looked as if they would slash her throat to steal a ring without a twinge of regret.

"Finn, is that you?" a loud female voice called out.

A woman with wild, unbound red hair, laughing eyes, and a generous bosom that threatened to spill out of her ill-fitting bodice pushed men aside as she bounded toward them. She threw her arms around Finn and kissed him right on the mouth. And continued kissing him as if intent on sucking the life out of him.

The woman's brazen sensuality made Margaret feel painfully prim and uncomfortable in her own skin. Unlike her, this young woman clearly enjoyed her appeal to men. She would be surprised to learn Margaret envied her that.

Of course, her envy had nothing to do with the particular man the woman had her lips locked on at the moment. After what seemed an unnecessarily long time, Finn removed the woman's arms from around his neck. Then he nodded toward Margaret as he spoke to the woman.

The woman shot sour looks at Margaret while she and Finn continued their whispered conversation. Then she called a couple of men over, and they all talked some more.

"Found a ship sailing in the morning," Finn said when he returned to Margaret's side. He paused and peered more closely at her. "I'm sorry if that embarrassed ye. The lass meant no harm."

"She appears to know ye rather well," Margaret said. "Do ye come this way often?"

"I came here once, two or three years ago," he said, and took Margaret's arm.

"Must have been a memorable visit," Margaret murmured beneath the noise of the tavern as he led her out.

"The lass helped me find someone to buy the horse as well," Finn said as he untied his horse outside the tavern. "He makes his living hauling goods to and from the boats and lives just up the path here behind the tavern."

"You'd sell your horse?" Margaret asked.

"I need the money to pay for our passage," he said as he rubbed the horse's forelock. "And he's not mine."

"Whose horse is he?"

"I don't know," he said with a shrug. "I stole him from the palace stables."

She laughed despite her shock. After her husband and brothers, who always tried to hide their selfish motives and unsavory acts, his frank admission had a certain charm.

When they reached the cottage, she counted five children outside, who were either pulling weeds in the small vegetable garden or hanging clothes out to dry. Their father watched them approach with narrowed eyes.

"Remember, ye promised to give me no trouble," Finn said in a low voice. "Don't try to run off on me."

Where would she go?

While Finn and the man haggled over the price, the children stopped working and came over to greet Margaret and Ella and pat the horse. The contrast between these happy, boisterous children and Ella, who cautiously peeked out at them from behind Margaret's skirts, worried her. Fortunately, the men did not take long to conclude their deal for the horse.

"Be good to him," Finn said and rubbed the horse's ears.

Once they were on their way and out of earshot, Margaret said, "Ye do know that horse was worth far more than what ye sold him for."

"Aye, but the man could not pay what the horse is worth without taking food out of the mouths of his children," he said. "As it was all gain to me and enough for our passage, it was a good bargain for us both."

While the two men bartered, she had watched the other man closely and was certain he would have paid more, whether he could afford to or not. She was accustomed to men of vast wealth who squeezed their tenants for every farthing with never a thought for how their families would suffer for it. And yet her kidnapper, who did not appear to have an extra penny to his name, had shown kindness toward a stranger out of concern for the man's children.

She found herself increasingly at ease with this Highlander, which was a mistake. She reminded herself that, while he appeared to have a soft heart for children, he was also a womanizer, a charmer, a horse thief, and a kidnapper. Such an unpredictable man just made it more difficult to anticipate the dangers.

Finn took another long pull from his flask as he watched Margaret put her sleeping daughter to bed in the basket, leaving the two of them alone in the night before the fire. How in the hell did he get himself in this situation? He had not thought through what it would be like traveling with Lady Margaret Douglas. He shook his head as he recalled the frozen look on her face when they were in the tavern.

He should never have taken her into the tavern.

He never should have taken her at all.

"You should go to sleep as well," he told her.

He'd wager she had never slept on the ground in her life before this. No doubt, the maids fluffed her pillows each night. Probably took two maids to comb out her hair and strip her of her fancy gown—*ach*, he should not think about that.

When he agreed to this, he thought the widowed Douglas sister would be older. Matronly. Definitely unattractive. It was just his bad luck she was impossibly beautiful. Hell, if she was going to look that good, she ought to at least be difficult. He'd expected his highborn hostage to be complaining, demanding, and generally unpleasant. *Ach*, was that too much to ask?

Lady Margaret was trouble, all right. But the wrong kind of trouble.

He felt her eyes on him as he took another long drink. Without the bairn for distraction, she could not quite hide her unease at being alone with him in the dark. Unease? Hell, she must be scared witless. He was a horse's arse for not realizing it sooner.

"Don't worry, lass, you're safe from me," he said. "You're not my kind of woman."

"What is your kind?" she asked after a long silence. "Women like the one in the tavern?"

"Exactly. I like hot-blooded women who want a good time"—he paused to take another swallow—"and nothing more."

Lady Margaret was careful, contained, and highborn to boot. She could not be further from the sort of woman he liked. And yet he wanted her so much his teeth ached.

CHAPTER 10

Margaret ought to be relieved she would not have to fight off her captor's amorous advances. Instead, his lack of interest made her feel wooden inside, as if she was lacking something other women had. William told her so often enough.

You're cold as a fish. Would she never get his voice out of her head? She had more important concerns now. She had a daughter to worry about. She lay down with her hand resting on Ella's basket and watched the Highlander, who had moved farther away and leaned against a tree wrapped in his plaid.

He was brooding and drunk tonight. One would think a man so deep in his cups would not still be attractive. But he was as handsome as ever with the firelight playing across his face, broad chest, and long, outstretched legs. With looks like that, she imagined he had no trouble finding willing bed partners. No doubt he took advantage of that and had carnal relations with an abundance of women.

She had let down her guard earlier, drawn in by his humor, his easy conversation, and how good he was with Ella. But she must remember he was not her friend, and she could not rely on him. He would protect her and Ella only because it was in his interest to deliver his hostage unharmed. If that changed, he would leave them to the wolves.

The next morning, Finn was his charming and cheerful self again, and she found it hard to hang on to her resolve of the night before. He made them breakfast, letting Ella help again, and then they walked down to the harbor.

"Good morning to ye!" Finn called out to the men who were on the beach loading barrels onto the boat.

The sailors did not look any less rough and dirty to Margaret than they had the day before in the tavern. Finn walked with one arm around her while carrying Ella in the other.

"Try to look like you're my wife," he said in a low voice.

"How would your wife look?" she asked.

"Satisfied."

She couldn't help laughing, he was such a rogue. When they got to the boat, which was pulled partway onto the shore, he lifted Margaret into it and handed Ella up.

"Sit in the bow, where you'll be out of the way of the oarsmen," he said. "I'll join ye shortly."

Finn spoke with an older man she remembered from the tavern who was giving orders to the others, then he joined the men as they lined up on either side of the boat. On the older man's signal, they heaved and pushed the boat into the sea, and then hoisted themselves over the sides. Finn joined the others at the oars, and the men rowed hard until the boat cleared the point at the north end of the bay.

Once they reached deep water, they unfurled the sail and pulled up their oars. The sailors, who had been fully occupied with their efforts until now, suddenly seemed to have nothing to do but stare at her. Her heart lurched, and she held Ella tighter as a huge man with the arms of a blacksmith and a jagged scar across his cheek took a step toward her.

"I wouldn't mind a bit of that," he said.

The next thing she knew, the man flew over the side of the boat. It took her a moment to realize Finn had come up behind him and flung him over. He was holding the man over the waves with an arm around his neck.

Good heavens, how did Finn do that? As the sailor cursed and kicked, he started to reach for something at his belt.

"Looking for this?" Finn said, holding out a dirk with a long, wicked blade.

"I can't swim," the man pleaded. "Let me up!"

"Are ye prepared to treat my wife with respect?" Finn asked. "Otherwise, the fish can have ye."

"Aye!"

"What's that?" Finn said, turning his head. "I'm not sure I heard ye."

"Aye, damn it!" the man shouted. "Aye!"

Finn hauled the man back into the boat and dumped him on the bottom. Then he turned toward the other men with a smile on his face and a blade in each hand. "Can I count on the rest of ye to behave as well?"

The men turned their gazes away and settled onto the benches.

"Good," Finn said and took his seat beside Margaret and Ella.

"I thought ye said we'd have no trouble with these men, so long as they believed I belonged to you," she whispered.

"We won't have any trouble." Finn turned and winked at her. "Sometimes men just need a reminder to be courteous."

"You enjoyed that, didn't you?"

He leaned back and folded his arms. "It was rather satisfying."

Margaret shook her head, but she could not help smiling at his cockiness. "Can ye tell me now where you're taking us?" she asked.

"We sail to Aberdeen, which will take two days," Finn said. "From there, we're headed to Huntly Castle."

"Huntly?" she asked. "The Gordons are behind this kidnapping scheme?"

"Aye. Your brother took over the guardianship of the young Earl of Huntly from the queen," he said. "The Gordons want their chieftain back."

"I saw young Huntly often at Holyrood," she said. "He seemed happy to be there."

"There are some who mistrust your brother's intentions," he said. "They fear he'll misuse his position—and Gordon lands."

"No doubt he will," she said.

Finn laughed. "I didn't expect such an honest assessment of your own brother."

"I understand why the Gordons want a hostage to trade for Huntly," she said. "But why were you chosen to undertake the task?"

"As I told ye before," Finn said. "I didn't have a choice."

"Men always have choices," Margaret said as she stared off at the horizon, "though they may pretend they don't."

The easy camaraderie they had enjoyed earlier vanished, and Margaret turned away from him.

"Since you're doing this for the Gordons, I assume you're one of them," she said, still not looking at him. "Ye needn't worry I'll tell my brother who ye are so he can track ye down. I never will."

It would be utterly foolish to trust her assurance that she would not tell her brother, even if she meant it at this moment. But her sudden coolness toward him bothered him, like a burr poking through his sock.

"My full name is Finlay Sinclair Gordon," he told her. "My mother is a Sinclair and my father a Gordon, two clans that gravely mistrust each other—and that's on a good day."

"If ye were caught taking me, ye might well be put to death. How did they persuade ye to do it?" she asked, turning back to face him. "Was it the reward of lands alone? Or was it escape from punishment for some wrong ye committed?"

"'Twas both," he said.

"Ye told me there was a long tale behind your reason for kidnapping me," she said. "We have two days on this boat, and I'd like to hear it."

She listened attentively as he told his sorry tale of how he came to be here, starting with his decision to join the Sinclair chieftain's fight to regain Orkney and ending with the Earl of Moray promising Finn both lands and redemption with his Gordon clan.

"So where are these lands you've been promised in exchange for delivering me to Moray and the Gordons?" she asked.

"On the north coast of Sutherland," he said. "'Tis beautiful, wild country up there."

"I can understand your wanting a home so much," she said in a wistful voice, "that you'd take a great risk to have it."

"What I want is the freedom that comes with owning lands." He was not sure why her saying he wanted a home got his back up, but it did. "I'll owe my allegiance to my chieftain, and gladly fight for him when called. But with lands of my own, I'll not be dependent on another man for a bed to sleep in, a roof over my head, and food on my table."

He would have a place that was his. A place he belonged.

He'd only wanted to make her at ease with him again and maybe make her laugh, not spill his guts about why he wanted lands so much. When the captain ordered the food brought out for the midday meal, Finn was relieved to have an excuse to leave her to collect their share of the bread, dried meat, cheese, and ale.

The sparse meal was a far cry from the endless courses of fancy dishes and fine wine Margaret was accustomed to at Holyrood Palace, but it was all he had to give her. She ate delicately, holding the food with the tips of her fingers as if she was at court instead of among rough sailors. Ella, on the other hand, shoveled it in her mouth with both hands as if she feared it would be taken away.

No sooner had they finished than a storm came out of nowhere and swallowed the boat in a swirl of wind and waves that set it bouncing like a cork. The men dropped the sail and took the oars. Finn was going to join them, but Margaret was shaking from the cold despite the blanket he draped around her and Ella.

"Here, let me warm ye up." Though he knew full well this would ruin his peace of mind, he joined them under the blanket and wrapped his arms around them.

Margaret stiffened and started to pull away until the next wave crashed over the side, hitting them with an icy spray. Margaret held wee Ella on her lap and neither complained, but they had to be miserable.

"How are ye holding up?" he asked, and steeled himself for the criticism he deserved for endangering her life and Ella's by choosing this sea journey.

"At least the sailors are too preoccupied with the storm to stare at me," she said.

This lass was entirely too forgiving.

When another wave sprayed over the side, Margaret huddled against him and burrowed her head into chest. *O shluagh!* Even in the midst of a gale, her lithe body pressed against his drove him mad with desire.

This Lowland noblewoman, his captive, should not feel so good—so damned right—in his arms. She was a dangerous lass. If he had any sense, he'd be praying the storm would pass quickly so he could release her, instead of hoping it would last all the way to Aberdeen.

Margaret was far too cold to object when Finn put his arms around her. As his warmth enveloped her, she finally stopped shaking, but she also became all too aware of his body, the hard muscles of his thigh pressed against hers, the strong arms around her, and the broad chest beneath her head.

The storm ceased to frighten her. Inside the cocoon of his embrace with Ella on her lap, she felt safe. For the first time, Margaret imagined what it would be like to share responsibility for this precious child with a man and to make a family of three, rather than just the two of them.

That was just a foolish dream left over from her childhood. Though the Highlander was willing to give them protection from this storm on their journey north, he would not be there for the other storms of life. No one would.

She would have to be strong for Ella, for they were good and truly alone in the world.

CHAPTER 11

Margaret felt as if she were still at sea and the ground was rolling under her feet as she attempted to cross the wooden dock at Aberdeen. Finn caught her arm and steadied her. So much for her plan to keep a respectful distance between them after she'd practically glued herself to him on the boat for the last two days and nights. Naturally, now that they were on shore, the skies cleared.

"Are ye ready to meet a good friend of mine?" Finn asked Ella as they started into the town. "Most lasses are quite partial to him."

Margaret's pulse jumped. "Someone else is traveling with us?"

"Don't fret, lass, I'm only speaking of my horse," Finn said. "I boarded him with a tavernkeeper here when I sailed from here to Edinburgh to find you."

She thought she'd kept her alarm from her tone, but Finn was disturbingly perceptive.

"I named him *Ceò*, which means mist," he told Ella, "because he's gray and can creep up on an enemy like a Highland mist."

After paying for his horse's keep and extra oats inside the tavern, Finn took them around to the stables behind it. A handsome gray horse snorted and stamped its foot as soon as it saw Finn.

"I know you're annoyed with me for leaving ye, *gràdhan*," *darling*, Finn murmured to the horse as he rubbed his nose and fed it a handful of oats, "but I told ye I'd be back."

Margaret sighed. Finn was even charming to his horse. Did he have to make it so difficult to remember she must not let her guard down and trust him?

He saddled *Ceò* and tied on his blanket and supplies. When he attempted to tie Ella's enormous basket as well, the horse shied, stepping sideways with wild eyes.

"Ye can't blame a fine animal like *Ceò* for refusing to be treated like a mule," Finn said and carried the basket himself as he led the horse out of the stables.

They continued through the town until they reached a church that sat on a small square.

"There's something we need to discuss, wee one," Finn said, crouching down beside Ella. "Ye see that woman over there on the steps of the church holding a babe? Looks to me as if she hasn't got much and could use a bed for her babe. As you've grown too big for your basket, I wondered if you're willing to part with it."

Ella sucked harder on her thumb as she shifted her gaze to the woman in the ragged cloak. This was a battle he was sure to lose. Margaret was tempted to intervene, but Ella was not afraid of Finn, and he would not push her too hard.

"I'm taking ye to stay in a big castle," he said, stretching his arms out wide. "You'll have a fine bed to sleep in with piles of blankets and soft feather pillows."

After turning to look at the woman and babe one more time, Ella gave a slow nod. He patted her on the back. When he stood up with victory shining in his deep blue eyes, Margaret's heart actually fluttered. The man was sinfully handsome and dangerously charming.

"My mother warned me about silver-tongued devils like you," Margaret told him in a low voice. "Do ye always succeed in persuading females to do what you want?"

"I do my best," Finn answered with a wink.

But if he were that persuasive, he and Margaret would be in bed in a room above the tavern right now. By the saints, having Margaret in his arms during the storm had driven him to the point of madness. When they finally got off the boat, he wanted to kiss the ground, grateful his torture was over.

Margaret responded with an amused smile as she gave Ella the rag doll and blanket from the basket to hold. They were so ragged and dirty that Finn wondered again about the woman Margaret had entrusted with her daughter. At first, he assumed Margaret was more concerned with keeping her secret than with assuring her daughter's wellbeing. Now he knew she was just too damn trusting, for she was clearly devoted to the bairn.

"I'll take the basket to the woman," Margaret said, and picked it up.

Finn watched her carry it across the square to the church, exchange a few words with the woman, and coo over the babe. Before Margaret set the basket down, she slipped a small leather pouch out of it and hid the pouch inside her cloak. He was curious what was in it that she did not want him to see.

When they resumed walking through the town, Finn kept catching himself about to run his hand down her back or around her waist. It was only because he'd become accustomed to touching her on the boat—and lust, of course.

As they passed the townsfolk on the street, women gave them warm smiles, and men looked at him with envy, believing Margaret was his wife. It felt odd to have people look at them and think they belonged together, that they were a family. He would never be that man, the husband and father they saw.

Tomorrow they would reach Huntly Castle, and he'd be on his own again, as it should be.

As Finn set up camp in the growing darkness that night, he realized just how wrong he'd been to think his torture was over when they got off the boat. Having Margaret's sweet bottom between his legs all day on the long ride was bad enough, but tonight would be worse.

He and Margaret would be alone all night, except for Ella— and Ella slept like the dead. Before they took the boat, Margaret was so uneasy around him that there was no risk of anything happening between them, but she had warmed toward him *considerably* since then. Even if she wanted to, it would be wrong to roll around the blanket with her when she was his captive.

Wouldn't it?

After supper, they sat side by side in front of the roaring campfire with Ella fast asleep on the blanket behind them. Tension sizzled between them hotter than the flames. It was not just him. The sidelong looks Margaret gave him made the air crackle. He was more than ready to give in to temptation, but he waited for her to make the first move.

And waited.

He sighed. Evidently, she did not wish to act on the attraction between them. While this was verra wise on her part, he hoped to God she changed her mind.

He remembered the wistfulness in her voice when she said she understood wanting a home. Naturally, she would miss being mistress of her own grand castle, but did the husband she lost still hold her heart? Was that what held her back?

"If ye don't mind my asking, what happened to end your marriage?" There must be more to that story, for he could not imagine how her husband could leave her.

"I failed to give him an heir." She wrapped her arms around her knees and stared into the fire. "Once my family fell from power as well, I was no use to him at all."

What a sack of shite to leave her when she most needed protection.

"He said I was worse than useless," she said softly. "I was a rope around his neck."

"The cruel bastard! How could he say that to his wife?" Especially to a sweet lass like Margaret. Finn wanted to gut him with his dirk and leave him for the wolves to finish off.

"'Tis not so very different from what you said," she said.

"What I said? I'd never—" Then he remembered comparing a wife to having an anchor tied to his neck. "The difference is I don't have a wife. And if I did, I'd never say that to her."

"Ye wouldn't have to say it," she murmured as she stared into the fire. "She'd know."

"He had no excuse for mistreating ye like that," Finn said, and rested his hand on her arm. The bloody idiot should have thanked his lucky stars to have such a woman.

"I put his lands and position in danger." Margaret turned and gave him a sad smile. "So, ye see, he had no choice."

Finn winced, for he'd used the same excuse of having no choice the night he took her from the cottage. She did not throw his words back to him in anger but with a sad resignation that made him feel worse. They sat in silence for a long while, but eventually his curiosity got the better of him.

"If ye lived together as man and wife for years," Finn asked, "how could your husband obtain an annulment?"

"We're third cousins, which is within the church's prohibited degree of consanguinity."

"But he must have known that before ye wed," Finn said.

"Of course he did. Half the marriages among the nobility are the same." She poked a stick into the fire. "Still, 'tis grounds for a nobleman who is wealthy and well connected to rid himself of a barren wife."

A barren wife. If her husband believed that, then neither of them must have known she was with child when he abandoned her. And Finn had blamed her for not telling the bastard about Ella later.

"You're well rid of the horse's arse, but I'm sorry ye lost your home." His words felt painfully inadequate.

"That was the least of what I lost," she said in a faraway voice.

"What else did you lose?" he asked.

She just shook her head and looked so full of sorrow that he regretted asking.

"I have Ella. I won't ask for more," she said, then she lay down beside her daughter. "Good night, Finn."

If he was hoping she would succumb to his charms, he could not have picked a worse topic of conversation than her broken marriage. While Margaret's interest in him had faded to nothing, his desire had not lessened one whit. He'd never wanted a woman this much—not even Curstag, who he'd followed around like a starving dog when he was a lad of sixteen.

With her long, fair hair glinting in the firelight, Margaret looked like a faery queen who had fallen asleep on his blanket. Even in her sleep, she cast her magic over him, and he stayed awake just to watch her.

99

He had told Margaret she was not his kind of woman. But the truth was that he was not her kind of man. He had no castle, no servants, no means to provide her with fine gowns and jewels. If they had given in to temptation tonight, Margaret would surely regret it.

And he could not have borne to see that regret in her eyes in the morning.

In the morning, Margaret felt tired and unsettled. Strange how she slept so well on the boat, despite the storm, but last night she couldn't settle down and tossed and turned half the night. It was almost as if she missed having Finn's arms around her while she slept.

"We're nearly to Huntly Castle. It's just on the other side of this wood," Finn told her after they had been riding a couple of hours. "Before ye know it, you'll be back in Edinburgh."

She knew he meant to reassure her, but the prospect of reaching their destination so soon only made her feel more on edge.

"Moray promised me you'll be treated as an honored guest, as befits your station," Finn said. "So you've nothing to fear."

She thought she had hidden her unease, but Finn seemed to be able to read her better than anyone, except her sisters. He was wrong at least in part, however, about the reason for her disquiet. What had her stomach tied in knots was the prospect of parting from him. She tried telling herself it was only because she'd grown accustomed to him and she was about to be thrown into an unfamiliar situation with strangers.

But it was more than that. She felt safe with Finn. Not just safe from outside dangers, but safe to be herself. In truth, she'd never felt so at ease with a man. With Finn, she did not to have to be careful of every word she spoke. She could even tease him. And he made her laugh.

She would miss him. And what about Ella? He'd won her fearful little daughter over entirely.

"Will ye remain with us at Huntly for a time?" she asked him.

"Nay," Finn said, dashing her hopes. "I'll head north to Sutherland as soon as I can."

More than anyone, she could understand that he was anxious to settle onto his new lands. Like her, he longed for a home of his own and the independence that would give him. Even though she could not have that for herself, she was happy he would.

But she was not ready to part with him. It should not be that, after knowing him for so short a time, the thought of bidding him farewell *forever* made her chest hurt.

"Could we stop and have an early lunch before we get there?" she asked, keeping her voice light and cheery. "Ella's hungry."

That was a white lie, but hungry or not, the child would eat when food was put in front of her. It broke Margaret's heart to know it was probably because she had not always had enough to eat. She wished she had realized how dire Ella and Brian's circumstances were and done more to help them.

Finn spread their blanket amidst the bluebells on the forest floor. The smell of spring filled the air, dappled sunlight filtered through the new leaves on the trees, and a burn gurgled a few yards away. After they finished their simple lunch of oatcakes, dried venison, and apples, Margaret and Finn sat in silence while Ella played with her doll.

Margaret ran her gaze over Finn's now-familiar features—the strong jaw, broad cheekbones, black slash eyebrows, and the shadow of a beard that made him dark and dangerous.

When he passed her his flask, their hands touched, sending a jolt of awareness through her. She rarely drank whisky, but she took a long drink and felt the burn down her throat. The first drink did nothing to ease the tension bubbling inside her, so she took another.

Finn helped her up and started to pack up their things. She loved the way he moved with such confidence and ease, whether it was a simple task like this or dangling a huge sailor over the side of a boat.

"*Ach*, Ella has fallen asleep," he said, smiling down at her daughter. "I hate to wake the wee thing. Shall we let her nap a bit longer?"

"Aye." Margaret felt relieved and yet uneasy.

If she was honest with herself, unease did not accurately describe this feeling gnawing at her gut. But what was it? The realization hit her with the force of blow. *Regret.* That was what she felt.

Regret that she had not let him touch her like he wanted to. Though he never asked in so many words, she saw the question in his eyes every time he looked at her, felt the desire vibrating off him whenever he was near her.

Regret that she did not know what it felt like to rub her palm against his rough cheek, or drag her fingers through his black hair, or run her hands over his chest.

She did not know what to do with all the emotions swirling inside her—regret mixed with this painful longing. To cover her confusion, she stooped and picked one of the bluebells. The color matched his eyes. When Finn took the sprig from her and stuck it in her hair, her gaze fixed on his full, sensuous lips. She wished she knew what it was like to be kissed by that mouth.

When she lifted her gaze and their eyes locked, it was as if a flame shot between them, connecting them with a ribbon of white-hot fire. Her chest felt too tight to breathe, and she asked herself what would happen if she ignored the voice that always warned her *be cautious, be careful, be safe*.

The desire Finn had been resisting since the first moment he laid eyes on Margaret Douglas burned through his veins like whisky on an empty stomach. It was wrong to want her like this when she was his prisoner. It would be worse still to act upon his desire.

When the longing in her eyes told him she wanted him too, that nearly did him in. But Margaret had such a kind and gentle spirit that he feared he would sully her by the violence of his lust for her. It was lucky for them both that they would part today. He could not last much longer without giving in to the need building between them.

He ought to be galloping to Huntly with her now. Delay was dangerous. And yet he found himself incapable of moving with her standing so close and looking at him with such longing in her large brown eyes. Even if he could pry his feet off the ground, he could not bear to cut short this last hour he would have her to himself. After today, he would *never* see her again.

"We won't be alone again," she said, echoing his thoughts.

He saw her intention in her eyes even before she moved, and he could have turned away. He knew he should. But when she took a step closer, his resistance melted like candle wax to a hot flame. Then Margaret rested her hand on his chest, a light touch that had the force of a ten-foot wave crashing him against the rocks.

"Kiss me," she said, looking up at him with her lips parted.

One kiss. Surely there could be no harm in one kiss freely given. He knew that was a lie even as he lowered his mouth to hers. Though he barely brushed his lips against hers, a jolt of need shook him to his core and made him forget any thought he had of taking just one sweet kiss.

He lifted her off her feet and crushed his mouth against hers. When he thrust his tongue inside, she responded with a moan that sent him reeling. If she'd only pushed him away, he would have stopped. Instead, she wound her arms around his neck, spread her fingers in his hair, and kissed him back with a fervor that sent all his blood to his cock.

Lust blinded him to all reason and consequences. He backed her against the nearest tree. He ran kisses along her jaw and sucked on her neck while his hands feverishly sought the soft curves and dips of her body, as he had in his imagination a thousand times.

"*O shluagh,* ye feel even better than I imagined," he moaned in her ear as he cupped her breasts. But she had on far too many clothes. "I need to see you."

Somewhere in the far recesses of his mind he knew that if they took this any further, there would be no turning back, but his whole body pulsed with his need for her. He jerked her bodice down, revealing two small, perfect breasts with rosy tips begging to be touched. When he paused to drink in the sight of them, Margaret suddenly went rigid and crossed her arms over her chest.

He leaned his forehead against the tree trunk, panting, and squeezed his eyes shut. He could almost feel the soft mounds and hard nipples of her breasts against his palms. Slowly, he lifted his head to look into her face and try to understand what had suddenly gone so wrong. Her lips, red and swollen from their kisses, were as inviting as ever.

But when his gaze reached her eyes, the fear in them stopped him cold.

"I didn't mean to frighten you, *leannain*," *sweetheart*. He cupped her cheek and ran his thumb across it. "I would never hurt you."

"I'm the one who asked ye to kiss me," she said, dropping her gaze.

"And that's all ye asked for," he said. "I shouldn't have pushed ye for more."

"Ye didn't push me." When she lifted her gaze again, her eyes no longer held fear, but regret. "I'm sorry, but I can't do this. I just can't."

"I know," he said. "I've known from the start."

Some nobleman with vast lands and wealth would make her his wife and the lady of his great castle, while Finn had nothing to offer her but an afternoon of pleasure. That would never be enough for Margaret. For the first time since he was a lovesick lad of sixteen, Finn was not certain it would be enough for him.

Luckily, they would part today, and he would never know the answer to that question. Still, he suspected it would be a long, long time before he forgot Lady Margaret Douglas.

CHAPTER 12

In a daze, Margaret touched her fingers to her lips. Good heavens, what had happened to her? She could still feel the sensation of Finn's mouth on hers, his hands running over her body, and the unfamiliar, blinding rush of desire.

And yet she could not recall pulling up her bodice, straightening her skirts, or waking Ella, though she must have done all those things, for she was now walking down the trail with Ella and Finn, who was leading *Ceò*. One glance at Finn's clenched jaw told her he had decided to walk rather than ride to avoid touching her.

"'Tis less than a half-mile now," he said, with his eyes fixed straight ahead.

She tried again to understand how she had come so close to disaster. How could she nearly risk pregnancy and another miscarriage just to lie with a man she would part with before the day was over? From the moment Finn crushed his mouth against hers, she lost her reason. She had never felt anything like that mindless, all-consuming passion before.

Fortunately, she had come to her senses just in time. But her body still tingled with the sensations, and her arms longed to reach for him.

She could see the clearing at the end of the wood ahead of them when Finn suddenly shoved her and Ella behind him and drew his sword.

"Finn!" The shout came from the wood.

A moment later, a ginger-haired youth emerged from the trees leading a horse and wearing a wide grin. Finn embraced the lad, then put him in a headlock and rubbed his head with his knuckles before releasing him.

"You're traveling with a woman?" The lad's eyes went wide as he took in Margaret and Ella. "A woman *and* a bairn?"

"This is Alex Òg Gordon," *young Alex Gordon,* Finn said, turning to Margaret, "my troublesome fifteen-year-old cousin and the future Earl of Sutherland."

Alex blushed and dipped his head.

"This is Maggie and her daughter Ella," Finn said. "Why were ye hiding in the brush?"

"I've come out here the last two days and waited for ye for hours," Alex said. "I wanted to catch ye before ye went into the castle."

"Why?" Finn asked. "What's happened?"

"Moray keeps asking if you've arrived yet."

"That's no surprise," Finn said. "He's expecting me."

"'Tis the *way* he asks," Alex said. "I think ye may be in trouble."

Finn pulled his cousin aside, and the two spoke in low voices Margaret could not make out.

"I'll go into the castle alone first," Finn told her when he returned to her side. "Alex will look after ye until I come back."

"What's wrong?" she asked, doing her best to remain calm.

"I just want to make sure there are no surprises." He leaned close so that Alex would not hear and added, "After all, last time I was here, I got sent off to kidnap a lass."

His attempt to make light of whatever trouble waited in the castle did not reassure her.

"I won't be long," Finn said, but when he took her hand and raised it to his lips, it felt like goodbye.

As she watched Finn disappear from sight, she suppressed the urge to call out after him, *Don't leave me.* Men did what they were going to do, regardless of how it affected anyone else, and Finn had decided to leave her and her daughter alone in the middle of the Highlands with no one but a stranger who was barely more than a boy.

A burst of laughter drew her attention to her protector, who was engaged in a lively game of peekaboo with Ella.

"I finally got a smile out of her," Alex said, grinning at Margaret.

"Ella is usually shy, but I can see you've won her over already." And that went a long way toward winning over Margaret as well. She sat down on the log beside him and asked, "Are ye staying long here at Huntly Castle?"

"I left home without my father's permission," he said, "so I expect I'll be sent back soon."

"Why did ye come without his permission?"

"Because he wouldn't give it," Alex said. "I had to come, ye see, because there's a lass here that…well, I'm in love with her."

She could not help smiling at how very forthcoming Alex was. Since Finn had left her with his chatty cousin, he had no one but himself to blame if she used the opportunity to learn more about him. "You and Finn are close?"

"Aye. Finn fostered with my father, so he spent a good deal of time with us at Dunrobin Castle. That's our home up north in Sutherland," Alex said. "Finn is like a big brother to me—the good kind of big brother."

"Ye seemed quite surprised to find him traveling with me and Ella," she said.

"Finn is not one to be with a lass long enough to travel with her." Alex paused to do another peekaboo for Ella. "And he's never with a lass who's looking for a husband."

"What makes ye think I'm looking for a husband?" she asked.

"Finn says a lass with a bairn always is," Alex said, as if Finn was the authority on all things female.

"The last thing I want is a husband," she said.

"That's good," Alex said. "Much to my mother's frustration, Finn is dead set against taking a wife."

As Finn approached the gates of Huntly, he wondered if he would ever leave the castle again. Hopefully, Alex was wrong about trouble awaiting him, but Finn had not survived this long among his Gordon and Sinclair relations by ignoring warnings. He'd made Alex promise that if he did not return, Alex would arrange for Margaret and Ella to be taken safely to Edinburgh. He hoped his young cousin was up to the task.

The change in plan had made Margaret anxious, but she did not complain. She never did. On the chance he would not see her again, he had kissed Margaret's hand as an excuse to touch her and to look into her soft brown eyes one last time.

Evidently, Moray was as anxious to see him as Alex claimed. The guards at the gate ushered him into the castle and straight into the private room behind the hall where he'd met with Moray before.

Moray was not a man easily rattled, but when he looked up from the parchment he was reading and saw Finn, tension rolled off him in thick waves.

"Where's Lady Margaret?" Moray asked in lieu of a greeting as soon as the guards closed the door behind Finn.

Something was seriously amiss here. Though Finn had no notion what it was, he went with his instincts and decided to lie.

"I did try to kidnap her, Your Grace," he said, spreading his hands out. "But I couldn't get near the lass. She was too closely watched."

"Praise God for that!" Moray said, and drained his cup, though he was neither particularly religious nor a drinker. "The odds were against you succeeding. Still, I feared you had."

"And I feared you'd be disappointed," Finn said as he accepted the cup of wine Moray poured for him. "What changed your mind about wanting a Douglas kidnapped?"

"As I told you before, the council decided to rotate custody of the king's person among four magnates to avoid giving any one faction too much power," Moray said. "Douglas was given the first three months."

Finn waited to hear why Moray was telling him all this again.

"Douglas's rotation is coming to an end." Moray folded his long, elegant fingers on the table. "He's refusing to relinquish the king to the next custodians."

Finn sat up straighter. "Refusing? Can he do that?"

"He has the king in his possession, and my sources tell me he keeps a close guard on him at all times," Moray said. "Douglas claims it's his right as the king's stepfather to be his sole custodian and that the king wishes this as well."

"Does the king wish it?" Finn asked.

"After his mother filled the lad's ears with venom about Douglas for the last three years? I sincerely doubt it," Moray said. "I'm told, however, the king's cage is a gilded one designed to divert a young man—with feasts, gambling and, of course, women."

"I would think that would give us all the more reason to want leverage over Douglas to force him to return young Huntly," Finn said.

"Archibald Douglas has won the battle, and the kingdom is in his hands now, which changes the calculation considerably," Moray said. "For however long Douglas holds the king, it's in young Huntly's interest to remain in Douglas's care as well."

"Something tells me you're not leaving him there for the feasts and the women."

"Huntly will be the king's constant companion throughout his ordeal—and the king will come to view this time when his step-father keeps him under his thumb and rules in his name as an ordeal, despite the feasts and women," Moray said. "No matter what Douglas does, the king will eventually become a man and rule, and the special bond between Huntly and the king will be of value to him, the Gordons, and their allies for many, many years to come."

Finn was not surprised that such dramatic news of the king had traveled faster than he did among the nobility or that news of Margaret's disappearance had not. The Douglases would want to keep Margaret's disappearance quiet while they searched for her to avoid rumors that such a valuable marriage prize had run off with a lover.

"Tell me," Finn said, tilting his head, "what would ye have done if I had succeeded and come here with Lady Margaret?"

"What do you think I'd do?" Moray asked.

"Put the blame on me and throw me in chains," Finn said. "You'd have Douglas in your debt for rescuing his sister from a damned rogue you would say tried to exchange her for gold."

Moray leaned back in his chair and smiled. "My mother said you were clever."

"*Ach*, not as clever as all that," Finn said. "If I had succeeded in kidnapping the lass, I would have walked right into the trap and ended up in your dungeon." *Or dead.*

"I would have sincerely regretted having to do it," Moray said as he refilled Finn's cup. "My mother would have been rather angry with me. But what else could I do?"

Moray's remark reminded him of what Margaret said. *Men always have choices, though they may pretend they don't.*

They finished their drinks companionably enough. Finn had known from the start Moray was guided by interests larger than Finn's fate, and the man held no true malice toward him. But for all his trouble, Finn had gained nothing and would have to go to France or Ireland after all. He should have known this was where it would end.

But this meant he would have to return Margaret first. He rubbed his hand over his face as he thought of the days and nights of temptation ahead. Still, it would be good to see the relief on her face when he told her she was going home.

Since his audience appeared to be over, he started to get to his feet, but Moray stopped him.

"Were you aware," Moray said, "that, before your *unfortunate* decision to fight for the Sinclairs, your uncle the Earl of Sutherland intended to make you captain of the guard at Dunrobin Castle?"

Damn it. Would the consequences of that decision never end? Captain of the guard was a position of great honor and responsibility. Yet Finn had to admit that even if he'd known at the time, he probably still would have been fool enough to give in to the lure of lands on Orkney to fight with the Sinclairs.

"I received a message from your uncle indicating he is most anxious for his son Alex Òg to return home," Moray said. "I think it would be wise for you to be the one to take him."

"I'm not certain I'd be welcome at Dunrobin," Finn said. "Besides, his father would insist on an escort of at least ten men."

"Sutherland was very particular in asking me to provide an escort of only one or two guards so as not to draw attention to his departure," Moray said, tapping the tips of his fingers together. "In fact, he mentioned you by name, as he knew I expected you here, though I did not tell him why."

"Is Alex in danger?" Finn asked, leaning forward.

"All I know is your uncle wants his son brought home as quickly and as quietly as possible," Moray said. "If you want to persuade your uncle of your loyalty to him and your clan, you'll take Alex Òg and make haste for Dunrobin Castle."

How in the hell was he supposed to do that and return Margaret at the same time?

Moray drew out a clean piece of parchment, ink, and a quill from the drawer in his table.

"I'll send a message with you advising your uncle," Moray said, as his quill scratched across the parchment, "that you have my trust and, in my judgment, are worthy of serving on his guard."

Moray was a powerful ally of the Gordons, and his endorsement would go a long way with the important men of the clan, particularly Finn's uncle.

"I'm verra grateful for this," Finn said.

"I know," Moray said with a small, satisfied smile. "I may have need of you again."

Finn caught sight of Margaret as he hurried up the path. Though time was short, he paused to watch her as she sat on a fallen log with Ella on her lap and chatted with Alex as if they were old friends. She'd shown such grace throughout their journey, despite being ripped from her home and family, dragged across half of Scotland, and forced to endure days and nights of rough travel.

After everything he put her through, Finn knew what he had to do. Before he took Alex to Dunrobin, he must give her back her life and return her home. He owed her that, even if it meant he lost the chance of gaining his uncle's trust and a place in his guard.

Margaret smiled when she saw him and stood, waiting to hear his news.

"Mind Ella while I have a private word with Maggie," he told Alex, then he led her a few steps away and explained the situation to her. "So ye see, you're no longer needed as a hostage."

"I'm not?" Her eyes were wide with alarm. "What will ye do with me?"

"Don't fret," he said, taking her hand. "I'll take ye back to Edinburgh."

"But I don't want to go back to Edinburgh," she said, and pulled her hand from his.

"Then I'll take ye to Blackadder Castle or Tantallon," he said.

"Nay, I don't want to go there either," she said, her voice rising. "I don't want to go back at all."

"What?" He thought he must have heard wrong, but she was stepping backward and shaking her head. "Why not?"

For a moment, the ridiculous thought entered his head that he—and those few moments of reckless passion against the tree—had something to do with her not wanting to leave. Even more ridiculous, the thought did not send panic rushing through his veins.

"I *cannot* go back," she said.

He glanced at Alex, who was shamelessly attempting to overhear them, and drew her farther away. "Tell me, what is this about?"

"Ella isn't really mine," Margaret said, twisting her hands in her gown. "I mean, she's mine now. But she wasn't always."

Wasn't always? By the saints, had Margaret stolen the bairn? Something had seemed off from the very start. It had been too easy to persuade her to come with him, but he had put that down to her cool head and calm facade. And she had not seemed to know her own daughter very well, but he dismissed that when she told him Ella had been in the care of a village woman.

"Explain this to me, *leannain*." Finn rested his hands on her slender shoulders and spoke in a soft voice. "How can Ella be yours, but not yours?"

"I didn't give birth to her," Margaret said in a tight voice. "She was…a…a gift."

"A gift?" People did not give away children. He cupped Margaret's cheek with his hand. "Oh, lass, what have ye done?"

She proceeded to tell him a wild tale of a murdered mother and a desperate lad who brought Ella to her on the very night Finn kidnapped her. His head was spinning.

"Do you believe me?" she asked, looking at him with those big brown eyes that appeared to hold no guile.

Finn would be a damned fool to believe her. And yet he did.

"Ye cannot take me back," she pleaded. "My brothers will use me to forge an alliance. They'll force me to marry again!"

Jealousy rammed him like a raging bull as Finn imagined another man touching her velvety skin...sliding his hands over her soft curves...tasting her lips...

"No nobleman my brothers would choose for my husband will accept the child of poor villagers as my adopted daughter."

She was talking about Ella, but his mind was still stuck on the notion of a husband who would wake to see Margaret's face every day and lie with her each night.

"Do ye understand?" She gripped the front of his tunic in her fists, forcing him to hear what she was telling him. "If I return, my brothers will take Ella away from me! I'll never see her again."

"I'll not let that happen." He pulled her into his arms and kissed her hair. "I promise."

He gave her his word without thought because he could not bear to see her so distressed and because it would be wrong to part her and Ella. But what in the hell was he going to do with them?

He'd never wanted to be responsible for a woman or a bairn—and he'd never been in a worse position to do so. He would protect them with his life, but he had little else to offer them. He had no home he could take them to and no certain means of providing for them.

With a deep sigh, he rested his chin on her head. How did he get himself into this mess? Their lives had become entangled like his fingers in her hair. There was nothing he could do now but bring them with him to Dunrobin and pray his uncle would take him into his guard.

He felt a tug on his tunic and looked down to see Ella with her arms raised, wanting him to pick her up. He tossed her into the air, which earned him a rare laugh from the bairn. When he turned to Margaret and saw her face glowing with happiness and relief, his doubts fell away.

No matter what it took, he would find a way to take care of them until Margaret decided what she wanted to do next.

Margaret was overjoyed that Finn would not abandon them or try to return her to her brothers. But the smile froze on her face as she recalled their wild moment of passion no more than an hour ago. If she had known she and Finn were not parting today, she never would have asked him to kiss her. Her cheeks grew hot as she recalled how quickly that kiss led to having her back against a tree, her skirts around her waist, and Finn staring at her bare breasts.

Her hand flew to her chest. She had not even considered the consequence of Moray's change in plans to Finn.

"Forgive me for only thinking of myself," she said. "This must mean ye won't receive the lands ye were promised for kidnapping me."

"*Ach*, I'm no worse off than I was before," Finn said with a shrug.

She was not fooled. This was a hard loss for him.

"I'm sorry," she said, resting her hand on his arm. "I know how much ye wanted that land."

If he had no home, where he would take them? She did not care where so long as she could keep Ella. From the tale Finn told of how he came to kidnap her, however, he might not be welcome with either his father's or his mother's clan.

Though Finn surely wanted to be rid of them, it would be a lot to ask him to take her and Ella across the Highlands and through mountainous terrain to Eilean Donan Castle. And what if Sybil and her husband had changed their plans and were not there when they arrived? Still, she was about to suggest it when Finn spoke.

"I'm glad I don't have to choose between taking you all the way back to the Lowlands and taking Alex north to Sutherland."

Finn turned around and caught his young cousin inching closer, obviously bent on overhearing their conversation.

"We're leaving for Dunrobin Castle at once," Finn told him. "Your father wants ye home."

Alex groaned. "Do I have to go?"

"You're my means of redemption, so aye, ye do," Finn said with a grin, and put an arm around his cousin's shoulders. "Your father is so anxious to have ye brought home that he just may be willing to overlook my excursion with the Sinclairs and take me into his guard."

"At least it's you taking me," Alex grumbled. "I'm surprised my father didn't send thirty warriors to escort me, as if I couldn't make it home by myself."

"You're the future earl, and he's your father," Finn said. "Ye cannot blame him for wanting to protect ye."

"It was bad enough before," Alex said. "But since that wee accident, he treats me like a bairn."

"Just what was this *wee* accident?" Finn asked.

"I found shards of glass in the bottom of my cup," Alex said with a shrug. "A servant must have broken something in the kitchen and not noticed that some pieces fell into the cup."

Finn's teasing manner disappeared. "When and where did this happen?"

"Here at Huntly Castle when my family was here for the gathering after the old earl died," Alex said. "You'd already come and gone before we arrived."

"The castle was verra crowded for the gathering," Finn said.

Judging from his grim expression, Finn suspected the shards were no accident. And in a crowded castle, it would be difficult to discover who the culprit was.

"'Twas an accident, and I didn't swallow the shards," Alex complained. "But ye know what my da is like."

"I do," Finn said, his humor returned. "He suspects everyone is as sly and conniving as he is. And yet your father trusts me to take ye home."

"That's because Da knows you'd never harm me," Alex said.

"He also knows I left the gathering before ye had your *wee* accident."

"That may have enhanced his trust in you," Alex agreed with a smile.

"Lucky for you, I've nowhere else to go," Finn said, and ruffled Alex's hair, "so we're off to Dunrobin."

"I need to go back to the castle first to bid farewell to someone." Alex darted a glance at Margaret and blushed, confirming her guess that the someone was the lass he thought he was in love with.

"We can't risk alerting anyone who may want to follow us," Finn said, shaking his head. "If someone here does mean ye harm, they'll be watching for ye to gather your things and make your goodbyes."

Alex groaned but did not argue this time.

"When danger is chasing ye, always do the unexpected," Finn told him with a wink. "Mount your horse—and you can tell me on the way who the lass is."

Though he spoke in a light tone, Finn clearly took the threat seriously and was anxious to get Alex safely home to Dunrobin Castle.

Asking Finn to take her to her sister Sybil was out of the question, at least for now. Even if Alex's safety were not at risk, she could not ask Finn to give up the chance to earn a position in his uncle's guard and acceptance back into his clan.

"Where is Dunrobin?" she asked him as they rode off.

"In the far north, up in Sutherland."

He was taking her farther from the Lowlands, her brothers, and her past life. And that was all she needed to know.

CHAPTER 13

Margaret started to object when Finn lifted Ella onto Alex's horse, but Ella seemed happy to ride with him. Though Alex was a few years older than Ella's brother Brian, Margaret suspected she took to Alex so quickly because she missed her brother. A wave of sadness swept over her at the thought of Brian. She touched the bag of broken onyx tied to her belt and told herself they would see him again one day.

Finn kept a vigilant watch, scanning the hills as they rode. They spoke little and did not stop until late in the afternoon, when they reached the sea.

"Where are we?" Margaret asked, trying to get her bearings.

"This is where the North Sea meets Moray Firth, the large inlet that reaches inland to Inverness," Finn replied.

"We'll pass through Inverness?" Margaret asked.

"Nay, 'tis faster and safer to sail across the firth," Finn said. "To reach Dunrobin by land, we'd have to travel all the way west to Inverness and then ride along the far shore of the firth for another forty miles or so, much of it through the lands of unfriendly clans."

This information might be useful later. Castle Leod, the MacKenzie stronghold on the easternmost part of their clan lands, was somewhere near Inverness. In several weeks, Margaret's sister Sybil and her family expected to return there. While forty or fifty miles was no small distance, particularly on these rough Highland trails and traveling alone with a small child, it was not *impossible*.

"How will we find a boat this time?" she asked.

"I left mine hidden here when I sailed over," Alex said.

Alex's boat was just large enough to hold the two horses and them. After Finn and Alex raised the sail, Alex took the rudder, and Finn sat beside Margaret with Ella on his lap. Despite the uncertainties ahead, she enjoyed the sail. It was June and the days were long, so they still had a few hours of sunlight. Ella seemed livelier, even squealing with delight when she saw seals in the water. Watching her daughter smile and laugh made Margaret's heart feel lighter. She wrapped her arms around her daughter from behind and pressed her cheek to Ella's while Ella pointed at another seal.

Margaret turned and caught Finn watching her with an unexpected tenderness that made her heart flip in her chest. His eyes quickly darkened with desire, making her wonder if she had imagined that look of tenderness. As their gazes held, the memory of their heated kisses was like a tantalizing buzz under her skin.

"Ye truly believe Alex is in danger?" she asked, forcing her thoughts in another direction. "'Tis hard to imagine who would want to harm such a sweet lad."

"The Gordons of Sutherland have enemies, some with good reason," Finn said. "Ye could say our grandparents—Alex's and mine—swindled Dunrobin Castle and the Earldom of Sutherland from the Sutherland clan."

"Really?" she asked, leaning forward.

"Our grandmother was a Sutherland herself, daughter of the earl," Finn said. "After she married our Gordon grandfather, the two of them told the king her father had gone mad. They persuaded the king to declare her father incompetent, and he gave them control of all of the Sutherland lands until her younger brother came of age."

"Was her father mad?"

"He'd ruled his clan for many years before then, but who's to say?" Finn said.

"Ye shouldn't be so suspicious of your grandparents," she said with a smile.

"A few years later when our grandmother's brother came of age"—Finn paused and waggled his eyebrows—"they had him declared incompetent as well."

"Madness sometimes does run in families," Margaret said.

"And sometimes people are greedy and ruthless," Finn said with a laugh. "Despite his *incompetence*, her brother somehow managed to name my grandmother as his heir."

"I suppose that does look suspicious, but ye ought not assume they were ill intentioned."

"Her brother died rather mysteriously a month later," Finn said with an amused smile. "And that's how our grandmother became the Countess of Sutherland and the earldom passed to the Gordons."

"Your grandmother had no other brothers to inherit before her?" she asked.

"She did have a half-brother, Robin, who was twenty-odd years younger and still a boy when all this came about." Finn gave her a sideways glance and lifted one black eyebrow. "Robin was placed in the guardianship of one of their close allies, who *persuaded* the lad to renounce his claim. Once he came of age, however, Robin claimed he'd been coerced and that he was the true heir to the Earldom of Sutherland."

"As a son, surely he had the better claim?" Margaret said.

"Aye, but the Gordons had all the power," Finn said. "Our grandfather's brother was the Earl of Huntly, the so-called Cock of the North who was the king's sheriff. Huntly was not ever going to rule for this young Robin Sutherland over his brother and sister-in-law."

"Was that the end of the dispute?" she asked.

"Nay, this young Robin Sutherland captured Dunrobin Castle not once, but twice," Finn said, with a grin. "According to the tales about him, he was a clever and charismatic leader, and he had the support of most of his Sutherland clansmen, who were not pleased to have a Gordon for their laird."

"What happened to him?"

"'Twas a sad ending for both him and the Sutherlands," he said. "Robin was eventually caught, and his head put on a spike above the gates of Dunrobin."

"Your grandparents do sound rather ruthless," Margaret said, attempting to keep her voice light. "Will they be at Dunrobin?"

"After their schemes secured the Sutherland lands and title for their line, they washed their hands of the far north," Finn said. "Grandmother relinquished the title to Alex's father, and they lived their remaining years in peace on their Gordon estates near Huntly Castle."

"I confess I'm not sorry I won't meet them."

"Fair warning," Finn said, leaning close, "like madness, ruthlessness runs in families."

"Alex certainly isn't ruthless," she said with a laugh.

"That's because he takes after his mother," Finn said. "My Aunt Helen has a good heart."

"And Alex's father, the earl?" she asked.

"My uncle treated me fairly while I fostered with him, and I was lucky to have such a skilled warrior train me." Finn paused and squinted at the horizon. "But I would not want to be between him and something he wanted."

His uncle sounded like all the men of her family.

"There's Dunrobin." Finn pointed to a large fortress that came into view as they rounded the headland. "We'll be ashore soon."

"I forgot to tell ye," Alex shouted over the wind as he guided the boat to shore. "Your family is here at Dunrobin as well."

Finn narrowed his eyes at his cousin. "You *forgot* to tell me?"

Alex gave him an impish grin. "They all traveled north with my parents."

"*All* of them?" Finn asked, his voice rising.

"Aye," Alex said. "They're staying several weeks for the hunting."

His parents! Margaret's hand went to her throat. Finn had told her about his grandparents and Alex's parents, but not a word about his own parents. She did not even know if he had siblings. She had a hundred questions, but they were nearly to the shore. Men from the castle were already coming down to the shore to help haul their boat in.

"Who will ye say I am?" she asked.

Instead of telling her ancient family history, they should have made a plan.

Shite, shite, shite! Finn pulled out his whisky flask, tipped his head back, and let the burning liquid pour down his throat. How in the hell would he explain Margaret to his family? He had to think fast.

He pulled several strands of hair loose from Margaret's neat braid. When he attempted to tug her bodice lower, she slapped his hand away.

"What are ye doing?" she hissed.

"We must make ye look like the sort of woman I would bring home," he said, "or my mother will be suspicious."

"No one will suspect who I really am dressed like this." She spread out the skirt of her plain gown. "I look like a simple villager."

"An innocent village lass is not the sort of woman who'd be traveling with me," he said. "God's bones, bringing a lass like that to my mother would be like throwing a puppy to the king's lions."

"You can tell them I'm a poor widow looking for work as a servant in the castle," Margaret said.

"I could say that if it were just my aunt and uncle," he said. "They would both be polite and pretend to believe I brought a stunningly beautiful lass to their home to scrub floors. But my own family won't even pretend to believe it."

Besides that, she would actually have to scrub floors to keep up the pretense, and he could not have Lady Margaret Douglas doing that.

"So, ye wouldn't bring a respectable servant to your aunt and uncle's home, but you'd bring a woman who dresses like a tavern wench?" she asked. "That would not upset your family?"

"Aye, it would upset them, but not surprise them." Finn could not help laughing at her appalled expression. "Trust me, I'm giving my family exactly what they expect of me."

CHAPTER 14

Surely Finn was jesting. His family could not truly have such low expectations of him.

"Stop teasing me." Margaret slapped his hand away again and tucked the loose strands back into her braid as best she could. "You're making me more nervous about meeting them."

She wished they had time to settle on the particulars of her story, but it was too late now. The men from the castle were wading out to the boat. All too soon, they had hauled it in, Finn lifted her and Ella down, and they were surrounded by more men who escorted them through the gates and into the castle.

Before she knew it, they stood before the massive wooden doors at the entrance to the castle's great hall. Margaret held Ella's hand tightly and reminded herself she must appear to be in awe of the castle. While Dunrobin was a good-sized castle made of a lovely red sandstone, she had lived in far larger ones.

"Let me do the talking and play along," Finn whispered as the doors swung open.

Margaret intended to enter behind Finn and Alex, as a serv-ant would, but Finn put an arm firmly around her waist and pulled her along. When they came to a halt before the three well-dressed couples waiting for them, Finn had a smile on his face, but his wide stance made it look as if he was going into battle.

She could have guessed which were Alex's parents even if they had not rushed to greet him. His father, the earl, was a tall, well-built man in his forties who exuded authority, and his mother had Alex's ginger hair and lively green eyes.

While she waited to be introduced, Margaret turned toward the other couples, and her polite smile froze on her face. Well-bred people were supposed to at least feign graciousness when they greet-ed guests, but she had never seen a less welcoming foursome in her life.

Finn's mother, a tall woman with gray-streaked black hair and pursed lips, examined Margaret with penetrating black eyes that made Margaret instinctively hold Ella more tightly. The woman had Finn's black slash eyebrows, straight nose, and angular jaw. But while Finn's charm and good nature shone through to make his handsome face even more appealing, his mother's pinched expression made Margaret think of a beady-eyed crow picking over a carcass.

His father had the blotchy skin and baggy eyes of a drunkard, but at least he did not stare at her with a sour expression as the other three did. The younger man, who must be Finn's brother, had his mother's cold black eyes and a sly look about him. The woman on the brother's arms, a dark-haired beauty with cupid lips and a buxom figure, ran her gaze up and down Margaret as if calculating the worth of a horse.

"Praise God you're home," the earl said to Alex as he squeezed his son's shoulder.

While Alex's mother embraced him again, the earl spoke quietly to Finn, and Finn handed him a sealed parchment, which the earl tucked inside his tunic.

Margaret's cheeks hurt from holding her smile by the time Finn finished exchanging formal greetings with his aunt and uncle, as was appropriate to the rank. Finn gave her a reassuring wink, obviously pleased they would not be turned out immediately, and then turned to introduce her to his family.

"Who is this that ye brought uninvited?" Finn's mother said before he could speak.

"This is Maggie," Finn said, giving her shoulders a squeeze. "Maggie... Fletcher. And that's her daughter, Ella, behind her."

Fletcher? Apparently, she came from a family of arrow makers. She supposed it could be worse.

"Ye should know better than to bring one of your women here," his mother said through thinned lips.

"Maggie is not like the others." Finn was smiling, but he had ice in his eyes. "She's a good woman, and I expect ye to treat her as such."

123

"Hmmph!" His mother uttered one of those expressive Highland grunts. "You'd have us believe this one is decent? What would make a respectable lass come away with the likes of you?"

Margaret stifled a gasp—and hoped Finn had come up with a plausible explanation for how she came to be here with him.

"My sweet Maggie was in a bad way when I found her and wee Ella in Edinburgh," Finn said, shaking his head. "Her husband had died and left her destitute. With no family to turn to, the poor lass was driven to the point of desperation."

"God's blood," his mother hissed, "you've brought a whore into your uncle's home."

Margaret jabbed Finn hard with her elbow.

"*Ach*, no, Maggie hadn't sold herself—yet," he said. "But she was desperate when I found her on the streets."

"That's our Finn, always jesting," Margaret interjected with a forced smile. "Of course, I was not on the streets but praying in the abbey church when he first saw me."

"Praying she wouldn't have to sell herself to feed her young bairn," Finn said. "I guess ye could say I was the answer to her prayers."

"I was not *that* desperate," Margaret said between clenched teeth. She could see Finn was accustomed to using humor to cope with his mother, but she did not appreciate the jest.

"So I took it upon myself to rescue the young widow and her wee bairn." He put his hand over his heart. "'Twas the only Christian thing to do."

"You've sunk low, even for you," his mother bit out, "making a desperate mother your whore."

Margaret gasped aloud this time. Even more than the woman's rudeness in insulting her to her face, Margaret was shocked Finn's own mother actually believed Finn would take advantage of a woman in such dire straits. How could she know her son so little? He was not that sort at all.

Instead of responding with another jest, Finn's jocular manner was replaced by a dangerous stillness.

"Oh my," Margaret said quickly, "I'm afraid ye misunderstand altogether."

Everyone, including the earl and the countess, turned to look at her as she tried desperately to think of an explanation for her presence that his mother would accept and would not reflect badly on Finn—or make her out to be a prostitute.

"What do I misunderstand?" his mother asked, her black eyes glinting with malice.

"Well…ah…" Margaret swallowed. The woman was a bit frightening. "Finn began meeting me and Ella outside of the abbey church every day to walk us home, which was a great kindness, as the only room I could afford was in a dangerous part of the city."

She was rather proud of herself for adding that bit about the dangerous part of the city to support Finn's claim she had been in difficult straits.

"As ye know, Finn is easy to talk to," she said. "In a short time, we came to know each other quite well."

"I'm sure ye did," Finn's brother said in a snide tone.

Well, that one certainly took after his mother.

Margaret was desperate to bring her meandering tale to an end, and yet she had to come up with an ending that would explain why she was here. She never thought she would regret having so little practice at lying. If only her sister Sybil was here to help her.

"Finn told me he simply must carry me off with him to the Highlands."

That much was true, but as soon as she said it, she realized how they would interpret it. She rushed on before his brother or mother could make another rude remark.

"As Finn needed to go north and wished to have matters settled between us quickly," she said, "he suggested the Highland custom of handfasting."

If she had surprised them before, it was nothing to what she had done now. They all stared at her with their mouths open, including Finn, but it was too late to stop now.

"So that's what we did," she said, "right there on the steps of the abbey church."

"Ye married her?" Finn's mother asked him. "She's your *wife*?"

The silence stretched out for so long that it was apparent Finn was too stunned to answer.

"Isn't it wonderful?" Margaret said with a bright smile. When Finn still said nothing, she leaned into him with her hand on his chest and looked up with what she hoped passed for adoration.

"Aye," Finn finally croaked out. "That's just how it happened."

He looked as if he'd been hit over the head with a brick, as if marrying her was the worst fate imaginable, which was rather insulting. She had always been good at swallowing her pride and biting back a clever response, knowing it would cause more trouble than it was worth. Why this, of all the slights and insults she had suffered in her life, pushed her over the edge, she could not say.

But it did.

"My darling Finn took an oath and swore by all that is holy that he would never touch another woman." She felt a sense of satisfaction when his entire family sucked in startled breaths. "Aye, he pledged to me—and these were his verra words—*If I ever so much as look at another woman with lust, may God strike me blind!*"

Good heavens, what had come over her to make up such a lie? And when had she developed such a wild imagination?

"I'll wager Finn will be blind inside a week," Finn's brother said with a guffaw, while his wife glared at Margaret with daggers in her eyes.

The silence stretched out so long then that Margaret had an urge to confess. Fortunately, Alex's mother intervened.

"I'm sure you're weary after your journey," she said, taking Margaret and Finn firmly by their arms. "I'll show you two newlyweds upstairs to a guest bedchamber."

Margaret ventured a glance at Finn's still-stunned expression and swallowed hard.

"I'll send servants up with refreshments and hot water for a bath," his aunt said as she marched them toward the stairs. "No need to rejoin the family until morning. We'll celebrate this *happy* news another day."

CHAPTER 15

Their steps echoed against the stone walls of the spiral stairwell. None of them spoke as they climbed round and round the wheeled stairs until they reached the top floor, where there was a narrow landing with a door on either side.

When Finn's aunt opened the door on the left, an old woman inside looked up from her stitching.

"Your daughter will sleep in here with Una," Finn's aunt said. "Una can serve as her nursemaid while you're here."

"That's kind of ye, but I cannot leave my daughter with a stranger," Margaret said in a low voice so as not to offend the elderly woman.

"Una Murray was my son's nursemaid," his aunt bristled. "Ye couldn't ask for better."

"Una weaves magic with children." Finn lifted Ella out of Margaret's arms and carried her into the chamber before Margaret could object, then he leaned down and kissed the elderly woman's cheek. "You're as beautiful as ever."

"Let me show you your chamber," his aunt said, and gently but firmly pulled Margaret toward the opposite door.

Margaret barely had time to duck her head under the low doorway before she found herself in a tidy chamber with a vase of flowers on a small ledge above the bed and a view of the sea from a window in the thick castle wall.

"What a cozy chamber!" Margaret's immediate delight with the room faded as she realized she would be sharing it with Finn. Now the small chamber seemed cramped rather than cozy—and it had only one bed. "'Tis lovely. Thank you, Countess."

"You can call me Helen," his aunt said, giving her a friendly smile. "I'm glad the chamber pleases ye, Maggie."

"This is all very kind of you," Margaret said.

"You're a lucky lass to catch Finn," Helen said with a conspiratorial wink as Finn joined them. "Many a lass has tried. I worried this one would never settle down."

"I never thought I would," Finn said, and pulled Margaret against his side. "Maggie certainly surprised me."

She had indeed, and his cheerful countenance did not fool her that he was pleased about it.

"Make the most of these early days of your marriage," Helen said, then added with a glint in her eyes, "and the nights."

Margaret avoided looking at Finn.

"Oh, I intend to enjoy my bride quite thoroughly," Finn said, and nuzzled Margaret's neck.

"I'll be off, then," Helen said, then she looked at Finn and nodded toward the door, indicating she wanted a private word.

Finn followed his aunt into the stairwell, but he did not quite close the door. Margaret could not help that, if she stood close to it, she could hear every word.

"If ye were ready to wed," Helen said, "ye should have asked me to find ye a bride."

"Ye think I needed help?" Finn asked in an amused tone.

"She's a charming lass, and I wish ye well," Helen said. "But after your foolishness with the Sinclairs, a wife from a solid Gordon—or even a Sutherland—family of unquestioned loyalty would have gone a long way to smooth your path."

"There wasn't a Gordon or Sutherland lass I wanted to wed," Finn said. "And what's done is done."

"Ye know I'm verra fond of ye," his aunt said, "but it will be no easy task to win your place here. The men are suspicious."

"I know they are," Finn said. "I'm grateful my uncle seems willing to give me a chance to prove myself."

"He won't give ye a second one," she said. "So there can be no running off again!"

When Margaret heard Helen going down the stairs, she braced herself to face Finn. Before he had a chance to confront her about her tale of being handfasted, however, servants came up the stairs carrying wine, bowls of savory soup, and a platter with cheese, sliced pork, oatcakes, and honeyed nuts.

Finn instructed them to set the food and drink out in Una's chamber, which was no bigger but had a small table between the two cots. Margaret could barely eat, but Finn and Ella ate as if it was their last meal. When they were finished, Una turned to Ella.

"I'd wager this wee lassie would like to hear a story about trouble Finn got into when he was a bairn," Una said. "*Ach*, he got into so much mischief 'tis hard to know which tale to start with."

Ella crawled into Una's lap, the deserter.

"There's no need for ye to keep Ella," Margaret said. "She can sleep in our chamber."

"Nay, we need our privacy, being newlyweds and all, *mo leannain*," Finn said as he pulled Margaret to her feet. "Fair warning, Una. Ye may need to hold the pillow over your head tonight to sleep through my wife's screams of pleasure."

The elderly nursemaid slapped Finn's arm. "I've known this charming devil since he was a lad, and he's not half as bad as he seems," she told Margaret. "Don't fret over Ella. I'll take good care of this sweet bairn."

Before Margaret could argue, Finn pulled her into their chamber, closed the door, and stood in front of it with his arms folded. The time for reckoning had come.

"What made ye say we're handfasted?" he asked, raising one black eyebrow.

"What made *you* attempt to paint me as a woman who was willing to sell myself?"

"I said it because no one would believe I hadn't bedded ye when we'd traveled together," he said.

"Women find ye that irresistible, do they?"

"Anyone would think a lass who was willing to travel alone with a man would also be willing to share his bed," he said. "By saying ye were a desperate widow, I put the best face on it I could."

"Nay, *I* put the best face on it," she said. "I couldn't have your mother, of all people, thinking ye brought a prostitute home to the family. Don't ye care what she thinks of ye?"

"My mother wants to believe the worst in me." He blew out his breath and spread his arms. "I don't know why I feel compelled to find out if she actually will, as she always does."

"So ye make sure she does," Margaret said.

"Don't be angry with me about that." He gave her that smile that probably got him extra sweets when he was a bairn—and sexual favors later on. "I'm sorry I insulted ye, but it would never have occurred to me to say we were wed."

Would never have occurred to him. As apologies went, that was not a very good one.

Finn lifted her to sit on the bed and took her hands between his. "Ye do know what handfasting is?"

"'Tis a Highland custom whereby a couple enters a trial marriage by making vows to each other," she said. "They have a year and a day to change their minds and dissolve the marriage if they wish."

"So ye did know what ye were doing." He heaved a sigh. "I suppose it could be worse. Ye could have said our marriage was blessed by the church. Then we'd be bound *forever*."

"Being blessed by the church did not ensure my marriage was forever," she said, folding her arms.

"Well, I'm no rich Lowland nobleman, so there would be no getting out of it."

Finn obviously thought being bound to her for life would be the worst possible fate that could befall him. That should not irritate her, as marriage would be the worst possible thing for her as well. All the same, it did.

"'Tis all a lie anyway, so what does it matter?" she said.

"What matters is that ye convinced everyone else of your lie. So here we are, *m' eudail*," *my treasure*, he said with a slow smile and a devilish twinkle in his eye, "forced to share a bed."

Margaret's skin felt hot under his gaze. She never should have kissed him this morning. Never should have let him touch her like he did. Never should have run her hands over his chest or clutched his hair in her fingers. Because now, when he was looking at her like this, all she could think about was how wonderful it felt to have his mouth on hers and his hard, muscular body pressing her against the tree.

It had been a grave mistake to initiate that kiss. Yet, try as she might, she could not persuade herself to regret it. The memory drew her body toward his, as if pulled by a rope.

Rap, rap, rap.

The knock at the door saved her from herself. This time the servants arrived with a tub and buckets of steaming water, breaking the spell Finn cast over her and giving her a chance to come to her senses. She shook her head, determined not to let it happen again

Finn never thought he'd like being married—but playing at it definitely had its advantages.

Now that he and Margaret were sharing a chamber—*and a bed*—he was certain they would make love tonight. After the way passion exploded between them with their first kiss outside of Huntly Castle, there was no denying the attraction between them. *Ach,* Margaret had been on fire in his arms. Sharing such close quarters, it was inevitable they would be lovers.

He was more than ready to get naked, but he understood now he must go slowly and give her time. Margaret was a cautious woman who liked to keep a tight rein on her emotions, and that explosion of passion between them had frightened her. It sure as hell had surprised him.

"You can bathe first," he said after the servants left them alone. "I'll wash your back for ye."

"I can manage on my own, thank you," she said, giving him an amused smile.

Finn stretched out on his side on the bed, propped his head on his elbow, and watched her through the steam rising from the tub between them. This bath would be his undoing. And he was looking forward to it.

"You're not staying in this room while I bathe," Margaret said. "You can wait in Una's chamber."

"If the household is to believe we're newlyweds, I'm afraid I must stay." He gave her a wide smile. "Una is a wonderful nursemaid, but a dreadful gossip."

She rolled her eyes. "Turn around then and promise not to look."

"Ye can't mean it," he groaned. When she did not relent, he reluctantly rolled onto his other side and faced the wall.

"Wait," she said, causing his hope to rise—along with his cock. "Could ye unhook my gown first?"

He leaped to his feet. After sweeping her hair to the side, he slowly unfastened the first hook. Who knew the nape of her neck could be so irresistible? He had to fight the urge to press his lips there. As he slid his fingers along her skin from hook to hook down her back, her breathing grew shallow, and he smiled. He was not alone in being affected by their closeness.

"With all your experience," she said, "I thought you'd be quicker at this."

"Some things are better savored," he breathed in her ear.

She shivered beneath his fingers as he slid the gown off her shoulders, and he thought perhaps she would let him wash her after all…

But, alas, she turned around holding the loosened bodice over her breasts and said, "I can do the rest myself."

He heaved a loud sigh and stretched out on the bed again—facing the wall. The next half-hour was pure torture as his imagination filled in what he could not see. He heard the rustle of her gown as she slipped it down her body and the soft *whoosh* as it hit the floor. His pulse raced as he envisioned how the candlelight would reveal her silhouette beneath the thin fabric of her shift.

What would she do next? Probably sit on the stool and remove her stockings with one long leg crossed over the other. He was already breathing hard when he heard her step into the tub. His heart nearly stopped at the sound of another soft *whoosh* and he envisioned her pulling her shift over her head and tossing it on the stool.

She paused then, making him wonder if the water was too hot. Things were certainly too hot where he was. In his mind's eye, he saw her standing in the tub with the steam rising up her long, slender legs. Knowing how modest she was, Margaret would be holding one hand over the juncture between her legs and her other arm across her breasts, which only had the effect of adding to the allure of the image.

Before he could continue his mental journey over her naked form, she sank into the water with a deep sigh. He hoped to make her sigh like that many times before this night was over. Mesmerized by the light trickle hitting the tub of water, he imagined her squeezing the sponge. She would run it down her arms and then along her throat, causing beads of water to stream down the valley between her breasts with their tips rosy from the heat.

The next time, she would let him bathe her, and he would kiss those rosy tips…run the sponge down the length of her leg…suck on her wet toes…pleasure her with his hand and watch her come. Aye, it had to happen. He was sweating and lightheaded from all the blood rushing to his cock when her voice interrupted his daydream.

"Oh my, that was lovely."

She had no idea.

"'Tis your turn," she said. "The servants left another bucket of hot water. I'll pour it into warm the bath up for ye."

What he needed was a dip in an icy loch. Nay, he needed her with him in the tub. Or on the bed. Or on the floor. Or against the wall.

When he turned around and saw her, his heart did a flip in his chest. She had donned the simple night shift the servants had brought for her. Though it revealed nothing but her pretty bare feet and ankles, just knowing she was naked beneath it nearly killed him. And she smelled like heaven.

Jesu, he was not strong enough to survive this.

"I don't mind if ye wish to watch me bathe." With that devilish glint in his eye, Finn unfastened his belt, let it fall to the floor, and started to pull his tunic and shirt over his head.

Margaret whirled around before she caught an eyeful of brawny, naked Highlander. Though she was tempted to watch him bathe, Finn would take it as encouragement that she would do what she absolutely could not allow herself to do tonight.

Still, she could not help but wonder if he was as beautiful without his clothes as he was with them. If she turned her head to look out the window and happened to catch a glimpse of him from the corner of her eye, that would not be the same as actually watching him...

"You're peeking," he said.

"I'm not," she said, and fixed her gaze straight ahead again. "I was concerned ye might be flooding the floor."

For a man who could sneak into a cottage without making a sound, he seemed intent on making certain she was aware of his every motion by splashing in the tub.

"I'm out," he said after a while. "'Tis safe to look now."

She turned around and swallowed hard. Nay, it most certainly was not safe to look.

Drops of water glistened on his sooty eyelashes and fell from his black hair in tantalizing rivulets down his muscular shoulders and broad chest. More drops glistened on the hair on his abdomen above the drying cloth he'd slung low around his hips.

"Shall I take this off so ye can have a better look?" he asked, giving the drying cloth a slight tug.

Her cheeks burned hot and her gaze flew to his face. He wore a wide grin.

"If you're done staring," he said, "ye can hand me that clean *léine* my aunt sent up."

"I wasn't staring," she said. "I merely wondered why ye did such a poor job of drying yourself."

"Do ye have any notion what a poor liar ye are?" he asked with a laugh.

She held the shirt out to him and turned her head as he dropped the drying cloth.

When she looked again, he had donned the *léine*, the loose linen shirt Highlanders wore, which hung to his mid-thighs, clung to his damp skin, and exposed an expanse of his chest through the gap down the front.

"Sit on the stool and let me comb your hair for ye," he said.

Finn's offer seemed harmless—and she would not have to struggle to keep her eyes off him while he stood behind her—so she sat down and handed him the comb.

Harmless? Heavens, no. Margaret could not help the occasional sigh as Finn took his time, combing with smooth, rhythmic strokes that he drew out and lengthened. She was surprised by how intimate it felt to have Finn do this for her. In five years of marriage, William never had. It never would have occurred to him. She was the one who was always expected to cater to him.

"Your hair is the color of moonlight shimmering across a loch on a clear night," Finn said as he paused to let strands of her hair slide through his fingers.

When Finn began massaging her temples, her eyes fluttered closed. *Don't stop*, she silently pleaded, because it felt so good. She felt the whisper of his breath on the side of her neck, followed by his lips, a soft touch that caused a tantalizing thrill and made her nipples tighten. She tensed with delicious anticipation as he continued down her throat toward her breasts...

Good heavens! She opened her eyes with a start as she suddenly recalled how quickly she lost her head the first time they kissed—and ended up with her skirts around her waist and her back against a tree. She sprang to her feet and spun around to face him.

"Are ye ready to go to bed, *leannain*?" he asked, and ran his hands down her arms, a gesture that made it difficult for her to breathe.

"Aye, 'tis getting late," she said, her voice coming out unnaturally high.

She opened her mouth to ask which side of the bed he preferred, but the words died on her lips when he cupped her face between his large hands and leaned down to kiss her. Her will to resist him slipped away and her body bent toward his.

Instead of hot and demanding like the last time, these were slow, sensuous kisses that made her feel drugged, bewitched. Her head fell back, and her mind could focus on nothing but the journey of his lips and tongue as they traveled along her jaw, below her ear, and down the side of her throat. He lifted her onto the bed and enfolded her in his arms, then his mouth was on hers in another smoldering kiss that left her head spinning.

He paused to lean over her, his deep blue eyes dark with desire, and brushed a stray strand of hair from her forehead with his fingers.

"I'm beginning to think," he said in a hoarse voice, "that telling everyone we are handfasted was a verra good idea after all."

She wanted to pull him down into another mindless kiss, to not think of risks and consequences. She'd never been kissed like that before, where time seemed to stop, and it felt as if he wanted to kiss her forever. But time did not stop. She knew where Finn expected these kisses to lead—where they would inevitably take them—and she could not let herself go there.

"We can't do this," she forced herself to say, and pressed her palms against his chest.

His brows shot up. "Why not?"

"Because we're not truly wed," she said, though that was not the reason that stopped her.

"If we must act as if we are," he said, "we ought to have the *one* benefit of this pretense of a marriage."

"But it is only a pretense," she said.

"M' eudail," my treasure, he said, giving her a wicked smile that made her stomach flip, "ye cannot truly believe the two of us can share this chamber—*this bed*—and not enjoy ourselves in it."

"Of course I can," she said. "Why shouldn't I?"

"Because I think ye want me, and God knows I want you." His expression grew serious. "I have since the first time I saw ye looking like a faery princess in a sparkling gown at Holyrood Palace. And I've wanted ye more every day since."

Oh my. She ran her tongue over her dry lips. "But ye said I wasn't your sort of woman."

"You're the wrong sort of lass in every way," he said, brushing his thumb across her cheek. "But I cannot help myself."

With his black hair falling over one eye, Finn was dangerously appealing, and she was all too aware of his hard-muscled body against hers through her thin night shift. If his kisses were a hint, and she suspected they were, then making love with Finn would be nothing like having William grunt over her. She was sorely tempted to find out…

"There's no reason to deny ourselves when everyone here thinks we're wed," he said. "And there's nothing to fear since ye cannot bear a child."

Ye cannot bear a child. Finn had hit upon the open wound in her heart and the true reason she could not say aye to him. Though she longed for his touch, his kisses, and more, she could not risk another pregnancy and miscarriage. She just could not face that heartache again.

"This will not happen." She rolled away from him and lay against the wall, taking up as little space as possible.

He deserved an explanation. But she was not ready to tell him about her deepest sorrow, her failed pregnancies. She might never be. The wound was too deep, her failure too painful to share.

The room was so quiet she could hear his every breath. She was overly aware of her own breathing as well, even her pulse. It would take so little for the tension between them to ignite into something she could not control that she was afraid to move. Finn was right to question how long they could share this bed without giving in.

Staying here with him was dangerous. It was not Finn she feared, but her weakness for him. No other man could tempt her this way. Despite her efforts to resist, he had breached her defenses.

It would be unfair to ask Finn to take her halfway across Scotland to her sister Sybil so soon after they arrived and when so much was at stake for him. His aunt's warning still rang in her ears.

It will be no easy task to win your place here…no running off again!

She had no money or jewels to pay someone else to take her. Even if she did, she would not know whom to trust to take her. It was a great distance, and she had a young child to consider.

In truth, she would not trust anyone but Finn. He could have abandoned them when Moray no longer wanted her kidnapped. Instead, he had brought them to this place, far from her brothers' reach. For as long as she and Ella needed to stay here, they would be safe.

Until she was able to leave, she would just have to manage this...*situation* with Finn. She had navigated the perils of her marriage for years—catering to William's demanding nature, soothing his erratic moods, and suffering his relentless criticism.

After that, she should have no trouble containing what was nothing but a simple attraction between her and Finn.

CHAPTER 16

Margaret awoke alone in the bed and sat up, looking for Finn. He was gone, and she had no notion where he was. After she refused him last night, she ought to feel relieved to avoid the awkwardness of waking together. Instead, she felt unsettled. Of course, it was only because she was accustomed to having him nearby. Except for the hour he went inside Huntly Castle, he had been her constant companion since the night he took her from Old Thomas's cottage.

Judging by the sunlight shining through the narrow window, she had slept late. She dressed quickly, wishing she had a clean gown to put on, and went to find Ella. When no one answered her knock on Una's door, Margaret pushed it open. Panic welled in her throat as she took in the neatly folded blankets on the pallets and the empty room.

Why had she let Finn and his aunt persuade her to leave Ella with a stranger? She did not know these people! She ran down the stairs and entered the hall breathless. When she saw Ella at the table eating porridge, the relief that poured through her body was so intense it made her limbs feel weak.

She had not realized becoming a mother would make bouts of terror a regular part of her life. But then Ella looked up from her breakfast and broke into a smile, and Margaret knew the worry was a small price to pay for the joy her daughter brought her.

Servants had cleared away most of the dishes, and the men were gone. She suspected the four women who had remained at the table were waiting for a closer inspection of Finn's new bride.

"Good morning," Margaret said as she slipped into the seat beside Ella and put a protective arm around her.

Finn's Aunt Helen and Una greeted her with warm smiles that showed they were prepared to like her. His mother and sister-in-law, however, wore hard expressions that seemed to say they had already decided Margaret would meet their worst expectations.

"What with all the...*excitement* of Finn bringing home a bride, I'm afraid we failed to introduce ye to his mother Isabel and his brother's wife Curstag," Helen said, nodding toward the two women. "Now, shall I have the cook prepare some eggs and bacon for ye?"

"No need to go to the trouble," Margaret said, knowing the kitchen servants would be busy preparing the big noon meal. "If there's porridge left in the pot here by Ella, that will do fine for me."

That earned her a nod of approval from Helen, which confirmed that the question had been a test to see if Margaret was the demanding sort of guest who created extra work for the hostess and her household.

"Did ye know Finn makes a perfect porridge?" Margaret said to fill the awkward silence as she served herself from the pot.

Helen beamed at her. "I taught him."

"You cook?" Curstag asked, wrinkling her nose as if she smelled something foul. "The only time I enter the kitchen is when I find it necessary to reprimand the cook."

Margaret suspected that occurred all too often and felt sorry for the cook.

"'Tis a useful skill," Helen said. "Ye never know when it may come in handy."

"Why would *you* ever need it?" Isabel said. "You're a countess with a large castle full of servants."

Goodness. Margaret regretted mentioning Finn's talent with porridge. She began eating the lukewarm porridge with the goal of finishing it as quickly as possible.

"Is that Finn's bastard?" Isabel asked, looking at Ella.

Margaret nearly choked on her porridge, then she pushed the bowl aside and lifted Ella onto her lap. Thankfully, Ella did not appear to understand what Isabel said.

"Isabel, this is my house, and you'll treat my other guests with courtesy," Helen said, which gave Margaret the moment she needed to gather herself.

Margaret was as shocked by Isabel's lack of subtlety as by the insult itself. At court, insults could be just as cutting, but they were nearly an art form in their sophistication.

"My daughter is not a bastard. Nor is she Finn's child." Margaret paused to kiss the top of Ella's head. "As Finn told ye last night, I'm a widow."

"Hmmph," Isabel grunted, and fixed her steely black eyes on Margaret. "Finn is a philanderer of the worst sort. He'll bring ye no happiness."

"Looks like a fine day, and Ella and I could do with some fresh air," Margaret said, and stood up with Ella on hip. "Can ye suggest a walk nearby?"

"There are paths through the wood next to the castle," Helen said. "Just don't go too far and get lost."

"I'll ask Finn to take us," Margaret said.

"I'm afraid he can't today," Helen said. "The earl has him practicing with his personal guard."

Margaret was happy to hear it. Surely this was a sign Finn's uncle was likely to ask him to join his guard. "I won't disturb him then."

"I've told my husband how pleased I am to have Finn back with us," Helen said with a twinkle in her eye.

While Finn's mother may not say a word on his behalf, his aunt was on his side—and she was the earl's countess.

"Curstag," Helen said, "would ye be so good as to accompany Maggie and her daughter on their walk so they don't lose their way?"

Margaret expected Curstag to make an excuse, but she readily agreed. When Margaret excused herself to fetch their cloaks, Helen and Una came upstairs with her and Ella.

"I have a few gowns packed away from when I was young and thin," Helen said, taking her arm as they climbed the stairs. "I don't know why I kept them for so long, as there's not enough fabric to let them out to fit me now. Would ye like to have them?"

The back of Margaret's eyes stung with the threat of tears at Helen's kindness. The countess evidently had noticed Margaret came with nothing. Instead of thinking worse of her for it, Helen took pains to offer the gowns in a way that would not embarrass her.

"That is most kind of ye," Margaret said. "I'd be grateful if ye would lend them to me until I can make my own."

"Keep them—consider them a marriage gift," Helen said, with a wave of her hand. "And try not to mind Isabel's sharp tongue. There's no bride Finn could bring home who would please her, but I can see now he made a good choice."

"Thank you." Margaret felt like a fraud for deceiving this sweet woman.

"I could tell from the moment ye entered the hall that the two of ye were bound by true affection, and that counts for something," Helen said. "My son speaks very highly of ye as well, and Alex has his mother's good judgment."

Before going back downstairs to meet Curstag, Margaret tied the pouch of broken onyx to her belt. Though it was foolish, Finn's sister-in-law made her uneasy, and the onyx reminded Margaret of her mother's strength and love. From the way Ella clutched her old rag doll and hid behind Margaret when they met Curstag downstairs, she felt apprehensive too.

Curstag was blessedly silent as she led them out of the castle and onto a path into the wood. The weather was still cool this far north, but the bluebells were lovely and thick beneath the trees, and the birds were chirping overhead. As they trailed behind Curstag deeper into the wood, Margaret began to relax and enjoy herself. But then Curstag came to an abrupt halt and spun around to face her.

"You're one sly bitch," Curstag said.

"What?" Margaret stared at her. Curstag might be more careful in public, but she was as rude as her mother-in-law.

"Ye may fool the countess with that feigned look of innocence." Curstag made her eyes big and blinked several times in what Margaret assumed was meant to be a mocking imitation of herself. "But ye don't fool me."

"I think it's time Ella and I returned to the castle," Margaret said, hoping to avoid any further unpleasantness.

When she started to turn back, however, Curstag stunned her by shoving her against a tree with surprising force. Margaret was too astonished to react.

"I didn't come out here for a damned stroll in the wood," Curstag said, bringing her face mere inches from Margaret's. "I came to find out how ye got Finn to agree to marry ye."

"I haven't forced Finn to do anything." It never paid to rile an angry person, so Margaret kept her own voice calm. "He's the one who insisted I come with him to the Highlands. In truth, he absolutely refused to leave me behind."

"Are ye with child?" Curstag shot a glance down at Margaret's belly before returning her glare to Margaret's face. "That must be it. Finn never wanted a bairn. *Never.* But knowing him, he'd feel obligated if a lass got herself pregnant."

Margaret refrained from telling Curstag that women did not get themselves with child.

"Not that ye have any right to know, but I'm not with child," Margaret said. "So perhaps ye can take your hands off me now?"

"Then I'd wager ye lied and told him ye were," Curstag said, nodding to herself. "Aye, that's it."

"Whether I'm lying or not, surely this is a matter between Finn and me," Margaret said. "I fail to see why it would be any of your concern."

"Finn and I have always been close," Curstag said. "I don't want to see him made a fool of."

Close? Margaret felt a jab of jealousy right under her ribs. She was not Finn's true wife, or even his lover, so she had no rights to him. No claim at all. And yet she wanted—nay, needed—to know just how close he and Curstag had been.

And were they still?

"Ye won't keep him in your bed for long," Curstag said. "You're too dull for a man like Finn. He'll be bored within a sennight, if he isn't already."

Curstag was right. It would take a woman with a wild, passionate nature to hold Finn, but Margaret certainly was not going to give her the satisfaction of admitting it.

"And you'll never have Finn's heart," Curstag said with a smile curling her full red lips. "He gave that away a long time ago."

Margaret did not want to believe Finn had bedded his brother's unpleasant wife—or even worse, given his heart to her—but she had to admit Curstag was the sort Finn liked. Though better dressed, she had the same blatant sensuality and voluptuous figure as the tavern maid who had flung herself at Finn when they went to find a boat.

Before Margaret could dwell any longer on that ugly thought, she caught sight of Ella and gasped. Her wee daughter was curled up on the ground with her hands covering her ears. After the violence the child had seen in her home, seeing Margaret get pushed and shouted at must have frightened her badly.

"Get out of my way!" Margaret shoved Curstag so hard she fell on her rear end, which served her right for frightening Ella.

Margaret rushed to her daughter, dropped to her knees, and gathered Ella in her arms.

"'Tis all right. You're safe. I'm here," she murmured. "I'll not let anything bad happen to you."

"Find your own way back," Curstag said, and stormed off.

Margaret ignored her and continued rocking Ella and murmuring reassurances until the bairn finally stopped shaking.

"She's bad," Ella said, looking up at her with watery eyes.

"I'm sorry I let her frighten ye," Margaret said, wiping Ella's tears away. "Curstag has a foul mouth, but she can't hurt us."

Ella did not look persuaded.

"Come, let's go back to the castle, and I'll find a special treat for ye in the kitchen."

Margaret looked around then and realized Curstag had left them in the middle of the wood. Worse, she had gotten turned around and was not at all certain which way led back to the castle.

She gave Ella what she hoped was a reassuring mother-knows-what-she's-doing smile, and the two of them started off, hand in hand. After a while, the wood seemed to grow darker, and then a long, doleful cry that sounded like a wolf or wild dog stopped her in her tracks. *Ow-oooo, ow-ooo.* She picked up Ella and held the bag of broken onyx in her fist as she tried to hear where the sound was coming from over her pounding heart. *Ow-ooo, ow-oooo.*

Then, behind them in the distance, she heard the cry of sea-gull, a welcome sound that would lead them to the sea—and back to the castle. The path back split twice, but she knew which way to go by the cry of the gulls. Though Ella grew heavy in her arms, Margaret ran until she finally saw the clearing at the end of the wood.

"We're almost there," she told Ella, and pointed. "See, there's the castle."

The men were in the field between the wood and castle practicing with their claymores, the heavy two-handed swords Highlanders favored. Curstag stood watching them with her back to the wood. When she looked over her shoulder and saw Margaret and Ella, her expression turned sour. Apparently, she was disappointed they had found their way out of the wood.

Margaret wanted to strangle her, but she forgot about Curstag when she caught sight of Finn. Even for a Highlander, he was tall, but it was his skill with the sword that made him stand out among the men. He was simply breathtaking in motion, the ideal of masculine beauty and prowess, as he swung the deadly weapon with smooth, rhythmic strokes.

Clang, clang, clang.

Despite the chill wind coming off the sea, he had removed his shirt, and his muscles rippled and bunched as he swung his sword. He fought as if he knew instinctively where his opponent did not expect the blow, striking high and low and high again, but always pushing the other warrior back and back and back.

With one final, powerful swing, he knocked the other warrior to the ground with the flat of his sword. No sooner had he defeated him, than another came at him. Only then did Margaret notice there was a line of warriors waiting to fight him.

"Finn!" Ella danced with excitement and pointed at him. "Finn!"

He glanced up, and a thrill went through Margaret when his gaze caught on hers and held. His opponent took advantage of his distraction, however, and knocked him flat.

Finn took it with good humor and was laughing as his opponent offered him a hand. Finn took it, flipped the other warrior onto the ground, and stood over him with a wide grin. After signaling to the next man in line to wait a moment, he waved at her and Ella.

Margaret had forgotten Curstag was there until the woman looped her arm through hers and waved back at Finn with a bright smile. As soon as he returned to the practice, Curstag released her arm and flounced off toward the castle gate. On her way, she passed Una without a word.

"Mind that one," Una said when she joined them. "She thrives on trouble like seed on a dung heap."

"What's between her and Finn?" Margaret asked.

"'Tis not me, but your husband ye ought to ask." She paused, then added, "If you're certain ye want to know."

If there was nothing, surely Una would have just said so.

When Alex, who had been practicing with the men, came over to greet them, Ella let go of Margaret's hand and ran to meet him. Margaret was relieved that her daughter seemed to have recovered from the incident in the wood. Alex, however, was limping.

"What happened to you?" Margaret asked.

"My horse got a thorn in his hoof and threw me," he said. "'Twas my own fault for riding near the brambles."

"We ought to go inside and see to your leg," she said.

"Nay, it barely hurts at all." He paused to lift Ella high in the air, which made her laugh. "Don't tell my father. The way he's been lately, he'll question everyone in the castle over a wee thorn."

To her mind, the earl behaved like a man with lands and responsibilities who had only one heir.

"*Ach*, look at Finn!" Alex said, turning to watch the practice. "He's better than all of them."

"Why are the other guards lined up to fight him?" Margaret asked.

"Because he's the best," Alex said. "And they're angry with him—but he's already winning them over."

She could see his impressive fighting skills and good humor were bringing them around. By the time Finn faced the last warrior in line, however, he had welts on his arms and torso from the blows he had taken. Though he must be exhausted as well, he moved with grace and speed, as if he could do this all day.

She swallowed hard when the last man stepped up to challenge Finn. He was huge, with legs the size of tree trunks and a vicious look in his eyes.

"Treat?" Ella interrupted, tugging on Margaret's skirts.

Margaret beamed at her. Just a few short days ago, Ella was afraid to draw attention to herself or to ask for anything. In Ella's home, she had learned it was safest for a child to be neither seen nor heard. It would take a long time to overcome her fears, but this was a good sign.

"Of course, sweetling," Margaret said, though she wished she could watch Finn a little longer to be sure he survived his last fight without serious injury.

"I'll take the wee lassie inside," Una said, then leaned down to speak to Ella. "Cook has made a plum pudding, and it's still warm. Shall we have some before your nap?"

Ella nodded with a shy smile.

"Warm plum pudding?" Alex said. "I'll go with ye."

Margaret's heart swelled as she watched her small daughter walking between the old woman and Alex, holding their hands. Despite the incident in the woods with Curstag, Ella was learning to trust—or rather, she was learning who she could trust, and that was still better.

Finn winced as he pulled his torn shirt over his head.

"Mercy!" Margaret gasped. "What have they done to you?"

"For the men to accept me," he said, "I must prove myself—and take a wee bit of punishment for leaving to fight with the Sinclairs."

"This is a *wee bit*?" She raked her gaze over his bare chest and back as she circled him.

If he'd known a few cuts and bruises would overcome her shyness, he'd have asked the men to beat on him sooner. This was nothing, but why tell her that?

148

"I'd like to give those men a piece of my mind," she said. "I'll see if Una has a salve for those cuts, but we'd best get ye washed first."

This was sounding better and better. The notion of Margaret sliding her soapy hands all over his body was verra appealing.

"Can't wait to get clean," he said with a grin.

"Good," she said in a clipped tone. "You wash up while I get the salve."

The cuts stung like hell as he washed, so he made quick work of it and was sitting on the stool with the drying cloth wrapped around his waist when she returned. She took a long and thorough look at his bare torso and legs, which made her blush and him get hard. Pretending that had not happened, she smoothed her expression and set about tending to his wounds.

"How long do ye suppose it will take to prove yourself?" Margaret asked as she dabbed the salve on his cuts with gentle fingers.

"The men respect my skills as a warrior, and most of them have known me since I was a lad," he said. "But 'tis a serious offense to fight for an enemy clan."

"Even if that clan is also your blood relation?"

"My Sinclair blood is what makes me suspect in the first place," he said with a smile.

As Margaret leaned across him to apply salve to a cut on his shoulder, her breasts were barely an inch from his face, and he blessed the man who struck that particular blow. The lavender in her hair filled his nose, and he could almost taste her skin on his tongue.

"They ought to understand ye fought for a chance to gain your own lands," she said.

"These men are content with the honor of serving in their laird's guard, and some of them resent me for wanting more," Finn said. "Being close kin to three earls, though it gains me little, also sets me apart."

"So they make you pay by battering you?" Margaret blew out her breath and shook her head. "What about your uncle? Is there more ye must do to win his trust?"

149

"I suspect there is, but he hasn't told me yet."

Her fingers and hands rubbing salve over his bare skin was driving him mad with lust. The lass no longer showed any unease with his near nakedness. In fact, he was beginning to think she was touching him more than strictly necessary with the salve...

Perhaps this would lead to more. God, he hoped so. With another woman, he knew it would. Last night, he thought he could get past the barrier Margaret raised between them by going slowly and giving her time. But she'd left him frustrated and confused. Though he hated to admit it, her rejection hurt him as well.

"Ella and I went for a walk in the wood with Curstag," she said.

He groaned inwardly at the thought of the two women talking. Margaret may as well have poured a bucket of cold water over his head.

"What's the cause of the trouble between you and your brother?" Margaret asked. "Has it something to do with his wife?

Damn, what had Curstag told her? Though Margaret's careful tone held no accusation, he could read her well enough now to tell from the tension in those pretty, slender shoulders that the lass cared very much about his answer.

He wanted to tell her the truth about Curstag. And he would, one day. But now, while they were stuck here together with his family, was not the right time. Before he told Maggie about his past with Curstag, he needed to convince her she could trust him. Telling her the truth now would make it that much harder to persuade her.

"Bearach and I have never gotten along," he said, and hoped to leave it at that.

"And Curstag?"

"What about her?"

"Well," she said, casting her gaze to the side, "she watches you as if..."

"As if what?"

"As if the two of you were lovers. She said as much today." Margaret quickly added, "Of course, it's not any of my concern."

Margaret sounded jealous. Now that was promising.

Finn rested his hands on her hips and met her gaze. "She's nothing to me."

"Would Curstag say the same?" she asked.

"Doesn't matter what she'd say," he said. "You're the one I want."

He wanted her? There was nothing special about that. Men had been wanting to bed her since she was thirteen. But Finn was the first man *she* wanted.

If ye had me, what then? She was tempted to ask him, but she already knew the answer. He would be disappointed. Beauty drew men to her, but William had shown her that was not enough.

"You're so beautiful ye take my breath away," he said, which was like jabbing her with the point of his blade.

When he reached for her, she turned her back.

For once, she wished a man wanted her just for herself. She wanted Finn because of everything he was. His good heart, charm, and humor drew her as much as his fine looks—though they were very fine, indeed.

She sighed. It did not matter why he wanted her anyway. The risk of another failed pregnancy and heartache was too great to give in to temptation.

Late that night, as they lay side by side in the bed, the tension was thick between them.

"I don't know which will kill me first," Finn muttered, "frustration or lack of sleep."

"Death seems unlikely," she said.

He chuckled, which eased the tension for a moment.

"Ye know this can't go on forever," Finn said, turning on his side to face her. "Just what was your plan?"

He was far too handsome in the glow of the candle he'd left burning, so she decided it was safer to keep her gaze fixed on the ceiling.

"I had no plan beyond not being labeled a whore," she said.

151

"I don't mean when we arrived here at Dunrobin," he said. "What was your plan at the verra beginning when ye decided to go along with the kidnapping?"

"I don't recall ye giving me a choice."

"All the same, ye wanted to come with me," he said.

"Ella's brother only brought her to me an hour before ye came to the cottage," she explained. "I'd decided I must escape with her, but I'd no time to make a plan beyond that."

"Ye took a chance running off with a kidnapper," he said. "Evidently, it wasn't because ye find me irresistible."

He was very nearly irresistible, which was the problem.

"In truth," she said, "I've never done anything so bold in my life as the things I did that night."

"Do ye regret coming away with me?"

"Nay," she said. "Not for a moment."

If not for Finn, she would almost surely have been caught, lost Ella, and been forced to wed a powerful nobleman her brother needed as an ally.

"I'm grateful to ye," she said.

"Gratitude is not what I want from ye," Finn said in a strained voice.

Though Finn was not like William, the discord her refusal caused between them made her feel tense and vulnerable. She knew Finn would never force her or make her pay in other ways for not complying with his wishes. And yet she could not forget the lessons she learned from her years of marriage so easily.

There was one lesson she'd learned from William, however, that might be useful here.

"There is something"—she hesitated—"I could do to help ye sleep."

"What, sing to me?" he asked. "I doubt that will help, but if ye wish to tr—"

He abruptly stopped speaking when she got on her knees and began to slowly pull the bedclothes down his body. The gaze he fixed on her held such heat it scorched her skin. That gave her more confidence that Finn would welcome this means of resolving his problem, and they could both get some much-needed sleep.

As she dragged the bedclothes farther down, they caught on his erection for a moment, and then his shaft sprang free. She swallowed. He certainly was ready.

She pushed away the memories of William holding her head down and forcing her to do this. Gingerly, she wrapped her hand around his shaft, which was thick and long and already wet at the tip.

"*Jesu,*" Finn moaned on an exhale.

That was encouraging. This should not take long. Leaning over him carefully so that no other part of their bodies touched, she brought her mouth toward his shaft.

Finn reached out to touch her hair.

"Don't," she blurted out.

Finn dropped his hand. William had never heeded her requests, so she had quit making them. Instead, he gave her endless instructions until she learned to do this—not well, but well enough.

Not like that! What is the matter with ye? 'Tis fortunate you're beautiful because you're utterly useless in bed.

###

Finn was more confused than ever. He longed to touch her, but she would not even let him touch her hair. When she leaned down, he could not breathe. Nay, he could not be mistaken as to what she meant to do. Her hair fell over her shoulder and the ends brushed against his hip, sending a sweet thrill of sensation across his skin like a shimmer across a loch.

Desire hit him so hard he had to clench his fists when she ran her fingertips down the column of his manhood.

"*O shluagh, please,*" escaped his lips as he watched her slowly lower her mouth.

When she glanced up at him, she stole his breath away—God help him, she was so beautiful, and she was holding his cock...but...was that alarm in her eyes?

"Maggie, what's wro—"

She took him in her mouth and every single thought left his head. Nothing existed except the glorious sensation of her lips cap-

153

turing his cock, her tongue sliding and flicking, toying with him, teasing him, driving him to madness.

Aye. Aye. Aye! He did not know if he said the words aloud or just moaned them when she took him fully into her mouth and sucked. *Ach*, it felt so good that he was going to explode if he did not stop her, and this would all end far too soon.

He took hold of her shoulders as he sat up and pulled her against his chest.

"Did I not do it right?" She looked at him with wide, frightened eyes.

Good God, of all things, why would she say that? Then Finn knew why—there could be only one explanation—and he wanted to kill her former husband for it.

When Finn touched her cheek, she jerked away. He needed to tread carefully here.

"The truth is," he told her, "I feared I'd die of pleasure."

She tilted her head. "Then why did ye not let me finish?"

"Because ye don't really want to," he said. "You're only doing it to keep me from touching you."

"If it gives ye pleasure, what does it matter why I do it?"

"Because I want to give ye pleasure, not just take it. I want to touch ye, to feel your body against mine, to be inside ye and hear ye cry my name," he said, resting his palm against her cheek. "I want to make love to you."

Her eyes went dark and she bit her lip, and he caught a glimmer of the lass who had pulled him into a deep kiss outside of Huntly Castle. She was tempted, but something was holding her back.

Just what was she afraid of?

"Ye can't have a child, so ye needn't worry you'll end up bound to me," he said.

"Or you to me," she said in a tight voice.

Then why the hell not? And what did she mean by that, anyway? He was desperate to have her in his arms, but she was cooling by the moment.

"If you require a true handfasting to do it, I'm willing." He nearly choked on the words, but he didn't see where pretending and actually being handfasted would be much different. Either way, they'd be sharing this bed, and he could not have any other women.

"Although I'm flattered by such a *heartfelt* proposal," she said, "I must refuse, for your sake as well as mine."

Judging by the way she picked up the pillow and fluffed it rather vigorously with her fist, he must have phrased that badly. With all the blood drained from his head and filling his cock, he could not think properly.

Ach! He was even more confused and frustrated than before. The only thing he knew for certain was that Margaret was not going to reveal her secrets tonight. When she turned her back to him again, he felt as if she'd drawn an invisible line down the bed between them that he dare not cross.

And he had never felt lonelier in his life.

CHAPTER 17

Finn could take the punishment the men meted out at practice each day. At least he felt he was making progress with them. But after three more nights of tossing and turning beside Margaret, Finn could not take much more. And Margaret showed no signs of changing her mind.

He was in a foul mood and well on his way to getting stinking drunk when his brother plunked down beside him. The other men in the hall had taken one look at Finn and had the sense to leave him alone with his whisky.

"Ye look terrible," Bearach said, giving him a harder-than-friendly slap on the back. "That bride of yours must be riding ye hard."

"Mind your tongue." Finn kept his gaze fixed in front of him and willed his brother to disappear.

"*Ach*, that Maggie is something to look at," Bearach said. "Acts all quiet and proper, but I'd wager she's a wildcat under the blankets."

"Don't speak about her like that." Finn's head began to pound as he slowly turned to face his brother. "In fact, I'd ask ye not to foul her name by speaking of her at all."

"If you're having trouble satisfying your bride, little brother," Bearach said, "I'd be happy to take a turn and show her what she's missing."

Finn grabbed Bearach by the throat and lifted him off the bench. Speaking each word slowly, he said, "Stay away from her."

"It won't matter if I do," Bearach said with a smirk. "She'll come to me, just like Curstag did."

"Is minic a bhris béal duine a shorn." Many a time a man's mouth broke his nose.

Finn was very close to planting his fist in his brother's face when he heard the rustle of a gown and looked over his shoulder to find his mother fast approaching.

"Let go of him!" his mother shouted from still several feet away. "What in God's name is wrong with ye, Finn?"

"I mean it. Stay away from my wife," Finn said an inch from Bearach's face before dropping his brother back onto the bench.

"Ha, you've fallen for the bitch, haven't ye?" Bearach laughed and slapped the table. "Thought you'd learned your lesson. You're a damned fool."

Finn did not often agree with his brother, but he was indeed a fool. Margaret would not have him, but he could not enjoy himself with any other lass because that would dishonor his *wife*. Worse still, he had no interest in bedding any other lass. No one could be more surprised than Finn was to learn that Margaret was the only woman he wanted.

Finn had no hope of sleep again that night. Watching Margaret in the moonlight shining through the window made him feel as if something heavy was pressing against his chest.

He tossed aside the bedclothes, got dressed, and headed down the stairs. He needed fresh air. A thorough swiving was what he really needed. It would not be hard to find a willing lass, but word would go around, and that would shame Margaret.

As he descended the dark stairwell to the floor above the great hall, he saw a shaft of light under the door to his aunt and uncle's private solar. Who would be in there in the middle of the night? Imagining someone rifling through his uncle's locked drawers, he eased the door open only to find his uncle sitting alone drinking.

"Sorry to disturb ye," Finn said. "Just wanted to make sure nothing was amiss."

"I'm surprised to see the new bridegroom out of bed at this hour," his uncle said. "Come in and have a whisky with me. I've been wanting to have a quiet word alone with ye."

Finn hoped this was good news for him and took a seat while his uncle poured him a cup.

"Tomorrow we're going up to our hunting lodge at Helmsdale," his uncle said. "We'll stay there for a few weeks."

"Ye should have good hunting up that way." Finn could barely hide his relief. With the family gone, he would not have to keep up a pretense of newlywed bliss.

"I'll leave most of my men behind to protect Dunrobin, as usual," his uncle said. "But you and your lovely bride, of course, will come with the rest of the family."

Damn, damn, damn.

"Ye must come to Helmsdale," his uncle said, apparently noticing Finn's lack of enthusiasm. His uncle leaned forward. "I need ye there to keep Alex safe."

"You're still worried someone may try to harm him?" Finn asked. "Even here in Sutherland?"

"There are still Sutherlands who wish one of their own ruled their clan and its lands instead of a Gordon," his uncle said as he poured himself more whisky.

"You're half Sutherland," Finn said, though that did not carry water with those Sutherlands who considered the earl's mother—and Finn's grandmother—a traitor to her clan for usurping the earldom from the rightful heir. "I thought the resentment died down long ago."

"Tensions have increased as of late." His uncle sighed as he twirled the golden liquid in his cup.

"Why now?" Finn asked.

"Who knows what set them off this time?" his uncle said with a shrug. "And if not the Sutherlands, it could be the Sinclairs and the Mackays, who would also hope to gain if I lost my only son and heir."

If the earl had no heir, there would be a fight among every Sutherland who had a weak claim to be the next earl. The chaos and infighting that would ensue would leave the clan vulnerable, and the Sinclairs and the Mackays would take advantage of that.

"I'll do anything ye ask to protect Alex," Finn said. "But with you and your guard at Helmsdale, I'm not sure why ye need me."

"I'm his father. The men won't respect Alex if they see me watching over him like he's a bairn in leading strings," his uncle said. "But no one will think twice when they see Alex sticking close to his older cousin, a warrior admired by the men for his fighting skills and—if the rumors are true—liked even better by the lasses."

"Ye ought not believe all ye hear, uncle," Finn said with a laugh. "But if the men know the threat to Alex's life, they'll not think any less of him because ye want to keep a close watch on him. In fact, they'll expect it."

"I haven't told the other men." His uncle paused and stared into his cup. "I can't be sure one of them has not been bought off by our enemies."

This was disturbing news, indeed. Finn hoped this was just his uncle's suspicious nature and not that he had good reason to mistrust the loyalty of his own guard.

"There's been another *accident*, and it happened here at Dunrobin," his uncle said. "Alex was thrown from his horse."

"Alex told me it was just a thorn in the horse's hoof."

"Someone could have put it there," his uncle said.

That seemed unlikely, but Finn was persuaded there could well be a risk to Alex from the other clans.

"It would be better if more of your men were aware of your concerns and were keeping watch on Alex," Finn said. "But I appreciate that ye trust me."

"I know ye love my son as much as I do." His uncle gripped his shoulder and looked Finn in the eye as he spoke. "And you're the best warrior I've got."

Finn was surprised by the compliment. His relatives did not hand them out often, particularly to him.

"'Tis a damned shame my brother doesn't see what a fine son he has in you." His uncle shook his head. "That Sinclair mother of yours has poisoned his mind."

It would take a stronger man than Finn's father to withstand his mother. But no good would come of dwelling on that.

"As for that brother of yours," his uncle said with a grimace, "he's all Sinclair."

That poisoned Sinclair blood ran through Finn's veins too.

###

Margaret felt out of sorts all morning. After Finn left their bed during the night, she lay awake for hours imagining him with another woman—as if she was not miserable enough after her disastrous attempt to pleasure him.

She had no claim on him and certainly no cause to blame him for seeking out a woman who would give him what she could not. It should not trouble her in the least that he did. In fact, she should be relieved.

And yet it did trouble her, and she was anything but relieved.

The woman Finn went to last night—and may still be with this morning—would be the sort he was accustomed to, the kind he liked, and nothing like Margaret. She would be a voluptuous and bold woman who reveled in her sensuality and knew just how to please him. Despite herself, Margaret imagined him kissing the other woman's lips and throat the way he had kissed her, running his hands over the woman's bare skin the way Margaret wished she could let him touch her.

She was not ready to face Finn and whomever he had been with first thing, so she asked Una to have one of the servants bring breakfast up and ate alone with Ella. She could not, however, hide upstairs any longer. Bracing herself to see Finn without showing the hurt she felt, she went down to the noon meal with Una and Ella.

Finn arrived late and sat with the guards rather than with the family at the high table. He looked disheveled and tired. Evidently, he had not slept much either, though for a different reason.

Margaret suddenly realized Helen had been speaking to her, perhaps for some time, and she had not heard a word. "I'm sorry, what did ye ask me?"

"Are ye packed and ready to go?" Helen said.

Margaret's heart lurched in her chest. Was Finn sending her back? She struggled to calm herself. He had cause to be upset with her, but surely he would have told her himself. And Helen would not be asking if she was ready with a pleasant smile if they were kicking her out.

160

"Finn hasn't told ye yet?" Helen asked, raising her eyebrows.

Margaret felt a blush creep up her cheeks. She could not very well say Finn had not spoken to her since he left their chamber in the middle of the night.

"I suppose he got distracted," Helen said in a conspiratorial whisper. "*Ach*, newlyweds. I remember those days."

Margaret managed a weak smile. "Where are we going?"

"To Helmsdale, our hunting lodge fifteen miles up the coast," Helen said. "We leave in an hour and will reach Helmsdale before supper."

A short time later, Margaret was in their chamber packing when Finn came in.

"Your Aunt Helen was kind to give me these so that I have something appropriate to wear," she said to cover the awkwardness between them as she folded one of the gowns and put it in the satchel.

"Ye heard we're going to Helmsdale?" he asked.

"Aye, for hunting," she said.

Finn was standing too close. It was so distracting that she made a mess of folding the gown and had to start over.

"I don't hunt," she said. "Perhaps I could stay here."

"And have everyone know I can't keep a wife happy for even a fortnight?"

"They'll know it's me who can't keep you happy since you're already bedding other women." She clamped her mouth shut, appalled at herself for saying that out loud.

"Bedding other women?" Finn spun her around to face him. "Did Curstag tell ye that?"

That was not a denial.

"I have no right to ask, but I hope you'll be discreet," she said. "Your aunt has taken a liking to me, and she'll think ill of ye if she hears of it."

"There's nothing for her to hear," Finn said. "I haven't been with another woman since we met."

She wanted to believe him. It should not matter so much to her when she could never be what he needed.

"If you're asking about last night," he said, "I had a talk with my uncle."

"Ye did? What did he say?" she asked, turning around to face him. "Did he accept ye into his guard?"

She hoped so. Finn deserved that and more.

If the earl failed to make him a member of the guard, however, she could ask Finn to take her to her sister at Eilean Donan Castle. The prospect of leaving made her chest feel tight. She told herself it was only because it meant so much to Finn to have a place here—and not because she wanted to stay. Even if that was a lie, it was not safe for her to have what she wanted.

"He didn't exactly tell me about being in the guard." Finn paused. "He wants me to watch over Alex."

"He believes there's still a threat to Alex?" she asked.

"Aye, and he suspects he may have a traitor in his own household."

She knew all too well that it was usually someone close to you, someone you trusted to protect you, who betrayed you.

"The earl is right to be cautious," she said. "I should finish packing."

Turning her back to him, she attempted to withdraw the pouch of stones from where she had hidden it beneath the feather mattress without him seeing.

"What's in that wee bag?" he asked, leaning over her shoulder.

"Nothing of value," she said, but she should have known her attempt to discourage his interest would only fan the flames.

"'Tis the only possession ye brought with ye, so it must have value to you," he said.

"There's nothing in the bag but bits of broken stone."

"Can I have a look at them?" he asked.

She stifled a sigh. Since he probably would not give up until she showed him, she upended the pouch into her hand.

"The stone was in a pendant my mother gave to me," she said as she watched the pieces of black onyx fall into her palm. "My mother believed it had magical protective powers. She gave one to each of my sisters as well."

"Onyx is a hard stone," Finn said, picking up a piece between his thumb and finger. "How did it break into such small pieces?"

"My husband smashed it."

Margaret swallowed against the emotion that clogged her throat as she was flooded with memories from that terrible day. Though she had begged William to let her stay home because she had been so unwell during that pregnancy, he insisted she go with him to Edinburgh. She miscarried in the midst of the Battle of the Causeway.

In her mind, she was once again lying on sweat-soaked sheets, listening to the sounds of the battle outside the shuttered window and fretting about her cousin Lizzie, who had gone out before the fighting began to fetch a midwife. She felt as if her heart had been torn out with the loss of the babe. And deep down, she felt guilty for wishing her husband would be lost too.

William, however, returned before Lizzie. The maid must have told him the child was stillborn. Without waiting to remove his weapons or bloodied tunic, he stormed into the bedchamber, shouting and berating her for her failure. When that was not enough to satisfy his temper, he grabbed the pendant from her neck, snapping the silver chain.

Don't take it from me! she cried. *Please!*

This stone was supposed to bring good fortune, he said, clenching it in his fist. *But all it's brought is the devil's own luck.*

He dropped it on the floor and pulled the axe from his belt.

Not my pendant, she pleaded. *Please, not that!*

She should have known it was precisely because the pendant was the possession she valued most that William had to destroy it. When he slammed the wide end of the axe down with all his strength, bits of the stone shot across the floor.

After he stormed out, she crawled across the floor, weeping as she gathered the broken bits. Lizzie found her passed out on the floor with the broken pieces still clenched in her hand.

Margaret came slowly back to the present.

"I'm sorry he destroyed something so precious to ye," Finn said. "I hope one day you'll trust me enough to tell me the whole story."

Finn closed her hand over the broken pieces of stone in her palm and enfolded her hand in his. She did not even know she was weeping until he wiped the tears from her face. Despite the time and distance from that day in Edinburgh, she was still as broken as her stone.

###

Finn's thoughts were on Margaret as he went to the stables to collect *Ceò* for the journey to Helmsdale. Her former husband deserved a slow and painful death, and Finn would like to be the one to give it to him. How could he smash her pendant when he knew it would hurt her so much? As for Margaret's family, they had been cruel to wed such a kind and gentle lass to a brute like that.

"I may not be good enough for her," he confided to *Ceò* as he saddled him, "but I'm better than the wealthy and titled arse she was married to."

After being at the mercy of such a volatile man, it was no wonder she built a cocoon around herself, hiding her feelings behind a mask of calm. Finn wished he could prove to her that she could trust him, that he would never hurt her.

He led *Ceò* out of the stable behind one of the lads who was bringing another horse out. When he saw who the lad was bringing it to, he groaned. Curstag was waiting in the courtyard, slapping her gloves against her palm.

"Finn!" Curstag called, and waved to him.

Finn gave her a nod as he passed her and continued leading *Ceò* toward the tower steps where he was to meet Margaret and Ella.

"Finn!" Curstag called again. When he turned, she gave him a pointed look, evidently expecting him to help her mount.

"Let the lad do it," he said.

Curstag, however, was a lass accustomed to getting her way. She took the reins from the lad and brought her horse to Finn.

"I thought we could ride to Helmsdale together," she said. "For such old friends, we've hardly had a chance to talk since ye arrived."

"Don't play games, Curstag. Ye know damned well that would make Bearach jealous." God only knew why his brother was so sensitive when she had chosen him over Finn. "Go ride with your husband."

"Bearach isn't going with us to Helmsdale." Curstag tilted her head and looked up at him from under her eyelashes. "He's gone to visit your Sinclair cousins at Girnigoe Castle."

"I hope he enjoys his visit with them more than I did," Finn said.

"I fear I'll be desperately lonely while he's gone," she said as she ran her fingertips down his chest. She was teasing him as she used to, but he was no longer interested.

"If you're lonely, get yourself a dog," he said, and removed her hand.

"I know you're still angry with me after all these years, but I want to make it up to you." She rose on her tiptoes to whisper in his ear, "Tonight I'll give ye what ye always wanted."

"You're married." Then he remembered to add, "And so am I."

"If we're careful, they won't find out," she said with a light laugh, and laid her hand on his chest again.

He suddenly realized they were standing in the courtyard where anyone could see them and get the wrong idea. By the saints, Margaret might see them. He grabbed Curstag by the wrist and pulled her behind the stables where they would be out of view from the tower.

"Listen to me well," he said, pressing her against the wall by her shoulders. "I would never do that to Maggie—or to my brother."

"Come, Finn, ye know ye want me," she said, cocking her head. "Ye always have."

"I used to. I don't anymore." He meant it. For years, he had envied his brother and imagined Curstag's face on other women he bedded. But no more.

"I don't believe ye," Curstag said.

"I was blind to your wicked heart for years, but now I see ye for who ye are," he said. "Maggie is the only woman I want."

"Ye don't look like a satisfied man to me." Curstag gave him a sly smile as she touched her fingertip to his bottom lip. "I know you, Finn, and a wicked woman is exactly who ye want in your bed."

He heard a sharp intake of breath behind him. Nay, his luck could not be this bad. With a sinking feeling, he turned around to find Margaret standing there.

"Good afternoon, Curstag," Margaret said without a flicker of annoyance in her voice, but when Finn started to help her up onto *Ceò*, she stepped back from his reach.

"There's no need for *Ceò* to carry us all," she said, fixing her gaze somewhere over his shoulder. "I'm sure the earl can spare a horse for me and Ella to ride on our own."

Margaret had definitely seen them and drawn all the wrong conclusions.

"Maggie!" Finn called after her when she turned her back on him and walked toward the stables. He caught her arm when she was just inside. "That wasn't what it looked like."

"I'm not a fool," she said. "Ye can do what ye like. I don't care who ye bed."

"I think ye do."

"All I asked was that ye be discreet for the sake of your family as much as for me," she said. "But it's your business if ye want to embarrass yourself with your brother's wife."

Despite his intention to be patient and understanding, he was beginning to become irritated. Hell, he'd done nothing wrong. He had not even looked at another lass, let alone bedded one, since they met. Even if he had, Margaret would have no cause to complain, since she did not want him. At least, she did not want him enough to lower herself to bed a mere warrior.

"I've told ye you're the one I want, but I'm no monk," he said. "How long do ye expect me to live like one?"

"Bed as many women as ye like," she said. "Bed them all!"

By the saints, they were having a real argument. In all the time he'd known her, Margaret had never once shown she was angry, let alone shouted at him. Though he wished Curstag had not upset her, it was rather refreshing not to have to guess what was going on inside Margaret's head.

This was the same lass who had faced her former husband in front of a crowd of gossiping nobles at court without letting them see a hint of the humiliation and hurt she felt. No matter her denials, her loss of control told him the truth.

He smiled to himself. Margaret cared very much whether he was bedding someone else.

CHAPTER 18

Angry tears burned at the back of Margaret's eyes, making her grateful for the darkness of the stables. She was horrified that she had lost control and revealed how upset she was.

"I shouldn't have raised my voice," she said.

"Ye can shout at me all ye like. I don't mind," Finn said in a soft voice as if he was calming a frenzied horse. "A little shouting is good for the soul."

She did feel better for it, but she was not about to admit that. "Una will be here with Ella any moment. It would have upset Ella if she heard us arguing."

"'Twould be good for that wee lassie to do a bit of shouting herself," Finn said.

What was wrong with her today? Finn's remark very nearly made her burst into tears, because he was right. Ella was far too quiet and careful. Margaret did not want her daughter to be like her, always protecting herself, afraid to cause trouble or make demands.

"Don't worry about Curstag," Finn said, resting his hands on her shoulders. "She's just bored."

From the way Curstag glared at her during the ride, Margaret suspected Finn was not sleeping with her—yet. But as he had pointed out himself, he was no monk. It was unreasonable for her to expect him to resist temptation for long, whether from Curstag or someone else. The thought of him with another woman should not make her feel sick to her stomach.

Fortunately, the journey to Helmsdale was not long. The rugged coastline was stunning, but the trail was rough and skirted steep cliffs that dropped to the sea. Besides the family, only the earl's personal guard of two dozen warriors and half the household servants traveled with them, while the rest were left behind at Dunrobin.

The hunting lodge turned out to be a small tower castle built on a hill overlooking the sea beside the mouth of a river. A wall enclosed the tower and a small courtyard, where Finn helped her and Ella down from their horse.

"We'll have a cold supper tonight," Helen announced once everyone had dismounted. "It will be ready soon, so don't be long."

Finn remained outside with the other men while Helen led the women inside and showed them to their chambers. Once again, Helen gave Margaret and Finn a chamber at the top of the tower—because newlyweds need their privacy—and Una and Ella had the other chamber on that floor.

While Margaret unpacked her and Ella's meager belongings, a servant brought in a pitcher of water and a basin. Margaret quickly washed the dirt from their hands and faces. Before going downstairs, she peered out the arrow-slit window and caught sight of Finn waist-deep in the river, laughing and talking with the other men while they washed.

A small, high-pitched yelp escaped her lips when Finn dove under and then sprang up out of the water looking like a sea god from the old Norse tales, with water streaming from his shining black hair and down his muscular shoulders and chest.

As he climbed out of the river, she realized he was complete-ly naked. *Oh my.* He was so far away that she had to lean forward, but then some bushes blocked her view. Only after Finn was dressed and climbing up the slope to the castle did she notice that other men on the shore were naked.

Ella tugged at her skirts, breaking her reverie. *Good heavens,* how long had she been staring at him?

"What is it, sweetling?" she asked.

"I'm hungry," Ella said.

"'Tis good to speak up and tell me," Margaret said, smiling at her. "Let's find Una and go eat."

Nearly everyone was seated by the time Margaret returned to the hall with Ella and Una.

"The bairn must sit with me," Una said, and did not wait for Margaret's approval before leading Ella to one of the trestle tables where the servants and members of the guard were seated.

Margaret had not figured out if Una was treated as one of the family or as a servant. She seemed to choose whichever role suited her at the time. Just now, Margaret wished she could do the same and sit with them. One glance at the high table told her that meals at Helmsdale would be a more intimate affair than at Dunrobin, where the high table could accommodate thirty or forty people.

Here, the earl sat with his wife and son at one end of a small rectangular table, while Finn's father sat at the other end flanked by Isabel and Curstag. Margaret was about to sit next to Helen when Finn appeared at her side and, with a mischievous wink, guided her into the seat next to his mother before squeezing in between her and Helen.

"Isn't this delightful?" Helen said, beaming at them. "I always enjoy getting away to Helmsdale with the family."

Delightful. Margaret had Isabel beside her exuding hostility from every pore, and Curstag glaring at her from across the table. She took a large gulp of her wine.

On her other side, Finn's thigh rubbed against hers, and his black hair was still wet from his swim, making it impossible to get the image of him rising out of the river out of her head.

She took another gulp of her wine.

That night, Margaret was too restless to sleep. When she turned on her side, the moonlight streaming through the window illuminated Finn, who appeared to be sleeping like a rock.

She propped her head up, leaning on her elbow. Though she felt a wee bit sinful taking advantage of his sound sleep to examine him closely, that did not deter her. There was not a thing she would change about Finn's face. She ran her gaze over the dark slash eyebrows, square jaw shadowed with dark stubble, the strong planes of his cheekbones, and his full lips that were so often curved up in amusement. A sigh escaped her as she recalled how soft and warm those lips felt on hers.

Though the chamber was chilly, Finn had kicked the bedding half off in his sleep, leaving his chest, the side of one hip—she paused there and swallowed—and one long leg free of the bedclothes. He was long and lean and all hard muscle. When he was awake, she had to be on her guard to resist the desire that radiated from him. But asleep, even his powerful frame did not intimidate her. In fact, she was tempted to touch him.

Finn was sleeping so soundly, she could surely risk a small touch. She bit her lip and watched his face to be sure he did not awaken as she ran her fingertip ever so softly down his arm. It felt so different from hers, from the rippling muscle of his upper arm to the masculine hair on his forearm to his hand with its calluses from so many hours of swinging a claymore. She smiled, recalling how safe she felt when this big hand encompassed hers.

Her desire to touch him surprised her. She had never felt this yearning to feel a man's bare skin beneath her hands before. Though she had touched her husband countless times, she never once wanted to.

After trailing her finger down Finn's arm did not wake him, she grew more daring. She sat up and ran her hand lightly over his broad chest, a wall of solid muscle. When her fingertip dipped into a scar, she bit her lip at the thought of how often he fought in battles and risked death. Unlike her, he seemed utterly fearless.

The hair on his chest tickled her palm, sending tendrils of pleasurable sensation up her arm and down to her belly. She should stop now, but her fingers seemed to move on their own, drifting down to his flat, hard-muscled belly.

Well, there was one part of him that was not asleep. His shaft pushed the sheet up as if begging for her notice. She was tempted to pull the sheet off the rest of the way, but that was far too bold. Instead, she ran her finger along the surprisingly soft skin on the side of his bare hip.

She gave in to temptation and very carefully began to pull on the sheet. Her breathing grew shallow as she dragged it down inch by inch.

"*Jesu*, are ye trying to kill me, lass?"

"Oh my God, you're awake!" she said. "I shouldn't have—"

"Don't say that." Finn sat up and pulled her against his chest. "Don't even think it."

He covered her face with kisses, ran more down the side of her throat, and pushed her night shift aside to kiss her shoulder as well. Then his mouth was on hers in a kiss filled with so much hunger it stole her breath away.

171

As he deepened the kiss, she felt as if he was unlocking something inside her. She had always been so careful, so afraid of offending and being hurt. Tonight, she could not make herself pull back. And she did not want to. Instead, she wrapped her arms around Finn's neck and kissed him back with a desperation that matched his own.

As they rolled across the bed, his hands moved over her body, caressing, squeezing, possessing. She let a wild and mindless passion take her. There was no tomorrow, no consequences. There was only now and this raging fire consuming them and melding her body into his.

Sparks flew off her skin as he ran his tongue and hot mouth along her throat. Between frantic kisses, he pulled her shift over her head, and suddenly, they were skin to skin. She reveled in the feel of his hard muscles beneath her hands, his chest against her breasts, and the taste of his skin on her tongue when she kissed his neck. When he cupped her breasts, she tensed for a moment with the memory of William complaining that her breasts were too small.

"By the saints, ye feel so good," Finn said, his breath hot against her skin, banishing her fear.

When Finn began rubbing her nipples between his thumbs and fingers, she heard herself moan. Finn moved down her throat with his lips and tongue until his mouth replaced his hand on her breast. *Oh God!* His tongue teased her nipple, sending rivulets of pleasure all the way to her toes. William had never touched her like this, never filled her with this wanton desire.

Finn drew her breast into his mouth and sucked, sending a stream of almost painful pleasure straight to her core, and she ceased to think about William or other times or anything else except the sensations sizzling through her body. Just when she thought she could not take any more, he sought her mouth again.

She pulled him into a deep kiss and gave herself wholly to the all-consuming and fiery passion she longed for, body and soul. She was lost in endless kisses, their tongues entwining, thrusting, when she felt his hand between her legs.

"*Ach*, you're hot and wet for me," he groaned against her ear.

God in heaven, his fingers had magic in them. Her breathing grew quick and shallow, and her skin felt too tight. As the tension coiled inside her, she writhed, tossing her head from side to side.

"I want ye so much," Finn said in a ragged voice, "I can't go slowly this first time."

"Please," she gasped, not even knowing what she wanted from him.

Her breath hitched and her mind went blank when she felt his hard shaft pressing between her legs. Every muscle in her body tensed with anticipation.

But he halted with the tip just inside her.

"Are ye sure?" he asked in a hoarse voice.

She did not want to talk. Did not want to think. A wild desire thrummed through her veins, and she lifted her hips and pulled on his shoulders.

"Aye," she said, and they both gasped with the rush of sensation as he slid inside her.

Then he leaned back, his weight on his elbows, and held her face between his hands. With his eyes locked on hers, he began moving inside her, excruciatingly slowly, thrusting deep and coming almost all the way out, then thrusting deep inside her again.

Intense and confusing emotions swirled and spun inside her. She felt as if the barriers that protected her were falling, exposing every secret and vulnerable part of her.

"Mo chridhe," my heart, he said against her ear as he thrust faster and harder. *"M' eudail, mo rùin."* My treasure, my love.

A need that was at once passion and more than passion gripped her, making her hold on to him with all her strength. She never wanted to let him go. Tension mixed with a painful longing grew and grew inside her until she thought she would burst into a thousand pieces.

She gasped as her body clenched in unexpected waves of pleasure. Finn surged against her, crying her name, and she fell over the edge with him like shooting stars through the night sky.

Tears spilled down her cheeks before she could stop them. The emotions inside her were just too big to contain. She had known making love with him would be different from what she knew before, but she had no notion it would be so wonderful and devasting at the same time.

"God have mercy, that was—" Finn started to say as he lifted his head. His eyes went wide, then his expression quickly changed to worry. "What's wrong?"

173

"I shouldn't have done this," she said.

"I don't understand, *leannain*." He rolled off her and cupped her face with his hand. "Tell me."

She shook her head, unable to speak, and curled up on the far edge of the bed, alone in her grief. In the heat of passion, she had let herself forget the foolish risk she was taking. It was not death she feared, though she had nearly died with her last miscarriage. What she could not face was the excitement and hope and then the inevitable crushing disappointment of losing a child again. She simply could not bear it.

Not Finn's child.

But her grief was not just over the risk of another failed pregnancy. She had never longed for a man before, never truly understood her sisters' desire for their husbands. She had not known what she was missing. Now she did. Making love with Finn had made her want things she could not have.

She was shaken by the discovery that in the throes of passion she had no protection against Finn. With her husband, she went through the motions, did what he said, and let him use her. He touched her body, but that was all. She kept the core of herself safe. She never let herself feel too much, never let him see more than she was willing to show him.

But when Finn was inside her and looking into her eyes, she had no defense, no last wall of protection. And that was what scared her most.

She could not let him that close again, let him spawn dreams and hopes, when he would eventually find a reason to abandon her. Men always did. If it was not her inability to give him children, something else would come along that was more important to him than she was, and he would tell himself he had no choice.

She could not let that happen. If she did, Finn would cause her more pain than William or her brothers ever had. He would break her heart.

Finn was stunned. He had never felt so much or felt so close to anyone as when he was inside her. He felt as if he was on the brink of having something wondrous, something beyond anything he knew or even hoped for—only to be pushed over a cliff and smashed on the rocks below.

One moment they were one in scalding passion, and the next she was weeping. The change happened so quickly that his heart still pounded from the explosion of his release, even while a sense of utter desolation settled over him like a dead weight.

When he tried to touch her, she scooted farther away.

"Maggie," he said, "what did I do?"

"It wasn't anything ye did," she said in a voice he could barely hear.

If it was not what he did, then it could only be who he was.

Or rather, who he wasn't. After losing herself to the throes of passion, she remembered he was not a nobleman with lands and castle to give her. He was only a landless warrior who must earn his keep by his skill with a sword. She was not his wife Maggie, and never could be.

He should have known better. He did know better. And yet he had fallen headlong in love with Lady Margaret Douglas.

The long-forgotten memory of the day his father sent him away to live with his uncle came to him. He was given no explanation. But even then, at eight years old, he did not need one. He knew they just did not want him. No one in his family even came out to bid him goodbye.

CHAPTER 19

It was a good day for hunting. And an even better day to be away from the castle.

Finn's back hurt like hell from sleeping on Una's floor. After Margaret made it clear she never wanted him to touch her again, he could not share a bed with her—not without losing his pride and begging. Fortunately, Una was not really a gossip, but he had to put up with the old woman giving him an earful about resolving his problems with his *wife*. As if he could.

Finn slung his bow over his shoulder and motioned for Alex to follow him up the hillside. They had tied their horses half a mile back to stalk a stag.

"He came right through here." Finn squatted on the ground and pushed the heather back to reveal the stag's tracks more clearly.

"*Ach*, looks like he's a big one," Alex said, squatting beside him. "Maybe even big enough to have antlers worthy of hanging at Helmsdale."

Finn knew how badly Alex wanted a prize set of antlers to display on the walls of the hunting lodge with those from the most impressive stags his father and grandfather had killed.

"Aye, but this fellow did not live this long without being cagey," Finn cautioned him. "But perhaps we'll have luck on our side today."

They were downwind from the stag, and it was blowing hard, so they had a good chance of getting close enough before the stag smelled or heard them.

Finn heard a movement behind them and tapped Alex's forearm to warn him. Though it was probably an animal moving through the gorse, the wind that worked in their favor as stalkers would also favor anyone stalking them from behind.

He strained to hear over the harsh wind whistling across the hillside. There it was again, a faint rustle.

In one motion, he stood, drew his sword, and whirled toward the sound. A figure emerged from behind a boulder. When he recognized the man was Seamus, the son of Duffus of Sutherland, Finn relaxed—until Seamus started toward them with his sword drawn and murder in his eyes.

"What is the matter with ye, Seamus?" he shouted. "'Tis me, Finn."

"'Tis not you I'm after, but him," Seamus said, pointing his sword at Alex. "Step aside, Finn."

"I can't do that," Finn said. "Alex is my cousin."

Seamus was a big bear of a man and a seasoned warrior, but he was a scholar by nature. Finn wondered what had gotten him so riled up.

"The Gordons owe me a blood debt," Seamus said. "Ye ought to help me collect it instead of standing in my way."

"Tell me what's happened," Finn said, making sure he was between Seamus and Alex. "Whatever it is, Alex is an innocent."

"My father's dead," Seamus said. "Murdered!"

"I'm sorry to hear that. Your father was a good man," Finn said, and he meant it. "But murdered? Are ye certain?"

"A blade in the back is no accident," Seamus said.

"I would have to agree with ye there," Finn said. "How did it happen?"

"He was killed up in Thurso. Murdered by the Gunns."

Why would the Gunns commit such a crime? It made no sense. They were a small clan that would not benefit from Duffus's death, at least not directly.

"How do ye know it was the Gunns that did it?" Finn asked.

"We caught one of them," Seamus said. "He admitted they were bribed by the Bishop of Caithness, Andrew Stewart."

That was unfortunate. The culprit was a Stewart *and* a bishop, which meant obtaining justice would be no easy matter. But a bribe would explain why the Gunns did the killing.

"If it was the bishop," Finn asked, "why are ye here threatening my cousin Alex Òg?"

"Ye know as well as I do that the bishop did it at the behest of his kinsman, that sly Gordon dog, the Earl of Sutherland," Seamus said. "The Gordons are at the root of this conspiracy to murder my father."

When Seamus stumbled forward a step, Finn suspected he'd been drinking.

"Ye don't know the Gordons were involved," Finn said. "And I can promise ye Alex had nothing to do with it. Did ye, Alex?"

"Nay!" Alex called out behind him.

"My father had a claim to the Earldom of Sutherland," Seamus said, weaving on his feet as he waved his sword. "His father had mine murdered to make certain the Sutherland lands and title passed to him."

Unfortunately, that did sound like a plausible explanation.

"Justice demands I deny that Gordon scum what he hoped to gain by this murder and kill his only son and heir," Seamus said. "An eye for an eye!"

"Come, Seamus, ye don't have the stomach to kill an innocent lad who's not even full grown," Finn said.

"I must avenge my father," Seamus said, but Finn could tell he was weakening.

"I'd hate to have to kill ye over this, but we both know I'm the better swordsman," Finn said, and pulled out his flask. "Let's have a drink and discuss how ye can obtain justice against the men ye know are guilty—the Gunns and the bishop."

When Seamus finally dropped his sword, Finn drew in a deep breath. It took an hour and all of his whisky to persuade Seamus to go to the King's Council in Edinburgh to make his allegations against the bishop and demand justice. He'd be lucky if he persuaded the council to punish a couple of the priests who assisted the bishop, but Seamus was well suited for that kind of fight.

And it would keep Seamus out of the reach of Finn's uncle.

Finn pushed aside the guards posted outside his uncle's chamber and flung the door open.

"I need a private word with my nephew," his uncle said, dismissing the guards who had followed Finn inside with their swords drawn.

"Did you and the bishop have Sutherland of Duffus murdered?" Finn demanded as soon as the guards closed the door.

His uncle raised one eyebrow and asked in a pleasant tone, "Is he dead?"

Finn shared what Seamus had told him of the murder.

"I doubt the bishop was involved," his uncle said. "But if he did undertake this vile act to protect my family's interests, he did so without my knowledge."

Finn did not know whether to believe him. But one thing was certain—if his uncle was involved, no one could ever prove it.

"While I had no part in Duffus's murder," his uncle said, raising his cup, "I'm glad he's dead."

"Why?" Finn asked. "Duffus was an old man. In all these years, he never challenged your right to the title."

"He could have, so there was always a risk he would," he said. "As I told ye before, many of these Sutherlands would prefer to have one of their own serve as their laird, and they resent how the title passed to a Gordon—though it was entirely legitimate."

"Entirely." Finn did not bother to keep the sarcasm from his tone.

"I'll forgive that remark as well as your baseless insinuation that I was involved in this murder, because ye protected my son to-day," his uncle said. "I was right to trust in your loyalty to him."

His uncle motioned Finn into the chair opposite and poured them both a cup of whisky. Finn drank it down. Charging in here and accusing his uncle was a mistake. Did he expect his wily uncle to confess? All he had accomplished was risking his uncle's goodwill and his newly regained place in the clan.

"I need to know," his uncle said, examining him through narrowed eyes, "if this Seamus is still a threat to Alex."

Seamus would not live long if the earl believed he was.

"Seamus gave me his oath that neither he nor the Sutherland men who follow him will attempt to harm Alex."

His uncle raised a skeptical eyebrow. "How did ye manage that?"

"I persuaded Seamus to pursue the prosecution of the bishop instead," Finn said. "He's headed to Edinburgh now to petition the King's Council."

"You silver-tongued devil!" His uncle threw his head back and laughed. "Seamus hasn't a bloody chance in hell of succeeding. The bishop is a Stewart, for God's sake."

"Seamus denied he made any attempt to harm Alex before today," Finn said, after his uncle's laughter subsided. "The broken

179

shards in Alex's cup at Huntly and the thorn in his horse's hoof must have been accidents."

"I suppose you're right. But if not for that, I wouldn't have had ye here to protect Alex today." His uncle raised his cup to him. "You'll always have a place in my household. I'll not forget what you've done and the debt I owe ye."

Finn should be happy. This was what he had hoped for, but his troubles with Margaret dragged his spirits down even now.

"Helen is worried that there's some trouble between you and your bride," his uncle said, stopping Finn as he started to leave. "Maggie's a good woman. Don't let yourself lose her."

"I don't deserve a good woman like her."

"None of us do," his uncle said. "But ye must tell yourself you're better than the man who's likely to take your place."

With all his flaws, Finn was better than some Lowlander laird like her former husband. But Margaret had made her choice.

She did not want him.

CHAPTER 20

At supper that night, his aunt embraced him and gushed over how he'd saved her son, and the men toasted him until Finn was drunk enough to decide to take his uncle's advice to try to hold on to Margaret—and drunk enough to believe he had a good chance of succeeding.

Alex told the story about Seamus two or three times, embellishing the tale more each time, as any good Highlander was expected to do. Then Alex told them again about the stag they were tracking when Seamus interrupted their hunt.

"Ye should have seen the size of him!" Alex said. "Finn said we'd go back tomorrow and try to pick up his trail again."

"I'm sure Finn will get that stag," Curstag said in her throaty voice. "A brave man can get what he wants."

Finn hoped so. When he caught Margaret darting glances at him, he smiled to himself. Now that he was the hero of the day, she just might be willing to overlook his shortcomings for another night together. One night could lead to two, and two could lead to more.

True, things had ended badly last night—*verra* badly—but Margaret had a cautious nature. Perhaps she just needed time to become accustomed to the notion that they would be together.

His thoughts came to an abrupt halt when Margaret rested her hand on his arm. As she leaned close, the light scent of wildflowers from her hair filled his nose. Lord above, he wanted to have her in his arms again, to hear her soft moans when he kissed her breast and—

"Can ye come to our chamber after supper?" she whispered.

"Aye, lass!" He could not help grinning like a fool. She wanted him. He could tell by the way she blushed.

As he followed her up the stairs, he watched the graceful sway of her hips. He was sorely tempted to pull her sweet bottom against him and kiss her neck, but then he recalled how last night had ended and decided it would be wise to follow her lead. He was usually good at reading women, particularly in bed. But if Maggie had shown any sign of distress before bursting into tears last night, he'd missed it entirely—and unlike now, he'd been stone cold sober.

When she closed the bedchamber door behind them, he leaned against the bed, folded his arms to keep from reaching for her, and waited to see what she'd do. Her delicate features were strained, suggesting she had not slept any better than he had last night. She held herself very still, attempting to hide her tension.

"Ye did a fine thing today," she said. "I'm so happy neither you nor Alex was hurt."

Despite her complimentary words, he had an inkling this conversation might not be leading to the two of them rolling around on the bed. But that was all right. He could be patient. She was worth waiting for.

"No need to be nervous," he said, glancing at her clenched hands. "'Tis just me."

"I think it's best I leave," she blurted out.

"Leave?" Finn could barely get the word out. "What in the hell do ye mean, leave?"

"I want ye to take me to my sister Sybil's," Margaret said. "She's married to the MacKenzie."

"Ye never told me ye had a sister with the MacKenzies," he said, though her failure to mention that was the least of his concerns.

"I didn't tell ye about Sybil because she's all the way at Eilean Donan Castle, and I knew ye couldn't take me before." Margaret paused and licked her lips. "But now that you've proved yourself and the earl is so grateful to ye for saving Alex, I thought—I hoped—ye could take me."

Her sister. The MacKenzie. His mind was making no sense of the words.

"Are ye leaving me?" he asked.

Finn told himself not to assume the worst, but when she would not meet his eyes, fear like he'd never known on the battlefield clutched at his stomach.

"Ye can hardly call it leaving ye when we're not truly married," she said.

"Ye can't mean it," he said, gripping her arms. "Look at me and say it."

When she raised her gaze to his, her brown eyes were damp, but her voice was firm. "I have to go."

He was suddenly sober—and wished to God he was not. How could she leave him now that he wanted her so much? He'd begun to think she actually cared for him.

"Staying will only make us both miserable in the end," she said.

"Don't speak for me," he bit out. "But if you're set on leaving, I'll take ye."

If she thought he'd beg her to stay, she was mistaken. He'd salvage what little pride he had left. He should not be angry with her, but he was.

He was angry that she did not think he was good enough. Angry that she was not willing to sacrifice a life of servants and fine things to be with him. Angry that she would not give him a chance to prove he could make her happy despite all he lacked.

Her decision may be practical and wise. But it was still wrong.

"I'd take ye right now—tonight, if I could," he said. "But I need to speak with my uncle."

"Of course," she murmured, dropping her gaze to her laced fingers.

"I'm sure he'll grant me leave to go," Finn said. "I promised to hunt for that stag with Alex tomorrow. But first thing the next morning, I'll take you—and Ella."

It tore at his heart to realize he was losing Ella as well, which made him all the angrier that Margaret would do this. He slammed the door as he left.

Margaret brushed the tears from her cheeks and pulled the satchel out from underneath the bed. She hated to leave, but the longer she stayed, the harder it would be to go. Finn deserved a woman who could give him many children. He would make such a wonderful father.

She wondered where he slept last night after storming out and slamming the door. If she stayed, she would spend countless restless nights and long, long afternoons wondering who he was with. She had no faith she could keep his interest or weather his disappointment when she failed to give him the sons that every man wanted. Leaving was the only thing she could do.

When she heard the chamber door open, she looked over her shoulder to see Una standing in the doorway with her hands on her hips.

"What are ye doing, lass?" Una asked in a tone that could only be called disgusted.

"I'm packing," Margaret said, and returned to the task.

"What's Finn done?" Una asked.

"Nothing."

"Then 'tis just your own foolishness to blame?"

"Aye."

"'Tis plain as day ye don't wish to go," Una said. "Tell me the reason you're throwing away what ye want for what ye don't."

Margaret shook her head and swallowed back her tears.

"Put on your cloak. I'm taking ye to the spring," Una said, and turned toward the door. "I'll fetch Ella from her nap."

"Why the spring?" Margaret asked, calling Una back.

"To see if I'm right about your future."

"I don't understand." Did the old woman think she was a seer? And what did a spring have to do with it?

"There's a pool fed by the spring that comes out of a faery hill," Una said in a hushed voice, though no one could hear them.

"A faery hill?" These Highlanders and their faeries.

"Aye, the faeries come out of the hill to play in the water," Una said. "If they favor ye, they'll sprinkle their magic healing dust over ye."

"If we go, how will I make the faeries favor me?" After all, Margaret could not be sure there were no faeries.

"*Ach*, do ye know nothing of faeries, lass?" Una shook her head.

Margaret searched her memory for stories her old nursemaid had told her about faeries. "They like shiny things, like silver coins."

"Aye, though ye never really know with the faeries," Una said, and then pointed her finger at Margaret. "Just be careful not to insult them, or instead of sprinkling their magic dust, they'll cause ye to lose your footing in the pool and drown."

The old woman had been kind to her and her daughter, and this seemed important to her, so Margaret put on her cloak.

As they started down the path along the river, Ella skipped ahead gathering flowers as usual. Seeing how happy her daughter was, Margaret felt guilty for taking her away. Ella was blossoming here, and she'd become attached to Una and Alex—and, of course, Finn.

Ella adored Finn.

Ella came running back, her smile gone, and lifted her arms to be carried. When Margaret looked up the path to see what had frightened her, she saw Isabel kneeling on the ground with a basket, gathering herbs. Margaret could not face the surly woman today.

She and Una exchanged a look.

"We'll take the other path," Una said under her breath, and without another word, they changed directions before Isabel saw them.

"Is the spring much farther?" Margaret asked when she noticed Una was leaning heavily on her cane.

"'Tis a bit longer this way," Una said. "This is the path to my grandson Lachlan's cottage, but it will take us by the spring."

A short time later, Una ducked through the bushes beside the trail. Margaret followed, holding Ella's hand, down a gentle slope shrouded in greenery

"'Tis lovely!" Margaret gasped when they pushed through the last tall bushes to find the dark pool with white and pink water lilies floating on the surface.

Margaret could imagine little winged faeries leaping from lily to lily. Whether it was truly magical or not, it was a beautiful, restful spot.

Una placed a small silver coin on a flat rock among the reeds at the edge of the pool.

"Do we have a gift for the faeries?" Ella looked up at Margaret expectantly.

Una had been filling Ella's head with stories of faeries since they met, and Margaret did not want to disappoint her. Besides, if faeries did exist, this was a place they would be—and Margaret could not afford to offend them.

In her former life, she had more silver jewelry than she could ever wear—combs, brooches, necklaces, bracelet, rings. Even the box she kept them in was made of silver. She removed the bag of onyx from her belt, picked out two small shiny pieces, and gave one to Ella.

"We have no silver or sparkling trinkets to give you," Margaret called out, facing the pond. "Instead, we brought bits of magical stone imbued with a mother's love."

Una gave a nod of approval as Margaret and Ella set their bits of onyx next to the coin. The old woman's gaze darted and flicked across the pond, as if she was watching a bee fly from lily to lily or a stone a child skipped across the water.

Ella laughed and clapped her hands, as if she saw whatever Una did.

"The faeries are verra pleased with your gift," Una whispered. "They grant ye permission to go into the water. 'Twould be a grave insult not to accept."

Margaret removed her shoes and stockings, lifted her skirts, and gingerly stepped into the edge of the pond, expecting it to be cold.

"'Tis warm!" She'd heard of warm springs but never been in one before.

"That won't do—ye must bathe in the pool for the faery dust to do its work," Una said, "unless 'tis only your feet that need healing."

"Bathe?" Margaret asked. "Ye mean without my clothes?"

"Of course," Una said, and glanced heavenward.

"But I don't need healing. In truth, I've never been healthier."

"Some wounds can't be seen." Una extended her arm. "Hand me your gown."

Margaret reluctantly gave in and was immediately glad she did. The warm water felt like liquid velvet on her skin.

"Ella, come in!" she called to her daughter, who was dangling her feet in the water beside Una.

Ella shook her head, her golden curls swinging side to side.

"I told her we mustn't tempt the faeries by putting such a pretty bairn in their pool," Una said. "They've been known to take a bairn through the spring to their home in the faery hill and leave a changeling in its place."

Margaret wished Una would not frighten Ella with such tales. Still, now that she'd heard the tale herself, Margaret was glad Ella did not want to join her in the water.

As she floated on her back with her eyes closed, she felt as if her troubles were drifting away.

"Ye ought not let fear make ye run from Finn," Una said.

So much for leaving her troubles. Margaret closed her eyes again and hoped Una was done talking.

"There aren't many good men, but you've found one," Una said. "Don't be afraid to take a chance at happiness."

"I couldn't keep his interest for long," Margaret said, echoing what Curstag told her. And she'd never have his heart.

"So you're leaving him before he can leave you," Una said.

He would leave her. If Margaret stayed, she would lose more of her heart to him each day as she waited for him to tire of her or find some other reason to cast her aside. And all the while, she would risk conceiving and losing another babe. Nay, it was better to go now.

She sank beneath the surface and let the dark silence of the pool encompass her. As soon as she lifted her head above the water, Una continued talking.

"Ye think Finn will throw ye to the wolves like some men will," Una said. "But Finn is not like that. What has he done to cause ye to judge him so harshly?"

It was true that Finn could have abandoned her when he learned Moray no longer needed a hostage. But he'd had nothing to lose by taking her along. If he had more at stake, a cost to pay, would Finn make the same choice? Neither her husband nor the men of her family ever thought she was worth giving up a single thing they wanted.

"What if it's me?" Margaret asked in a choked voice. "Perhaps I'm not worthy of sacrifice."

"*Ach*, don't speak such nonsense," Una said with a dismissive wave of her hand.

Nonsense or no, the men Margaret should have been able to rely on had used her for their own ends and then abandoned her when she needed them.

"Live while ye can," Una said, "for you're a long time dead."

After that bit of Highland wisdom, Margaret got out of the water, dried off, and dressed. And still, Una would not leave the subject alone.

187

"My own dear husband died just a year after we wed," Una said as they started back to the castle. "But I wouldn't give up that year if I'd known I'd lose him. Nay, I would have squeezed every bit of happiness I could have from every day I had with him."

"Would ye not suffer all the more when ye lost everything?" Margaret said.

"Ye can't give up what happiness this life has to offer out of fear of sorrow," Una said, leaning on Margaret's arm as they walked. "Sorrow will come, as it does to all of us, and that's all you'll have to remember."

Margaret had spent so much of her life pleasing others and expecting little for herself. Believing she had no choice but to accept her burdens, she'd tried to do it without anger or resentment. Was she losing too much by leaving now? Was it worth the pain she would suffer later to have some happiness now, however brief?

She was abruptly pulled from her thoughts when Una pinched her.

"Ouch!"

"Hush," Una whispered. "*Ach*, this is bad luck, but a pinch helps ward it off."

"What's wrong?" Margaret picked Ella up and looked around them, but she saw no danger.

"There," Una whispered, and Margaret followed her gaze to a branch overhead on which a single bird was perched. "Two magpies mean good luck for a wedding. One foretells trouble coming."

There was no mistaking the magpie. It had the black feathers on its head, neck, and breast, pure white ones on its belly and shoulders, and a long black tail with a sheen of deep blue.

"*Feasgar math*," *good day*, Una said to the bird.

Margaret's nursemaid had told her one must show the magpie respect and greet it to ward against the bad luck. Then again, the nursemaid had also suggested telling the magpie *I defy thee* seven times, which did not strike Margaret as at all respectful.

Margaret told herself she did not believe those superstitious tales. And yet, when the magpie tilted his head and looked straight at her with his dark, beady eyes, she felt a chill in her bones, as if someone was walking over her grave.

Squawk! Squawk! Squawk! The loud, harsh sound made her jump.

"Death is coming," Una said as they watched the bird fly away.

CHAPTER 21

Margaret usually managed to contain her emotions, but she could not sit still. She was anxious for Finn to return, though she still was not certain what she would tell him or even what she wanted. It might be too late to change her mind about leaving, anyway. He was so angry with her after she told him she wanted to leave that she may have ruined her chance.

She pushed aside her worries about Finn when she heard Ella sniffling.

"Has my poor lamb caught a cold?" Margaret said as she wiped Ella's nose.

"'Tis nothing to fret over," Una assured her. "But we'll have an early supper here in our chamber and go to bed."

"Then I'll eat here as well," Margaret said.

"No need for that," Una said, waving her hand. "I'm a wee bit tired from our walk and am happy to stay with her—and you need to talk to Finn."

Margaret kissed Ella's forehead. She did not seem to have a fever. "Do ye want me to stay here with ye, sweetling?"

"Shall I tell ye the tale of how I outwitted the wolf?" Una asked Ella as she lifted her onto her lap. "Or the one about my escape from the faery prince who fell in love with me?"

"Both," Ella said, then stuck her thumb in her mouth and rested her head against Una's chest.

Ella was in good hands, so Margaret gave her one more kiss and slipped out. After asking one of the servants to take a platter of food and hot drinks upstairs to them, she joined Helen, who was doing needlework by the hearth.

"Is there mending I can help with?" Margaret asked.

"There's always mending to do, isn't there?" Helen said with her son's smile, and gestured to the basket beside her. "I'd be grateful for the company as much as the help."

Margaret thought she had escaped Isabel, but a short time later, Finn's mother came up the stairs from the undercroft where the kitchens and storerooms were.

190

"I hope the men are back from their hunt soon," Isabel said. "The cook has made a stew with that lamb that fell into one of the ravines, and it smells delicious."

Margaret was surprised by Isabel's cheerful tone. Good heavens, the woman even smiled at her. Rather than being pleased that Finn's mother was pleasant for once, her unusual behavior made Margaret uneasy. Margaret could never like the woman because of the way she treated Finn. Perhaps she was being uncharitable, but she did not trust her either.

"Ah, here they are now," Helen said when loud, boisterous male voices reached them from outside.

"They'll be hungry after being out in this weather all day," Isabel said. "I'll tell the servants to get ready to serve the meal."

Honestly, the woman was so high-handed. It was Helen's place to direct the servants when to serve the meal.

Margaret set her needlework aside and stood to watch for Finn as the hunting party entered the hall in twos and threes. The men had obviously been drinking to stave off the cold. If their hunting was half as successful as their drinking, there would be meat for the household for weeks.

When the door closed behind the last man, Margaret asked him where Finn was.

"He and Alex were still stalking that stag," he said. "'Twas near dark and we were starving, so we left them to it."

"You left them?" she asked.

"*Ach*, you've no cause to worry," the man said. "Finn knows what he's about. The lad is safe with him."

It wasn't the lad she was thinking of. But he was right. Finn knew what he was doing and would not put his cousin at risk.

"'Tis just like Finn to inconvenience everyone by arriving late," Isabel snapped. "Bearach would never be so inconsiderate."

Margaret bit back a reply. Since the men were hungry, Helen ordered the meal served without waiting for Finn and Alex. The earl and Helen sat at one end, as usual, with an empty seat for Alex, while Margaret found herself stuck alone with Finn's parents and Curstag at the other end.

She was distracted through supper, watching the door. As the meal dragged on, she could hear a storm brewing outside and began to worry.

191

"What's happened to those two?" Isabel asked. "They should have been back long before this."

Isabel seemed truly anxious about Finn. Perhaps she did love him in her own way. He was a son Isabel ought to be proud of. More than his superficial charms, of which there were many, he had a good heart. And yet his parents and brother did not recognize his worth.

No matter if she stayed or left, she needed to tell Finn how she felt. Given how little his family thought of him, she did not want him to think she did not care. The problem was she cared too much.

Her gaze went to the door yet again, but her attention was jerked back to the table when the earl abruptly stood up in the midst of the meal.

"Poison!" he shouted, his voice filled with rage. "I've been poisoned!"

The earl gripped the tablecloth as he swayed on his feet, sending cups and crockery clattering to the floor. Margaret was out of her seat and reached him first. She held his elbow and tried to steady him.

"Let's get ye to your bed," she said in a soothing voice, and prayed the earl was wrong about being poisoned.

"Which of my enemies did this?" The earl's eyes were wild, and he clutched at his throat as he demanded, "Who here is the traitor who helped them?"

Margaret's gaze followed his as it traveled down the table and back again, where it came to a halt on his wife. Helen's skin had gone pale and glistened with a sheen of sweat.

Poisoned. Margaret now feared it was true. Her mother had told them a hundred times every detail of her sisters' deaths. All three sisters were poisoned to ensure the death of the one the king wished to marry against the advice and interests of his powerful nobles. Her own mother only escaped their fate because she missed breakfast.

"Quick, help me!" Margaret shouted when everyone else was still staring at the earl in shock. "The earl and his wife must be taken upstairs and purged at once!"

Her plea spurred his guards into action. They lifted the earl, but when they started to carry him off to his bedchamber, he grasped Margaret's arm.

"My son. Warn my son." His fingers were like iron claws digging into her arm as he pulled her close and gasped in her ear. "He's in danger!"

"God help us," she whispered. "Ye believe the poison was meant for Alex as well?"

"Of course," the earl said, his breathing harsh. "Don't let Alex touch any food or drink here. Finn must take him away to Dunrobin!"

"I'll tell Finn," she said, trying to calm him.

"Promise me," he demanded, his feverish eyes drilling into her. "Promise!"

"I promise," she said. "Finn will take Alex to safety."

Only then did the earl release his grip on her arm and allow his men to carry him upstairs to his bedchamber, where his wife had already been taken.

Margaret told herself others would care for the ill couple and resisted the urge to help. The earl feared someone here had intended to poison Alex as well—and still meant him harm. She had to warn Finn and Alex.

Ella! Panic raced through Margaret's veins at the thought of her daughter. What if the poison was in their supper? She ran up the stairs to their bedchamber and flung open the door.

Her heart pounded in her ears as she took in the scene, which seemed unnaturally ordinary. Una was stitching. Ella was on the floor playing with her doll. Her gaze caught and held on the tray of half-eaten food on the table.

"You've not fallen ill?" she choked out.

"Ella just has a wee cold," Una said, "but you look like a banshee chased ye up the stairs."

Margaret knelt beside Una and quickly told her what happened in a low voice so that Ella would not hear.

"If it was poison, 'twas a kind that works its evil quickly," Una said. "Ye needn't worry about us. We ate our supper long before the rest of ye. As ye can see, we've no ill effects."

"Praise God!" Margaret grabbed her cloak from the back of the door. "I'm going to wait for Finn and Alex in the stables. I must hurry if I'm to catch them before they come inside."

Before she reached the bottom of the stairs, however, she heard their familiar voices. Finn locked his gaze on her the moment she rushed into the hall, and she could tell he had already realized something was dreadfully wrong at Helmsdale.

"Ye should see the size of the stag I got," Alex boasted. "Finn says it's the biggest…" His voice trailed off as he looked about the room, which had fallen into a deadly silence.

"What's happened?" Finn asked, taking Margaret's hands when he reached her.

Before she could explain, she heard Isabel behind her telling Alex about his parents.

"Your father and mother have taken ill, and I'm afraid 'tis rather serious," Isabel said, her tone surprisingly gentle. "Come, they'll want to see ye while there's still time."

The earl did not want to see Alex—he wanted him sent away. Margaret spun around in time to see Isabel put her arm around Alex and lead him toward the stairs.

When she saw a cup in Alex's hand, her blood froze in her veins. He was ten feet away and lifting it to his mouth.

"Nay!"

Finn was stunned when Margaret shouted and charged into Alex. She hit him with such force that the cup flew out of Alex's hand and splattered wine in a wide arc over Alex, Isabel, and half a dozen others before clattering against the wall.

Margaret, who was usually so cool-headed, would not do anything so dramatic without good cause. While the others were still staring slack-jawed at the spilled wine or wiping it from their clothes, he drew Margaret and Alex aside so she could tell them the reason.

"Ye must leave at once," Margaret said in a hushed voice. "Alex's parents have been poisoned, and—"

"We don't know that," Finn's mother interrupted as she joined them. "I expect 'tis just a passing fever. Or even more likely, spoiled meat—Helen has no skill at managing servants."

"Alex is in danger here," Margaret whispered to Finn. "I'll explain as we go to the stables for your horses."

"If my parents are ill, I must see them," Alex said.

Finn saw the panic in Margaret's eyes when Alex started for the stairs and caught Alex in an iron grip. Together, he and Margaret half dragged Alex out of the hall. Outside the door, they were met by a curtain of rain. The storm was growing worse by the moment.

"Your father fears for your life, Alex," Margaret shouted over the wind as they splashed through puddles in the yard to reach the stables. "He gave me orders that Finn is to take ye away at once."

While Finn saddled their horses by the light of a lantern, Margaret told them all that had transpired.

"How can I leave them like this?" Alex asked.

"Ye must do as your father says," Finn said, resting his hands on Alex's shoulders. "Your duty to your parents and to your clan is to save yourself."

"I promise, Alex, I'll see that everything possible is done to save them," Margaret said.

Like hell she'd see to it. Finn pulled her aside and told her, "You're coming with us."

"I can't leave Ella, and we'd slow ye down," she said. "The earl was adamant that whoever did this intended to murder Alex."

"I'll not leave ye here with a murderer," Finn said, trying and failing to keep his voice down.

"If they'd wanted to poison me at supper, they could have," she argued. "But if the earl is right and the villains want to murder Alex, then riding with you would be far more dangerous for me and Ella than staying here."

She was right, damn it. He and Alex could have armed men chasing after them or already waiting in the dark to ambush them. Still, Finn hesitated.

"I'm no threat to anyone. As far as anyone knows, I'm an impoverished widow with no ties to a rival clan," she said. "The only people at Helmsdale the killer lacked the opportunity to poison are Alex *and you.*"

Finn ran his hands through his hair.

"Please, ye must go!" she pleaded. "Ride hard for Dunrobin before they catch you."

"I'll be back in a few hours," he said, giving in. "Lock yourselves in Una's chamber and don't leave it until I return."

"Be careful." Her beautiful brown eyes were filled with worry. Did she care for him after all? He could not help but hope.

"I will, *mo chroí,*" *my heart.* He cupped her face between his hands and kissed her hard on the mouth.

CHAPTER 22

"What in God's name have ye done, sending them off?" Isabel greeted Margaret the moment she reentered the hall. "Alex should be here to comfort his parents."

"I did as the earl bid me," Margaret said as she removed her rain-soaked cloak.

"Of all the foolish things," Isabel huffed. "If there is a murderer at Helmsdale, we need our men here to protect us. Go fetch them back!"

"They've already gone," Margaret said. "How do the earl and Helen fare?"

"Not good," Isabel said through pursed lips. "I've sent for the priest. He'll be here in the morning."

Margaret ignored Finn's instructions and hurried up the stairs to the earl and Helen's chamber. As she entered the room, she cast sidelong glances at the two men guarding the door and the maids attending the ill couple. Was it one of them who poisoned their laird and his wife?

She was shocked at the earl's transformation. An hour ago, he looked like a man in robust health with his ruddy complexion and powerful presence. Now he was covered in sweat, and his face was ashen with pain.

When the earl saw her, he attempted to sit up, but he was too weak. "Did ye—"

"Rest easy." She waved the maids away from the bed and leaned down to whisper in his ear, "Finn and Alex are on their way to Dunrobin. They rode off a short time ago."

"He...didn't..." the earl attempted to croak out the question.

"No food or drink passed his lips, I'm certain of it," she said in a hushed voice, and took the earl's hand between hers. "Finn will keep him safe."

"Aye, ye can count on Finn when it matters," the earl said, forcing the words out between harsh breaths.

His eyes drifted closed, and she thought he had fallen asleep, the poor man.

"But he needs a good woman. Told him to…hold onto Maggie," he said in a voice so weak she had to lean down to hear him. "Didn't know…how lucky he was…to lose Curstag."

Lose Curstag? Finn had told her there was nothing between them. She could not think about that now.

She turned when one of the maids tapped her on the shoulder.

"I've done everything I know to help them," the maid said, wringing her hands. "Una is wise in matters of healing. Could ye ask her to come?"

"Of course. I'll fetch her now," Margaret said.

She was relieved to see Ella safely ensconced in their chamber, lying on her pallet and listening to Una's stories behind the barred door. While Una went down to the earl and Helen's chamber, Margaret rocked her sleepy daughter on her lap. After all that had happened, it was such a comfort to hold her that tears came to her eyes.

"I love ye so much," she murmured as she rubbed her check against the top of Ella's head. "You're a blessing."

"Where's Finn?" Ella asked, looking up at her.

Through the narrow window, she heard the wind and rain pounding against the thick walls of the castle. She prayed silently that Finn and Alex would reach Dunrobin safely.

"He'll be back tonight," she said as she brushed a curl behind Ella's ear.

Ella smiled and laid her head down. She was sound asleep in Margaret's arms when Una returned.

"Ye weren't gone long," Margaret said.

"They don't need a healer," Una said. "They'll be dead in two days' time, and nothing can be done about it."

Margaret gave a sigh as a wave of sadness washed over her. "I'll go sit with them."

She laid Ella on her sleeping pallet, careful not to wake her, and placed a gentle kiss on her cheek.

"Let this be a lesson to ye," Una said, stopping her at the door. "Ye never know how long either of ye have in this world."

"What if I can't bear the loss that comes after?" Margaret asked.

"Pain and sorrow come to us all," Una said, patting Margaret's hand. "But fear will lead ye to miss the joy."

Una's words went around and around Margaret's head as she sat at the bedside of the dying couple. And they *were* dying. The most she could do for them was ease their suffering by wiping their brows. Every hour or so, she looked up to find Isabel standing in the doorway, her piercing black eyes fixed on her brother- and sister-in-law.

Finn and Alex rode through the storm at a reckless pace on the muddy trail along the coast. Finn was determined to get his cousin to Dunrobin before whoever was behind the poisoning had time to send men after them to finish the job. Luckily, they both had ridden this trail between Helmsdale and Dunrobin countless times and knew every dip and curve. It was growing dark, however, and the storm was pounding in their faces and blowing debris on the trail.

"Fallen tree!" he shouted. He leaned low over *Ceò*'s neck as his horse sailed over it, then turned to make sure Alex's horse cleared it too.

All through the treacherous ride, questions spun through Finn's head. Who was behind this heinous act? How many were involved in the plot? Plenty of men had reason to seek vengeance against his uncle. But if the intent was to erase his family and leave no Gordon heir to Sutherland, that bespoke of both hatred and ambition.

Finn was more than glad to hear the Dunrobin Castle gate bang closed behind them. After gathering everyone into the great hall, Finn watched their faces as he told them about the poisoning of their laird and his wife. Was someone here party to this crime? Someone whose look of shock was not caused by the news about Alex's parents but by Alex's escape?

"Every one of ye must be vigilant to protect your laird's heir," Finn said. "I want four men guarding his door at night."

With four, they could keep watch on each other.

"You and you," he said, pointing at two warriors at random, "will taste Alex's food and drink before it's served to him."

Finn was anxious to return to Helmsdale. After speaking briefly with the man his uncle had left in charge of the castle, he drew Alex aside to bid him goodbye. His cousin looked young and scared.

"You'll be safe here," Finn said, and squeezed his shoulder.

"Whether my parents are alive or…no," Alex said, choking on the words, "I want them brought home to Dunrobin."

Finn prayed his aunt and uncle would live, but he would not give Alex false hope by assuring him his parents would survive.

"It may not be wise to move them right away," Finn said. "But I'll return with them as soon as I can."

The storm swirled around him, the darkness pierced by bursts of lightning as Finn rode back alone. It was long after midnight when he finally reached Helmsdale.

"Give *Ceò* a good brushing and extra oats," he said as he threw the reins to the stable lad, then he patted his horse's shoulder. "Ye did well, *mo caraid*." *My friend*.

He rushed inside and ran up the stairs. As he started past his uncle and aunt's chamber, he saw Margaret curled up in a chair beside the bed and drew his first easy breath since he'd left her.

She must have sensed his presence, for she turned toward the doorway where he stood muddy and dripping wet. Her eyes went wide, and then she surprised him by leaping to her feet and throwing her arms around him. Praise God she was safe. He closed his eyes and held her for a long moment before either of them spoke.

"I've been so worried about you," she said against his chest.

That was so like her to fret over him when she ought to be angry that he'd left her alone with his ailing relatives—and with a murderer on the loose.

"I see ye didn't follow my instructions to lock yourself in with Ella and Una," he said, leaning back to look into her face.

"I wanted to do what I could for your aunt and uncle," she said. "I'm afraid they're not doing well."

He turned his gaze to the couple on the bed. *Oh, God,* they did look bad.

"Thankfully, the pain seems to have eased, and they've gone to sleep," Margaret said. "Is Alex safe?"

"Aye, he is, but let's talk upstairs," he said. "Ye need your rest. Let the maids take care of them for a few hours."

Margaret woke one of the maids who was sleeping on a pallet on the floor and whispered instructions to her.

"There's no doubt it was poison?" Finn asked as they climbed the stairs.

"Una is certain, and your aunt and uncle show all the signs," Margaret said.

"Any notion how it was done?" he asked.

"The men fed what was left of the supper to the dogs, hoping to find out which food or drink contained the poison," she said, wrinkling her nose in disapproval, "but none of the dogs became ill."

"Then either my aunt and uncle consumed all of whatever food was poisoned," he said, "or someone got rid of what was left."

"One of the servants—a man who helped serve our supper—has gone missing," Margaret said.

"Damn it," Finn said. "When Alex and I left, I told the men at the gate not to let anyone else leave."

"He was probably already gone by then," she said. "The hall was in chaos after the earl began shouting that he'd been poisoned. The culprit could have easily disappeared in the confusion."

"I expect this missing servant was bribed to do the deed," he said. "But I'd wager someone else is behind it, someone with a good deal more to gain than a piece of gold."

"Who do ye suspect?" she asked.

That depended on whether the motive was vengeance or gain. Either way, there was no shortage of possibilities.

"I don't know, but I intend to find out," he said. "In the morning, I'll question everyone in the castle."

When they reached their chamber, Finn took off his cloak and hung it on a peg on the back of the door. He wondered if Margaret would leave now to sleep with Una and Ella.

"You're soaked through," Margaret said. "Let me help you out of those wet clothes and find ye a dry shirt to wear."

If Margaret were a different woman, he might think this was an excuse to get his clothes off. Alas, thoughtful Margaret just wanted him warm and dry before she left him for the night.

After he donned the dry shirt, she sat him on the stool and stood behind him to dry the rain out of his hair. Humming softly, she rubbed his head with a cloth, then combed his hair.

He did not fool himself that any of this meant she had changed her mind about leaving him. It was just Margaret's kind nature that made her want to comfort him after the tragedy that struck his family. Kindness, however, was not what he needed to soothe his troubled soul tonight.

200

He wanted to get lost in fiery passion, to bury himself inside her until he forgot himself, forgot that his aunt and uncle lay dying, forgot his terror that Margaret might be murdered while he rode through the storm—and forgot that she would leave him.

But he knew better than to expect that.

When Margaret slid her arms around him from behind, his heart nearly stopped in his chest. Did this mean what he hoped it did? He was afraid to move for fear she would stop.

Her hair spilled over his shoulder and onto his chest as she leaned over him. He closed his eyes to concentrate on the delicious sensation. When he felt her breath on the side of his neck, his every muscle tensed with anticipation. Then her lips grazed his skin, sending a shock of desire coursing through his body.

He turned on the stool, pulled her onto his lap, and looked into her eyes, willing her to answer the question burning in his blood.

"I want us to make love," she said.

He did not ask her why, did not want to know it was because of the terrible events of this day. Did not want to know that she felt sorry for him or wanted to comfort him. He needed her so desperately that it did not matter why she would have him, just that she would.

"You're certain this time?" he asked.

"Aye," she said. "I want this. I want *you*."

That was all he needed to hear. He crushed his mouth against hers. Margaret was bound to leave him. It may not be tomorrow or the next day or the day after that, but she would go.

But tonight, she was his.

And he was going to make damned sure she did not forget him.

The shadow of death had passed too close to them both for Margaret to ignore Una's advice—and her own desire. Tonight, she would not let fear hold her back. Tonight, she would let down her defenses. Tonight, she would risk pain and sorrow to take all the pleasure and passion Finn could give her.

She wanted to drown in his kisses, to hear his harsh breaths in her ear, to feel his heart beat wildly beneath her hand. For once, she would hold nothing back. She would embrace life and love and give herself fully.

After that first scorching kiss, she expected the mindless rush and torrent of passion like the last time, but Finn surprised her by pulling back.

"I'm going to be slow and thorough this time," Finn said with a wicked gleam in his eye that sent her pulse racing. "But first, to make up for torturing me the night we arrived at Dunrobin when ye took your bath, I want to watch you undress."

Margaret thought he was teasing her to allay any fears she still harbored, until he stood back and leaned against the bed with his arms crossed.

She took a deep breath. Time to embrace life fully. Sitting on the stool, she removed her shoes, but when she started to pull off her stockings, he interrupted her.

"Slowly," he said.

Her breath hitched at the heat in his eyes as she rolled down one stocking and then the other. When she stood and he walked toward her, her whole body tingled in anticipation. Instead of wrapping his arms around her, however, he stepped behind her and undid her gown, sending shivers along her skin with his fingers. She felt his warm breath and then his soft lips on the side of her neck, and she leaned back against him.

When he reached around and cupped her breasts, she became acutely aware of her nipples pressing against his palms, his strained breathing in her ear, and the length of his manhood pressed against her backside. Surely, he would carry her to the bed now. His body was more than ready. But Finn surprised her again and returned to the side of the bed.

"Now the gown," he said.

Swallowing hard, Margaret slowly eased the gown off her shoulders and down over her breasts, and then past her hips until it fell to the floor around her feet in a soft swish. She was standing in just her shift now.

"Take it off," Finn said in a strained voice.

When she slipped one strap down and heard his sharp intake of breath, she felt a sudden surge of feminine power. Finn's reaction made her feel sensuous, desirable. She let the other strap fall and then inched the shift down to almost her nipples. They were peaked and sensitive to the brush of the thin fabric, and she gave the shift another tug to fully reveal her breasts.

When she looked up, the air around Finn seemed to vibrate with the force of his desire, and that gave her the courage to let the shift drop to the floor.

"Jesu, Mary, and Joseph." The heat of Finn's gaze burned her skin as it traveled over her from head to toe and back again.

He shed his own clothes with remarkable speed. *Oh my*, he was a beautiful man—and fully erect—but he barely gave her time for a proper look before he enfolded her in his arms and the torrent of passion she expected. But then he changed the pace and gave her a long and languorous kiss. Beneath that kiss, she felt the power of his lust held in check and wondered what on earth he was waiting for.

Then he lifted her onto the bed and began to show her. She'd never had anyone show her such tenderness. He kissed and caressed up and down her body, as if he wanted to know and claim every inch of her. Then he paused to flick and circle her nipple with his tongue, while he tortured her with his magic fingers between her legs, drawing moans from her throat and causing an aching need low in her belly.

When he stopped, she wanted to weep, but she was distracted by his kisses down to her belly.

"I've been wanting to taste ye forever," Finn said, pausing to look up at her.

Taste her? What did he mean? The breath went out of her when she felt his mouth on her most private part. William had definitely never done this.

She gripped the bedclothes in her fingers as Finn kissed and licked and circled his tongue over the sensitive nub between her legs. Good heavens, nothing had ever felt like the exquisite sensation of his mouth and tongue. The tension grew until it became unbearable. She wanted to beg him to stop and not to stop, but she could not form words.

She cried out as liquid waves of pleasure rocked her body. Before she recovered, she felt an urgent need to have her arms around him, to feel him inside her, to have their bodies joined. To be one with him.

When she pulled on his shoulders, he drew up until they were face to face.

"I need ye inside me. Now," she said in a ragged voice. "Please, *now*."

"*O shluagh*," he said.

Her hips lifted of their own accord, her body ready for his. She bit her lip as he thrust inside her, filling her. She clamped her arms and legs around him, urging him on.

Heaven help her.

"*Mo leannain*," he said, pausing to rest his forehead against hers, "You're going to kill me."

His shaft throbbed inside her as he gave her a long, deep kiss. When he began to move inside her, every nerve and muscle in her body strained against him.

"I need... I need..." *Could he not go faster?*

Instead, he rolled with her until she was on top of him.

"Show me how ye want it." He coaxed her to sit up, straddling him. Gripping her hips, he rocked her against him, helping her find her rhythm.

His gaze raked over her as she moved, setting her skin on fire. For the first time in her life, she felt wanton and truly free. This was not like her. And yet she felt as though this was how she was meant to be.

As she rode him, he covered her breasts with his hands and pinched and rubbed his thumbs over her nipples. *Oh God!* She leaned over him, hands on his chest, straining against him. It was happening again. When he reached between them and rubbed the sensitive nub between her legs, she felt as if she was about to fall over the edge of the world.

"Look at me!" he said.

As they locked gazes and their bodies rocked together, she felt as if their souls touched. Instead of fear, she was filled with wonder.

Oh, oh, oh! Waves of blinding pleasure rolled through her as he thrust faster and harder, again and again, until he surged against her one last time, and they cried out together.

She collapsed on top of him, sweating and out of breath. She had never lost control like that. She suspected she had even screamed. Nothing had ever felt so good, but she feared she must have shocked him.

"*Mo chridhe*," *my heart,* Finn said, holding her close. "That was beyond anything I imagined."

She sighed as he kissed her hair and ran his hand up and down her back.

Making love with Finn was a revelation. Instead of making her feel used and inadequate, he had made her feel gloriously sensuous. She never dreamed a man could be so generous or make her feel that she was what he wanted, just as she was.

"Why now?" Finn whispered.

Because I love you. But she could not tell him that.

"I don't want to let fear keep me from this—and from you," she said, which was also true. "Not anymore."

"Ye needn't fear me," he said. "I would never hurt you."

Though he would not mean to, she knew Una was right. Pain and sorrow were bound to come. But Margaret was determined to take the joy while she could.

In the morning, Finn lay against the pillows with his arms around her, watching her sleep in the first light of dawn filtering through the narrow window. Margaret was breathtakingly beautiful with her flawless skin, angelic face, and silvery blond hair spread over the pillow. Last night, he watched in wonder as she first discovered and then reveled in her sensuality. In all his life, with the countless women he'd had, he'd never had a night like that, never felt so much, never needed a woman so. She was an amazing lass, his Maggie.

It pained him that he had no hope of keeping her. He was still a landless warrior with no proper home to give her. If anything, his uncle's probable death made his future even less certain than before.

During the night, he had turned to her again and again, each time making love as if was the last time. Because he knew it could be. He feared she would change her mind and decide this was a grave mistake, and he might never hold her in his arms again.

And each time he was inside her, he lost another piece of his heart to her, until she had it all.

CHAPTER 23

Though Margaret sensed it was near dawn, she snuggled closer to Finn and refused to open her eyes. She never wanted this night to end. She had never felt so close to anyone—or such intense pleasure or tenderness—as when they made love.

She would hold the memory with her always.

If only they could stay in their chamber, just the two of them, a little longer. But their troubles would not wait. When Margaret finally gave in and opened her eyes, she found Finn watching her.

"Thank you for last night," Finn said, and gave her one last kiss that was so tender it made her heart weep. "'Tis early. Stay and get some rest. I'll go see how my aunt and uncle fare."

"I'll go with ye." If the earl and Helen had passed on during the night, she did not want him to face that alone.

They dressed quickly and went to his aunt and uncle's bedchamber.

"They're resting nice and peaceful," one the maids told them, which sounded to Margaret like the end was near.

"Thank you," Margaret said in a hushed voice. "Get some sleep. I'll stay with them."

Finn held his aunt's hand and spoke to the couple, though it was doubtful they could hear him.

"Alex is safe," he assured them. "I give ye my word that, no matter what comes, I will look after him."

Helen's eyelids fluttered briefly, so perhaps she did hear and Finn's words gave her some comfort. Margaret hoped so.

Finn heaved a sigh and got to his feet. "I'll question everyone, starting with the guards at the gate, to see if I can find a clue as to who did this and why."

Margaret wanted to hold him in her arms again, but it was not comfort he needed now but answers. "I'll send for ye if there is any change."

After adjusting the ill couple's bedclothes and wiping their foreheads, she curled up on the chair next to the bed. She had gotten almost no sleep and had to struggle to stay awake. She must have drifted off because she was jolted awake by screams.

She sat up, disoriented, and looked about the room for the cause of the alarm. The ill couple still lay unmoving on the bed. As her mind cleared, she realized the screams were coming from a distance.

She ran down the stairs. In the hall, the men who slept on the benches and floor were lurching to their feet and grabbing their weapons. But then, almost as one, they halted in place, as if uncertain what was required of them, as it became clear the screams were not the sounds of an attack but of a lone woman wailing in grief.

When the men saw Margaret enter in the hall, their relief was almost palpable.

"Come with me," she said, pointing to two of them. "I may need your help."

She followed the wretched sound down the separate stairs into the dark undercroft, where the kitchen and storerooms were. The woman's wails echoed against the stone walls, filling the enclosed space with a misery so wretched it made Margaret's eyes sting.

What tragedy awaited her? A young maid came running from the opposite direction and nearly knocked her over. Margaret caught the maid by her shoulders and spoke with a calm she did not feel. "Tell me what's happened."

"I had to fetch her!" the maid babbled. "He told me not to, but I didn't know what else to do. Don't ye see, I had to!"

What Margaret could see was that she was not going to get anything sensible out of the maid. "I'll take care of it," she told her. "Go sit in the hall."

Margaret lifted her skirts and hurried past the kitchens toward the pitiful sounds until she reached an open door. Light from a lamp inside revealed a storage room containing bags of oats, a barrel, and two cots that she assumed were used by kitchen servants.

A woman was on her knees beside one of the cots and holding the hand of someone lying on it. Margaret gasped when she saw the woman's profile and realized who it was. What in heaven's name was Isabel doing down here?

"Isabel," Margaret called softly.

When Isabel spun around, the sharp planes of her face were distorted with anguish.

"He's dying!" Isabel cried. "My son is dying!"

For one terrible moment Margaret thought she meant Finn, and her heart stopped in her chest. But it could not be Finn. He was outside questioning the guards. And his mother would never weep like this for him.

When Margaret stepped closer, she saw that the man on the cot was Bearach. His limbs were tangled in the bedsheet from tossing and turning, and his chest glistened with sweat, but his eyes were alert.

"For God's sake, shut her up!" Bearach said.

"Let me help," Margaret said, resting her hand on Isabel's shoulder. "What can I do?"

"My darling son is dying!" Isabel wailed. "He's dying!"

"I'm ill, not dying," Bearach growled. "Now get out, before Curstag hears your yowling. If she finds me here, she'll know I was with one of the maids again."

"You're supposed to be at Girnigoe Castle," his mother said. "Why did ye come back?"

"When the weather turned nasty, I decided the visit could wait another day and turned around," he said. "I slipped into the kitchen while everyone else was at supper and persuaded that bonny lass with the fiery hair to spend the night with me."

"Have ye had any food or drink since ye returned?" Margaret asked.

"Why?" Bearach asked in surly tone.

"Your aunt and uncle are gravely ill," Margaret said. "We suspect they were poisoned at supper."

"Tell me ye touched nothing," his mother pleaded.

"I stole the earl's best wine that he saves for himself, the selfish bastard," he said, and pointed at an ornate silver flagon on the floor.

Margaret recognized it as the one that was always placed at the earl's end of the table.

"Nay! Nay!" Isabel wailed, tearing at her hair. "Why did ye drink it? Why did ye come back?"

From the look of panic on Bearach's face, he finally understood why his mother was wailing. Neither panic nor wailing, however, would help the situation.

"We don't know that the poison was in the wine," Margaret said, attempting to calm them.

"He's dying!" Isabel cried, louder than before. "My son is dying!"

"Listen to me." Margaret pulled Isabel to her feet and gave her shoulders a shake. "Even if there was poison in the wine, that doesn't mean Bearach will die."

"You're lying," Bearach said. "My aunt and uncle are already dying from the poison, aren't they?"

"You're not as ill as they are, which probably means ye consumed far less of the poison," Margaret said in a firm voice. "Besides that, you're young and strong, so you've a good chance of surviving this."

She prayed it was true. Though she could find nothing to like about either Bearach or Isabel, they did not deserve this.

"Aye, ye will recover," Isabel said, finally gaining her composure. "Being half Sinclair, you've stronger blood than the earl and Helen."

"We need to move ye up to your bedchamber." Margaret signaled to the two men who had followed her and were waiting just outside the room. "You'll be more comfortable there." And easier to care for.

"Don't tell Curstag...where ye found me," Bearach said between gritted teeth as the men helped him to his feet and slung his arms around their shoulders.

"Everyone will say," Isabel ordered, glaring at the men and Margaret, "that Bearach returned during the night and slept in the hall so as not to disturb his wife."

How Bearach and Isabel could connive to deceive Curstag in the midst of this was beyond her. In any case, the lie proved unnecessary.

Curstag had slept through all the commotion. When the men banged open the door as they hefted Bearach inside, Curstag leaped out of bed in her night shift.

"God help me, he's wounded!" she shrieked, and covered her face with her hands. "I can't bear to see his blood! I can't, I can't!"

Seeing that Curstag would be no help, Margaret hurried to pull down the bedclothes so the men could help Bearach into bed.

She turned back around in time to see Isabel slap her daughter-in-law hard across the face.

"He's not bleeding, he's poisoned, ye fool," Isabel said. "Calm yourself and stay out of the way."

Good heavens. "Isabel," Margaret said gently as she stepped between the two women, "your son needs you."

In a flash, Isabel's expression went from angry to stricken. While she rushed to her son's bedside, Curstag fled from the room, still wearing nothing but her thin shift. Margaret sent a maid after her with instructions to give Curstag a draught of whisky and put her to bed in one of the other chambers.

"What can I do for ye, *mo chridhe?*" *my heart,* Isabel asked as she ran her hand over Bearach's forehead.

"Leave me alone," Bearach groaned and pushed her away.

"There must be something I can do," Isabel said, desperation in her voice.

"We gave the earl and Helen mugwort and a tincture of fennel seeds boiled in wine," Margaret said. Though these common remedies for poisoning had not helped the ill couple at all, Isabel needed to feel she was doing something to help her son. "There's some left in the kitchen."

"Of course," Isabel murmured to herself, then she stood up and pointed a long, bony finger at Margaret. "Don't give my son any of your useless remedies. I'll make a tincture myself."

With that, Isabel scurried out of the chamber, leaving Margaret alone with Bearach. While she waited for Isabel to return, she straightened his bedding. When she leaned over to fluff his pillow, he locked an arm around her waist.

"I knew you'd crawl into my bed sooner or later," he said, his sour breath in her face.

She was so startled that she did not react quickly enough, which gave him time to squeeze her breast before she shoved him away. She'd become accustomed to men leaving her alone because of Finn and let her guard down.

"Have pity on an ill man," Bearach said.

"You'll mind your hands if ye don't wish to be injured as well," she said.

He laughed at her, which caused him to wheeze and then fall into a long coughing fit. That sapped his strength, and he soon fell into a sound sleep.

She was waiting for Isabel to return so she could go check on Ella when she heard running footsteps coming up the stairwell. A moment later, Finn burst through the doorway. When he saw his brother on the bed, he staggered backward as if from a blow.

"Is it true, then?" he asked. "He's been poisoned too?"

Margaret went to him and touched his cheek. "I'm so sorry."

"Why?" Finn asked, gripping her arms. "Why Bearach?"

"I don't believe he was an intended victim," she said in a low voice so as not to wake Bearach. "Your brother drank the wine that was in the earl's silver flagon."

As she told him the rest, Finn clenched and unclenched his jaw.

"Your father doesn't know yet."

"I'd better go find him and tell him," Finn said, clearly dreading the task. Before leaving, he approached the bed and stared down at his brother. "Poor Bearach."

"Get out!" Isabel shouted from the doorway. "I'll not have ye near him."

Isabel rushed into the room, stood between the bed and Finn, and flung her arms out as if warding off an attack. Margaret was too stunned to move.

"'Tis bad luck to have ye here when ye wish him dead," Isabel said.

"How can ye say that?" Finn asked. "Bearach is my only brother. I've never wished him ill, and I pray now that he'll soon recover."

"That's a lie!" Isabel's hands were shaking, and her eyes were dark and wild. "Ye hope to take his place as heir."

"Isabel, please stop," Margaret said.

"Ye want Garty for yourself!" Isabel shouted at Finn.

"After the misery I suffered at Garty, ye think I want it?" Finn said as he backed toward the door. "I never want to see that goddamned place again."

"I swear ye won't have it! Bearach will recover," Isabel shouted. "Get out! Get out!

But Finn was already gone.

###

Finn tore out of the room, stunned by his brother's poisoning and his mother's accusations. In his blind rush, he nearly crashed into Curstag in the dimly lit stairwell. At the last moment, he caught her. When he tried to release her, she wrapped her arms around his waist and buried her face in his chest, sobbing.

He wanted to beat his fists against the wall and run until his heart could take no more. Most of all, he wanted to be alone. But Curstag feared she was losing her husband. She needed and deserved what comfort he could give her. Tamping down the feelings raging inside him, he forced himself to put his arms around her and hold her while she wept.

"I feel so alone," she said. "What will I do if…"

"Shh. You're not alone," he said as he rubbed his hand up and down her back. "And ye mustn't give up hope."

He heard a light step above him and looked up. Around the curve of the wheeled stairs, he saw Margaret's silhouette outside his brother's door. With the light behind her, her face was in darkness and he could not make out her expression.

Before he could untangle himself from Curstag, she disappeared back inside his brother's chamber. He told himself Margaret was a levelheaded lass, and she would see this for what it was.

CHAPTER 24

Margaret spent the rest of the day moving between the two chambers of the ill, directing the servants and giving what comfort and help she could. Most of the time she was too busy to dwell on what she had seen in the stairwell, but every time she went up and down the stairs between the two chambers, the image of Curstag in Finn's arms came back to her.

With three members of the household poisoned and fighting death, it would be petty to let that embrace trouble her. Curstag was in need of comfort, and it would be unkind for Finn not to give it. And yet Margaret could not help thinking there was something between those two that Finn had not told her.

By the end of the day, Margaret was weary to her bones. Most of the household had already gone to bed, and the castle was quiet as she climbed the stairs one last time to take a fresh pitcher of water to Bearach's chamber and ask Isabel if she needed anything else for the night. Isabel could not be persuaded to leave Bearach's bedside and let the servants care for him even for a few hours so she could rest.

The door to his chamber was slightly ajar, and a thin shaft of candlelight shone through the crack into the dark stairwell. When she heard voices, Margaret paused outside the door. Despite the vinegary concoction Isabel had forced down Bearach's throat, his condition had worsened through the day, and Margaret was hesitant to intrude on what could be one of their last conversations.

"What have ye done, Mother?" Bearach's voice reached her through the crack. "What have ye done?"

Was he upset that Isabel had turned Finn away? Perhaps, fearing death, Bearach wished to reconcile with his only brother. Margaret hoped so. Isabel only wept in response.

Careful not to make a sound, Margaret left the pitcher beside the door and left.

The image of Finn holding Curstag came back to her once again as she climbed the last set of stairs to the bedchamber she shared with Finn. Even if that embrace meant nothing, it was a reminder that she was one of a long string of women Finn had taken to bed. That day outside Huntly Castle, Alex had told her Finn was not the sort of man to stay with one woman for long.

That should not make her feel like a blade was piercing her heart, since their affair could not last anyway. Once this crisis with his family passed, Finn could take her to Sybil, and that would be the end of it. She had risked too much already and ought to end it now. She had a glorious night to remember, and that would have to be enough.

Her resolution melted like butter on a hot skillet when she opened their door and saw Finn leaning against the bed waiting for her. The moment their eyes met, that fiery blaze ignited between them again.

Without a word, she walked into his arms and into the flames.

The earl and Helen died the next morning.

Finn sat with his father while the women prepared the bodies for the eventual burial, washing them and dressing them in their finest clothes. Once again, Curstag and Isabel left the task of organizing the women to Margaret.

Finn did not know what they would have done without her. The last two days had been hellish. While Curstag lay in bed making demands on the servants, and his mother alternately wept and forced more of her vinegary concoction down Bearach's throat, Margaret took care of the sick and kept the household running.

All Margaret had wanted was escape, and he had brought her to this. As if his family were not difficult enough on their own, there were poisonings and a murderer on the loose. And now, she was washing dead bodies.

He rubbed his forehead against a pounding headache and stole a glance at his father. Though it was not yet noon, his eyes were bleary, and his sweat smelled of whisky. His father was coping with Bearach's illness and the death of his brother and sister-in-law the same way he coped with all of life's challenges and disappointments.

"At least we have a bit of good news about Bearach," his father said, raising his flask.

Whether it was Isabel's odd remedy or Bearach's strong constitution, he did appear to be improving.

"Aye, we've cause for hope," Finn said. "Margaret told me Bearach sat up in bed and ate for the first time since the poisoning."

After that brief exchange, they fell into another long silence. Finn's relationship with his father was not acrimonious, but they had never been at ease with each other.

"Alex wants his parents' bodies brought to Dunrobin," Finn said at last.

"Isabel says they must remain here for a couple of days so the folk in this part of Sutherland can pay their respects." His father cleared his throat and attempted a faint smile. "My brother was their chieftain, and he'd want to remind them of that even in death."

"He would, indeed," Finn agreed. And for Alex's sake, it would be wise to remind all the Sutherlands that they owed their allegiance to the new earl.

For the next two days, every man, woman, and child within walking distance passed through the hall where the bodies were on display. Whether it was out of respect or merely curiosity because of the poisoning, Finn could not say, but he spoke with every one of them. With Alex at Dunrobin and his own father off drunk somewhere, someone had to greet the mourners on behalf of the earl's family.

Finally, it was time to take the earl and Helen home to Dunrobin.

"I promised Alex I would bring them myself," Finn told Margaret that night when they were at last alone in their chamber. "But I don't feel right leaving when my brother is so ill."

"Why not let other members of your uncle's guard escort their bodies home?" She put her arms around him. "Bearach is not out of danger. I'm sure Alex will understand."

Remembering how young and scared Alex looked when he left him, Finn still felt torn, but he could not leave while his brother's survival was still uncertain. "I'll ask Una's grandson Lachlan to go along. He's a good man I know I can trust."

That night they again shut away the world for a few hours and made love frantically between bouts of restless sleep. They barely spoke at all, but he showed her how he felt with his body.

How much longer would she stay? He was under no illusion that this could last. Margaret needed an escape from her highborn life for a time, but he'd always known she would go back to it. She was not meant for the humble life he could give her.

And yet he could not envision his life without her. He had never let himself need a woman before. He did not want to need her now.

But it was too late.

He would get by after she'd gone, as he always did. But her leaving would break his heart, and he had a bad feeling the wound would never heal. Even if he could have foreseen the hole she would leave in his life, however, he would not have missed a moment of his time with her.

"I need ye now," he said as he pulled her against him, when what he meant was, *I need ye forever.*

CHAPTER 25

Finn awoke to someone knocking on their chamber door and squinted at the window. It was barely dawn, and all he wanted to do was stay in this warm bed with Margaret. He buried his face in her hair and cupped her breast, unwilling to face the troubles of the day quite yet.

"It could be about your brother," Margaret said sleepily.

He dragged himself out of bed, tossed his shirt over his head, and opened the door a crack. An anxious maid waited there twisting her hands in the skirt of her gown.

"Lachlan just rode in from Dunrobin," she said. "Says 'tis urgent he speak with ye."

Finn's blood turned cold. *Alex was in danger.*

Margaret pulled on her robe while he finished dressing, and they hurried down to the hall together. The household was unsettled after the dramatic events of the last several days. Despite the early hour, the warriors and servants who slept in the hall were stirring as word spread that a messenger had arrived. The news had even reached Finn's mother and father, who came down the stairs behind them.

Lachlan stood in front of the great hearth, steam rising from his rain-soaked cloak.

"What's happened?" Finn asked him.

"George Sinclair, the Earl of Caithness, arrived at Dunrobin with a fleet of ships full of warriors," Lachlan said. "*Ach*, there must have been fifty boats!"

O shluagh. George could not have chosen a more opportune time to attack, with Alex's father not even in his grave and Alex too young and inexperienced to lead. Finn never should have left Alex's side.

Alex's parents had died only three days ago. How did the Sinclair chieftain learn of the earl's death and take advantage of it so quickly? George was prepared to act as soon as he heard the news, which meant the bastard must have had a hand in their murder.

"The Sinclair chieftain demanded entry as Alex's guardian," Lachlan said.

"As his what?" Finn demanded.

"He claims guardianship over Alex now that his parents are dead," Lachlan said.

"That's an outrage!" Finn slammed his fist against the mantel. "I know for certain Alex's father named his sister's husband, the Earl of Athol, in his will to be Alex's guardian should one ever be needed."

"Apparently, Athol sold him the wardship."

"Sold it? That bastard!" Finn could not believe his ears. "Alex's father should never have trusted someone not of his blood."

"The Sinclair chieftain said if we refused to hand over his ward, it would be treason."

"When ye refused, the Sinclairs laid siege to the castle?" When Lachlan did not answer right away, a cold rage filled Finn's belly. "Don't tell me the men complied."

"The Sinclair chieftain threatened to burn down Dunrobin with all of us in it if we did not open the gates," Lachlan said, fidgeting under Finn's glare. "That's when Alex ordered us to let them in."

"*A' phlàigh oirbh Sinclairs!*" *A plague on the Sinclairs!* Finn wanted to have George Sinclair's thick neck between his hands and squeeze the life out of him. "This cannot stand. I'll not allow Alex to remain in the clutches of that foul man."

"If Athol sold it, the King's Council is bound to approve it, you'll see," his mother said, nodding. "My Sinclair cousin is a wise choice for Alex's guardian."

"A wise choice?" Finn felt as if his head would explode. "I'd wager my last farthing that George had a hand in the murder of Alex's parents. And now he has the bollocks to claim to be his guardian?"

He was vaguely aware that Margaret was tugging at his arm, but he could not be diverted with all this anger pulsing through his body.

"There's more, I'm afraid," Lachlan said.

Whatever it was, it could not be worse news than this.

"The Sinclair chieftain has forced Alex"—Lachlan paused to clear his throat—"to wed his daughter Barbara."

Finn staggered on his feet. Nay, it could not be. Not to Barbara. She'd destroy his naïve, sweet-natured cousin.

"'Tis a fine match," his mother said, folding her arms. "After all, Barbara is an earl's daughter and a Sinclair."

"Alex is fifteen!" Finn said. "Barbara is more than twice his age—and a vicious snake."

His blood froze in his veins as he imagined Barbara's cold gray eyes taunting him while she strangled his cousin, just as she had killed his dog so many years ago.

Margaret found Finn throwing dirks at a wooden stake in the field where the men practiced behind the castle.

"I'll get Alex back," Finn said. "I have to."

"Now that Athol has sold the wardship and George Sinclair has Alex in his custody," she said, choosing her words carefully, "that will be difficult."

"I don't care how difficult it is," Finn snapped, and threw another dirk, hitting the stake squarely with a *thunk*.

"Come inside where we can talk," she said, taking his arm.

"*I* should be Alex's guardian before that damned George," he said, stabbing his thumb against his chest. "*I'm* a closer blood relation."

"I'm afraid that will not carry enough weight with the King's Council." She paused, knowing he would not like what she had to tell him. "That is not how these matters are decided."

"What could be more important than blood?" he demanded, his eyes like blue fire.

"Alex is an earl," she said. "The council will not grant his wardship to someone without rank."

"Then my father can be the guardian in name," Finn said. "He has a rank and title."

"What I should have said"—she paused to lick her lips—"is that the council will not grant the wardship of an earl to someone of *lesser* rank. Alex and his properties can only be placed in royal guardianship or with another earl."

"You're saying even your brother would be chosen over me," Finn said, turning to glare at her, "though he does not even know Alex and would not have Alex's interests at heart?"

"For certain," she said.

"Then the council can go to hell," Finn said, and started to march off.

"This won't last forever," she said, struggling to keep up with his long strides. "Alex will come of age in less than three years."

When he swung around to face her, his eyes held such fury that she had to fight the urge to step back.

"Ye don't understand," he said between clenched teeth. "Alex is not safe with the Sinclairs."

Then he stormed off into the woods, leaving her standing alone in the muddy field. She stared after him, wishing there was something she could say or do to ease his fear for Alex. She was worried about Alex too, but wardships could be bought and sold, and the council would view an earl with adjacent lands as an appropriate guardian. Even if they did not, they were too absorbed in their own power struggles to take on a fight in the distant far north with the powerful Earl of Caithness.

With a sigh, she turned around and headed back inside. After passing through the gate, she saw Isabel ahead of her climbing the steps into the keep like a scurrying rat.

"I shouldn't have taken my anger out on you," Finn said when he returned hours later. "'Tis not your fault if the King's Council will allow such a travesty to stand."

"And 'tis not your fault the Sinclairs have Alex," she said.

"It is," he said. "I made a deathbed promise to my uncle and aunt that I would take care of Alex."

"Ye saved his life by taking him to Dunrobin after the poi-sonings," she said. "Ye did all ye could."

"I left him," he said. "He needed me, and I left him."

Things remained strained between her and Finn as the days passed and bad news continued to arrive. George Sinclair wasted no time before he began using his position as guardian of Alex's estates to pillage Sutherland. As always, those who suffered most were the common folk. With each new tale that reached them, Finn's spirits sank lower, and Margaret felt more helpless.

It broke her heart to see him like this. No matter how she tried to tell him that none of it was his fault, he blamed himself for the danger he believed Alex was in. He erected a wall between them and would not let her past it.

At times when they made love she felt as if that wall was so thin she could almost break through. But Finn retreated like an injured bear, hiding the gaping wound in his underbelly.

And now, Bearach's health was failing. Eight long days after he drank the poison, Isabel's vinegary tincture did not seem to be working anymore.

Needing to escape the castle for a while, Margaret took Ella on a walk along the river. Their progress was slow, as Ella stopped every few feet to watch a bird or pick a flower.

"Don't eat them," Margaret told Ella when she caught her tasting a bluebell.

Margaret's thoughts returned again to Finn as they walked. She had put off leaving for too long. The longer she stayed, the greater the chance she would become pregnant. She could not ask him to take her while his family was in upheaval. Besides, making the long journey together would be too painful. If she could get a message to Sybil, her sister would send someone for her.

"Pretty!" Ella said.

Margaret turned to see her daughter pulling with both hands on a stalk with yellow, bell-shaped flowers and green leaves with points. *Henbane.* Margaret's heart went to her throat.

"Ye mustn't touch that one!" Margaret lifted Ella off her feet and rushed her down the slope to the edge of the river, where she vigorously washed Ella's hands and face. "'Tis a very, very bad plant!"

Ella's bottom lip trembled as she looked up at Margaret with tears in her big blue eyes.

"'Tis all right, sweetling," Margaret said, trying her best to keep the panic from her voice. "But ye must tell me if ye tasted that plant with the yellow flowers—or if ye even touched it to your mouth."

"Nay! Too stinky!" Ella made a face and extended her arms to show how she'd held it.

Praise God! Margaret sank to the ground and pulled Ella onto her lap.

Ella put her small hands on either side of Margaret's face and peered at her with frightened eyes. "Don't go away."

"I won't," Margaret said. "What makes ye think I would?"

"Mam was scared, and she went away."

The poor child must think her mother left her. How could she explain to Ella that her mother didn't abandon her, but was dead?

"I was only frightened because that flower could make ye ill," Margaret said. "I will never leave you. Never."

Ella was quiet for a time as she appeared to take this in, then she looked up at Margaret with her wide blue eyes, and asked, "Will Finn leave us?"

Margaret drew in a shaky breath. In making her plans to leave, she had failed to fully consider how attached Ella was to Finn. And he to her. But the longer they stayed, the harder it would be on all of them when the inevitable parting came.

"Finn is verra fond of you," Margaret said, because she could not bring herself to tell Ella yet that they would be the ones leaving.

With her thoughts on Ella and Finn, it was not until they were nearly back to the castle that it occurred to her they may have discovered the poison the murderer used. Anyone at Helmsdale could have collected the henbane from along the path. Because the plant was commonly used—carefully and in small doses—to relieve pain, particularly toothache, someone gathering it would raise no suspicion.

She debated whether to trouble Finn with what she discovered, as there was little chance it would help reveal who the poisoner was. Everyone at Helmsdale had walked that path at one time or another. She herself had done so many times before today.

When she and Ella entered the hall, she saw Finn sitting alone with his father, which was unusual. Her skin prickled, and she feared more bad news had come to Helmsdale. Worry creased Finn's handsome face as he got up and started toward her and Ella.

Before he reached them, wailing coming from upstairs stopped him in his tracks. A moment later, Curstag came flying down the stairs and threw herself into Finn's arms, weeping loudly.

"He's dead!" Curstag cried. "Bearach is dead!"

Margaret watched in horror as Finn's father clutched his chest and fell to the floor.

CHAPTER 26

Frustration and guilt gnawed at Finn's belly as he climbed the stairs. Someone had murdered three of his closest kin right under his nose. Not only had he failed to prevent it, he had not even succeeded in finding out who the murderer was. And ever present in his mind was his worry about Alex. With each day that passed without more news from Dunrobin, the weight of Finn's unfulfilled oath to protect his cousin grew heavier and heavier on his shoulders.

He ought to grieve for his brother, but he felt nothing. Though they had buried him yesterday, Finn still could not quite believe he was dead. Bearach had survived so long after the poisoning that Finn had been convinced he would recover.

Thankfully, the shock to his father's heart had not killed him as well—at least not yet.

Finn tapped on his parents' bedchamber door, hoping Margaret would answer it. She and Una had been caring for his father since his heart failed him, and she had not come to bed again last night.

When Una opened the door a crack, he saw Margaret on the far side of the room. She had her back to him, wringing out a wet cloth, and did not see him, but Ella, who was playing on the floor at her feet, gave him a smile and a wave.

"Gilbert is resting," Una said in a hushed voice, which was the same thing she'd told him the last time and the time before that. "Sleep is the best healer."

He needed to be doing something. Anything. Instead of pounding his fist into the wall, he climbed the stairs to wait for Margaret in their chamber. When he opened the door, he found Curstag lying on their bed.

"What in the hell are ye doing in here?" He spoke in a harsh tone before he remembered she was a grieving widow.

"I can't verra well be in my own bed, now can I?" she said, and sat up. "Isabel has locked herself in there again, weeping and smelling his clothes."

Finn tried and failed to get that image out of his head.

"I'll let ye be, then," he said, but when he started to go, she leaped off the bed and grabbed his arm.

"Talk to me," she pleaded. "I can't bear to be alone just yet."

Jesu. Curstag was the last person he wanted to have a conversation with, aside from his mother. But he did not want to be heartless, so he let her pull him inside.

"Ye know what this means, don't ye?" she asked.

He had no notion what she was talking about.

"It means," she said, running her hand up his chest, "we can be together at last."

"What?" Finn said, and pushed her away. "Bearach is barely in the ground."

"Ye know you're the one I wanted," she said. "I only married him because he had the title and lands."

No one could accuse Curstag of being subtle. The lass did not have a kind or sensitive bone in her body.

"Ye can't blame me for making a good marriage," she said. "Any lass with an ounce of sense would do the same."

He did not fault her for choosing the position and security she believed his brother could give her, but for toying with him when he was too naïve to know that would inevitably tip the scales against him.

"But now that you're the heir," she said, tilting her head in a way he once found fetching, "there's nothing to keep us apart."

"Nothing?" he said. "You're forgetting I have a wife."

"You're only handfasted," she said. "Ye don't have to wait the whole year to set her aside."

"Maggie is the only woman I'll ever want," he said. "Don't ye understand? I love her."

The words that fell out of his mouth were true. He was hopelessly in love with Margaret. No other woman would ever do for him now.

"Love? *Ach*, you're still the romantic ye were at sixteen." She gave a light laugh and shook her head. "I give it a month before ye tire of her and come begging—"

"Don't let me find ye in here again." Finn pushed her out the door and shut it behind her.

Ironically, he had reason to be grateful to Curstag. In the midst of so many dark days, she had given him hope by pointing out

224

that the barrier that kept him from making Margaret his true wife was gone. He was no longer a landless warrior who must always live by his sword.

He was his father's heir.

Margaret lay sprawled on the bed beside Finn, unable to move her limbs. This was so unfair. Just when she had decided it was time to ask Finn to take her to her sister's, he tore down the wall he'd erected between them and made love to her until her body felt like soft wax melded to the mattress—and he held her heart in his hands.

She could not leave him while his aunt, uncle, and brother were dying, nor while his father's fate was uncertain. But now the dead were buried, and his father, though still weak, was recovering. Sadly, there was nothing Finn could do for Alex until his cousin came of age.

The crises were passed. It was time to leave.

And yet she did not want to go.

"Your father has been asking for ye," she said. When he groaned in response, she kissed his shoulder and brushed the back of her fingers along the side of his face. "I know things have never been easy between the two of ye, but he's lost a brother and a son. He needs you."

"Ye take care of everyone, whether they deserve it or no." He gave her a tender kiss on the lips. "I promise I'll talk with him."

She groaned her objection when Finn got out of bed, but he was back a moment later and pulled her up to sit up beside him on the edge of the bed.

"The blacksmith helped me make this for ye," Finn said, and handed her a small wooden box.

"A gift?" she said. "Ye needn't have."

She hoped he had not wasted what little money he had on jewelry he could ill afford. She once owned jewels worth a small fortune, but the only piece that meant anything to her was the onyx pendant her mother gave her. The others were ornaments given not out of affection, but to accentuate her beauty and enhance her status as a worthy prize.

"Just open it," he said in an indifferent tone that did not fool her.

The lid fit snugly, and it took her a moment to work it off the box. When it suddenly gave way and she saw what was inside, she gasped.

"Ye don't like it?" Finn asked.

She blinked back tears as she picked up the brooch and ran her fingertip across the shiny black stones embedded in a circle made of silver. The irregular broken pieces of her onyx had been transformed into a thing of beauty.

"*Ach*, I knew I should have asked ye before I did this with your bag of stones," Finn said, misunderstanding her tears entirely. "I can melt it down and remove the stones."

Her throat was too tight for her to choke out words to reassure him, so she just put her arms around his neck and wept.

"Does this mean ye like it?" he asked.

When she nodded with her face buried in his chest, he enfolded her in his arms and kissed her hair.

"I wanted ye to wear your magical onyx for protection, as your mother intended, instead of hiding it in a bag under the mattress," he said. "The silver adds extra protection from witches and fairies."

"'Tis the most perfect gift you could ever give me," she said, and kissed him softly on the lips.

This was going well so far. Surely Margaret knew what he meant by this gift.

"I think," he said, and cleared his throat, "we ought to stop pretending we're husband and wife."

"Why?" she asked, her eyes going wide.

In for a penny, in for a pound. "We ought to pledge ourselves. Become truly handfasted."

Finn held his breath as he waited for her answer. He hoped she was not remembering that he'd offered this once before when he was just desperate to bed her. This time, he meant it. He wanted it with all his heart.

"Ye don't have to do this just because ye took me to bed," she said. "That's no reason."

"I'm asking because I want to take ye to bed for the rest of my life," he said. "I want ye to be my wife."

"We can't marry," she said softly, and touched his hand. "I'll not have ye bind yourself to me."

Finn felt as if he'd been kicked in the stomach.

"But I'm heir to Garty now," he said, sounding desperate to his own ears. "I can give you a home."

"A home you don't want," she said. "You told your mother you never wanted to see it again."

"I'd do it for you," he said, clasping her hands between his. "For you and Ella."

"You need a wife who can give you children," she said. "Especially now that you'll have a title and property, you need heirs, and I can't give them to you."

Finn knew what she really meant. He still was not good enough to be her husband. She put it as though she was refusing for his sake, but those were just words. Though she was different in other ways from Curstag and his mother, just like them, she would never willingly accept a husband beneath her.

"And you, Maggie? What do *you* need?" he asked, angry now. "A man to pleasure ye until ye find a husband who can give ye the kind of life ye had before?"

"I don't need a husband," she said. "And I want one even less."

"There is one thing ye do want from me, isn't there?" He pulled her against him and kissed her hard on the mouth. She melted into him, but he forced himself to release her.

He wanted everything from her—her head on the pillow beside him at night, her smile in the morning, her counsel in times of trouble. And most of all, he wanted her heart.

He wanted it all, and he wanted it every day for as long as he lived. And all she wanted from him, however, was a few nights of passion before leaving him. She could not love him.

That had gone terribly wrong. Margaret had not meant to wound Finn's feelings. She wanted to make him understand why she could not face the pain of marrying again, even to him. Perhaps to him most of all. She could not live through the years of always hoping she would become pregnant—and fearing it at the same time—and then suffering the disappointment, both hers and Finn's.

227

Perhaps if Finn knew how hard her miscarriages had been for her, it would help him understand her fears.

"Ye said ye hoped one day I'd trust ye enough to tell ye the whole story of when my pendant was shattered," she said. "If ye still want to know, I'll tell ye now."

He was silent, which she took as an aye. She wrapped a blanket around herself and went to the window to stare out at the sea. Then she began her sorry tale of being caught in Edinburgh during the Battle of the Causeway.

"Everyone knew trouble was brewing," she said. "I'd wanted to stay home, but William insisted I come with him to the city."

She winced as she remembered the sounds of the fighting outside the shuttered windows.

"My cousin Lizzie was with me," she said. "When I started to bleed, she went to fetch the midwife."

"The midwife?" he asked.

Lost in the terrible memories, she told him about losing the child and William returning soon after. She could not bear to repeat all the horrible things he'd shouted at her, especially the worst one.

At least it was just a girl.

"William was angry and smashed my pendant with his axe." Such a simple statement could not begin to convey the horror of that moment. Before she could finish her tale, Finn spoke and pulled her out of her memories.

"You were with child?" he asked.

Startled by his angry tone, Margaret turned around to face him.

"I thought ye could not conceive," he said. "Ye told me so yourself!"

"I never said that."

"Ye led me to believe it," he said. "Ye said your husband had your marriage annulled because ye couldn't give him an heir."

"I *couldn't* give him an heir," she said.

"If ye couldn't, then how is it ye were pregnant?"

"I lost the babe!" How thick headed could a man be?

"But if ye can conceive," he said, "that means ye could be carrying our child now."

Aye, and she would lose this one too. Tears stung her eyes, and she had to bite her lip to hold them back. She started for the

228

door. She had to get out and away from him before she broke down completely.

Finn caught her wrist and pulled her back. "Are ye with child now?"

"I don't know," she said, which she knew was a mistake the moment the words left her mouth. Why had she never learned to lie easily? She wrenched her arm free and went to the door.

"Ye can't go now," he said. "We need to talk about this...this...situation!"

"There's nothing to discuss," she said without turning around. "Ye needn't trouble yourself about me or the *situation*."

"But we must do something," he said, his voice full of alarm. "There's no choice now. Ye must marry me."

No choice? She *must* marry? When he used the same words as the men who had controlled and used her before, a burst of anger exploded in her chest.

"Nay, I don't have to," she said.

"Ye do," Finn said, leaning forward with his hands on his hips.

She would not be ordered to wed. She would not put herself under a man's thumb, to be told what to do and when and how. Never again.

"I'm going to my sister Sybil and the MacKenzies," she told him. "If you can't take me, I'll find someone who will."

Finn was so flummoxed by the news that Margaret could conceive—and might even now be carrying his child—that he was slow to grasp that she still actually intended to leave him.

When he heard her shut the door behind her with a firm *click*, he ran to catch her. He was so distracted, however, that he failed to notice his foot was tangled in the sheet.

"Ooomph!" He tripped and crashed to the floor. "Goddammit!" he shouted as he struggled to extract himself. Finally, he managed to wrap the torn sheet around himself and jerk open the door, but Margaret had already escaped into Una and Ella's chamber.

He knocked on the door with laudable restraint so as not to awaken Ella. This was not an argument the bairn should hear. But, no matter how much Margaret wished to avoid it, this was an argument they were going to have.

Rap, rap, rap. He knocked again, a wee bit louder. "I know ye can hear me," he said against the door.

"She won't speak to ye tonight." It was Una's voice. "Go back to bed and let the poor lass be."

The poor lass? He pounded a little louder.

Margaret opened the door just far enough to show her face.

"I understand all ye wanted from me was a bit of fun under the blankets," he said. "But the pretending is over. Ye will marry me!"

"I will not be forced to wed anyone ever again," she said.

"A child changes everything," he said, trying to make the damned woman see reason. "Whether either of us likes it or no, we're going to be wed."

"I've been through this before, and I can get through it again if I must," she said. "But I cannot do it with you. That would be more than I could bear."

"You've done this before?" he said. "What in the hell does that mean?"

"I've been with child three times. Each time, I miscarried," she said, speaking slowly as if to a slow-witted fool. "So there will be *no* child and *no* cause for us to marry."

With that, she shut the door and slammed the bar across it.

CHAPTER 27

Finn stomped into the stables intent on taking *Ceò* out for a hard gallop. Margaret had slept on Una's floor again last night and avoided him all day, not even showing her face at meals. She had never shown such stubbornness before. Apparently, she was not going to change her mind about marrying him.

"Finn!" he heard someone call to him from a dark corner of the stables.

He had his dirk ready in his hand but sheathed it when Una, of all people, emerged from the gloom.

"Your father needs to speak with ye today," she said.

"Ach, ye came out here to tell me that?"

"Mind your tone with me," she said as if he were still a bairn. Then she glanced behind them and said in a hushed voice, "I came to tell ye my grandson Lachlan has news from Dunrobin."

Lachlan was wise to be discreet and send a message through his grandmother. Until they knew every single person who either played a part in the poisoning or sent word of it to George Sinclair, they had to assume there could still be a traitor inside Helmsdale.

"News about Alex?" Finn asked.

"Aye," she whispered. "Lachlan is waiting for ye a half mile down the coastal trail."

For an old woman, Una could move quickly when she wanted. Before he could ask any more questions, she was gone.

He found Lachlan pacing beside the trail. After looking up and down the path to be sure no one was coming, Lachlan signaled for Finn to follow him behind a clump of aspen where he had tied his horse.

From Lachlan's grim expression, the news from Dunrobin was not good.

"What's happened?" Finn asked. "Is Alex all right?"

"I've learned that the Sinclairs plan to murder him," Lachlan said.

"Murder? Why would they do that?" Finn said. "They need Alex alive. 'Tis only through him that they have control of Sutherland."

"They don't need Alex if they have his heir."

"*Mìle marbhphàisg oirbh Sinclairs!*" *A thousand death shrouds on the Sinclairs!* "Barbara is with child?"

"It's her lover MacKay's," Lachlan said. "But the Sinclairs will claim it's Alex's and say the babe came early."

"How did ye hear this?" Finn asked.

"One of the Sinclair men got drunk and told a maidservant he was trying to bed," Lachlan said. "First chance she had to leave the castle, she came and told me."

"We can't wait any longer," Finn said. "We must rescue Alex."

"Aye," Lachlan said. "Ye can count on me and my clansmen."

"Good," Finn said, gripping Lachlan's shoulder.

Finn was glad he could rely on the Murrays, who were longstanding allies of the Gordons, bound by their mutual hatred of the Sinclairs. It went without saying that they would have to rescue Alex without the help of any men who were at Helmsdale at the time of the poisoning, including the Gordon guards.

"If we could get word to Alex," Finn said, "would he be able to meet us outside of the castle?"

"The Sinclairs never allow him to take a horse out," Lachlan said. "But I'm told they let him walk along the shore in front of the castle."

"Then we'll ask him to meet us on the strand, down the shore from the castle," Finn said. "We can have a boat waiting there and spirit him away."

"The problem is getting the message to Alex," Lachlan said. "We're asking him to take a big risk running for it from the beach. I wouldn't do it unless I got the message from someone I trusted."

"Aye, you or I need to go into Dunrobin," Finn said.

"Not you," Lachlan said. "George Sinclair and his family know ye too well."

"They'll not recognize me dressed as a peddler," Finn said, with a grin.

"'Tis too risky," Lachlan said, shaking his head.

"Alex trusts me and will do as I tell him," Finn said. "Besides that, I fostered with my uncle at Dunrobin and know the castle better than you."

"I should do it. They don't know my face like they know yours."

"Nay, it has to be me," Finn said. "I want to be the one to steal Alex out from under George's nose. That will make the victory all the sweeter."

After all the damn sitting and waiting, he could finally do something. He could save Alex. And he would.

Before leaving, Finn forced himself to climb the stairs to his father's chamber, where he found Una sitting beside the bed. He had to hide his shock when he saw his father. Gilbert had aged twenty years in the week since Bearach's death. His ruddy complexion had changed to a chalky pallor. Through years of heavy drinking, he'd retained a warrior's muscular build. But now, he looked hollowed out and caved in on himself as he lay on the bed.

"He wants to speak with ye alone," Una said, and gestured for Finn to take her seat next to the bed.

Finn sank into it, dreading another awkward talk with his father. His father's eyes flickered open when the door clicked shut behind Una.

"I'm here." Finn took his father's hand, something he could not remember doing even as a bairn.

"I must tell ye something before I die," his father said. "And don't tell me I'm not dying. I know I am."

Finn did not want to hear his father confess his regret that he had not done more for him, had not protected him from his mother's bile or done any of the other things a father should. None of it mattered now, but if it would ease his father's passing, Finn could not deny him.

"I'm listening," Finn said. "What is it ye wish to say to me?"

"The truth!" The force with which Finn's father expelled the word caused a coughing spell that racked his body.

Finn retrieved the cup Una had left on the small table and lifted his father up to help him drink.

"Make it whisky next time," his father said as he collapsed back on the pillows.

He lay still with his eyes closed for so long that Finn thought he had gone to sleep and Finn could leave. But then he opened his eyes again and said the last thing Finn expected.

"I'm not your father."

Finn wondered if in his weakened state his father did not recognize him.

"When I brought ye home as a wee newborn babe, I told Isabel ye were my bastard," his father said. "To save her pride, she agreed to pretend ye were hers, but she never forgave me."

Well, that explained a lot. Finn supposed that deep down he always suspected he was the bastard of one of the many women his father had on the side. He thought of how Margaret showered love on a child not her own, but Isabel was not capable of that.

"I know Isabel mistreated ye because of it," his father said. "But she would have killed ye in your cradle if she knew the truth."

"What truth?" Finn asked.

"The truth that your mother made me swear an oath on her deathbed to keep secret," he said. "Isabel was not the only one who would have wanted ye murdered if they knew."

Finn felt as if he were standing in the shallows, fighting to keep on his feet as wave after wave crashed into him. The mother whose angry resentment had shaped his life was not truly his mother. And the woman who gave birth to him was long since dead. He would never have a chance to know her.

"Who was she, this woman ye say was my mother?" Finn asked. Knowing his father, she was probably a poor tavern wench he barely knew.

"Isabel's sister."

"Her sister?" Finn was lucky he was already sitting down. "I didn't know she had a sister."

"Her name was Deirdre," his father said. "Our fathers were keen on making an alliance and arranged a marriage between us. She was the sister I was supposed to marry."

God's bones. Finn could hardly take it in.

"Deirdre was the most beautiful lass I'd ever seen," his father said with a wistfulness Finn had never heard in his voice before. "She was full of laughter. That lass had a sparkle in her eye that made ye believe your life would be golden if only ye could have her at your side."

"Ye loved her?" Finn asked.

"Aye, but Deirdre told me she wouldn't have me because she loved someone else," he said. "But as I said, it was all arranged."

Finn braced his elbows on his knees and ran his hands through his hair. What next?

"When Deirdre ran off with her lover, our fathers salvaged their alliance by making Isabel take her place as my bride."

Finn got up and started pacing the room. No wonder his father and mother were never happy. He was in love with her sister, and she knew it.

"So who did this Deirdre"—Finn could not yet call her his mother—"run off with?"

"Ye must remember hearing tales about your grandmother Sutherland's half-brother Robin, who was twenty years younger than she?"

"Aye. He claimed to be the rightful heir to Sutherland and took Dunrobin Castle twice." Finn had heard the tales all his life. The Sutherlands considered Robin a hero, while the Gordons labeled him a rebel.

"He was wild and fearless and darkly handsome." His father paused to cough and gasp for air. "What man could compete with that?"

"Are ye saying that's who she ran off with?" Finn asked. "But that would mean…"

"Aye. Robin Sutherland was your father."

"But how…" Finn had a hundred questions but could not seem to find the words. His head was spinning. His mother was not his mother. His father was not his father.

"Not long after Robin was finally captured and killed, I received an urgent message from Deirdre asking me to meet her at Duffus Castle in secret," his father said. "In truth, I got my hopes up she'd have me now that Robin was dead. When it came to Deirdre, I had no pride."

"Why Duffus Castle?"

"The Sutherlands, being Robin's clan, were protecting her," his father said. "Duffus himself was away, but his sister Mary, the one who was married to the Sinclair chieftain, was there. Mary warned me Deirdre was dying before she took me to see her."

235

Tears ran down his creased face, but his father—nay, Gilbert—either did not notice them or was past caring.

"Even near death, she was beautiful. She had a babe in her arms. She feared ye would never survive to be a man if it was known ye were Robin's son, with a claim to the earldom," Gilbert said. "Deirdre was a clever lass and had decided that the best way to protect her son from the Gordons was to make them believe you were one of them."

All this time, Finn was not a Gordon at all. He was hidden among them like a cuckoo hides its egg in another bird's nest.

"She begged me to raise ye as my son and made me swear not to reveal your true parentage," Gilbert said. "Once ye were grown, I was to tell ye and let you decide if ye wanted the world to know. She said it was to be your choice."

Finn had been grown for some time, but there was no point in saying that. If he'd known Gilbert and Isabel were not his parents, at least he would have understood why he never felt he belonged.

"I know I should have done better by ye," Gilbert said. "But I could see so much of both of them in ye that it pained me to look at ye. Still does."

"Who else knows the truth about who I am?" Finn asked.

"Mary Sutherland, of course, but that woman knew how to keep a secret," Gilbert said. "Mary put the word about that Deirdre and the babe both died in the birth. Una served as the midwife."

"Una?" Finn asked

"Aye, she married into the Murray clan, but she's a Sutherland by birth," Gilbert said. "There were others among the Sutherlands who had their suspicions that the babe was sneaked out of Duffus Castle and hidden away, but none of them would guess the babe was hidden with a Gordon."

"Does Isabel know?" Finn said.

"I told ye she doesn't," his father—or rather, Gilbert—said, but Finn was not convinced.

"It would be hard for a man to keep a secret like that from his wife for twenty-seven years," Finn said. Especially if the man was a drinker and his wife was Isabel. "I wouldn't blame ye if ye did tell her, but I need to know."

"Not telling her was the one thing I did right," Gilbert said. "In her eyes, your claim to the earldom, even if it was a failed cause, would give ye higher status than Bearach."

Isabel would have made him suffer all the more for that. Finn was grateful Gilbert had kept the secret from her.

"Why tell me now, after all this time?" Finn asked.

"Because ye have a choice now that Bearach is dead and Alex is a prisoner of the Sinclairs," Gilbert said. "Ye can say nothing of this and be heir to Garty, or ye can claim your place as the Earl of Sutherland."

Finn pressed the heels of his hands to his temples. This was too much to take in. He did not have a drop of Gordon blood in him. His true father was Robin Sutherland, the legendary rebel who was likely the rightful heir to Sutherland. And that made Finn...

"Nay," Finn said, shaking his head. "Alex is the earl now."

"I've kept this hidden since Deirdre gave it to me." Gilbert pulled a silk pouch from inside his shirt and held it out to Finn. "Here is your proof that you're Robin's son. It has his seal."

A surge of emotion clogged Finn's throat when he upended the bag and held the ring that had belonged to his true father.

"The earldom is yours for the taking," Gilbert said. "Ye have the better claim, and with Alex captive and too young to lead, the men would follow you."

Finn knew in his heart this was true. He could take it.

"If you were the earl," Gilbert said, "Dunrobin Castle and all the wealth of Sutherland would be yours."

Finn did not care about the wealth or the title or the power for himself. One thought, one truth alone, pounded in his head.

The Earl of Sutherland would be good enough for Lady Margaret Douglas.

Finn is the rightful heir to the earldom of Sutherland.

Margaret swayed on her feet and nearly dropped the pitcher before easing the door closed. She had not expected Finn to still be in his father's chamber when she opened the door quietly in case Gilbert was sleeping. Finn had told her he was in a hurry, and the two men rarely had more than two words to say to each other.

She should not have stayed to listen to their intimate conversation. But when she heard Gilbert say Finn was the son of Robin Sutherland, she could not tear herself away.

The news could not be worse.

The weight of disappointment crashing down on her made her realize she had harbored the hope that Finn could convince her to stay. But now, even more than before, she had to leave him.

Because she knew from bitter experience about men and their ambitions. She wanted to believe Finn was different, that he would not be willing to cast aside loyalty, honor, and those he loved. But if he would fight for a rival clan and kidnap an innocent woman for a chance to own a small bit of land, what would he do to gain the riches and power of an earldom?

The more power men had, the more they wanted—and the more casualties they left behind. Even if Finn tried to resist, an earl would inexorably be drawn into court intrigues and shifting alliances, the dangerous games of the most powerful men. She hated that life. If she had wanted it, she would have stayed with her brothers.

Even if she were willing, an earl's first duty was to sire heirs. Not having an heir with so much land and power at stake caused wars and chaos over succession. An earl could even claim it was his duty to set aside a barren wife. Finn may not know it now, but after fighting to gain an earldom, he would *want* a son to leave it to.

She leaned her head back against the wall. Somehow, the dream of a quiet and happy home with Finn and Ella and a love that lasted forever had crept into her heart without her knowing it and against her better judgment. If it was not utterly hopeless before, it was now.

She suddenly realized she had been standing outside the door far too long. Before she could gather her wits to run up the stairs, Finn opened the door.

"I was just going to see if your father needs anything," she managed to say.

"I have to leave Helmsdale for a bit," he said in a low voice. "I could be away for a few days."

She wondered if he was already going out to gather Sutherland men to his cause.

238

"I can't blame ye for not wanting to be my wife." He gripped her hand and stared intently into her eyes. "But promise me ye won't leave while I'm gone."

"Oh, Finn, it's not that I don't—" She cut herself off. The pain in his blue eyes tugged at her heart, but it would not serve either of them to tell him how she felt about him. "I'll be here when ye return. I promise."

"We'll talk then," he said. "If ye still want to leave me, I'll see ye safely to the MacKenzies."

He turned to go down the stairs. She just could not let him go yet.

"Finn!" she cried.

When he turned around, she threw herself into his arms and held him, not knowing if she would ever hold him like this again.

"Be careful," she said. "I'll be here waiting for you."

Before she broke down into tears, she released him and started up the stairs. When she was out of sight, she paused until she heard his footsteps, then she turned back for one last look.

"Goodbye, my love," she whispered as she watched Finn disappear down the stairs.

CHAPTER 28

Margaret surreptitiously wiped her tears away as she packed, hoping Ella would not see them. She wanted to be ready to leave when Finn returned.

Ella tugged at her skirts. "Why do ye weep?"

"Because it makes me sad to say goodbye to our new friends here," Margaret said, stooping down to talk to her daughter. "We're going to go live with my sister."

"Don't want to!" Ella said and stamped her foot.

Margaret was taken aback. Ella was always so compliant. She'd hoped that Ella would feel safe enough to throw a tantrum like other children did on occasion, but now was not the best time.

"I know, sweetling," Margaret said. "But sometimes we must do things we don't want to."

"Want to stay here!" Ella shouted, clenching her little fists.

"What's all this blathering about?" Una said from the doorway.

Ella ran to Una and wrapped her arms around her leg. When the old woman picked her up, Ella buried her face in Una's chest and refused to look at Margaret.

"I see you're packing again." Una narrowed her eyes at the satchel, then turned her glare on Margaret. "You'd leave Finn now? *Ach*, I thought better of ye."

With that, she turned around and took Ella into her chamber. Margaret swallowed back her tears over Ella's rejection and took several deep breaths to calm herself. Before she lost her will to leave, she reminded herself of the long, dark hair she found in the bedclothes, a hair too long to be Finn's. She was not mistaken as to whose it was. Even the pillow smelled of Curstag.

When she finished packing, Margaret carried the satchel beneath her cloak down to the stables, where she hid it beneath some straw. She did not want the household to find out she was leaving before Finn returned, but having her bag packed and waiting helped her feel committed to her plan.

She went back upstairs and rapped on Una's door to fetch her daughter.

"Hush," Una said, sticking her head out. "The poor dearie has cried herself to sleep."

Margaret sighed. *Why not just stab me in the heart, Una?*

"Enough of this," Una said under her breath. Then she came out, shut the door behind her, and signaled for Margaret to follow her into the other chamber. "Now, tell me what foolishness has gotten into your head this time."

When Margaret told her about finding Curstag's hair in their bed, Una dismissed it with a wave of her hand, as if swatting at a fly.

"Curstag was probably snooping," Una said. "She's a nosey lass, that one."

"Snooping in the bedclothes?" Margaret said. "I've seen her in Finn's arms more than once. I tried to dismiss it as comforting the widow, but I don't believe Curstag is grieving all that much."

"That's true enough," Una said with a laugh. "I wouldn't be surprised if she poisoned Bearach herself."

"Don't say that," Margaret chided.

"Curstag goes after what she wants, which is a lesson ye could learn from her," Una said. "But this isn't really about Curstag, now is it? Tell me what's truly troubling ye."

Margaret hesitated to unburden herself and share her pain and shame.

"I can't give him children," Margaret finally said in a small voice.

"I knew from the start that ye didn't give birth to Ella because the two of ye were still learning each other's ways," Una said, her tone gentle now. "But tell me about these babes ye lost."

"How did ye know about them?" Margaret asked.

"I saw them when ye were in the healing waters of the faery pool."

Margaret blinked. Before she could ask how, Una began pressing her with questions about the times she was with child. The old woman clucked her tongue as Margaret admitted how very thin she became during her marriage, how she'd lost a babe during the stress of a raging battle, and how her husband had not waited for her to recover from that miscarriage before she became pregnant that last time.

"I'm an old wise woman, so pay attention," Una said. "Ye were not meant to have a child with that devil. But that doesn't mean ye can't have one."

"I can't go through that again," Margaret said, shaking her head. "And I can't put Finn through it, either."

"You're a strong and healthy lass now," Una said. "You've meat on your bones and a glow to your cheeks."

She had gained weight, it was true. And she had not felt so well in years.

"At the faery pool, I saw the children ye lost," Una said in a hushed voice. "And they were smiling because, like me, they saw ye with a babe in your arms."

Margaret took the handkerchief Una handed her and blew her nose.

"Even if ye don't believe ye can have children," Una said, resting her hand on Margaret's arm, "ye ought to let Finn make his choice."

"What he chooses now will be different from the choice he makes later." Margaret turned to face Una. "I know he's heir to the earldom. I heard Gilbert tell him."

"He should have told Finn long ago," Una said. "Finn is like his true father. Once Robin found the lass he wanted, he was true until death."

Margaret refrained from pointing out that Robin Sutherland had died young and before he gained the earldom.

"You're still afraid Finn will fail ye," Una said.

"How do I know he won't?" Margaret asked.

"Faith," Una said. "Ye must decide to trust him."

###

After wasting half the day fretting and stewing over what to do when Finn returned, Margaret decided she may as well be useful. She had not visited Gilbert as she had intended to earlier, so she picked up the same pitcher of water and headed down the stairs.

"Kind of ye to visit me," Gilbert said as she fluffed his pillows for him. "You're a surprise. Not at all the sort of lass any of us thought Finn would marry."

"I suppose not," she said, hoping he would drop the subject.

"Doesn't follow his head, but his heart," he said in a faraway voice. "I should have known he would."

She did not want to hear it now. "Is there anything I can get for ye before I go?" she asked. "How about something from the kitchen?"

"My blood's gone thin." He pointed at the large trunk at the bottom of the bed. "I believe you'll find an extra blanket in there."

It was a chilly day. Margaret should have thought to ask if he was cold. The lid of the chest was so heavy that she had to kneel to lift it.

"Here it is," she said, happy to find the blanket right on top.

"And if ye don't mind," he said, "I slipped an extra flask of my brother's best whisky in the bottom before we left Dunrobin."

Margaret rolled her eyes. This was what Gilbert had really wanted her to open the chest for. She felt uneasy about rummaging around Isabel's gowns and stockings and tried to move them as little as possible as she reached down along the sides in search of the damned flask.

At last, her fingers touched the smooth, hard surface of the whisky flask. When she pulled it out, however, it was not a regular flask, but a wide-mouthed jar with a stoppered top.

She opened it to see if he'd poured whisky into it. Instead of a liquid, it contained the long stems of a dried plant with distinctive yellow flowers. Her blood ran cold.

Henbane. Had she found the killer? Her hand shook as she quickly replaced the jar deep inside the trunk.

"The whisky isn't here," she said as she smoothed the gowns back into place over the jar. "Ye must have already drunk it."

Gilbert would not have asked her to look in the trunk if he had put the henbane there. That meant the murderer had to be…

Her heart leaped to her throat when she heard the door opening.

She dropped the lid of the trunk closed and looked up into Isabel's piercing black eyes.

Finn pulled the worn cap low over his eyes, slumped his shoulders, and led his peddler's mule and cart up to the gate of Dunrobin Castle. As he passed under the arched entry, he glanced up and wondered if his head would soon be displayed on a pike there, just like the father he never knew.

He pushed aside Gilbert's revelations about his true parentage and his troubles with Margaret, which had plagued his thoughts all the way here, to focus on the problem at hand—and not a moment too soon.

Across the castle yard, he saw two familiar figures headed straight toward him. They were none other than George Sinclair and his daughter Barbara. What bad luck. Saying a silent prayer that a peddler would not draw their attention, he turned the cart with slow, plodding steps.

Before long, he had a line of people waiting to buy or trade. Apparently, he had given his first customers too fine a bargain. How was he supposed to know how much to ask for a spoon or a ribbon? When he recognized two lasses he had slept with in the line, he pulled his cap low and regretted his pride in insisting on bringing the message into Dunrobin himself. But whether it was the ragged clothes or the false belly he'd given himself, the two lasses barely looked at him when they paid their pennies.

The line was gone, and he'd still not caught a glimpse of Alex when a rough-looking man with a real potbelly dragged a wee dog up to his cart.

"Lost my eating knife," the man said. "Will ye trade this dog for one? He has a good nose for hunting vermin."

The dog was a yappy terrier with one eye and matted fur. Finn had never seen such a pathetic looking creature.

"Shut up!" the man said, and tried to kick at the dog, but the terrier was too quick.

"Kick my dog again, and I'll flatten ye," Finn said, grabbing the rope from the man. "Now pick out your damned knife."

The dog attracted another customer. Finn hid his excitement as Alex approached the cart. Finn chose his moment when Alex leaned down to pat the dog and his face was hidden from anyone passing by.

"Don't look up," Finn said. "'Tis me, Finn."

Alex froze a moment, but then he had the sense to rub the dog's ears as Finn quickly told him of the danger he was in and the plan to rescue him.

"I knew you'd come for me," Alex said in a choked voice. "I'll leave supper early and meet ye while the others are still eating."

"Good," Finn said. "You'd better go now before someone gets suspicious."

To make sure no one connected Alex visiting his cart with his departure, Finn waited another half-hour before slowly rolling his cart toward the gate with his new dog trailing beside him. As he passed under the iron portcullis at the gate, he felt a prickle at the back of his neck. When he glanced over his shoulder, sweat broke out on his brow and palms.

Barbara Sinclair was standing in the middle of the courtyard with her head cocked to the side and her cold gray gaze fixed on his back.

"Good day to ye, Isabel." Margaret pasted on a pleasant smile on her face and got up from her knees holding the blanket. "Your husband was chilled and asked me to fetch this from your trunk."

Her years of protecting herself by hiding her feelings behind a smooth mask saved her from showing how scared she was. She told herself that so long as she gave Isabel no cause to believe she had discovered the henbane, she would get out of this room.

"Just what I needed," Gilbert said, giving her a wink as she spread the blanket over him.

Thankfully, Gilbert did not want his wife to know he'd had Margaret searching for his secret flask of whisky any more than she did.

"If there's nothing else ye need, I'll be on my way," Margaret said, meeting Isabel's icy stare with another bland smile.

Margaret's heart pounded as she forced herself to walk in measured steps past Isabel to the open doorway. As she crossed the threshold, alarm shot through her body, urging her to *run, run, run!* Instead, she hummed a tune and climbed the first step as she imagined Isabel coming up behind her with a long blade.

Isabel had already brazenly murdered people close to her, so she would have no qualms about eliminating another threat. Margaret's breathing seemed unnaturally loud as she strained to hear movement inside the chamber behind her. Now she imagined Isabel in the center of the chamber, standing as still as a stone and listening, just as Margaret was, for some sign that would reveal what the other knew.

At last, Margaret reached Una and Ella's door. Her pulse jumped when the latch made a soft *click* as she lifted it. Moving quickly, she slipped inside and drew the bar across the door.

Una dropped her stitching in her lap, and Ella stopped playing with her rag doll. Neither moved nor made a sound as they fixed their gazes on Margaret. These two, one old and one young, had acquired a keen sense for danger.

Sweat beaded on Margaret's forehead as she leaned her ear against the door. When she heard no footsteps coming up the stairs, she picked up Ella and held her close.

"Don't be frightened, sweetling. Everything will be all right, but can ye find your shoes and put them on for me?" Margaret said, then she lifted her gaze to meet Una's. "We need to leave the castle *now*.

While Ella struggled with her shoes, Margaret quickly told Una about finding the henbane.

"I suppose the wicked woman was gathering it when we saw her that day in the wood with her basket," Una said. "And she made that vinegary tincture for Bearach. Vinegar is used in many cures, but vinegar and mulberry leaves is for henbane poisoning."

"I don't think Isabel knows I saw the henbane in the trunk," Margaret said.

"If she even suspects you've found her out," Una said, "'tis not safe for ye here."

"Then 'tis not safe for you, either," Margaret said. "She'll assume I told ye."

"We'll go to my grandson Lachlan's cottage and wait for him and Finn there," Una said. "It will be no easy task, but Finn will see that justice is done."

"It will be hard for him to learn that the woman who raised him would do such a thing," Margaret said. "And she's probably already thrown the henbane down the privy."

"What I meant is that it will be hard because Isabel will claim you're the poisoner," Una said. "Someone has already planted that seed. It hasn't taken hold yet because the servants like ye. But I've heard whispers that you're a spy for the Sinclairs."

"Me? Why would anyone think that?"

"You're a stranger among us," Una said. "After no lass in Sutherland could capture Finn's heart—and many of them tried—he comes home bewitched by a mysterious lass who claims she has no clan."

Margaret swallowed hard. She was the perfect scapegoat.

"Of course, it will be far easier for her to blame ye if you're dead," Una said. "So let's be on our way."

"We shouldn't go together," Margaret said. "I want ye to take Ella first—pretend you're taking her to pick herbs and flowers, as usual. If I'm not with ye, Isabel will have no reason to follow ye."

Una nodded.

"I'll wait an hour and meet ye at your grandson's," Margaret continued. "Don't worry if I'm late. I'll have to wait until I can get away without being seen."

"Just be sure to come before dark," Una said. "If ye wander off the trail, ye can fall into a bog and never be seen again."

After sharing that unsettling bit of advice, Una donned her cloak and picked up the basket she used to gather herbs.

Margaret lifted Ella into her arms and kissed her on both cheeks.

"What's wrong, *a mamaidh?*" *Momma,* Ella asked.

It was the first time Ella had called her that. Margaret was already struggling to hold back tears and nearly lost the battle, but she sniffed and managed a smile.

"I'll be fine. Mind Una for me, and I'll join ye soon." She gave Ella one last hug. "I love ye with all my heart, my sweet daughter."

She watched Una and Ella until they were out of sight down the stairs, then went to the window to wait for them to emerge into the castle yard. The elderly nursemaid and her young charge gathered herbs and flowers most days, so no one should take notice of them. All the same, Margaret bit her lip until it bled as the pair slowly made their way to the gate. She continued watching long after they left the castle and entered the wood to be sure no one followed them.

Relieved that they were well on their way to safety, Margaret left their chamber and went into hers and Finn's to wait. When she shut the door behind her, it seemed so empty without Finn. How she wished he was here now. She always felt safe with him.

It was a chilly day and one of the servants had been thoughtful enough to pile extra peat on the brazier and start a fire. Margaret donned her boots and cloak, sat on the bed, and drummed her fingers. Perhaps she did not need to wait a full hour…

After a while, the heat made her feel so sleepy. She tossed off her cloak. Perhaps she should rest a bit while she waited…

She woke up with her head hanging over the side of the bed. On the floor beneath her, Ella's rag doll peeked out from under the edge of the bed. Ella would be upset that she left it. When Margaret tried to get up to pick it up, she rolled off the bed and crashed onto the floor. She blinked, attempting to clear her vision. But it only grew worse.

Her body felt so heavy. Something was wrong with her. What was it? The answer was there, just outside her reach…

CHAPTER 29

Margaret saw the old rag doll beside her on the floor and clutched it in her hand. *Ella. Ella was waiting for her.* She had to get to her daughter. She struggled to get up, but the floor tilted, and her limbs refused to obey her.

She had to get out…had to get to Ella. She pulled herself along the floor to the door. Though she strained with all her might, she was unable to lift herself high enough to reach the latch. She collapsed with her face pressed between the floor and the base of the door.

A draft from the stairwell blew through the crack onto her face, and she drew in deep breaths of the sweet, cool air. *Poison. Murder.* She felt as if she was sinking into a bog as she struggled to grasp the fleeting thoughts floating through her head and put them together.

Isabel. A few more deep breaths through the crack under the door, and she remembered what Isabel had done.

Poison. That was the answer she'd been searching for. She'd been poisoned.

Death was coming for her in this chamber.

With a surge of strength, she crawled up the door and shoved the bar back. When the door fell open, she fell onto the stone floor of the stairwell. The metallic taste of blood was in her mouth and her elbow throbbed, but she forced herself to her hands and knees.

She did not know how Isabel had done this to her—but she knew she would come back to make certain her dark deed had succeeded.

Isabel is coming for me.

Margaret refused to die here. Her daughter needed her. And she needed Finn. She needed to tell him she loved him. Holding on to the wall, she fought a wave of dizziness as she stumbled to her feet. Her head and elbow throbbed from her falls, but the pain helped keep her alert as she slowly made her way down the stairs.

Somehow, she found herself at the gate with no memory of crossing the hall or the courtyard.

"Are ye all right, Mistress Margaret?" a guard asked as he peered into her face.

She nodded.

"Will be dark soon, and the weather is turning," he said, looking off at the horizon. "Don't be long."

"I must hurry," she said, her voice sounding faraway to her own ears.

Concentrating on keeping her walk steady, she made her way into the wood. She felt her senses slowly returning as she followed the path through the wood until it opened up onto the vast moorland. She shivered in the wind and realized she had left her cloak behind.

It was growing dark. Remembering Una's advice, Margaret kept her eyes on her feet and quickened her pace. As she hurried along, she tried to figure out just how she had been poisoned. She remembered how hot it was in the chamber and the extra peat on the brazier. It would not be difficult to add a powdered poison to the peat that gave off noxious fumes when burned. If Isabel had acted quickly, she could have done it while Margaret talked with Una in the other chamber. She had already shown herself to be a decisive killer.

Margaret came to an abrupt halt when she suddenly found herself on the edge of a deep chasm, a giant fracture that split the earth in front of her. She must have veered off the path, and she had no notion how long ago she'd left it. How could she make such a mistake?

Her heart beat frantically in her chest as she scanned the horizon, searching for the path or a landmark of some kind. But there was barely any light left, and this land of peat and bog seemed to stretch forever in a dark, beautiful sameness.

When she heard a rustling behind her, she whirled around.

Piercing black eyes set against white skin filled Margaret's vision for an instant before Isabel shoved her. Margaret screamed and flailed her arms as she fell backward into a black abyss.

Finn and Lachlan stood side by side staring up the shoreline. Alex was two hours late, and Finn was worried he would not make it.

"We'll take him to Dornoch Castle," Lachlan said. "He should be safe there. Even the Sinclairs would not dare to attack a bishop's home."

Dornoch belonged to the Bishop of Caithness, the Gordon ally who most likely procured the murder of Duffus of Sutherland as a favor to Alex's father. It was the closest safe place to take Alex.

"We'll have to move him from there as soon as we can," Finn said. "A bishop isn't good enough to protect Alex for long. He needs an earl."

Finn did not trust the bishop to withstand pressure from both the Sinclairs and the King's Council to return Alex to his guardian. And from what Margaret had told him, it would take another earl to challenge George Sinclair for the guardianship.

"Take him to the Earl of Moray," Finn said. "He'll see that Alex gets to Huntly Castle, where he'll be safe in the midst of Gordon lands."

"Looks like Alex won't make it today," Lachlan said, and clasped Finn's shoulder. "We'll come back and hope he makes it out tomorrow. Let's tell the men waiting with the boat to make camp."

"Wait, there he is!" Finn said, pointing as a figure emerged in the distance, coming toward them at a dead run.

Finn ran down the beach with his new dog yapping at his heels and lifted his cousin off his feet in a bear hug.

"I heard shouts behind me," Alex said, looking over his shoulder.

Finn and Lachlan pulled him off the beach and onto a trail that cut across the headland to the inlet on the other side, where the boat was hidden.

"I see ye kept the dog," Alex said as they ran along the trail.

"I'm giving him to Ella," Finn said. "A bairn should have a dog."

"She'll like him," Alex said. "He's as raggedy as her doll."

The first half of the trail was uphill. When they reached the top and Finn had a good view of the shoreline on both sides of the headland, he stopped.

"Lachlan will take ye to Dornoch," he told Alex. "I'll keep watch and divert the Sinclairs if need be while ye get away."

Finn lifted Alex's cap off his head and put it on, covering his hair as best he could. Though he was considerably taller than his cousin, people generally saw what they expected to see. The Sinclairs did not know yet that Alex had friends meeting him and were likely to follow a lone man running away from them.

"You're not coming with me?" Alex said.

"Lachlan will see ye safe." Finn gripped his cousin's shoulders and gave him a wink. "Remember, I've got a bonny bride waiting for me to come home."

She was waiting to leave him, but Alex did not need to know that.

"Ye ought to get rid of that dog," Lachlan said, "or he'll give ye away."

"*Ach*, no, he'll be quiet as a mouse, won't ye?" Finn said.

The dog barked in response—not a good sign.

"Hurry now!" Finn said.

He watched Alex and Lachlan scurry down the backside of the hill toward the cove where the boat was hidden. Luckily, the sky was growing dark with the coming storm, so they should be able to slip down the coast to Dornoch without being seen.

When Finn looked back the other way, he cursed. A line of men was on the shore coming from Dunrobin. He picked up the wee dog and put him in the bag he had slung over his shoulder and waited for the Sinclair men to spot him.

It did not take long. When he ran inland along the ridge, the Sinclairs started up the hill toward him. He could see Alex and Lachlan still scrambling down the hillside to the boat. *Run faster, dammit!* If the Sinclairs reached the top of the hill and saw them, Alex and Lachlan could not get to the boat and sail away before the Sinclairs raced down the hill and shot their arrows into the boat.

Finn had to keep the Sinclair warriors from cresting the hill, so he dropped down to their side. He shifted direction from side to side, but always making sure they could see him.

He glanced over his shoulder and grinned when he saw that every one of them was following him. Ha, George Sinclair was going to be furious when he learned Alex had escaped. Finn might not escape himself, but he would lead these Sinclairs on a good chase.

Margaret screamed as she bounced against the rock walls of the crevice. With a final, jarring thump, she landed in a heap at the bottom. She hit so hard it knocked the breath out of her. For one terrifying moment, she could not suck in air, then she gasped as pain hit her like an anvil.

Far above her, she could just make out against the night sky the darker outline of a figure leaning over the opening. Clenching her teeth to keep from moaning, Margaret forced herself to remain still. Though it was too dark at the bottom for Isabel to see her clearly, she could feel Isabel's cold gaze watching for movement.

How long would the wretched woman wait to be sure?

Finally, the figure disappeared. Isabel must have been satisfied that Margaret was either dead or too badly injured to survive. Or perhaps she was convinced Margaret could not escape and would die a slow death.

When the initial shock of pain subsided, she sat up and ran her hands over her body, checking for injuries. She was bleeding from cuts and scratches, her knee and hip were badly bruised, and her ankle was already swelling. Miraculously, nothing seemed broken, but every part of her body ached and throbbed. When she tried to stand, she could not put weight on the leg with the injured ankle.

The realization hit her that no one would find her here. Una was the only one who knew she'd taken the path to Lachlan's cottage. And she'd gone off the path, so even Una would not know where to look. If Margaret had any hope of surviving, she had to climb out.

Raindrops hit her face as she looked up at the daunting distance to the jagged edge of her prison. Then thunder cracked, and lightning filled the chasm with a flash of light, briefly revealing the steep wall of rock she had to climb. If she wanted to survive, she had to try.

Feeling her way up the wall for clefts and cracks, she started climbing. Gritting her teeth each time she had to put weight on her injured leg, she made her way up several feet. Reaching up, she grasped a brush growing out of the rock. As she pulled herself up, the brush came loose in her hand. She screamed as she careened down the side.

When she hit the ground, the pain in her ankle shot up her leg and nearly blinded her. Shaken and gasping for breath, she dropped her head onto her knees. She would have to wait until morning when she could see to climb before risking it again.

She clutched her knees, shivering against the cold. Her gown was wet from the rain and clung to her skin.

With a long night ahead of her, she had nothing to do but dwell on her regrets. When Finn returned and could not find her, he would think she had left him. She had told him she would. How could she have been so foolish? Rather than risk pain, she had thrown away happiness for them both.

She could die in this black hole. If she had the chance again, she would not waste another hour that she could have with him. Her only comfort was knowing Finn would take care of Ella. She had no doubt he would. If only she could be with them…

She felt a prick against her skin and looked down to find the brooch Finn had made for her with the broken bits of onyx hanging by a thread from her torn bodice. Bursting into tears, she clutched it in her hand and prayed Finn knew how much she loved him.

Exhausted, she rested her head against the cold wall of rock. She awoke some time later to the sensation of ice-cold water on her feet. Scooting away from the puddle of rain that had collected there, she felt around her for a drier spot.

Water was all around her.

Fearing the worst, she tasted her wet fingers. They were salty. She tried to remember how close the trail had been to the sea. *Too close.*

Panic closed her throat. Her rocky prison was filling with the incoming tide, and she had no way out.

CHAPTER 30

Finn walked the last few miles back to Helmsdale with rain and wind pelting his face like accusations. Now that Alex was safely away and Finn had lost the Sinclair men following him, he could no longer avoid thinking about his mistakes with Margaret.

With time and distance, he recognized that he could have responded better to the revelation that she was able to conceive a child. And he definitely should not have shouted at her and told her she *had* to marry him. That was not at all how he planned his marriage proposal to go.

He'd forgotten all about the wee dog until he whimpered.

"What do you have to complain about?" he said as he reached in to pat the dog. "You're warm and dry in there."

After another mile, he thought about the miscarriage she suffered during the Battle of the Causeway. It can't have been easy for her to share her pain from that day, and all he could hear at the time was that she was not barren. He thought she'd lied to him.

For the first time, it occurred to him that perhaps she had not rejected him because he was not good enough or because she did not care, but because she was afraid. Afraid of being under a man's authority again. Afraid of being mistreated and taken advantage of. Afraid of losing a child again. Afraid of being abandoned.

After what she'd been through, he should have known, but he'd been blinded by his own past. Though he pretended his family's rejection and Curstag's betrayal did not affect him, they made him believe he was unworthy of love and could never truly belong.

What if Margaret was with child now? His child. Surely many women who had miscarriages also had healthy children.

God knew he never expected to be a father, and Gilbert had set a poor example. But Finn would try his best. He wanted to be the kind of father he did not have. The kind who saw the good in his children, who laughed with them, and who was always there for them when troubles came.

But if Margaret lost the child, he could not bear for her to suffer alone. He needed to be with her, no matter what happened.

He leaned into the wind. The storm had not let up, and it was full dark now. He could not explain it, but an uneasy feeling settled in the pit of his stomach. A warrior learned to trust his instincts, and his instincts told him Margaret was in danger.

He started to run. He did not stop until he reached Helmsdale. He was out of breath as he passed through the gate.

"Finn—" The guard tried to speak to him, but Finn ignored him and continued across the yard without pausing.

Though he tried to tell himself he had no cause to fear for Margaret's safety, his pulse pounded, *find her, find her, FIND HER!* He burst into the hall, but she was not there. He took the stairs at a dead run.

When he opened the door to their chamber, it was empty. His stomach dropped to the floor when he saw that all her belongings were gone. He opened the door to Una's chamber and found it empty too. He sat down on the bed he'd shared with Margaret and held his head in his hands.

She had left him.

He was overwhelmed with regret. Regret that he had not told her he loved her. Regret that he had not made the most of every moment he had with her. Regret that they would not live to old age together and watch Ella and the other children they might have grow up.

The dog poked his head out of the bag and nudged Finn with his paw, as if prodding him to get up and do something. Here he was wallowing in remorse when Margaret could be in danger.

Even if she still wanted to leave him, she promised not to go before he returned. Something must have happened to make her decide she could not wait for him. Margaret would not break her word lightly, so that something must have been serious and unexpected.

And *how* did she leave? A beautiful woman like Margaret could always persuade some man to take her where she wanted to go. But would the man she chose keep her safe? Would *he* be a danger to her? Margaret was altogether too trusting.

Finn needed to find her and make sure she was safe. If she did not want to come back with him, he would see her safely to the MacKenzies himself. He started for the door, but something on the floor just under the edge of the bed caught his eye.

His hand shook as he picked up Ella's rag doll. The wee bairn had carried it across half of Scotland and could not sleep without it. They must have been in a terrible hurry to leave without it. He examined the room more closely now, looking for clues, and found Margaret's cloak wedged between the bed and wall. *O shluagh*, she had gone out on this cold and stormy night without it.

He was more certain than ever that something terrible had happened. Moving quickly, he tucked his axe in his belt, gathered her cloak and the other things he might need, and ran down the stairs to the hall.

"Has anyone seen my wife?" he shouted at the group gathered around the hearth.

Everyone, except for Isabel and Curstag, shifted their gazes to the floor or the ceiling, anywhere but at him. Curstag gave him a pitying smile and drew him aside.

"How well do ye really know this Maggie?" she asked.

"Why would ye ask that now?"

"I want ye to hear this from a friend who cares about ye," she said. "I'm afraid there's speculation about her since she disappeared tonight."

"Speculation of what?" he demanded, though he could guess that they all thought she'd run off with another man.

"I'm not saying I believe it," Curstag said in a hushed voice, as if everyone in the hall did not already know what she was about to tell him. "I like to see the best in people, but her sneaking away does appear to prove it."

"Prove what?" Goddammit, would the woman not get to the point?

"That your mysterious bride is the one who did it, of course," she said.

"I've no time for your games." Finn resisted the urge to shake her. "Speak plainly."

"They're saying Maggie is the murderer," Curstag said. "She used ye, and now that the black deed is done, she's gone and left ye."

"She is no murderer." He turned and shouted at the others, "I need men to help me search for my wife!"

He waited for someone to come forward. None did.

257

"There's no sense in looking for her till daylight," one of the men ventured. "Even if she's out there, we won't find her tonight in this storm."

Between the darkness and the storm, the odds were against finding her. But what these men were really thinking was that, whether Margaret was the murderer of no, she had left him and did not want to be found.

Belatedly, it occurred to Finn that someone in this room could be the reason she left in a rush without her cloak and Ella's doll. He could not take any of them with him, even if they offered. He needed to do this alone.

When he reached the gate, the guard was there.

"I was here when your wife left," he said. "She didn't seem right to me."

"What do ye mean, not right?"

"At first, I thought she'd had a few too many nips of whisky, but I don't believe that was it," the guard said, drawing his brows together. "Usually she greets everyone with a smile and a few words, but she was real quiet-like and acted as if she did not really see me."

"Did she say anything?"

"Just one thing," he said, after pausing to think. "After I told her the weather was turning bad, she said, 'I must hurry.'"

Was Margaret in a hurry because of the weather or some other reason?

"I was surprised to see her without that wee lassie of hers," the guard said.

"Ella wasn't with her?" Finn asked, alarm coursing through his body. "You're sure?"

"Aye," the guard said. "I saw Una take the bairn out in the afternoon, but I assumed they'd come back long since."

Questions swirled in Finn's head as he saddled *Ceò*. Was Margaret worried because Una and Ella were late returning with a storm brewing? If so, why had she not alerted the men and asked them to help her look for them? Instead, she had slipped out quietly on her own as it was growing dark without mentioning to the guard that they were still out and she was going to fetch them.

The guard said she acted strangely. Was she ill? Afraid?

Finn wondered again if she was trying to evade someone, to leave without that someone realizing she did not intend to return. If anyone saw her leave without Ella, they would assume she was going out for a short time, not departing. The same was true if they saw Una and Ella go out.

Why the subterfuge? As Finn was away at the time, it could not be him Margaret was attempting to evade. Who was she afraid of? And in this storm, where would she go?

He had to think. If Una was helping Margaret and Ella escape, he thought he knew where the old nursemaid would take them. He hoped to God he was right and that they were not out in this storm without shelter.

"We'll see if you're a hunter," he said, holding Margaret's cloak to the dog's nose. "Help me find her."

He tucked the dog inside the fold of his plaid with Ella's ragdoll then led *Ceò* out into the driving rain. Holding the lantern in front of him, he followed the path that led to Lachlan's cottage. It was four miles, a fair distance for an old woman with a young bairn, but Una knew every inch from walking it for sixty-odd years. And unlike Margaret, Una and Ella had left in daylight and before the storm.

Every few yards he called Margaret's name and paused, hoping to hear a response over the sound of the rough sea pounding against the cliffs.

Ruff! Ruff! Ruff! The wee dog stuck his head out of Finn's cloak and barked.

"What is it, laddie?"

The dog leaped down and sniffed frantically around Finn's feet. Before Finn could grab him, he darted off the path into the darkness. Where in the hell was he going?

"Get back here," Finn shouted.

Ruff! Ruff!

Ice lodged in Finn's heart. Surely, Margaret knew better than to wander off the path in the dark. But she was not from Sutherland. Had he warned her about the danger of the bogs here in the flow country? He could not remember.

Ruff! Ruff!

Finn went after the dog, stepping through thick gorse and slipping on moss-covered rocks. If the dog was chasing a damned rabbit, Finn was losing precious time—not to mention risking falling into a bog himself—but he had to take the chance that the dog had picked up Margaret or Ella's scent.

Surely, Margaret could not have gone more than a few feet before realizing she'd gone off the trail. He raised the lantern and peered through the rain but saw nothing that could give her shelter and entice her to come this way with darkness falling and the storm growing worse.

Annoyed with himself for letting the dog divert him, he turned around.

###

The sea had reached Margaret's perch on the highest part of the rocky floor and lapped around her as she lay curled on her side. But Margaret felt at peace. She was not cold anymore. She had ceased to feel her body some time ago.

As she felt herself drifting away, she saw Finn holding her sweet Ella on his lap. That made her heart glad—until she saw that Ella was weeping and Finn's face was etched with grief. When she tried to reach for them, she floated farther and farther away…

Maggie! Maggie! In her dream, she heard Finn calling to her. His voice was far away. She wanted to get up and look for him, but her body was so very heavy…

And she could not hear him anymore.

CHAPTER 31

"Damn it!" Finn nearly fell when he tripped over the damned dog. He thought the dog had not meant to do it, but then the wee thing growled and clamped its teeth on the back of Finn's boot.

"All right," he said, turning around. "I'll follow ye a bit farther."

When the dog ran ahead, nose to the ground, excitement grew in Finn's chest. Perhaps the dog had found Margaret's scent after all.

Luckily, the dog sat and waited for him in front of a giant crevice that split the ground, or Finn might have not seen it in time and fallen into the dark chasm. If Margaret did come this way, she would have to walk around this crevice in one direction or the other.

"Which way did she go? Show me!" he said, but the dog just jumped up and down barking.

Finn's blood ran cold when the thought struck him that Margaret could have fallen down there. Leaning forward, he held the lantern over the edge, but the light did not reach the bottom.

"Margaret!" he called, even while he prayed she was not down there but safe at Lachlan's cottage. "Maggie! Maggie!"

He lay flat on his belly and held the lantern as low as he could reach. On a scrub growing out of the rock several feet below him, a torn piece of cloth fluttered in the wind. He squeezed his eyes shut. *Mother, Mary of God, please help me. My Maggie is down there.*

He would not let himself think she was dead. She was hurt, and he needed to get to her.

"Maggie," he shouted again. "I'm coming down for ye!"

He retrieved his rope from *Ceò*'s saddle and, holding his lantern up, squinted into the driving rain, searching for a bolder or tree to tie it to. There was nothing nearby but clumps of brush.

"*Ceò*," he said, rubbing his horse's neck. "This will not be easy, but we need to save her."

After he tied one end of the rope to *Ceò*'s saddle, Finn hooked the lantern's handle over his arm so that his hands were free to hold the rope. Then he stepped backward over the edge and started down, letting the rope slide through his hands as he walked his feet down the rock wall.

"Steady, steady," he called out to *Ceò*.

His foot slipped on the wet rock and he slammed against the wall, jerking the rope. If his horse had bolted and ripped the rope from his hands, Finn would have fallen straight to the bottom—with no rope—but *Ceò* barely shifted under the strain.

Finn wiped the rain from his eyes and continued down. When he was halfway down, he heard the sound of water sloshing against the rock walls.

God's blood, this was a sea cave.

He scrambled the rest of the way down until he was just above the water. Holding the lantern high, he searched the dark surface, calling her name. He knew no one could survive long in this watery dungeon, but he could not give up. He tied the lantern to the rope and dropped into freezing seawater up to his chest.

On the far side of the cavern, he caught a glimpse of hair the color of moonlight floating on the water. His heart pounded in his ears as he splashed through the water to reach her.

He found her curled up on a ledge that was so close to being submerged that her hair and the skirt of her gown floated in the water. Praying hard, he gently lifted her in his arms and felt for a pulse.

Praise God, she was alive!

"I'll get ye out of here, *mo rùin*," *my love*, he said in a choked voice, and held her close.

"I was afraid you'd think I left ye," she said in a weak voice.

"Don't talk now, *mo chridhe*," *my heart*. "Ye must save your strength."

"I love ye, Finn," she murmured as her head fell against his chest.

Racing against time, Finn climbed the rope up the slippery rock with Margaret's limp body over his shoulder. He needed to get her out of this hellhole and warm. He had to leave the lantern to carry her, but he could gauge how much farther to the top by the dog's frantic yaps above him.

Finally, he hauled her over the edge and crawled out of the abyss and onto solid ground. Margaret was shaking violently. He ran to fetch her cloak and blanket strapped to *Ceò*'s saddle, wrapped her in them, and rubbed her body, trying to warm her. But it was not enough. She needed a roaring fire.

The storm had blown over and the moon shone brightly, lighting Finn's way as he galloped back to Helmsdale. Encircled in the heat of his body, Margaret seemed to revive somewhat on the short ride. When they reached Helmsdale, the guard saw him coming and opened the gate. He rode through and up to the steps of the keep, then slid off *Ceò* with Margaret in his arms.

"I'm all right now," Margaret said. "I need to tell ye something."

He ran up the steps without pausing. Though he was relieved to hear her speak, whatever she wanted to tell him could wait until he had her warm in front of the hearth and had checked her for injuries.

"Wait, Finn—" she said as he pushed open the door to the hall.

"Bring blankets and a hot drink!" he shouted as he carried her to the hearth. "We need more peat on that fire!"

"I must tell ye why I left," she said.

In his urgency to bring her back, he had forgotten that she had left in fear. The hall and everyone in it had been a blur when he rushed in. As he took in the room now, he could see that their sudden entry had disrupted a brawl. A man with a bloodied face was struggling against two men who held him.

"He's the traitor!" someone shouted. "The murderer!"

Finn recognized the man with the bloodied face now as the servant who went missing after his aunt and uncle were poisoned. So, they had caught the bastard.

"Kill him!" a woman shouted, and the others cheered.

"Finn!" Margaret gripped his arm. "Stop them. It wasn't him."

He thought at first she must still be out of her head, but she was sitting straight up and her eyes were alert.

"I'm telling ye," she said. "It wasn't him."

He suddenly knew why she had left the castle so suddenly in the midst of a storm. She had discovered the killer.

"Hold on!" Finn stood and raised his arms. "Let's hear what this man has to say."

"We already know he's guilty," one of the men said, and punched the already-bloodied man in the gut.

"Cut his head off!" a woman shouted.

"If ye cut off his head, he can't tell us who else was involved in the murders," Finn said. "Now let him go."

Finn stared them down until the men reluctantly released their captive.

"I came back to clear my name after I heard what was being said about me," the injured man said as he wiped the blood from his nose. "I didn't poison them. They were still well when I left."

"Then why did ye leave that night?" Finn asked.

"I was told to slip away after I served the wine and deliver a message to Girnigoe Castle," the man said. "I was given a gold coin to keep quiet about it."

"Who gave ye the gold coin and sent ye to Girnigoe?" The blood pounded in Finn's ears as he waited for the answer.

The man extended his arm, pointing. "She sent me."

The force of the man's accusation was like a lance clearing a path through the room in the direction he pointed until it landed on Isabel.

Isabel glared back at them with defiance in her eyes.

Finn should have known she would alert her cousin, George Sinclair, to the opportunity presented by the earl's poisoning and likely death. But taking advantage of the tragedy, bad as that was, did not mean Isabel played a role in the actual murders.

"He lies to cover his own dark deeds," Isabel said. "He admits to betraying his laird for a coin, but the gold he took was for poisoning him!"

"This man speaks the truth. Isabel is the murderer!" Margaret's voice rang out from behind him. "After I found henbane in the chest in Isabel's chamber, she tried to murder me as well."

Finn spun around to find Margaret on her feet, clutching the blanket. Despite her wet, bedraggled gown and the blanket clutched around her shoulders, she looked like a breathtaking avenging angel.

"She poisoned the peat in my brazier," Margaret said loudly enough for everyone to hear. "When I escaped before the fumes killed me, she followed me and pushed me into the enclosed sea cave where Finn found me."

After she finished speaking, Margaret's burst of strength was gone, and she seemed on the verge of collapsing. Finn wrapped his arms around her and stared at Isabel over the top of Margaret's head. Despite Isabel's past cruelties, constant barbs, and smoldering resentment, he never thought her capable of murder. By now, she would have removed the henbane from her chest and the poisoned peat from the brazier. With no proof, would the others take Margaret's word over Isabel's?

In the silence that followed, Gilbert emerged from the stairwell, leaning heavily on a cane. His face was deathly pale, and his hand shook, rattling the cane against the floor as he crossed the room to Isabel. Obviously shaken by the accusation against his wife, the ill man was coming to his wife's defense. Or so Finn thought.

"What have ye done, woman?" Gilbert said, standing before her.

"I did what needed to be done," Isabel said. "I did what you weren't man enough to do."

"Nay," Gilbert said, shaking his head. "This cannot be."

"I did it for our son. Bearach was meant to be an earl." Her black eyes glowed as she spoke. "Only three stood between him and the great earldom of Sutherland. I was patient. I bided my time for years. And when the opportunity came, I struck."

"My God, ye poisoned my brother and Helen?" Gilbert said, staggering backward.

"*Ach*, your high and mighty brother, always lording his wealth and status over us," she said. "He thought he was so clever, having Duffus murdered to eliminate his claim. Never occurred to him that with Duffus dead, all I had to do to clear the way for Bearach was to rid us of him and Alex."

Finn could not take it in. Isabel had murdered his aunt and uncle—and tried to kill Alex?

"I knew ye were spiteful, but I didn't want to believe ye were capable of such evil," Gilbert said. "God forgive me, I should have thrown ye out years ago instead of sending Finn away."

"You disgust me. You're a weak and pathetic man, not like my cousin George," Isabel said. "We planned it all together. He promised the Sinclairs would fight to support Bearach's claim once the deed was done."

"And what did ye gain by it?" Gilbert said. "Our son is dead at your hands. Dead!"

His words transformed Isabel's defiance to grief, and she sank to her knees.

"Bearach was supposed to be safe at Girnigoe," she wailed, holding her head. "I did not mean to kill him. Not Bearach. Not him. Not my precious son."

A horrified silence filled the room.

"An earl has been murdered. Only the Crown can decide her guilt," Margaret whispered in Finn's ear. "Without her as a witness, men who seek an advantage from the earl's death are bound to make false accusations against their rivals."

"And Isabel is the only one who can point a finger at George Sinclair," Finn said.

"Death to her! Death to her!" men suddenly began shouting, and several of the Gordon guards surrounded Isabel, who was still slumped on her knees on the floor.

Finn leaped in front of Isabel.

"We shall have justice, but not like this," he said. "She must be sent to Edinburgh and tried for her crimes."

CHAPTER 32

While Isabel was taken away and locked in one of the store-rooms, Finn sent someone to fetch Una and Ella. Margaret, the stubborn woman, refused to let him carry her upstairs to bed until Una and Ella arrived and she had held her daughter in her arms.

Una took over then, sending for hot water and checking Margaret for injuries over her objections that she was fine.

"Mind Ella while I clean up those nasty scratches and put her to bed," Una said, and shooed him out of the bedchamber

Finn waited in the other chamber with the door open. Though it could not have been long, it seemed like hours passed before Una stuck her head out.

"All she needs is rest. I'll send for ye when she wakes," Una said. "And stop your fretting, or you'll worry the poor bairn."

Ella took his hand and looked up at him. Hoping to make her smile, he pulled her doll out of the tuck in his plaid and held it out to her. When her bottom lip trembled, he saw that the thing was soaking wet from the seawater in the crevice and even sadder looking than before.

"She just needs a wee cleaning up," he said, then he remembered the dog he'd brought her. "I have a new friend for ye to meet."

He suddenly realized that after the dog had helped him find Margaret, he'd ridden off and left him without a backward glance.

"Don't want another horse," she said. "I like *Ceò*."

"Then let's go visit *Ceò*," he said.

When they stepped out of the keep, the wee dog was sitting at the bottom of the steps waiting. He was even more pathetic looking than her doll, with his raggedy fur and one eye.

Ella adored him. The bairn had a soft spot for broken things.

"This wee dog deserves a good meal after all he's done," Finn said, patting it on the head. "You two get acquainted while I go to the kitchen to get him some meat."

When he went down into the undercroft, he decided he needed to talk to Isabel one last time. He nodded to the two guards watching the door and went in.

"George will rescue me," she said as soon as he entered. "After I delivered Alex into his hands, he won't forget me."

"He doesn't have Alex anymore," Finn said.

Her eye twitched. She had not expected that.

"George doesn't need ye now," he said. "He'll let you take all the blame for the murders."

"I'm a Sinclair," she said, staring ahead. "He'll stand by me."

She would find out in time. "Ye didn't ask, but I thought you'd want to know that your husband isn't doing well."

"He never loved me," Isabel snapped. "All these years, he mourned my dead sister."

Finn wondered for a moment if she knew that her sister was his real mother.

"She ruined everything when she ran off with the man *I* was supposed to wed," she said, jabbing her thumb to her bony chest. "'Twas all arranged. She was to wed Gilbert, and I, as the elder sister, was to marry Robin Sutherland and become Countess of Sutherland."

"Ye would have become the widow of a rebel, not a countess," he said.

"With me as his wife, Robin would have succeeded in taking the earldom," she said. "Nothing and no one would have stood in our way."

"He chose love instead," Finn said. "They both did."

"He died for making the wrong choice," she said.

Finn was more than ready to leave, but she continued talking, as if he was not there.

"If I had to marry a Gordon, an enemy to my clan, it would not have been such an insult if he was the Earl of Huntly's first or second son," she said, bitterness oozing from her like black bile. "But nay, I was bound for life to the third son, a man of low stature and little property. And worst of all, a man my sister discarded.

"I needed to pay them back and take what should have been mine. When my sister came to me seeking forgiveness, I spat in her face and had her followed when she left. Then I told the Gordons where she and Robin were hiding."

"How could you?" Finn asked. "She trusted you."

"Robin was caught because of me," she said. "And yet I wept when I saw his head over the gate at Dunrobin."

268

Finn knew then that if she had found out his true parentage, she would have killed him in his cradle.

Later that day, he watched the Gordon warriors lead her in chains down to the boat that would carry her to Edinburgh for trial. Isabel had made his childhood a misery and never shown him a bit of affection. She murdered her husband's kin, a couple who had done nothing against her, while a guest in their home.

And yet Finn felt nothing but sadness as he watched her go. Her evil design to murder her nephew and his parents had led her to kill her own son. Finn watched until long after the boat disappeared on the horizon.

It was late in the day before Una sent word that Margaret was awake and asking for him. The old woman was waiting for him outside the chamber door.

"She's had no bleeding, God be praised," Una said, patting his hand.

"No bleeding?" His pulse jumped. "What's wrong with her?"

"She's a strong lass," Una said. "Stronger than she looks, for certain."

Her words only made Finn more worried. What was Una hiding from him?

You've every reason to hope for a healthy babe."

Margaret was with child? Finn suddenly felt lightheaded and had to rest his hand against the wall. He had known it was possible, but that was not the same as knowing for certain. The thought that she could suffer another miscarriage—and it was his fault—hit him like a punch in the gut.

Finn had not only left her at the mercy of a murderer, he did this to her.

When he went into the bedchamber, he found Margaret sitting up in the bed stitching. She set her needlework aside and gave him a warm smile.

"How are ye feeling?" he asked, taking her hands. It pained him to see the scratches on them.

"Remarkably well once Una brought me food," she said. "Ye should have seen how much I ate."

"Why did ye not tell me you're with child?" he asked.

"I didn't know for certain myself until Una told me," Margaret said.

"I'm so sorry," he said in a choked voice. "I know ye didn't want to go through this again."

"This time will be different, I know it," she said, squeezing his hands. "If I didn't lose the babe last night, I don't believe I will."

Despite the scratches and bruises, she did have a glow about her. Still, Finn could not forget the sadness in her eyes when she told him about her miscarriage.

"Can't ye see?" she said. "I'm happy to be carrying your child."

"Ye want a child with *me*?" he asked.

"Of course I do," she said, blinking back tears.

He pulled her into his arms and held her. God knew he was not fit to be a father. But if by some miracle Margaret had the child, he would try his best. And if she lost the babe, he would be there to comfort her. He needed to be with her, no matter what came.

"Ye came and found me," Margaret said, leaning back to look into Finn's eyes, "even though I told ye I was going to leave ye."

"I had to be sure ye were safe," he said.

Finn would never know what that meant to her, after the men of her family and her former husband had valued her so little.

"I never truly wanted to go to my sister's," she said. "I was afraid of so many things. Afraid to love you. Afraid you'd desert me when I needed ye most."

There was only one thing she was still afraid of.

"Una told me ye rescued Alex," she said. No matter his own ambition, Finn would not leave his cousin in danger. But that did not mean he did not want to become an earl in Alex's place.

Finn told her the tale of Alex's rescue then, though she suspected he left out the dangerous parts.

"Alex should be on his way to Huntly now," Finn said.

"You're a good man to save his life," she said.

"I gave my word I'd look out for him."

Finn would have rescued Alex even if he had not given his oath, just as he had rescued her.

"I have something to confess," she said. "I overheard Gilbert tell ye that Robin Sutherland was your real father."

A sudden wariness came into Finn's eyes.

"What will ye do?" she asked. "Will ye claim your rightful place?"

Fear tightened her belly as she waited to hear her future.

"I'm sorry, *mo rùin*, but I can't claim the earldom," Finn said. "That would cause a war between the Sutherlands and the Gordons, when we must fight together to push the Sinclairs out of our lands."

Relief flooded through her, until she noticed how wretched Finn looked.

"Besides, I couldn't take it from Alex," he said. "I can't do it, even for you."

"I should have known ye wouldn't sacrifice Alex, even though ye have the right to," she said, tears running down her face. "If I didn't already love ye, I would love ye for this."

"What?" Finn's eyes went wide. "Ye don't want me to claim it?"

"If I'd wanted to marry an earl," she said, "I would have stayed with my brothers."

Finn did not look persuaded.

"If you were an earl, ye couldn't avoid being drawn into the dangerous games and changing alliances of Scotland's most powerful nobles," she said. "You'd be expected to attend court and participate on the council, and we'd have other important nobles coming to visit. I don't want my brothers to find me and try to use us both, as they would be sure to do."

"I wouldn't let them," he said.

Finn had not lived in those circles as she had. No matter how he tried, he would be forced to choose sides. There was no neutral ground, just shifting sands among the most powerful nobles.

"Garty is a small property with a modest tower house." He brushed a strand of her hair behind her ear. "You were meant to be a countess and live in a great castle with a hundred servants and dozens of jewels and fine gowns."

"I don't need any of those things," she said. "What makes a home is love, and that's all I ever wanted."

Beneath his charm, Finn carried wounds from never feeling that he truly belonged. Though he had hidden it from himself for years, he longed for family and home as much as she did. He still did not believe he was worthy of love, but she would show him he was.

They would build a life together for themselves and their children and make a home that would be a sanctuary for them all.

"Marry me," she said, and kissed him. "Marry me, Finn."

Finn could not believe his good fortune and smiled at Margaret while they ate a late breakfast. When he caught Ella feeding the dog—whom she and Una named *Cù-sìthe*, fairy dog—under the table, he winked at her. His heart felt so full. He never expected to be this happy.

He looked up as a man in priest's robes burst into the hall.

"The Sinclairs have set fire to the town of Dornoch," the priest said. "The godless heathens even burned the cathedral."

The priest was shaking, and his face was charred with smoke.

"Sit down, father," Margaret said, taking his arm and helping him into a chair. Then she poured him a cup of whisky.

"Bless ye, lass," he said, and drank it down.

"Why attack Dornoch?" Finn asked. "Alex must be gone from there by now."

"The Sinclairs want revenge against the Murrays for helping Alex escape," the priest said. "When they chased them into Dornoch, the Murrays took refuge in the cathedral and the bishop's castle, thinking they'd be safe there."

The Sinclairs would risk excommunication attacking a cathedral and a bishop's residence.

"I fear the situation is dire," the priest said. "A few of the Murrays are holed up in the cathedral's tower. Lachlan and most of the others are trapped in the castle, which isn't stocked for a siege, as the bishop is gone and no one expected his home to be attacked."

The Sinclairs were exacting punishment on the Murrays for rescuing Alex.

"Who led the attack for the Sinclairs?" Finn asked.

"Their chieftain's eldest son John, Master of Caithness," the priest said. "He's a ruthless son of a bitch."

"He's not the worst of them," Finn said. "He may be willing to negotiate."

"That's why I've come," the priest said. "He says he'll parley with no one but you, Finn. If you're not there at noon on the morrow, he says he'll breach the walls and spare not a one."

"Why me?" Finn asked, though he suspected he knew.

"He says ye were the peddler responsible for Alex Òg's escape."

John Sinclair wanted Finn for more than the parley. The parley, the chance to avoid a bloody massacre of the Murrays, was the bait John knew would draw Finn out.

"He says if you don't come to him, he'll attack Helmsdale next."

The threat to Helmsdale was John turning the screw. Finn had no choice.

An hour ago, Finn saw a future beyond his dreams, a life with his beloved Margaret as his wife. He had allowed himself to imagine growing old with her and watching Ella and perhaps more children of their own grow up.

Tomorrow he would ride to Dornoch not knowing if he would return. Finn could not put his own happiness or even Margaret's above the lives of so many good men. The best he could do now for Margaret and Ella was to make certain they had a home on lands of their own, a haven where they would be safe.

"I'll go back with ye in the morning," Finn told the priest, then drew him aside. "But I need ye to do something for me tonight."

"What was it ye asked the priest to do?" Margaret asked after he brought her back upstairs to speak with her alone.

"I want us to wed tonight," he said, taking Margaret's hands. "We'll say our vows with the entire household as witnesses, have the priest bless our marriage, and celebrate with a feast."

Once the priest blessed their marriage, they were bound in the eyes of the church, and before so many witnesses, neither his relatives nor hers could challenge its validity.

"Ye expect a wedding feast with only a few hours to prepare?" she asked with a wide smile. "Surely we can wait until ye return."

"After all that's happened, we know how precious time is," he said. "I don't want to let another day go by without you being my wife."

"How dangerous is it for you to meet with the Sinclair chieftain's son?" she asked, drawing her brows together. "I thought this was just a parley."

Finn should have left out the part about time being precious. He hated to lie to her, but he wanted her to be happy at their wedding.

"*Ach*, 'tis just talking we'll do. I'll be fine," Finn said, giving her a smile and a wink. "But it would please me to know I have a wife and daughter waiting for me. I want the three of us to be a family now."

CHAPTER 33

Margaret expected grumbling from the servants over being given so little time to prepare a feast, especially for a marriage they believed had already taken place. But it turned out that the prospect of a wedding feast was a welcome respite from the dark cloud that had hung over Helmsdale since the tragedies struck.

The entire household embraced the idea of a wedding celebration and threw themselves into a frenzy of preparation. Men set up tables and carried wine and ale up from the undercroft, women helped in the kitchen, and children ran outside to gather flowers.

Laughing, the women pushed Margaret out of the kitchen.

"But there's so much to do," she objected.

"And all our hard work will be for naught if the bride isn't ready," Una said. "A hot bath is waiting for ye. And Ella could use a washing as well before the wedding."

Margaret gave in after she looked at Ella, who had stuck both hands in the pan of pudding that was cooling on the worktable and gotten more in her hair and on her face than in her mouth. Margaret sighed. At least pudding was easy to wash off.

After she and Ella had bathed, Margaret dressed Ella in a gown she had made and tied a ribbon in her hair. One of the gowns Helen had given her was too fine for every day, so she had never worn it. She ran her hand over it, thinking of Helen's kindness. It would serve well for her wedding gown.

"'Tis as if Lady Helen knew," Una said as she fastened the back. "The color blue is a lucky color for a bride, and the gown fits perfectly, another sign of good fortune."

One of the children brought sprigs of white heather for Margaret's hair, another symbol of good luck. Hope bubbled up inside her as she pinned the heather in her hair. Unlike her first one, this marriage would be a happy one.

If she had not suffered through that marriage, and if Wretched William had never thrown her out, she would not be here today, marrying the man she loved. The man she was always meant to be with.

Una held the looking glass up for Margaret to see herself. Her eyes sparkled with happiness. When she turned to smile at Ella, her daughter was watching her with big eyes. Though Margaret had worn gorgeous gowns countless times, her daughter had never seen her dressed like this.

"I want to be pretty too," Ella said.

"You are pretty." Margaret leaned down and stuck a sprig of the white heather in Ella's hair. "More than that, you're clever and kind and brave. You're the daughter I always wanted."

Someone pounded on the door, followed by giggles and a shout: "Everyone's waiting for the bride!"

Margaret touched the onyx brooch pinned to her bodice and closed her eyes for just a moment, wishing her sisters and cousin Lizzie could be here to see how happy she was. Then she took her daughter's hand and practically skipped out the door.

Her heart squeezed in her chest when she saw Finn. He was so darkly handsome in his plaid, and his eyes went soft when he saw her. Since everyone thought they were already handfasted, they could have made their pledges to each other in private and only received the priest's blessing before the witnesses here in the hall. When Finn wrapped the symbolic strip of linen around their hands, pressed palm to palm, and made his pledge, she knew he was right to insist they do it this way.

She wanted to shout that, against all odds, they had found each other. They took a lie and made it their truth. Transformed a kidnap and escape into redemption and refuge. Exchanged fear and mistrust for hope and love.

When she made her own pledge, she said her full name, Margaret Elizabeth Douglas, softly so that only she and Finn could hear it.

Ella was with Una at the front of the people that surrounded them.

"Come," Finn said, holding his arms out to her.

When Ella ran to him, he picked her up, kissed her on the cheek, and then lifted her up high for everyone in the hall to see.

"I claim this child as my own and give her my name," Finn said in a voice that filled the room.

Margaret had not thought it possible Finn could make her any happier, but now he had. Tears of joy filled her eyes. While she knew Finn loved Ella, Margaret had not expected he would formally claim her. When a Highlander claimed a child, that child had the same status and rights as any he sired within a marriage. Ella would not grow up as his stepchild from an unknown clan, never fully belonging.

"As my only child," Finn continued, "this wee lass, my daughter Ella, is my heir unless and until my wife blesses me with a son."

A shiver of fear went through Margaret. She understood now why Finn insisted their marriage take place this very day, why he made sure a priest blessed it, why he publicly claimed Ella—and for good measure, named Ella as his heir. It was this last, seemingly unnecessary proclamation that gave him away. As his wife, Margaret could not inherit Garty.

But his child could.

Finn had just ensured that Margaret and Ella would have a home if he should not return. She hid her worry, as she had so many times, and cheered with the rest.

Finn carried his wife over the threshold of their bedchamber and kicked the door shut, muffling the noise of the revelers still celebrating in the hall. When he set her on her feet, Margaret looked up at him with soft brown eyes and held his face between her hands.

"I love you, husband," she said. "I always will."

Finn swallowed against the surge of emotion clogging his throat. Plenty of women had enjoyed his company for a laugh and a good swiving, but he never expected to be wanted for more. Never expected to be loved. And to be loved by this sweet lass who held his heart in her hands was a blessing beyond measure. He did not deserve Margaret's love, but she gave it to him anyway.

"I can't believe you're truly my wife," he said. "You've made me a happy man."

As he had on the first night they shared a bed, he combed her hair, letting the long, bright strands glide through his fingers. He almost wept when he undressed her and saw all her scratches and bruises from the fall.

When her hair turned white and her face was lined, she would still be beautiful, for her true beauty came from inside. He prayed he would have the chance to grow old with her. But if he did not, he would count himself a lucky man, for he had been loved by this sweet lass, his Maggie.

He made love to her slowly, careful of her injuries. Over and over, he told her how much he loved her and tried to show her with his every touch how precious she was to him.

When she drifted off to sleep in his arms, a soft smile curving her lips, he left the candle burning until it was gone just so he could watch her. He stayed awake, savoring these last brief hours with his wife in his arms. Careful not to wake her, he ran his fingers through her hair and breathed in her scent. He did not think it possible he could fall more deeply in love with her, but his very heart beat for this lass.

His love, his *wife*.

In the morning, he made love to her one last time, trying not to let her see the desperation he felt at having to leave her. But he had to go. The lives of the men trapped in Dornoch, good men who had helped rescue Alex, depended on him.

They ate breakfast with Ella, but he could not delay his departure any longer. The priest was already mounted and waiting at the gate.

"Lachlan will be home soon," he told Una, who had come out into the courtyard with Margaret and Ella to see him off.

He lifted Ella up and tossed her into the air to hear her laugh, then he kissed her cheek and set her down. Finally, he enveloped Margaret in his arms and held her close. After one last kiss, he leaned back to drink in her lovely face once more.

"Time for me to go, *a chuisle mo chroí,*" *pulse of my heart.* "With luck, I'll be back by nightfall."

"I need ye to come back," Margaret said, her voice quavering, "so see that ye do."

He would be lost without her, but he was confident that if he did not return, Margaret would persevere through her sadness and loss. Her gentle nature and graceful form hid a strength that would carry her through.

Garty held none of the bad memories for her that it did for him. She would have her independence and, in time, could have a happy life there with Ella. Word might eventually reach her brothers, but the Gordons would watch over her. Alex would make certain they did.

CHAPTER 34

Smoke hung over the town and burned Finn's throat as he rode with the priest through the smoldering remains of the burned houses. Sinclair warriors surrounded the castle and the burned-out cathedral, which stood a few yards apart in the center of the town.

"A few of the Murrays are caught up there," the priest reminded him, pointing at the cathedral's tower, which was all that remained of the church.

As he came to a halt in front of the mass of armed warriors in front of the castle, Finn looked up and saw Lachlan among the Murrays peering down from the parapet.

"If this doesn't go well, take *Ceò* to my wife," Finn told the priest before he dismounted. Then he patted *Ceò*'s shoulder and walked toward the mass of armed warriors.

John, Master of Caithness, expected him, so the Sinclairs parted to let Finn through without a word. John stood waiting, his armor and face smudged with soot, in a small clearing at the center of his men. Behind him, two pews that must have been dragged out of the ruined cathedral were arranged face to face in the open air.

When John gestured toward one of the pews, Finn sat and stretched out his legs. Finn caught sight of the MacKay chieftain, Barbara's lover and close ally of the Sinclairs, standing nearby with a group of his warriors. He was not surprised that MacKay had joined in the attack, but he was relieved when John did not invite MacKay to join them.

At John's signal, the men widened the circle around the pews so that their conversation could be private. Finn waited to speak until they stepped back.

"'Tis one thing to raid some cattle and burn a few fields, but destroying the cathedral and threatening the bishop's home?" Finn folded his arms and shook his head. "You'll burn in hell for this, which means ye won't escape your father even in death, because we both know that's where he'll be."

"You're just angry that I succeeded in trapping your friends, the Murrays," John said.

279

"Your grandmother will be disappointed when she hears what you've done," Finn said. "Lady Mary still believes there's some good in ye."

"She died a fortnight ago," John said in a flat tone.

Finn was silent for a long moment as a wave of sadness passed through him. He'd always been fond of Mary, and now he knew the role she'd played in saving him when he was still a babe. And with her death, he'd lost an ally in appealing to John's better instincts.

"Come, John, ye don't want the blood of good men on your hands," Finn said. "You're not like your father."

"I am my father's son," John said. "Now let's get on with it."

"All right," Finn said. "Tell me what ye need to let these men go."

John bluffed and threatened, as expected, but they soon came to an agreement that would save the skins of the Murrays. In exchange for allowing the trapped men to leave Dornoch unharmed, the Murrays would agree not to challenge George Sinclair's control of Sutherland during Alex's minority. As was customary, John required three hostages to secure the promise.

"You'll guarantee the hostages safety?" Finn asked, though this was usual as well.

"Of course," John said, sounding offended. "I swear it."

Finn shouted the terms up to Lachlan and the other Murrays on the castle wall. It did not take long for them to discuss it among themselves.

"We accept the terms," Lachlan shouted down. "We'll draw lots for the hostages and send them out first."

"Since that's settled, I'll be off," Finn said, and got up.

"I have one more term ye must agree to," John said, "or I'll slaughter them all.".

Damn, damn, damn. Finn knew what it was without John telling him.

"Must ye do this, John?" he asked without much hope.

"Ye should have sent someone else to give the message to Alex," John said. "But ye had to be the one to come into Dunrobin disguised as a peddler and humiliate my father."

"What gave me away?" Finn asked.

"The dog," John said with a dry laugh. "Barbara saw ye take that one-eyed mongrel. After Alex escaped, she put two and two together."

It would be Barbara. At least Alex was safe at Huntly castle and free of her and the rest of the Sinclairs.

"Do ye believe this will finally win your father's approval?" Finn taunted him. "That you'll replace your brother William as his favorite?"

"My father will be grateful that I've caught the Murrays and forced them to surrender and agree to my terms."

"You're the better son, the best of his children, but you'll never change your father's mind," Finn said. "I was always the unfavored son, too, so I know."

"What I know is that I'm the son who's going to give my father what he wants," John said. "And what he wants is you."

When they reached Girnigoe, the three hostages were allowed to ride into the castle unbound. Finn, however, was forced to walk with a rope around his neck, removing any doubt that he was a prisoner, rather than a hostage.

He sensed something was wrong the moment they crossed the first gate of Girnigoe and the drawbridge was raised behind them with unnecessary speed. MacKay sensed it too, for he turned his horse and galloped over the half-raised drawbridge, sailing over the gap in the rock and landing on the other side.

"Run!" Finn shouted to the Murray hostages.

He pulled a dirk from the belt of the Sinclair warrior who held him and sliced the rope that tied them together. It was a hopeless attempt, of course, as he was on foot and too far from the drawbridge. He heard the drawbridge close with a *thump* as he was tackled to the ground by several of the Sinclair men.

This time, Finn's hands were bound, and John held the rope around his neck. Without hesitation, John rode through the next gate and into the inner courtyard where his father was waiting.

"Chain these prisoners together, hand and foot, and line them up," George ordered.

Finn struggled against the men who clamped irons around his ankles and wrists.

"The Murrays are hostages, not prisoners, Father," John said.

George turned on his son with such rage in his eyes that Finn had to give John credit for not stepping back as George walked up to him until they were nose to nose.

"*I* didn't agree to accept hostages," George said.

"You sent me to deal with the Murrays," John said. "I agreed to—"

"You let the Murrays go!" George said. "I did not tell ye to spare them."

"Ye gave me the task, and I did it," John said. "I did it well."

George extended his arm to the side and snapped his fingers. "My sword!"

One of his guards brought him his claymore. With barely a pause, George's powerful torso twisted as he swung it and cut the first hostage's head clean off his shoulders.

Jesu! Even George's guards looked shocked that their chieftain would violate Highland custom by brutally executing a hostage.

"Father, ye can't do this!" John shouted as George approached the next hostage in line. "I gave my oath that these hostages would not be harmed."

"I am chieftain of the Sinclairs, not you!" George roared.

"But I—"

Before the words were out of John's mouth, a second bloody head rolled across the ground.

"I know you're plotting against me," George said, turning back to John. "You're eyeing my chair. What made you think you're man enough to push me aside and take my place?"

"Nay!" John said. "I've always been loyal."

"The old witch foretold that my son would rebel against me, and now I see it's true," George said. "Ye made an alliance with MacKay behind my back, and the two of ye let my enemies go."

George stood before Finn and the last Murray hostage, his sword dripping with blood. This looked like the end. At least it would be quick. Finn closed his eyes, said a prayer, and drew up an image in his mind of Margaret holding Ella. His last thought would be of them.

He heard the *whoosh* of a sword and the third head roll.

###

The dungeon was pitch black, but Finn's eyes gradually adjusted until he could make out the outline of his fellow prisoner chained against the opposite wall.

"I should have stayed home with my bride," Finn said. "You're the last person I want to spend my final hours with."

"Don't worry. My father won't keep me here that long," John said. "You'll die alone."

"I wouldn't be so sure," Finn said.

"If my father wanted to kill me," John said, "he would have done it right off, like he did with the Murray hostages."

Perhaps even George Sinclair could not bring himself to murder his own son. But that did not explain why Finn was still alive. George either had some use for him or a special torture in mind. He strained against his chains, but they were bolted tight to the wall.

After a few hours, two guards brought food and ale.

"What about me?" Finn asked when they only gave it to John.

"You're to have none, ye Gordon devil," one of the guards said.

"I fought with your last chieftain!" Finn shouted after the guards as they climbed back up the stairs.

Each time the guards brought more, Finn waited for John to offer him some. After two days, Finn's tongue was thick, and his thirst finally overcame his pride.

"Will ye save a bit of that ale for me?" Finn asked. "If ye scoot the cup as far as ye can with your foot, I think I can reach it."

"'Tis bound to spill," John said. "And it would only delay the inevitable."

"Your prospects don't look so good either," Finn said.

He was beginning to think George had no purpose for keeping him alive except to give him a slow death in this dungeon. He could withstand hunger, but he was becoming delirious from thirst.

Margaret's image was so real to him. Imagining her was better than not seeing her at all. And he had so much to tell her. His tongue was so thick he could not speak, but she understood him without him having to say the words. She was in his head and in his heart.

In the blackness of the dungeon, he could not tell if it was night or day. He'd tried at first to gauge the passage of time by counting how often the guards came to feed John, but he'd long since lost track and had no notion how long he'd been here.

He had no real hope of ever escaping Girnigoe Castle. But he made up his mind to survive as long as he could, rather than give up the long conversations he had with Margaret in his head. He lay on the cold ground and imagined it was her lap, and she was running her fingers through his hair.

The next time the guards came down, Finn did not bother attempting to lift his head.

"The chieftain wishes to see ye," one them said.

"I knew my father would relent," John said, and held out his hands for the manacles to be removed.

"'Tis Finn he wants to see," the guard said, and turned to Finn. "He wants ye alert."

The guard set down a bowl of mush and a large cup of ale.

Apparently, George did want something from him after all. Finn drank the ale greedily, careful not to spill a single precious drop. Though he was ravenous, he took his time and ate only a few spoonfuls of the mush, knowing his shrunken stomach would rebel against more. The guards waited patiently until he set the bowl aside and drank the remaining swallow of ale that he'd saved for last.

Finn's chains clanged against the stone steps as the guards hauled him up the first set of steps and through a low arched doorway that led outside to the courtyard where the Murray hostages were executed.

George Sinclair was waiting for him there with a whip in his hand.

"Tie him up," George said. "And leave us."

When the news came that Finn was taken as one of the hostages, Margaret knew his life was in danger. The Gordon guards assured her the hostages would not be harmed so long as the Murrays kept the peace. Even the Sinclair chieftain, they told her, would not dishonor himself by violating that Highland custom.

Margaret did not believe them. The guards would not help her, but Una knew some Sutherland fishermen who were willing to take Margaret where she wanted to go.

The outline of Castle Girnigoe was barely discernable through the night fog. The fortress rose straight up from the sea atop a long point with sheer sides. Though Margaret was wet and freezing on the open boat, she was grateful for the fog and drizzle because they hid the moon and stars. The warriors inside the castle were less likely to see their small fishing boat before it turned into the inlet just before the one that bordered the castle.

Margaret held her breath until they entered the narrow inlet and were hidden from view. After the men hauled the boat ashore, she told them to wait for her there.

"Ye must leave well before dawn," she said. "If I'm not back before daylight, go without me."

There was no point in endangering these men more than she already was. If her plan failed and she was caught, the Sinclairs would search for the men who brought her. Even if they were fighting men, rather than fishermen, they could not resist the vast number of warriors in the Sinclair chieftain's stronghold.

She stood on the wet sand of the cove, replaying Finn's description in her head from that night on their journey north when he told her about leaving Girnigoe by a secret tunnel, with the help of Mary Sutherland Sinclair. He'd said it came out into a cave halfway up the bluff... There, she saw it!

Wind and rain whipped her hair across her face as she climbed the slippery black rock. She slipped and banged her knee and got up again. Once she finally stood inside the cave at the entrance to the tunnel, she reached inside her cloak and ran her fingers over the onyx brooch pinned inside her bodice. Then, taking a deep breath, she plunged inside.

She used her fingertips along the rough-hewn wall to guide her. She had thought the night was dark, but inside the tunnel it was so utterly black as to be disorienting. Fearing that Finn was in greater danger every moment, she wanted to run, but the floor of the tunnel was littered with loose rocks, forcing her to move slowly. She barely stifled a scream when something slithered over her foot. As the tunnel climbed higher, she heard beating wings. *Bats!* She felt the *whoosh* as one grazed her hair with its wing.

Did Finn say the tunnel was this long? She began to wonder if this was not the tunnel after all, but a long cave. As the walls seemed to close in on her, she feared she would be lost forever in an endless cave. But she kept going.

When her foot struck something solid, she knelt down. She felt one, two, three steps—and then her hand slid up a solid piece of wood.

She'd found the door into the castle.

Finn swam through a black sea of pain and gasped as he broke the surface. He thought he must be dead. Then he wished he was.

The excruciating pain of the rain pounding against his shredded back must have been what finally woke him. He had lost count of how many lashes George gave him before he passed out. He tilted his head back to catch the rain on his parched tongue. Then his mind went blank, but he woke and caught himself as he started to fall.

When he still was not dead after a time, Finn decided to take stock of his situation. It was dark, and he was cold, which made his mind slow. Eventually, though, he realized his arms and shoulders ached because he was hanging from the whipping post by the long chain attached to his wrists. Gritting his teeth with the effort, he pulled himself to his feet, then leaned against the post, gasping for breath.

He thought of Margaret as he waited for death to take him. What a surprise that highborn lass had been. Despite his pain, he smiled to himself as he recalled how she'd fooled him into believing he was kidnapping her when she was using him to make her escape. His Maggie was a resourceful lass.

In his mind's eye, he saw her and regretted how slow he'd been to trust her kind and generous heart. He was grateful for every moment he had with her. But he wanted more. And so, though it was foolish, he began to think of escape.

Squinting against the rain, he leaned around the post to see the hook on the other side that held his chain. He tried again and again, painfully swinging the chain with his arms, until finally the chain lifted off the hook and fell to the ground. But the chain holding his wrists was still around the post. Though he tried, he did not have the strength to climb the post to get the chain over the top of it and free himself.

Resting his forehead against the post, he considered the other end. The post was fixed into a square into the ground. If he could pull it out...

Each time he pulled on the post, he was blinded by the pain from his torn back. Still, he tried again and again until he blacked out and collapsed. He woke and pulled himself up and tried again.

He fell a final time and lay with the side of his face against the cold, wet ground. He drank like a dog from the puddle beside his face. But he could rise no more. His only comfort was knowing he had provided Margaret and Ella with a home of their own, as Margaret had always wanted.

She and Ella were safe.

Margaret put her ear to the door but could hear nothing. She had no way of knowing if that meant no one was on the other side or that the door was so thick it blocked the sound. Biting her lip, she pushed on the door, gently at first. When it did not budge, she pushed harder, to no avail.

There had to be a latch. The way Finn had told the story, the secret door was disguised as a panel, which mean the latch would not be in plain sight. There must be a knob or something to press. But what if the latch could only be worked from the inside? Tunnels like this were made for escape.

She felt all along the edge of the door with her fingertips, searching for a thin break in the wood or in the stone that framed it. Panic made her hands shake when she still could not find it. To be so close to Finn and not reach him!

She refused to give up. She was not leaving without him. Once again, she started at the top of the door and methodically worked her way down every inch. Her nail caught on a tiny crack. With her fingertip, she followed the crack as it made a one-inch square. Using both her thumbs, she pressed on the square, and the door moved.

She had done it. The door shifted just enough for a thin line of light to seep through, outlining the edge of the door. Quickly, she scraped the mud off her boots, removed her cloak, and tidied her hair under her head covering as best she could in the dark. She wore the simple servant's clothes she had stolen from Holyrood Palace in what seemed like another lifetime.

The household should be in bed, except for a few guards. If she ran into anyone, she hoped to pass unnoticed, just as she had at the palace. Most people saw what they expected to see, and they would not be expecting her.

Heart racing, she eased the door open far enough to peek through, and saw a small, empty room dimly lit by a torch fixed into a wall sconce. If anyone saw her coming through a secret doorway, there would be no mistaking her for anything but the intruder she was, so she had to do this quickly. Before she could dwell on the danger, she pushed through the door and shut it behind her.

In her haste, she closed the door harder than she meant to with a resounding *clump*. She let her breath out when no one appeared. Now to find Finn—without getting caught.

She had lived in and visited castles all her life, many of them with secret tunnels that were not so secret, so she ought to be able to figure out how to find him. This room was actually just a landing, with one door opposite the secret panel and a dark, narrow set of stairs on either side, one going up and one down.

These were not the stairs used by the Earl of Caithness, his family, and guests, but rather a back stairwell used by servants and perhaps guards. The dungeon would be below, in the bowels of the castle. That's where Finn would be.

If he's still alive. She forced that thought out of her head.

After a quick glance over her shoulder, she took a candlestick from her pocket, lit it from the torch in the wall sconce, and started down the steps. Partway down, she came to another landing, with an arched door on her right. Judging from the wind blowing under the crack, it led outside. She continued down the last steps until she reached the bottom and what she hoped was the dungeon.

"Who's there?"

She jumped when the deep male voice came out of the darkness.

"So my father has finally relented," he said. "Quickly now, get these irons off me!"

It had not occurred to her there would be other prisoners, though it should have. She surmised this prisoner must be one of the Sinclair chieftain's sons. She held up the lamp to light the rest of the dank, cavernous room, looking for Finn. But there were no other prisoners.

"You're the ghost Finn sees in his dreams," the prisoner said. "Get away from me! Go!"

Fear shot through her. His shouts could bring the guards. She blew out her candle and ran up the stairs, but partway up, she stopped. The prisoner mentioned Finn. He was here.

But if Finn was not in the dungeon, where was he?

She climbed the stairs back to where she had started. Rather than go up the next set of stairs where the bedchambers would be, she eased the door off the landing open a crack. The backs of two men blocked most of her view, but she could see that the room was the castle's great hall. At this hour, warriors and servants were asleep on benches and the floor. The two men with their backs to the door were talking of women, as men do. Just as she was about to look elsewhere, she heard Finn's name.

"Finn took it well, ye must say that for him," one of them said.

"He deserved a few lashes," the other said. "But it didn't sit well with me to see him lashed senseless, not after he fought for Orkney with our last chieftain."

Lashed senseless. Margaret's stomach dropped, and her hand went to her mouth.

"Aye," the first one said. "I wanted to cut him down, but I feared the chieftain would do the same to me."

"Ah well, Finn will be out of his misery soon. He won't last the night."

Finn was still alive. She had to find him soon, but where was he?

"Tied like a dog in the rain and cold," the other man said. "*Ach*, that's no way for a fine warrior like Finn to die."

Margaret flew back down the stairs to where she had noticed the wind whistling beneath the low arched door. When she pushed the door open, she was met by a curtain of rain. Shielding her eyes with her hand, she searched the enclosed courtyard, looking frantically left and right. A single torch outside the door and protected by an overhang provided barely any light at all.

When she did not see Finn, she wanted to scream. Against the far wall, she could make out an upright wooden beam… Her heart went to her throat. A limp form hung from the beam like a stag hung after a hunt.

She slid in the mud as she ran across the courtyard to reach him.

"Finn! It's me," she cried, falling to her knees beside him. "I've come for ye."

But Finn did not even lift his head.

What had they done to him? She wanted to wrap her arms around him and weep. Instead, she pressed her ear to his chest. Finn's heart still beat! *Praise God*. But how would she ever get him into the castle and up the stairs?

"I'm taking ye home, my love," she said, holding his head up between her hands. "But I need your help."

Her tears mingled with the rain pouring down her face as she kissed hm.

Finn's eyes fluttered open. He looked confused for a moment, then he smiled. "Maggie? *Ach*, I must be dead or dreaming."

"Nay, I'm really here," she said. "But we have to go. We're in danger."

"Danger?" He struggled to get up. "*O shluagh*, ye shouldn't be here."

"I have a boat waiting. We must get to the secret tunnel," she said. "Can ye walk?"

"I'm chained to this damned post," he said. "I can't reach the hook, and I can't pull out the post either. I've tried."

"I'll find something for ye to climb onto." She peered into the dark recesses of the courtyard, desperate for something, anything she could use. It was too dark, and they had no time. She dropped to her hands and knees. "Stand on my back."

"I'm too heavy," he said.

"For heaven's sake, I won't break. Your life's at stake!" When he still hesitated, she said, "And so is mine."

Finally, she felt his foot on her back and braced herself to take his full weight.

"What do we have here?" A voice came out of the darkness, sending a chill of ice-cold fear through her veins.

She scrambled to her feet. A few yards away, she could make out the outline of a man. No, there were two.

"I brought a drink for the prisoner," Margaret said. "I'm on my way back inside now."

"The chieftain would be angry if we told him," one of the men said. "No one is supposed to go near this one."

"Ye wouldn't want us to tell, now would ye, lass?" the other said.

The men were moving closer. Margaret's fingers itched to reach for the blade hidden in her boot, but she had to wait. Her only chance would be to surprise them at the last moment and stick it into one of them from up close. That would not help her against the second man, but she could not let herself think of that now.

If she and Finn lived through this, which seemed increasingly unlikely, she would make him teach her how to use her dirk.

When the men attacked, they moved so fast that they were on her before she could reach the blade in her boot. She kicked and bit and scratched at them, but in no time, one of the men had her arms pinned behind her back.

"You first," he said to the other one.

Fury exploded inside Finn, giving him a burst of strength. He pulled on the post and staggered backward when it came free with a loud *crack*. As the man closest to him turned toward the sound, Finn swung the heavy beam and crushed the side of his head.

He started toward the second man, who was holding Margaret from behind. "Release her!"

"Ye can't hit me with that post without hitting her too."

While her attacker's attention was fixed on Finn, Margaret raised her knee, pulled a dirk from her boot, and made a wild stab behind her. She must have hit him because her attacker yelped in pain. Without hesitation, Finn slipped his chain off the broken end of the post and ran hellbent at her attacker. Before the man could react, Finn had the chain around his throat and was choking the life out of the bastard.

His strength was fading fast, but he gritted his teach and managed to hold on until the man stopped struggling and his body became a dead weight in Finn's arms. Finn watched the limp body slide to the ground before darkness took him.

He awoke to his true love slapping him across the face.

"Put your arm over my shoulders," Margaret ordered him.

Somehow, she dragged him through the doorway, where he collapsed again. He was shaking violently.

"I won't make it. Ye must go, *mo rùin*," he said, speaking in short gasps. "Take care of our Ella. Don't die here with me."

He had accepted his death hours ago—probably even before he left Helmsdale. He was so very tired. He tried to keep his eyes open so that he could watch her leave, but they drifted shut again until Maggie shook him awake.

"Go," he told her again. "Save yourself. Do it for me."

"I did not come all this way, Finlay Sinclair Gordon, to leave ye to die," she said. "Now, you're going to get up and walk up those stairs."

"Can't ye see ye must go without me?" he pleaded. "Why won't ye leave me?"

"Because I need my husband, and Ella needs her father," she said in a choked voice. "We need *you*, Finn. Now get up before I get good and truly angry with you."

"All right, princess," he said, because she could not stay here. Every moment, she was in danger. Since she would not go without him, he had to find the strength to get to his feet and climb the stairs. Pain seared his back as he struggled to pull himself up, but he made it. He leaned against the stone wall to catch his breath before starting up the stairs.

"If only we had some whisky," he said between clenched teeth, "I'd run up these steps."

Margaret pulled a flask from inside her headdress, proving once again that she was the woman of his dreams.

Fortified by the liquid heat, he climbed the stairs with one arm around Margaret's shoulders, and the other braced against the wall. His back was on fire, and yet he was so cold he could not stop shaking. They were almost to the door to the tunnel.

They were going to make it.

"Just a few more steps," Margaret told Finn.

He was so heavy, and the long chain hanging from his wrists banged against her thigh with each step. But they were so close now that the torchlight from the wall sconce lit one side of the stairs. Another step up, and Margaret could see into the landing. It was empty, praise God.

C-r-e-a-k.

They flattened themselves against the wall of the stairwell that remained in shadow as the door from the hall swung open.

"Give me your dirk," Finn whispered as he eased his arm and the chain over her head.

She did not argue. Even injured to the point of near death, Finn was better with a blade than she was. In the courtyard, she had done little more than scratch her attacker, but at least she'd had the presence of mind to hold on to the blade.

She prayed whoever was on the landing would go upstairs. If he started down, he would see them. There was no time to run, even if Finn could have. Margaret saw one large boot on the stairs and then another. Finn struck so fast with the blade that the man went down before Margaret even realized Finn had done it. Then Finn fell on top of the downed man and held his hand over the man's mouth, stifling his dying scream.

"The two dead in the courtyard likely won't be found till morning," Finn gasped, as she helped him to his feet. "But we can't leave this body here."

Margaret did not know how Finn found the strength, but together they dragged the dead man up the last steps and through the secret door. She leaned back inside to wipe up the streak of blood leading to the secret door with her skirts. Finally, she shut the door and leaned her back against it for just a moment to recover.

They had made it out of the castle.

After his last burst of strength, however, Finn could barely stand. Holding on to each other, they began walking through the black tunnel. It had seemed long to her before, but it seemed ten times longer now.

Was it near dawn? She feared they were too late and that the boat had left them. Margaret felt as if she'd died a thousand deaths since she entered the castle and had lost all sense of time.

When she finally saw the end of the tunnel, her heart sank. The first streaks of dawn lit the sky. After all their efforts to escape, they had made it out too late. Struggling under Finn's weight as he leaned on her shoulders, she stumbled to the mouth of the cave.

The boat was there. The good fishermen had waited.

CHAPTER 35

"You'll heal," Una told Finn, "but you'll carry the scars from George Sinclair's whipping, *tuiteam gun èirigh dhut*." *May he fall without rising.*

Finn gritted his teeth while Una cleaned the wounds on his back and applied fresh bandages.

"Look at my baby," Ella said from where she was playing on the floor with the dog, *Cù-sìthe.*

Finn tried not to laugh when he saw she'd put a wee bonnet on him. *Cù-sìthe* gave him a pained look with his one eye. Like Finn, the dog would do anything for Ella, but he made one ugly, hairy-faced baby.

"Do your owies still hurt, Da?" Ella asked.

His heart melted whenever she called him that. Hell, he'd put on a bonnet for her too if she asked.

"Nay, not anymore," he lied, and winked at her.

"Did ye hear that Curstag left?" Una asked him. "Told me she found someone to take her to Edinburgh. She plans to become a famous courtesan there and cater to wealthy noblemen and merchants."

"Good luck to her," Finn said. "That would suit Curstag. I hope she succeeds and stays there."

He waited until after Ella scampered off with the dog to ask Una about Margaret.

"I'm worried about Maggie," he said. "It's been a week since we returned from Girnigoe, and she's still so tired. I fear it was all too much for her."

He felt racked with guilt that she'd put herself and their babe at risk for him.

"'Tis common for a lass to be tired in the first weeks," Una said. "As I've told ye before, Maggie is stronger than she was when she was married to the foul man."

Finn did not doubt that his wife was strong. Hell, she'd gone into Girnigoe alone to get him and then dragged him out with the sheer force of her will. But this was different.

"*Ach*, her husband should have been hung by his bollocks for what he did to her that last time she miscarried."

"The last time?" Finn asked. "Ye mean during the Battle of the Causeway?"

"That was bad enough, but I'm talking about when he threw her out," Una said. "On death's door, she was."

Finn jumped up, sending a roll of linen bandages across the floor.

"Death?" Finn gripped the old woman's arms. "Maggie almost died from a miscarriage?"

"Oh, aye, she was verra close indeed," Una said. "If she'd been properly cared for, I don't believe—"

He left Una and burst into the other bedchamber, where Margaret was sitting with her feet up.

"Ye should have told me ye nearly died from your last miscarriage," he said. "I would never have taken ye to bed if I'd known."

"Ye wouldn't have?" she asked, raising one eyebrow. "Then I'm verra glad I didn't tell ye."

"I wouldn't have risked your life." Finn knelt beside her and took her hands between his. "What if I've murdered ye by planting a child inside ye?"

"I've had three years to recover my health," she said. "I'm strong now."

She told him a harrowing story of becoming pregnant too soon after a previous miscarriage because her swine of a husband refused to wait the prescribed period for cleansing.

"The herbal tincture would have stopped the bleeding," she said, "but he forced me to leave before it could do much good."

Finn wanted to throw a chair against the wall as she described how she had ridden in the back of a horse cart, bleeding and with the storm pelting her face. If he did not have to leave her to do it, he would ride right now to her former husband's castle and put a blade through his black heart.

"I survived the sea cave and Girnigoe Castle," she said. "And Una is a gifted midwife, ye said so yourself. The babe and I will be just fine."

"Aye, ye will," Finn said, because he did not want her to worry, and he needed it to be true.

But he was terrified.

Several months later...

Margaret stood on the shore in front of Dunrobin Castle with her husband and daughter watching two boats on the horizon.

"Alex is sailing home on one of those boats," Finn said, leaning down to point them out to Ella.

"Alex! Alex!" Ella shouted, dancing from foot to foot.

Finn put his arm around Margaret's shoulders and rested a protective hand on her swollen belly. "This reminds me," he said, "of when we sailed across the firth and landed on this beach."

"And you tried to make me look like a tavern wench," Margaret said with a laugh.

"I had no notion how you'd change my life and bring me so much happiness," Finn said, and nuzzled her neck.

Margaret sighed and leaned back against him.

"I don't know why the Earl of Moray felt he had to bring Alex himself," Finn said. "I assured him it was safe for Alex to return to Dunrobin, and I sent twenty warriors to escort him here from Huntly."

With his uncle dead, the men of Sutherland had turned to Finn to lead them in the fight against the Sinclairs. First, Finn captured Dunrobin, just as his father Robin Sutherland had done years before. Then, under his leadership, the combined forces of the Sutherlands, Gordons and Murrays pushed the Sinclairs out of Sutherland altogether.

Finn did not do it for his own enrichment, but to protect the ordinary folk of Sutherland—and for Alex, the brother of his heart.

Margaret was worried that Finn had succeeded so well that Moray might have other uses for him. She put her hand over her belly, their miracle child, and prayed that Moray would not interfere with their plans. Once Alex was ready to assume his duties as laird alone, they wanted to set up their own household and keep as much distance as possible from royal politics and power struggles. She still worried that Garty had too many ghosts for her husband, and she wished it was farther away from Edinburgh, but it would do.

"I better go inside before the boats get any closer," Margaret said.

She had made sure everything was prepared for a visitor of royal blood, but she could not sit in the hall beside her husband to serve as hostess. Moray had seen her too many times at court for Margaret to take the risk that he would recognize her, even in her current, enormous shape. She hoped Moray's visit would be a short one.

"I'll take ye in," Finn said.

"I'm pregnant, not injured," Margaret said, and kissed his cheek. "I think I can manage to waddle inside all by myself."

She might tease him about being a wee bit too protective during her pregnancy, but after how little concern the men of her past had shown her, she was grateful to have a husband who was so thoughtful and caring.

"Go rest, *m' eudail*," Finn said. "I'll come up as soon as I can after the feast and my talk with Moray."

Two hours later, Margaret pressed her fist against her aching back as she walked back and forth across the bedchamber, waiting to hear the outcome of Finn's meeting with Moray. The feast she had meticulously organized should be over soon, and Finn and Moray would retreat to the laird's private solar.

When she heard the door latch behind her, she spun around, expecting Finn. Instead, a stunning woman of perhaps forty, dressed in expensive silk brocade that showed her voluptuous figure to advantage, stood in the doorway. Jewels glinted on the woman's fingers and at her throat, and the emerald green of her gown matched her eyes and set off her famous red hair, which was still striking, despite the streaks of white.

"God's blood!" The woman's hand went to her throat. "You're Margaret Drummond's niece, the missing Margaret Douglas."

Margaret hid the panic rising in her throat behind an outward calm. After keeping her identity secret for so long, she had been found out. She knew who her visitor was as well. This was none other than the infamous Lady Janet Douglas, the late king's mistress. She had not expected the Earl of Moray to bring his mother.

"Ye look so much like your aunt that I thought I'd seen a ghost," Janet said. "I heard ye bore a strong likeness to her, but the resemblance is rather startling."

"'Tis best we speak in private," Margaret said, and closed the door behind Janet before a passing servant overheard her. "Won't ye sit down?"

Janet's decision to enter her and Finn's private chamber un-invited was not only inexcusably rude, but it also imperiled their future. Margaret eased herself into a chair, folded her hands over her huge belly, and waited for what the woman would do next.

"Forgive my intrusion, but I was curious to meet the woman my friend Finn wed," Janet said.

Margaret suspected from the way Janet said *friend* that she had been more than that to Finn at one time. Was there no end to his former lovers? She reminded herself the past was behind them, and she had him now.

"In truth," Janet said as she sat down and smoothed her skirts, "I thought Finn had made you up entirely to keep me from pestering him."

Pestering was an interesting choice of word.

"I can't believe you're Finn's wife!" Janet threw back her head and gave a throaty laugh. "I'm pleased he took my advice to marry a wealthy woman, but I did not expect him to take it so far as to wed a Douglas."

"Please, no one can know who I am," Margaret said. "My brothers believe I died of a fever at Blackadder castle, and I don't want them to learn otherwise."

Exchanging letters with her sisters and Lizzy was difficult, but she had eventually received word from Alison telling her of the lie she and Lizzie had told to explain Margaret's disappearance.

"Now that ye mention it, I did hear a rumor that you were dead." Janet leaned forward. "'Tis best we keep your secret between us and not tell my son."

Margaret drew in her first easy breath since Janet appeared. Janet already knew the gossip about Margaret's first husband annulling their marriage, and Margaret told her briefly about her brothers' plans to use her before she escaped. Janet listened intently, tapping one manicured finger against her cheek.

"I don't want my brothers finding me and interfering in our lives," Margaret said.

"I, more than most, understand how dangerous a woman's connections to powerful men can be," Janet said. "I learned from your aunt's tragic example."

Janet went on to regale Margaret with tales of her youth. She'd had a fascinating life, but Margaret would not want it for the world.

"Do ye know why your son is here?" Margaret asked. "What does he want with Finn?"

When Janet told her, Margaret grew so tense that the baby rolled and kicked inside her. She took slow, deep breaths to calm herself while she tried to think what to do.

"Finn will never agree to what your son proposes," Margaret said. "But I have an idea."

She and Janet put their heads together to work out a plan.

"Take good care of that handsome man," Janet said with a wink, as she got up to leave. "Now I have business to attend to."

###

A great deal of whisky, wine, and ale had been consumed before and during the feast, so it took some time for the hall to quiet when Finn stood to make his toast.

"Welcome home, Alexander Gordon, the laird and earl of Sutherland!" Finn said, raising his cup. *"Gun cuireadh do chupa thairis le slàinte agus sonas." May your cup overflow with health and happiness.*

"Slàinte! Slàinte!" Shouts filled the room, and the floor shook from people stamping their feet. Finn grinned down at Alex, who sat next to him at the high table, and reflected on how his cousin had grown into a man.

Alex had filled out in the months he'd been away, but the changes went deeper than the physical. The murder of his parents and his brief captivity with the Sinclairs had destroyed Alex's youthful naivete. While he still showed moments of his old lighthearted self during dinner, Alex had become a serious young man who was determined to become a good laird for his people.

After numerous other toasts to Alex and to the departure of the Sinclairs, Moray, as the honored guest, stood to make the last formal toast.

"We'd be remiss in not recognizing the man who made your young earl's return possible," Moray said, then raised his cup to

299

Finn. "Let us drink to the hero who captured Dunrobin and drove out the Sinclairs!"

This time the shouts were even louder. Finn was not pleased that Moray had drawn attention away from Alex, who needed to be recognized and accepted as the new laird.

"I must speak with you alone," Moray said in Finn's ear before he returned to his seat.

When he and Moray settled into the solar a short time later, Finn wished Margaret could be there to help him. She understood the politics that motivated a man like Moray. One thing Finn knew for certain, however, was that Moray did not come all this way just to thank him for leading the forces that pushed the Sinclairs out of Sutherland.

Moray wanted something from him.

"Alex can petition the church for a divorce from Barbara Sinclair on the grounds of infidelity as soon as he turns eighteen and his wardship ends," Moray said. "I've already spoken to the bishop."

"That won't be necessary," Finn said.

"Why not?" Moray asked.

"After Barbara miscarried MacKay's child, she rode into Sutherland to join the Sinclair warriors in the fight for Dunrobin," Finn said. "A pack of wild dogs attacked her in the wood. Apparently, her horse threw her, for we found the horse unharmed."

"And Barbara?" Moray asked.

"She and dogs never did get along," Finn said. "I'm told there wasn't much left of her to bury."

Moray shuddered and took a gulp of his whisky. "What of the Sinclair chieftain and the rest of his family? I hear his sons are almost as dangerous as he is."

"The Sinclairs will always be a danger that must be controlled," Finn said, "but there was so much evil in that family that they turned on themselves."

"To what result?" Moray asked.

"Two of George's three sons are dead," Finn said.

After months in his father's dungeon, John persuaded two of the guards to enter a plot to free him. Before they could execute their plan, his brother William, George's favorite, discovered the scheme. Foiling the plot was not enough for William—he had to go to the dungeon to taunt John. When he stepped too close, believing John was too weak to be dangerous, John got hold of him and strangled him with his chains.

After John killed George's favorite son, George grew impatient for John's death and had him fed only salted meat and nothing to drink. John first went mad from thirst and then died.

"That still leaves George Sinclair, himself," Moray said.

"George was stabbed in the back and thrown over the wall into the sea. At least, that's what his men surmised when his body came in with the tide," Finn said. "Since George never saw anyone outside of his family without his guards at hand, the murderer was most likely his third son, who is chieftain now."

George misunderstood the old witch's foretelling, just as his father had when he killed that innocent shepherd boy on Orkney. George feared his eldest son would plot to take his place, but in the end, it was his youngest.

"That is good news, but as you say, the Sinclairs will always need to be contained—and there will be other threats." Moray paused and cleared his throat. "I want you to remain at Dunrobin. The people here need to see their young laird now and again, but I'll keep Alex at Huntly and out of your way."

"Out of my way?" Finn rapped his fist on the table. "Alex needs to be here. He can't learn to rule Sutherland from Huntly."

"You're the man the warriors here in Sutherland are willing to follow into battle," Moray said. "Once Alex is of age, he'll rule in name, of course, but I want you to remain here and in control."

"You're underestimating Alex," Finn said. "He has it in him to be the leader he needs to be."

While Finn was speaking, Janet entered the solar without knocking and took a seat.

"You've earned this by forcing the Sinclairs out of Sutherland," Moray said. "I want you to take it."

"I don't want it," Finn said between clenched teeth. "And I won't take it."

"Don't play coy," Moray said. "Is it gold you want to sweeten the pot or something else?"

"My son doesn't understand a man who lacks his kind of ambition," Janet interrupted. "As we don't have a good deal of time, let me suggest a resolution."

Before long, Finn had agreed to remain at Dunrobin to guide Alex until he came of age. Finn knew Margaret was anxious to make their own home, but she would understand that any other man Moray would choose would attempt to usurp Alex's role permanently. For his part, Moray seemed satisfied with the assurance that Sutherland would be secure for the next two years.

"Now," Janet said, turning to her son, "about that property ye have on the north coast that ye never visit."

Finn had taken a sip of his whisky and nearly choked on it. How did Janet know about the property Moray had promised him in exchange for kidnapping Margaret?

"Though Garty is worth more, I'd wager that Finn would be willing to exchange it for that property," Janet said. "'Tis your gain that Finn would prefer not to live in a place that would be a constant reminder of his murderous mother and the rest of his unpleasant and, thankfully, deceased family."

"Garty is mine now," Finn said, keeping his face expressionless.

Gilbert never recovered from the shock of Bearach's murder and died a few weeks later. Isabel was gone as well. After her conviction, she killed herself in her cell in Edinburgh the night before she was to be executed. With no proof beyond her word, however, George Sinclair was not called to justice—at least, not by the Crown.

"What do ye say to this exchange?" Moray asked him. "You could keep the peace in the north of Sutherland and be able to assist Alex here when needed."

Finn wanted to pound the table and yell, *Aye!* But Moray would not feel he got a good bargain if Finn seemed too happy, so he just nodded and said, "That will do."

"Now that we have that settled," Janet said, rising to her feet, "we should bid Finn farewell and be on our way."

Moray looked as surprised as Finn was that they were not staying the night after such a long journey.

"So soon?" Finn asked to be polite.

"Your wife is about to give birth," Janet said.

"Aye, 'tis close to her time," Finn said.

"This *is* her time," Janet said. "Just as I was leaving her to join you, her water broke, and she had me send for that woman, Una."

Finn's hands shook. As the months passed, Finn's concern that Margaret would die from a miscarriage had gradually subsided. But now, a torrent of fear exploded inside him. Women died in childbirth all the time.

"God's bones," Finn said, leaping to his feet. "Why didn't ye tell me sooner?"

"The first child is usually slow to come, and your wife wanted these matters settled." Janet smiled at him. "Ye made a better choice than a wealthy widow. *Is fheàrr bean ghlic na crann is fear-ann.*" *A wise wife is better than a plough and land.*

Ploughs? Finn did not know what in the hell Janet was talking about. He left them without another word and raced upstairs to their bedchamber.

"I'm here," Finn told Margaret as he sat beside her and took her hand.

Una told him his presence was neither customary nor useful, but he refused to leave his wife's side. All her life, Margaret had been abandoned by the men of her family when she needed them, and he was not going to do that to her. Not now, not ever.

For a lass who could hide her feelings with remarkable skill, Margaret screamed and cursed a great deal over the next few hours. Finn was encouraged by the strength of her voice—and her grip on his hand.

"Won't be long now," Una said with her head beneath the sheet.

"I'm glad you're here with me," Margaret said as Finn wiped her brow between contractions.

Una's calm demeanor, born of midwifing a hundred other births, helped them both as she guided Margaret through the hard contractions and pushing until, at long last, their child came into the world wailing his lungs out.

"Ye can be of some use after all," Una told Finn. "Hold your son while I wipe him off, but be careful—he's slippery."

When she handed him his child, Finn's heart swelled in his chest, and he was speechless with wonder. How had such a perfect babe come from his loins? He was certain it was all thanks to his amazing wife. Una wrapped the babe in a swaddling cloth and put him in Margaret's outstretched arms to suckle.

"A fine, healthy babe and mother," Una pronounced after she'd finished taking care of Margaret, then she wiped a tear from her eye. "*Ach*, your son looks just like you, Finn, when you were born."

Since Finn's mother had died giving birth to him, he was grateful he did not remember Una was his mother's midwife until now.

"I'll go tell Ella she has a new brother," Una said, and slipped out.

"Ye did well, *mo shíorghrá*," *my eternal love*, Finn said, and kissed his wife's forehead.

"I'm so happy, and I love ye so much," Margaret said. "Lie down with us."

Carefully, Finn eased onto the bed and put his arms around her and their son. Margaret was asleep a short time later when Ella tiptoed into the room. Ella crawled onto the bed on the other side and snuggled next to her mother with her hand on her new brother's blanket.

For the first time in his life, Finn felt whole and at peace. He belonged here with Margaret and their children.

He was home.

EPILOGUE

On the North Coast of Sutherland
Two years later (1528)

Margaret weeded her kitchen garden while Ella and wee Robbie played with the dog on the beach, under Una's supervision. She found it immensely satisfying to see the new plants poking through the ground and putting down roots, just as she was.

She paused to take in the beauty of the landscape outside her door—the quiet, sandy beach across from the house at the base of their inlet, the grassy, windswept slopes of the headland dotted with sheep on one side, and the path to the village through green fields on the other side.

The house behind her was not a grand castle, but it was solid and always full of love and laughter. At the moment, Finn was inside settling a dispute over a cow between two of the villagers, who were their tenants.

In a few weeks, they would return to Dunrobin to meet Alex's new bride, who was the Earl of Huntly's older sister, and they would visit her sister Sybil's family on the way. While Margaret looked forward to seeing them all again, she would always be happiest at home.

"*Mamaidh!*" *Momma!* Ella called as she ran up from the beach with *Cù-sìthe* yapping at her heels. "Someone's coming."

Margaret shielded her eyes with her hand and examined the young man walking up their path with a bag over his shoulder. She knew all the villagers, and he was not one of them. Besides, the young man was better dressed and wore expensive leather boots.

She could not put her finger on it, but there was something familiar about him. Perhaps he was someone she knew from Dunrobin, a messenger from Alex.

Margaret was surprised when she noticed Ella sucking her thumb, something she'd given up a long time ago. Her daughter's gaze was riveted on the young man.

The young man dropped his bag in the middle of the path and started running toward them. "Ella!" he shouted. "Ella!"

"Merciful God," Margaret cried. "It's your brother Brian."

Tears sprang to her eyes. When Brian reached them, Ella retreated behind Margaret's skirts, but Margaret threw her arms around him.

"Lady Marg—"

"I'm Maggie now," she said, smiling and brushing her tears away. "Ella, come greet your brother. He's come a long way to find you."

Brian waited patiently while Ella first peeked at him behind Margaret, then slowly inched her way out. Finally, she raised her arms, and Brian swooped her up off the ground.

"You're so big!" Brian said.

Brian himself had grown from a pale and skinny twelve-year-old lad to a strapping youth of fifteen.

"I was afraid she wouldn't recognize me," Brian said, looking at Margaret.

"We spoke about ye often so she wouldn't forget," Margaret said.

"This is my other brother, Robbie," Ella said, pointing, as Una and Robin joined them from the beach. "And my grandmother."

"I promise I won't impose on ye long," Brian said to Margaret. "But if I could sleep in your barn tonight, I'd be grateful."

"I'll not hear of ye sleeping in the barn," Margaret said. Before she could say more, she saw Finn bid the two village men goodbye and start toward them.

"He's my da!" Ella said, beaming at Finn.

Brian eyed Finn with suspicion as Margaret introduced them.

"Welcome!" Finn clasped Brian's shoulder, but immediately released him when Brian flinched.

"Ye must be hungry and thirsty from your travels," Margaret said. "The noon meal will be ready soon. Come inside, and I'll show ye your bedchamber where you can leave your bag."

Before going upstairs, Margaret asked the village girl she'd hired to help in the kitchen to put the food out and reminded Ella to set the table. Then she led Brian up to the small bedchamber at the top of the house.

"Thank you for taking such good care of Ella," Brian said when they were alone. "I can see she's happy here."

"She's a joy in our lives," Margaret said. "Looks like you've done well for yourself."

"I've sailed all over—to Ireland, France, even Spain," he said, his face lighting up. "You wouldn't believe the things I've seen."

"How did ye find us?" Margaret asked.

"I went to Blackadder Castle and asked to speak with Lady Alison. After I showed her my ring with the wee stone ye gave me," he said, holding out his hand so she could see the silver ring with the tiny black chip on his little finger, "she told me where ye were."

"I'm so glad you're here," Margaret said. "I hoped and prayed every single day that you would come to us."

Brian's cheeks colored, and she saw confusion in his eyes before he shifted them to the side.

"I almost forgot," Brian said, and leaned down to pull a folded, water-stained parchment from his bag. "Lady Alison wrote ye a letter."

Brian was quiet during the meal, his gaze flicking uneasily around the table as everyone else talked.

"Stop feeding the dog under the table," Margaret chided Robbie, as she tried to think of what else she could do to make Brian feel at home.

"Brian," Finn said, when they'd finished eating, "I could use your help with something behind the house."

Brian did not look as if he wanted to go anywhere with Finn, but he followed him out. While Una took the children outside to play, Margaret went upstairs to straighten the bedchambers. When she heard Finn's voice through the window, she looked out and saw Finn and Brian talking below her.

"Ye don't have to worry," Brian said. "I'll be gone in the morning. There's a boat waiting for me at Durness."

"You're Ella's brother," Finn said. "That makes ye part of this family."

Brian mumbled something she couldn't hear, so she leaned closer.

"You're a young man with a taste for adventure," Finn said. "Go on your travels, but know that ye have a home and a family here to come back to."

Brain sniffed and wiped his eye with the back of his sleeve. When Finn patted him on the back this time, Brian did not flinch.

"Come home as often as ye can," Finn said. "We'll always be here."

Finn turned away to give Brian a moment to gather himself, then they walked together toward the front of the house. By the time Margaret ran down the stairs to meet them outside, Ella and Robbie had taken Brian's hands and were pulling him toward the beach to see a castle they had made in the sand.

"You're a good man, Finn." Margaret put her arms around her husband and kissed him.

"I should have known ye were listening," Finn said, smiling down at her.

"Let's take a walk out on the headland," she said, taking Finn's arm. "Brian and Una can mind the children, and I'd like to read Alison's letter out there."

"You understand that Brian has to leave?" Finn said as they started out.

"Now that he knows we're here, he'll come home again," she said. "He'll always come home."

They walked the two miles through grassy hills and the occasional sandy dune until they reached the end, where they were surrounded on three sides by the sea. After taking in the glorious view of the stunning coastline on either side, they sat down in the tall grass, and Margaret pulled out the letter.

"Alison and David have had another babe—this time it's a girl," Margaret told Finn as she began reading it. "Our youngest sister, the one married to Lord Glamis, is widowed and having an affair."

"Ye don't mention that sister much," Finn said.

"She was just a bairn when I left home, so we were never close," Margaret said. "And her husband would not let her have anything to do with us after Archie was banished."

She turned back to her letter and read aloud.

"Wretched William has died of a painful and disfiguring disease. Though he got his heir and one to spare before he died, everyone says both boys are the spitting image of the castle steward."

"He deserved worse," Finn said.

"Good heavens, the king escaped to Stirling Castle!" Margaret exclaimed as her eyes raced down the page, then she read the next lines to Finn.

"The king had cannon brought from Edinburgh and bombarded Tantallon, where our brothers and uncle retreated. The walls held, however. In order to end his embarrassing, failed siege and be rid of the Douglas men, the king was forced to allow them to escape to France. All this has only made the king more furious."

If only Archie had mentored the king as Finn had done with Alex, instead of using him, Archie could have earned the king's favor and kept his powerful position and vast lands. But her brother always wanted more.

"Lizzy has disappeared!" Margaret said, grasping Finn's hand. *"The king sent men here looking for her, so at least we know he hasn't got her."*

"I'm sorry, *mo rùin*," Finn said. "I know you'll worry about her now."

"I *always* worry about Lizzy," Margaret said, "but she always manages to get out of trouble. My cousin is a verra resourceful lass."

Knowing Lizzy, she had found a good place to hide. Margaret prayed she had. After she put the letter away, Finn helped her to her feet, and they stood together facing the sea.

"I have some news of my own." Margaret took Finn's hand and placed it on her belly.

"Another babe?" he asked, as a grin spread over his face.

"Una killed a chicken and told me this one will be a girl."

"Another lass in the family!" Finn swung her around in a circle, laughing. "How did I ever get this lucky?"

"I'm the lucky one," Margaret said, smiling up at him.

She had been ready to settle for a small, lonely life of lost dreams before a charming and handsome rogue kidnapped her and changed everything. Because of Finn, her beloved husband, she had the home and family she'd always longed for—and, most of all, love.

"Let's go home," Finn said, nuzzling her neck. "We can sneak up to our chamber while Una and Brian have the children outside."

"Thought I wasn't your kind of woman," Margaret said, tilting her head.

"You've ruined me for my kind of woman, *m' eudail*," Finn said, and gave her a smoldering kiss that made her toes curl. "You're the woman I did not dare hope for."

Before they turned back, Margaret stood at the point facing the sea with her arms outstretched and the wind blowing her hair, and she laughed out of sheer happiness. She felt fearless and strong and free. No matter what troubles came, she and Finn would face them together.

She vowed that every day she would cherish the love he gave her and embrace the joy that filled their lives. Then she took the hand of the man she loved with all her heart, and they raced home together.

THE END

HISTORICAL NOTE

Most of the Douglases mentioned in this series are based on real historical figures. While I was researching the family, I discovered that Margaret's husband threw her out and had their marriage annulled after her brothers and uncle were charged with treason and fled the country. When I could not find out what happened to her after that, I decided to give Margaret a happily ever after with a worthy hero.

I set Finn, my fictional hero, in the midst of actual events involving the Sutherlands, Sinclairs, and Gordons, though I combined generations, condensed the timeline, changed a few given names, and made things up to suit my tale.

I was lucky to travel the coast of Sutherland and Caithness and visit Dunrobin Castle, as well as the ruins of Girnigoe and Wick. I spent a couple of nights at the bishop's castle in Dornoch, which is now a hotel. Helmsdale Castle is gone, but the Timespan Museum in the town is well worth a visit. I'm grateful to the staff there who were gracious in answering my questions about the Helmsdale murders.

Much of the history from this period, particularly Highland history, was passed down through oral storytelling. The result is that history is often mixed with legend and has gaps and differing versions, so take the historical facts below with a grain of salt.

If you haven't read the book yet, stop here—spoilers ahead!

Isabel Sinclair, the wife of Gilbert Gordon of Garty, confessed to and was convicted of the Helmsdale murders. Her cousin, who was the Sinclair chieftain and Earl of Caithness, denied her claim that he was involved. He purchased the wardship of Alex Sutherland, and he forced Alex to wed Barbara, who was more than twice his age.

Alex did escape with the help of the Murrays, but I gave my fictional hero the role of the peddler that was actually played by Gordon of Gight. Unlike in my story, George Sinclair retained control of the lands of Sutherland until Alex came of age. John, Master of Caithness, burned Dornoch and trapped the Murrays in retaliation for helping Alex escape.

George Sinclair kept his son John imprisoned for seven years, not just a few months. After John strangled his brother, George finished him off by feeding him salted meat until he went mad and died from thirst. Unfortunately, George lived a long life as chief of the Sinclairs. After he finally died, John's son became the next chieftain and murdered the two men his grandfather had made his father's jailors.

Turning to earlier events, it was Alex's great-grandparents, rather than grandparents, who finagled the earldom from the Sutherlands. Robin Sutherland is based on the history and legends about him, but I made up the romance and secret child.

Janet Kennedy and her son by James IV, the earl of Moray, and the earls of Huntly, both young and old, were significant players on the historical stage. James IV was rumored to be so in love with Margaret Drummond as a young man that he talked of marrying her, instead of making the expected marriage alliance with England or France. She and two of her sisters may have simply eaten spoiled food for breakfast, but I believe they were poisoned.

I invented the painful death that Margaret's husband, Drumlanrig, deserved.

Three years after Archibald Douglas refused to relinquish custody of his stepson, the king escaped. Ever after, James V had a burning hatred for the Douglases. Archibald, his brother George, and his uncle escaped again and left Scotland for many years. Lizzy's story, my next book in The Douglas Legacy, begins with the king's escape.

MAP

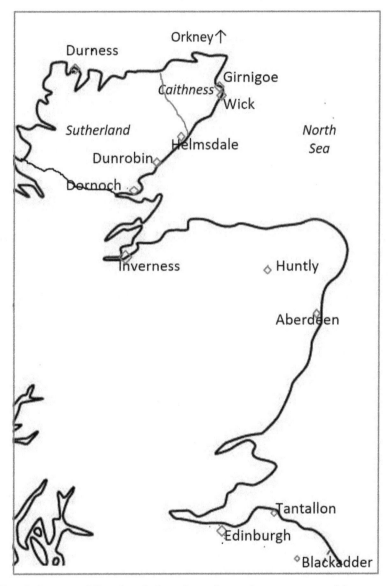

Partial map of Scotland showing places important to this story.

Excerpt from *CAPTURED BY A LAIRD*
(The Douglas Legacy #1)

Scotland
1517

Burning her husband's bed was a mistake. Alison could see that now.

Yet each time she passed the rectangle of charred earth as she paced the castle courtyard, she felt a wave of satisfaction. She had waited to commit her act of rebellion until her daughters were asleep. But that night, after her husband's body was taken to the priory for burial, she ordered the servants to carry the bed out of the keep. She set fire to it herself. The castle household, accustomed to the meek mistress her husband had required her to be, was thoroughly shocked.

"Do ye see them yet?" Alison called up to one of the guards on the wall.

When the guard shook his head, she resumed her pacing. Where were her brothers? They had sent word this morning that they were on their way.

As she passed the scorched patch again, she recalled how the flames shot up into the night sky. She had stood watching the fire until dawn, imagining the ugliness of the past years turning to black ashes like the bed. The memories did not burn away, but she did feel cleaner.

Destroying such an expensive piece of furniture was self-indulgent, but that was not why she counted burning it a mistake. While she could not tolerate having that bed in her home, it would have been wiser to give it away or sell it. And yet she simply could not in good conscience pass it on to someone else. Not when she felt as if the bed itself carried an evil.

Instinctively, she touched the black quartz pendant at her throat that her mother had given her to ward off ill luck. It had been missing since Blackadder broke the chain on their wedding night. After the fire, she found it wedged in a crack in the floor where the bed had been.

"Lady Alison!" a guard shouted down from the wall. "They're here!"

The heavy wooden gates swung open, and her two brothers galloped over the drawbridge followed by scores of Douglas warriors. *Praise God.* As the castle filled with her clansmen, Alison immediately felt safer.

One look at Archie's thunderous expression, however, told her that his meeting with the queen had not gone well. Without a word, her brothers climbed the steps of the keep, crossed the hall where platters of food were being set out on the long trestle tables for the Douglas warriors, and continued up the stairs to the private chambers. They never discussed family business in front of others.

"She is my wife!" Archie said as soon they were behind closed doors. "How dare she think she can dismiss me as if I were one of her servants?"

Alison tapped her foot, trying to be patient, while her brother, the 6th Earl of Angus and chieftain of the Douglas clan, stormed up and down the length of the room. When Archie's back was to her, she exchanged a look with George, her more clever brother, and rolled her eyes. This was all so predictable.

"I warned ye not to be so blatant about your affair with Lady Jane," George said in a mild tone.

"My affairs are none of my wife's concern," Archie snapped.

"A queen is not an ordinary wife," George said as he poured himself and Archie cups of wine from the side table.

Alison found it ironic that the Douglas clan owed the greatest rise in their fortunes to Archie's liaison with the widowed queen. Usually, it was the ladies of the family who were tasked with securing royal favor via the bedchamber.

Archie, always overconfident, had gone too far. While the Council had been willing to tolerate the queen's foolishness in taking the young Douglas chieftain as her lover, they were livid when the pair wed in secret, making Archie the infant king's stepfather. The Council responded by removing the queen as regent. She fled to England amidst accusations that she had tried to abscond with the royal heir.

"How was I to know my wife would return to Scotland?" Archie said, raising his arms. "Besides, I'm a young man. She couldn't expect me to live like a monk while she was gone."

Doubtless, the queen, who was pregnant with Archie's child when she fled, expected her husband to join her. But while the queen paid a lengthy visit on her brother Henry VIII, the Douglas men retreated behind the high walls of Tantallon Castle and waited for the cries of treason to subside.

That was two years ago. And now, Albany, the man who replaced the queen as regent, was on a ship back to France, and the queen was returning. Archie had gone to meet her at Berwick Castle, just across the border.

"Is there no hope of reconciling with her?" Alison ventured to ask.

"I bedded that revolting woman four times in two days—and for naught!" Archie thrust his hand out. "I had her in my palm again, I swear it. But then some villain sent her a message informing her about Jane."

"Must have been the Hamiltons," George said, referring to their greatest rivals.

"Despite that setback, I managed to persuade the queen— through great effort, I might add—that we should enter Edinburgh together as man and wife for all the members of the damned Council to see," Archie said, his blue eyes flashing. "But then she discovered I'd been collecting the rents on her dower lands and flew into a rage."

No wonder the queen was angry. After abandoning her, Archie had lived openly with his lover and their newborn daughter in one of the queen's dower castles—and on the queen's money.

"You're her husband," George said, leaning back in his chair. "Ye had every right to collect her rents. Still do."

Alison did not want to hear about husbands and their rights. She folded her arms and tamped down her impatience while she waited for the right moment to ask.

"Enough talk. We must join the men." Archie threw back his cup of wine. "We'll ride for Edinburgh as soon as they've eaten their fill."

George was already on his feet. She could wait no longer.

"Ye must leave some of our Douglas warriors here to protect this castle," she blurted out. "The Blackadder men are deserting me."

She hoped her brothers would not ask why. She did not want to explain that burning her husband's bed had insulted the Blackadder men and spurred many of them to leave. They disliked having a woman in command of the castle, and she had unwittingly given them the excuse they needed.

"I can't spare any men now," Archie said, slapping his gloves against his hand. "I must gather all my forces in a show of strength to convince my pigheaded wife that she needs my help to regain the Regency."

"The Hamiltons will attempt to do the same," George added.

"But what about me and my daughters?" Alison demanded. "What about the Blackadder lands Grandfather thought were so important that I was forced to wed that man? I was a child of thirteen!"

"For God's sake, Alison, we're in a fight for control of the crown," Archie said. "That will not be decided at Blackadder Castle."

"Please, I need your help." She clutched Archie's arm as he started toward the door. "Ye promised to protect us."

Archie came to an abrupt halt, and the shared memory hung between them like a dead rat.

"Mother did not need to remind me of my duty to my family," he said between clenched teeth. "And neither do you."

Unlike the Douglas men, who lauded Archie's seduction of the queen as a boon for the family, their mother begged him to end the affair. A generation ago, one of her sisters had been the king's mistress. After it was rumored that the king had fallen so in love that he wished to marry her, all three of their mother's sisters died mysteriously.

When Archie wed the queen in secret, knowing full well that every other powerful family in Scotland would oppose the marriage, their mother made one demand of her sons. Archie and George promised her, on their father's grave, that they would protect their four sisters.

"I'll find ye a new husband as soon as these other matters are settled," Archie said. "You'll be safe here until then."

Another husband was not what Alison asked for and was the last thing she wanted. "What I need are warriors—"

"Who would dare attack you?" Archie said. "Now that we are rid of Albany, I am the man most likely to rule Scotland."

Before she could argue, Archie pushed past her and disappeared down the circular stone stairwell.

"Don't fret, Allie," George said, and gave her a kiss on her cheek. "Your most dangerous neighbors were the Hume lairds, and they're both dead."

***

David Hume left his horse and warriors a safe distance outside the city walls and proceeded on foot. If the guards were watching for him, they would not expect him to come alone, or so he hoped. Keeping his hood low over his face and his hand on his dirk, he mingled with the men herding cattle through the Cowgate Port to sell in the city's market.

A month ago, David would have been amused to find himself entering the great city of Edinburgh between two cows. But his humor had been wrung from him. As he walked up West Bow toward the center of the city, the rage that was always with him now swelled until his skin felt too tight.

He paused before entering the High Street and scraped the dung off his boots while he scanned the bustling street for anyone who might attempt to thwart him. Then, keeping watch on the armed men amidst the merchants, well-dressed ladies, beggars, and thieves, he started down the hill in the direction of Holyrood Palace. He spared a glance over his shoulder at Edinburgh Castle, the massive fortress that sat atop the black rock behind him. If he were caught, he would likely grow old in its bleak dungeon. He'd prefer a quick death.

David had walked this very street with his father and uncle. With each step, he tried to imagine how that day might have ended differently. Could he have stopped it? Perhaps, perhaps not. Regardless, he should have tried. From the moment they entered Holyrood Palace, he had sensed the danger. It pricked at the back of his neck and made his hands itch to pull his blade.

The Hume lairds had been guaranteed safe conduct. Relying on that pledge of honor made in the king's name, David did not follow his instincts, did not shout to their men to fight their way out. Instead, he watched his father and uncle relinquish their weapons at the palace door, and he did the same.

Never again.

When he saw the stone arches of St. Giles jutting into the High Street, David's heart beat so hard it hurt. The church was next to the Tolbooth, the prison where the royal guards brought his father and uncle after dragging them from the palace. David's ears rang again

318

with the shouts and jeers of the crowd that echoed off the buildings that day. As he crossed the square, he did not permit himself to look at the Tolbooth for fear that his rage would spill over and give him away.

He turned into one of the narrow, sloping passageways that cut through the tall buildings on either side of the High Street and found a dark doorway with a direct view of the Tolbooth. Only then did he lift his gaze.

Though he had known what to expect, his stomach churned violently at the sight of the two grisly heads on their pikes. His body shook with a poisonous mix of rage and grief as he stared at what was left of his father. They had made a mockery of the man David had admired all his life. His father's sternly handsome features were distorted in a grimace that looked like a gruesome grin, his dark gold hair was matted, and flies ate at his bulging eyes.

David's chest constricted until his breath came in wheezes. He wanted to fight his way into the palace, wielding his sword and ax until he killed every man in sight. But Regent Albany, the man who ordered the execution, was no longer in the palace, or even in Scotland.

In any case, David had too many responsibilities to give in to thoughtless acts that would surely result in his death. He was the new Laird of Wedderburn, and the protection of the entire Hume clan fell to him. When he thought of his younger brothers and how much they needed him, he finally loosened his grip on his dirk, which he'd been holding so tightly that his hand was stiff.

The execution of the two Hume lairds and this humiliating display of their heads made their clan appear weak and vulnerable. That perception put their clan in even greater danger, and so David must change it. This first step toward that end required stealth, not his sword.

He would have his bloody vengeance, but not today.

While he waited for nightfall, he pondered how Regent Albany had managed to prevail over men who were better than him in every way that should matter. The first time Albany captured David's father and uncle, they persuaded their jailor, a Hamilton, to free them and join the queen's side. A furious Albany responded by having their wives taken hostage.

David wondered if Albany understood at the time just how clever that move was, or if he had merely taken the women out of spite. In any event, the trap was set.

By then, Albany was planning to return to France, which was more home to him than Scotland. David's uncle was inclined to wait and seek the women's release from Albany's replacement. But David's father and stepmother had a rare love, and he was tortured by the thought of her suffering in captivity. Because of his weakness for her, he persuaded his brother to accept the regent's invitation and guarantee of their safety.

"Free my wife! Avenge us!" his father had shouted to David as the guards dragged him away.

His father's final words were burned into his soul. While he kept his vigil in the doorway, they spun through his head again and again. He wanted to smash his fist into the wall at the thought of his stepmother living amongst strangers when she learned of her husband's death. Nothing could save the man who held her hostage now. Vengeance was both a debt of honor David owed his father and necessary to restore respect for his clan.

When darkness finally fell on the city, David gave coins to the prostitutes who had gathered nearby and asked them to cause a disturbance. They proved better at keeping their word than the regent. While the women created an impressive commotion, screaming that they had been robbed, David scaled the wall of the Tolbooth.

Gritting his teeth, he jerked his father's head off the pike and placed it gently in the cloth bag slung over his shoulder. He swallowed against the bile that rose in his throat and forced himself to move quickly. As soon as he had collected his uncle's head, he dropped to the ground and left the square at a fast pace. He could still hear the prostitutes shouting when he was halfway to the gate.

A short time later, he reached the tavern outside the city walls where his men waited for him. His half-brothers must have been watching the door, for they ran to greet him as soon as he opened it. Will threw his arms around David's waist, while Robbie, who was four years older, stood by looking embarrassed but relieved. David should admonish Will for his display in front of the men, but he did not have the heart. The lad, who was only ten, had lost his father and missed his mother a great deal.

"I told ye I'd return safe," David said. "I'll not let any harm come to ye, and I will bring your mother home."

Their mother was being held at Dunbar, an impregnable castle protected by a royal garrison. While David did not yet know when or how he would obtain her release, he would do it.

He planned his next moves on the long ride back to Hume territory. In the violent and volatile Border region, you were either feared or preyed upon. David intended to make damned sure he was so feared that no one would ever dare harm his family again.

He would take control of the Hume lands and castles, which had been laid waste and forfeited to the Crown. And then he would take his vengeance on the Blackadders, the scheming liars. While pretending to be allies, the Blackadders had secretly assisted in his stepmother's capture and then urged Albany to execute his father and uncle. It was a damned shame that the Laird of Blackadder Castle was beyond David's reach in a new grave, but his rich lands and widow were ripe for the taking.

And the widow was a Douglas, sister to the Earl of Angus himself. For a man intent on establishing a fearsome reputation, that made her an even greater prize.

ABOUT THE AUTHOR

Margaret Mallory, a recovering lawyer, is thrilled to be writing adventurous tales with sword-wielding heroes rather than briefs and memos. Her Scottish and medieval romances have won numerous honors and awards, including National Readers' Choice Awards, *RT Book Reviews*' Best Scotland-Set Historical Romance, and a RITA© nomination.

Margaret lives with her husband in the beautiful Pacific Northwest. Now that her children are off on their own adventures, she spends most of her time with her handsome Highlanders, but she also likes to hike and travel. Readers can find information on Margaret's books, as well as photos of Scotland, historical tidbits, and Margaret's social media links on her website, www.MargaretMallory.com.